Patricia is the million-c   [Lottie Parker
series. She always year.   ..a her full-time
work and raising a family she could never find the time or com-
mitment to fulfil that ambition. However, tragedy was to intervene
which caused a major shift in her life.

In 2009, after her husband died following a short illness, Patricia
had to retire from her job and found that writing helped her cope
through her grief. She then started to write seriously. Fascinated by
people and their quirky characteristics, she always carries a notebook
to scribble down observations and ideas.

Patricia lives in the Irish midlands with her children.

www.patriciagibney.com

ALSO BY PATRICIA GIBNEY

The Missing Ones
The Stolen Girls
The Lost Child
No Safe Place ✓
Tell Nobody

NO
SAFE
PLACE

PATRICIA GIBNEY

sphere

SPHERE

First published in 2018 by Bookouture, an imprint of StoryFire Ltd.
This paperback edition published in 2019 by Sphere

1 3 5 7 9 10 8 6 4 2

A CIP catalogue record for this book
is available from the British Library.

ISBN 978-0-75157-492-0

Printed and bound in Great Britain by
Clays Ltd, Elcograf S.p.A.

Papers used by Sphere are from well-managed forests
and other responsible sources.

Sphere
An imprint of
Little, Brown Book Group
Carmelite House
50 Victoria Embankment
London EC4Y 0DZ

An Hachette UK Company

www.hachette.co.uk
www.littlebrown.co.uk

For Marie, Gerard and Cathy
With love

Tuesday 9 February 2016, 3.15 a.m.

Her bare feet stuck to the frost, but still she ran. She thought she was screaming, but there was no sound coming from her throat. Her elbow smashed into granite, the pain minimal in comparison to her fear.

Chancing a glance over her shoulder, she found it was as dark behind her as the blackness that stretched before her. She had unintentionally veered off the path and was now lost among the limestone and granite. Feeling cold stones cutting her soles, she tried to raise herself over the kerb she knew must surely be there, but stubbed her toe and fell head first into the next furrow.

With her mind void of all thoughts except reaching safety, she hauled herself onto her bleeding knees and listened. Silence. No twigs breaking or leaves being thrashed. Had he left her alone? Had he abandoned the chase? Now that she'd stopped running, she shivered violently in the freezing night. A light down the slope to her right caught her eye as she scanned the near horizon. An enclave of bungalows. She knew exactly where she was. And in the distance, she saw the amber hue of street lights. Safety.

A hurried look around. She had to make a run for it. Silently she counted to three, getting ready to make her final dash to safety.

'Now or never,' she whispered, and without a care for her nakedness, she stood up, ready to run like a panther. That was when she saw the breath suspended in the frost of the night.

She felt his arm encircling her throat, crushing her windpipe, and her body being dragged against his jacket. The sweet smell of fabric softener mixed with the sour scent of anger clouded her nostrils. With one last bout of adrenaline, she jabbed her elbow backwards, thrusting it deep and hard into his solar plexus. A gasp of wind escaped his mouth as he loosened his grip, and she was free.

She screamed and ran. Banging and crashing into granite, leaping over frozen stones and low kerbs, she tumbled, still screaming, down the slope towards the light. Almost there. She heard his booted footsteps gaining on her.

No, please God, no. She had to get off this path. Veering to her left, zigzagging, she was almost at the wall when the ground disappeared beneath her. Down she fell, six feet into the cavern, stones and clods of clay tumbling with her.

Excruciating pain shot up her leg, and an agonised scream exploded from her mouth. She knew that the sound she'd heard had not been the breaking of timber but the bone in her left leg shattering with the fall. Biting hard into her knuckles, she tried to be silent. Surely he couldn't find her here, could he?

But as she looked up at the night sky with its twinkling stars heralding further frost, his face appeared at the edge of the hole. All semblance of hope disappeared as the first clatter of clay fell onto her upturned face.

And as she cried, big salty tears mingling with the dirt, she understood with terrible clarity that she was going to die in someone else's grave.

DAY ONE

Wednesday 10 February 2016

CHAPTER ONE

Lottie Parker woke to the sound of a child crying. She opened one eye and squinted at the digital clock: 5.30 a.m.

'Oh no, Louis. It's the middle of the night,' she moaned.

Her grandson, at just over four and a half months old, had yet to sleep for longer than two hours straight. Throwing back the duvet, she went to the bedroom next to hers. The night light cast a shadowy hue over her sleeping twenty-year-old daughter. Katie had a pillow over her head, the duvet rising and falling in rhythm with her breathing. Louis stopped crying when Lottie lifted him from his cot. She fetched a nappy and a bottle of formula from the bedside cabinet and left her daughter to her dreams.

Back in her own room, she changed Louis, nestled him into her arms and fed him. She felt the baby's heart beating against her breast. There was something so soothing and at the same time so grounding about it. Adam would have loved him. Her heart constricted when she thought of her husband, dead over four years now. Cancer. The void left after his passing refused to be filled.

She feathered her grandson's soft dark hair with a kiss, and as the baby twisted, pushing the bottle out of his mouth, Lottie winced with the pain in her upper back. She knew she couldn't afford to be off work. Even though things in Ragmullin were unbearably quiet at the moment, it wouldn't stay that way for long.

She winded her little grandson and he smiled up at her. She smiled back.

A good omen for the day ahead.

She hoped.

CHAPTER TWO

Mollie Hunter settled into her seat. She placed her laptop bag on the table, then rolled up her cotton scarf, scrunched it against the window and rested her head. Her eyelids slid closed, blocking out the impending breakthrough of dawn. Earbuds pumped soft music into her ears, muting the shuffling of her fellow commuters. As the train shunted out of Ragmullin station, she fell back into the sleep she'd risen from just thirty minutes earlier.

Her dreams resurfaced with the rhythm of the wheels, and unconsciously, she smiled.

'What's so funny?'

Mollie heard the question through the haze of sleep, and opened one eye. She hadn't noticed anyone sit down opposite her. But he was there. Again. The second morning in a row he had ignored other empty seats and occupied that one. Straight across from her. Slowly she closed her eyes again, determined to ignore him. Not that he was bad-looking. He appeared to be fairly ordinary, though his mouth wore a smug grin. He was maybe a little older than her twenty-five years. A mental image flared behind her closed eyes and she found herself awakening fully and staring at him.

Who the hell was he?

'What's your name?' he asked.

The cheek of him! There was an unwritten protocol on the six a.m. commuter service. No one annoyed anyone else. They were all in the same predicament. Up at all hours, half asleep, coffee hastily prepared and poured into travel mugs. Phones, earbuds, laptops and Kindles the only accessories of this tribe. So why the hell couldn't he shut up and let her sleep? Once they reached Maynooth, the carriage would begin to fill up and she could ignore him totally. For now, though, she couldn't.

His eyes were a cool blue. His hair was concealed under a knitted beanie. His fingernails were clean. Manicured? She wondered for a moment if he was a teacher. Or maybe a civil servant or a banker. She couldn't tell whether there was a suit jacket or a sweater under his heavy padded jacket, but she knew from previous mornings that he wore jeans. Blue, with an ironed crease down the centre of the legs. God, who did that any more? His mother? But he looked a little old to be still living with his mother. A wife, then? No ring. Why was she even thinking about it? A tremor of unease shook her shoulders, and immediately she felt afraid of him.

Closing her eyes, she allowed the music to invade her consciousness and the chug of the train to comfort her, hoping for sleep to help her through the next hour and ten minutes. And then she felt his foot touch her boot. Her eyes flew open and she drew back her leg as if scalded.

'What the hell?' she croaked. The first words she'd uttered since awakening that morning.

'Sorry,' he said, his eyes piercing blue darts. His foot didn't move.

And Mollie knew by the tone of his voice that he was anything but sorry.

*

He looked kind of cute, Grace thought. The way he bugged the woman who just wanted to sleep. She couldn't help smiling at him. He didn't notice her. No one did. But she didn't care. She really didn't.

She curled her fingers in her childish-looking mittens and shrugged her shoulders up to her ears, wishing she could pretend to sleep. But she was never any good at pretending. *What you see is what you get.* That was what her mum always said about her. And now she was stuck living with her brother for a month. Not that he was around too often. Thank God, because he was awfully fussy.

She looked down at the empty seat beside her to make sure her bag was still there. No one ever sat beside her until it was standing room only. I'm not going to bite you, she wanted to say, but she never did. She just smiled her gap-toothed smile and nodded. A nod usually put them at ease. You'd think I was a serial killer, the way some of them look at me, she thought. She couldn't help her anxious fidgeting, and she didn't care about what anyone thought, one way or the other.

I am me, she wanted to shout.

She remained tight-lipped.

CHAPTER THREE

'Chloe and Sean! Do I have to make myself hoarse every single morning? Up! Now!'

Lottie turned away from the stairs and shook her head. It was getting worse rather than better. At least next week they would be on mid-term break and she could escape to work without ripped vocal cords.

She unloaded the washing machine. The laundry basket was still half full, so she threw in another load and switched on the machine, then lugged the damp clothes to the dryer. At one time, her mother, Rose Fitzpatrick, used to do a little housework for her, but that relationship was more strained than ever before, and now Rose was feeling poorly.

Sipping a cup of coffee, Lottie allowed it to soothe her nerves. She swallowed three painkillers and tried to massage her back where the stab wound was doing its best to heal. Putting the physical injuries aside, she knew the emotional scars were embedded on her psyche forever. As she gazed out at the frosty morning, she wondered if she should fetch a sweater to keep out the cold. She was wearing a black T-shirt with long sleeves, frayed at the cuffs, and a pair of black skinny jeans. She'd dumped her trusty Uggs last week and was wearing Katie's flat-soled black leather ankle boots.

'Here, Mother,' said Chloe, strolling into the kitchen. 'I think you might need this today.'

'Thank you.' Lottie took the blue hoodie from her seventeen-year-old daughter. She noticed that Chloe was wearing pale foundation and a smoky eyeshadow with thick black mascara. Her blonde hair was tied up in a knot on top of her head.

'You know you're not allowed to wear make-up to school.'

'I do. And I'm not.' Chloe fetched a box of cornflakes and began shovelling them into her mouth.

'And that's lip gloss. Come on. You don't want to get into trouble.'

'I won't. It's not make-up. Just a soft sheen to protect my skin from the cold air,' Chloe said, picking cornflake crumbs off her sticky lips.

Lottie shook her head. Too early for an argument. She rinsed her mug under the tap. 'I'm just warning you in case the teachers notice.'

'Right!' Chloe said and turned up her nose. So like her father, Lottie thought.

'I worry about you.'

'Stop fussing. I'm fine.' Chloe picked up her rucksack and headed for the door.

'I can give you a lift if you like.'

'I'll walk, thanks.'

The front door shut loudly. Lottie wasn't at all convinced her daughter *was* fine. Being called Mother still rankled. It grated on her nerves, and Chloe knew it. That was why she did it. Only in times of extreme tenderness did she call Lottie Mum.

'I'd love a pancake,' Sean said, entering the kitchen holding out his school tie.

'Sean, what age are you?' Lottie looped the tie round her neck and began making a knot.

He looked out from under his eyelashes. 'I can't wait to be fifteen in April. Maybe then you might stop treating me like a kid.'

'I've shown you countless times how to knot your tie.' She handed it back.

'Dad never learned how to do it. I remember you always making the knot for him.'

Lottie smiled wistfully. 'You're right. And I'm sorry, but I haven't time to make pancakes. You've been watching too many American TV shows.' She flicked his hair out of his eyes and squeezed his shoulder. 'See you later. Be good at school.'

She zipped up her hoodie, grabbed her bag and coat and escaped towards the front door.

'Any chance of a lift?' Sean said.

'If you hurry up.'

She waited as he took a tub of yoghurt from the fridge and a spoon from a drawer.

Picking up his bag, he said, 'I'm ready when you are.'

Lottie shouted up the stairs. 'See you later, Katie. Give Louis a goodbye kiss from me.' Then, without waiting for her eldest child to reply, she followed her son out the door.

Just another normal morning in the Parker household.

CHAPTER FOUR

The train stopped at the university town of Maynooth. No one disembarked. Not unusual for the first Ragmullin to Dublin commuter train of the morning. No, the college students would crowd the seven a.m. train. The platform was full, though. Coffee steamed in the frosty air and commuters shuffled towards each other for warmth and seats as they boarded.

Mollie hoped the man sitting opposite her would get out. But she wasn't going to be that lucky. Like the other mornings, he was travelling to Dublin.

With his arms folded and his face turned to the window, she studied him again. Though his eyes were averted, she could feel them on her. Yuck, she thought with a shiver. Rubbing her hands up and down her arms, she tried to ward off the cold. But the feeling was something more than the open doors breathing in the outside air. The chill was emanating from the man sitting across from her.

She watched as he slowly turned away from the window and smiled. Thin pink lips turned up at the corners without the smile reaching his chill blue eyes with their dark pinprick pupils.

'Did you study at Maynooth University?' he asked.

His voice cut a shard into her heart. He sounded different from when he'd spoken earlier. Enquiring yet accusing. Gulping, she shook her head.

'What college did you attend?' he probed.

She really should tell him to bugger off. It was none of his business. Hell, she didn't know who he was. He didn't know her. Or did he? Furrowing her brow, she squinted at him. Was there anything vaguely familiar about him? No, she concluded. Nothing.

'Cat got your tongue?' That smile again. A smile that wasn't a smile at all.

Biting the inside of her mouth, she wished she could get off the damn train. As far away from him as possible. *You're being irrational,* her inner voice warned. *He's just being friendly. Making conversation.* But no one made conversation on the early-morning commute.

Wanting to move away, she looked around, but the train was filling up and she might have to stand. She glanced across the aisle and caught the eye of a young woman sitting beside the opposite window. There was a spare seat beside her. Should she move over there? Would it appear odd given that there was still an empty place right next to her? But she didn't know the man, so what did she care?

Pulling her black laptop bag towards her chest, she stood, grabbing her scarf before it hit the floor. She edged into the aisle and plonked herself down beside the young woman. But even as she exhaled with relief, she felt the cold air dissipate, to be replaced by the heat of an unspoken anger.

Blindly she stared straight ahead, hoping the girl wouldn't try to strike up a conversation. No such luck.

'My name's Grace, what's yours?' The young woman flashed a gap-toothed smile.

Mollie groaned and scrunched her eyes tightly shut. It was definitely one of those mornings.

✱

Two rows down, the man snuggled his chin into his scarf. He'd watched the young woman get up from opposite the annoying chatty man and sit over beside the gap-toothed girl. He knew it was a good thing that she was on edge. The guy had distracted her. Made her fearful. He smiled into the wool of the scarf. She was playing straight into his hands.

If that other bitch hadn't escaped, he wouldn't have need for her. But he always liked to be one step ahead of himself. His mother used to say that.

The thought of his mother caused his smile to slip, and he shoved his hands deeper into his pockets as the trembling began to shake his joints. It was cold, and the heat was always hit and miss on the train, but now he felt certifiably freezing. Shaking his head, he tried to dislodge the image of his mother and replace it with the girl gripping her laptop to her chest. She'd kept her jacket buttoned up and he wondered what she was wearing beneath it. Did she change her clothes when she arrived at work? He knew a lot about her, but he didn't know what she did once she walked through the doors of the nondescript office building on Townsend Street.

The train stopped and started at all the fiddly suburban stations and the carriage warmed up considerably with the pressing crowd. The aisle was now full of people clutching bags and phones, the air clogged with the smell of feet and body odour. It was so crowded that he could no longer see her. He closed his eyes, conjured her up from memory and touched her straight dark hair with an imaginary finger, all the while stroking himself through the pocket of his coat. He couldn't wait much longer. This evening he would see her again.

The train swayed and chugged, speeded up and then slowed down as it entered Dublin's Connolly station. An air of anticipation rose with the heated breath of the passengers as they readied themselves to disembark. He'd have a long day ahead thinking about her, waiting for her. But it would be worth it. Come 6.30 this evening, she would be his.

CHAPTER FIVE

At the garda station, Detective Inspector Lottie Parker climbed the stairs and made her way down the corridor. Her refurbished office was to the rear of the general area. The last piece of the puzzle that had involved three years of renovations and extensions. It even had a door that shut properly. But she couldn't get used to it, so she sat down at her old desk in the main office. Detective Sergeant Mark Boyd was seated opposite her in the cluttered space he shared with Detectives Larry Kirby and Maria Lynch.

'I can use it if you don't want to,' he said with a wink, indicating the empty office behind her.

'Not on your life,' she said. 'It's good to retreat in there when I want; to close the door and scream in peace.'

'You scream out here most of the time. We're immune to your outbursts.' He lined pages up in a file and shut it.

'What did you say, Boyd?'

'I'm only expressing out loud what we're all thinking,' he muttered under his breath.

'I know when I'm not wanted.' She picked up her well-worn leather handbag, shrugged it onto her shoulder and marched into her new office, closing the door behind her.

At her desk, she tapped the keyboard and the computer pinged into life. She opened the page she had been viewing the day before, clicked and zoomed up the photograph of twenty-five-year-old Elizabeth Byrne. Not officially classed as missing because it was too soon. But it was a calm week in Ragmullin, so she'd tasked Boyd with taking a cursory look into Elizabeth's suspected disappearance.

Crooking her chin in her hand, she studied the portrait picture, stared into the shining eyes of the young woman and wondered at the sheen on the auburn hair swept up behind her ear and hanging seductively across one brown eye. Instinctively her hand flew up to her own matted tresses. She needed a colour and cut. Payday was a week away, but she still couldn't afford the eighty-plus euros it would cost.

'Anything else you want me to do regarding Elizabeth Byrne?' Boyd stood half inside, half outside the door.

'I don't bite,' she said, trying to keep the smile from her lips.

'Really? I thought that was you sharpening your teeth a few moments ago.'

'Don't be a smartarse, Boyd. Come in and sit down.'

He closed the door and sat on the grey fabric chair, which she had strategically placed at an angle, ensuring he couldn't see what she was doing. Which wasn't a whole lot, if she was honest.

'Get anything from CCTV?' she asked.

Rustling through the file on his knee, Boyd scanned his eyes over a page then placed a black-and-white image in front of her.

'You know it's not official,' he said.

'I know.'

'It's not yet forty-eight hours.'

She nodded. 'Just tell me what you've got so far.'

'What has you so cranky this morning?'

'Boyd! Just tell me what I'm damn well looking at.'

He scrunched his shoulders and leaned over the desk. 'That's a screenshot of the CCTV from the train station. Taken as she purchased her weekly ticket, Monday morning at 5.55 a.m., before getting on the commuter train to Dublin. She works in the Financial

Services Centre, an administrator at a German bank. According to her colleagues, she was there all day and clocked out at 16.25 in order to get the 17.10 train back to Ragmullin. I asked a friend in Store Street garda station to help. He trawled footage from Connolly station CCTV but as yet he hasn't come across her.'

'Cameras on each platform?'

'Mainly on the DART lines. Other than that, they're focused on the general concourse and ticket offices.'

'Damn.'

'That's mild coming from you.'

'I'm cutting down on swearing. Katie says baby Louis will pick up on it.'

'Ah, for Jaysus' sake,' Boyd laughed. 'Any sign of her going back to college?'

'What do you think?' Lottie shook her head. 'She's hell-bent on heading off to New York to meet up with Tom Rickard, Louis' grandfather.'

'That might be a good thing.'

Mulling over Boyd's words, Lottie was reminded of the trauma her family had suffered the previous year with the death of Rickard's only child, Jason, Katie's boyfriend. A few months later, Katie, then nineteen years old, had discovered she was pregnant with Jason's baby. She'd deferred her college course, and now all her time was consumed with caring for her son.

Lottie had to admit that little Louis was a great tonic for the rest of the family. Chloe and Sean doted on him. But Katie was struggling, while stubbornly refusing all the help Lottie offered. She'd secured a passport for Louis, and was adamant she was heading to New York. There was still the conversation to be had about the cost. Tonight, maybe. Maybe not.

'A trip away might benefit her,' she said. 'But I'm not sure.'

'You're afraid she won't want to come home. Is that it?' he said, seriousness furrowing his brow.

She watched as he leaned back and folded his arms over his pressed blue shirt and immaculate navy tie. His greying hair was cut short as usual, and his leanness verged on being too thin, but not quite. Mid forties suited him better than it suited her, she had to admit. She liked sparring with Boyd and she knew he liked her, but her life was too complicated to embark on anything serious.

'I'm not sure about anything with regards to my children,' she said.

'One day at a time, eh?'

'Sure.' She picked up the CCTV image before Boyd began asking awkward questions. 'A twenty-five-year-old disappears without trace from the 17.10 Dublin to Ragmullin train on Monday evening. Are we positive she actually boarded that train?'

'She was a regular commuter. I talked to a few people leaving the station yesterday evening. Most said they saw her but then weren't sure of the day, but two people swear she was on it. They remembered her standing in the aisle before she secured a seat after Maynooth. Neither of those witnesses can tell us anything further, though, because they both disembarked at the next station, Enfield.'

Lottie said, 'But Elizabeth never arrived home.'

'Exactly.'

'Maybe she got off at Enfield too.'

'Enfield station CCTV confirms she did not.'

'So back to Ragmullin station. You have a CCTV image of her that morning. What about the evening?'

'All the cameras are focused on either the ticket desk or the car park. But we know she has no car so she must have walked to the station Monday morning.'

'She might have stayed on the train and ended up somewhere else.'

Boyd shook his head. 'I've checked with all the stations up to and including Sligo, where the train terminates, and there's no evidence she was on it other than the witnesses who *think* they saw her before Enfield.'

'The media will be calling this "the girl who disappeared from the train".' She printed off the photograph and handed it to Boyd. 'Tell me what you see.'

'A young woman. Hair cut to her shoulders. A scattering of freckles across her nose. Dark brown eyes and full lips. Can I say she's pretty?'

'Boyd! I'm asking about her personality.' She shook her head in exasperation.

'It's just a photograph. I'm not a psychic.'

'Try.'

He sighed. 'She looks sensible enough. No nose or eyebrow piercings. No visible tattoos, though it is only a head shot. Eyes appear clear and bright. Probably no drug use.'

'That's what I thought. Anything show up on her social media accounts?'

'Nothing since Sunday night.'

'What did that say?'

'Just a Facebook post with a GIF of a drowned-looking cat and the caption "Don't tell me tomorrow is Monday. Just don't."'

'Do you think she did a runner?'

'She lives at home and her mother says all her stuff is still in her room.'

Standing up, Lottie grabbed her jacket and bag. 'Come on. Let's have a look round her house and see if we can find out anything.'

'It's not yet forty-eight hours.'

'Are you a parrot? You keep repeating yourself.'

'Elizabeth is an adult. I think you're being a bit premature about this.'

'Oh, for Christ's sake, stop whingeing. Better this than being out in the freezing cold chasing boy racers or trying to get information about illegal bare-knuckle fights.'

'God help me,' he muttered.

She opened the door and looked back over her shoulder as Boyd slowly rose to his feet and joined her. Catching his soapy scent as he passed, she had to stop her hand from reaching out to his. She couldn't do anything that might compromise the contented truce they were experiencing at the moment.

'Why the sour puss?' he asked.

'None of your business,' she said with a smile, and marched through the main office, leaving the jangle of cooling radiators in her wake. In the corridor, she walked straight into Superintendent Corrigan.

'I was just coming to get you,' he said. 'My office. Now.'

Staring after his bulk, Lottie stood open-mouthed. She'd been good recently. Hadn't she?

'What did you do now?' Boyd said, retreating to his office.

'Nothing. I hope.' She crossed her fingers as she took off down the corridor after Corrigan.

'Sit down, Parker. You know it makes me nervous looking at you hopping from foot to foot.'

'I'm not …' Lottie clamped her mouth shut, folded her jacket over her arm and did as her boss commanded.

Superintendent Corrigan pulled his chair into his desk. With his belly suitably comfortable, he tapped a pen on the wood and looked up at her. She stifled a gasp as she noticed the worsening state of his eye. Last summer he'd sported a patch over it, and before Christmas he had declared it better. Better than what, no one asked, but now she thought it looked to have deteriorated considerably.

'Will you stop staring at my eye,' he said, rubbing it viciously, making it tear up and redden further.'

'Sorry, sir.'

'Well, actually, it's one of the reasons I called you in.' He paused. 'I had to visit another specialist. He didn't like it. Sent me for a scan. Found a bastard of a tumour sitting on the optic nerve. And …' His voice cracked and he stood up. She watched him walk to the window. Shit, this was bad news. And she felt there was worse to come.

'I'm going to have to take a break from duty.'

'I'm sorry.'

'Will you stop saying sorry? It's not your fault. One of the only things, I might add, that isn't your fault around here.' He turned around and she saw how much it was annoying him to have to leave work. 'I've contacted head office and they're sending a temporary replacement. No need for interviews or any of that feckin' shite.'

'Really? I thought it was obligatory to hold interviews for replacements, even short-term ones.'

'I've no feckin' idea how short or long my absence will be. My concern is focused on getting this bastard tumour out of my head.'

'I understand. Sorry, sir.'

'Jesus, will you give it up?'

'Sor—' Lottie stopped herself before she said it again. If they weren't holding interviews, shouldn't she get the temporary job of superintendent?

'And before you say another word, you are not going to be my replacement. Apparently your reputation for ballsing things up has reached people higher than me. Much as I try to keep our investigations local.' He took a breath before continuing. 'And how are you feeling since you returned to duty? Better, I hope.'

He wasn't just talking about her physical health. The injury she'd suffered at the hands of a killer had been the catalyst for astonishing revelations about Lottie's family history. Revelations she still couldn't deal with.

'I'm fine, sir. A month at home nearly sent me loopy, but I feel grand now.' She crossed her fingers that he wouldn't dig any deeper.

'That's good.'

'Who is deputising for you, sir? Anyone I know?'

'Detective Inspector David McMahon.'

Lottie shot out of her chair, dropping her jacket and bag to the floor. 'You can't be serious. McMahon! Holy Mother of Jesus, give me a break.' She just about stopped herself stamping her foot like an unruly child. 'If he arrives here, I'm leaving.'

'You're going to do what he says, and you're going to say nothing. Walk the feckin' line. Do you hear me?'

'Sir, you can't let this happen. I'll be the laughing stock of the district. It's preposterous to have an outsider from Dublin coming to deputise for you when I'm already here. It's uncalled for. It's … it's—'

'It's done. No more can be said about it.' Corrigan turned to look out of the window again. 'I hope you won't let me down. I expect you to behave.'

'I'm not five, sir.'

He spun round. 'Well in all honesty, at times you make me wonder.'

Lottie picked up her belongings from the floor. What was she going to do now? This was a disaster. She paused at the door. 'I hope your surgery will be successful, sir. And I promise I'll try to be good while you're gone.'

'Now you definitely sound like a five-year-old. But thanks. And please make McMahon feel welcome,' he added. 'Even though we both know he is an arsehole.'

Outside in the corridor, she leaned against the cool wall. McMahon. What had she done to deserve this? She needed to get out of the station and mull over the implications of the bad news. She shrugged her jacket on and went in search of Boyd.

CHAPTER SIX

Boyd hurried through the station and out the front door, but Lottie wasn't so lucky. A commotion at the reception desk warned her to keep going, but curiosity caused her to have a quick look just as the young woman who was shouting turned to face her.

'You there! You seem like someone who will listen to me. Can I talk to you for a minute?' The young woman had voluminous blonde hair with black roots, piled high on her head. Massive hooped earrings hung from her ears, and a child sucking his thumb rested in the crook of her arm.

'What's the matter?' Lottie asked, silently cursing herself for not being quick enough to disappear after Boyd.

In skin-tight jeans and knee-high black leather boots the woman strode towards her.

'That dope behind the counter won't take down what I'm saying. Will you tell her to write it down? I know once it's written you have to investigate it.'

Pointing to the wooden bench inside the front door, Lottie indicated for the woman to sit. She nodded knowingly to Garda Gilly O'Donoghue, who must have drawn the short straw for reception duty.

'What's your name?' Lottie sat beside the woman.

'My name has got nothing to do with anything. I just want to report what I heard, but no one will listen to me!'

'I'm happy to listen to what you have to tell me. But if you want me to take you seriously, I need to know your name and address.' Lottie extracted a notebook and pen from her bag.

'If I tell you that, you definitely won't believe me.' The woman folded her arms tightly around the child.

'Try me.'

'Right then. Let's see how unprejudiced you are. My name is Bridie McWard, and I live on the traveller site.'

'Okay, Bridie,' Lottie said calmly. 'What did you want to tell me?'

The young woman shifted uneasily on the hard seat, seemingly disconcerted that Lottie was prepared to listen.

'Little Tommy is cutting a tooth, see, and wakes up every hour on the hour. And Monday night, he was really bad. The tooth is just out, but all weekend he was a little hoor. Sorry. Don't suppose you'd know about a screaming baby?'

'You'd be wrong there. Go on.'

'Like I said, Monday night, he was a nightmare. I'd got up to him maybe three times, and that was when I heard it.'

'Heard what?'

'The screaming. Like I told that ditsy madam over there.' She pointed at Garda O'Donoghue.

Lottie smiled to herself. Bridie was a mile out in her conclusion. Gilly O'Donoghue was one of the brighter young guards at the station.

'Go on,' she said.

Bridie glanced at her. 'You know where the site is? The temporary accommodation. Temporary my arse. It's been there this twenty-five years. I was born there, and Mammy lived in a caravan on the site all her life, before the wee houses were even built. Reared eight of us, she did, until she had to go into the nursing home. I'm the youngest. Now we have the house. Temporary? No way. Anyway, I live right next door to the graveyard.'

'I know it,' Lottie said. She frequented the cemetery to visit Adam's grave, though not as often as she used to. She should go over soon and leave some red roses for Valentine's Day. Adam would probably turn in his grave laughing at her. They'd never bothered with Valentine's Day when he was alive.

Bridie continued talking. 'There's a high wall between the houses and the graveyard. And Monday night – well, it was really Tuesday morning – I heard screaming coming from beyond the wall. I thought the dead had risen up to haunt us. It was like a banshee. Mammy told me she heard it once, years ago. I grabbed Tommy out of his cot and turned to wake Paddy, my husband. Except Paddy wasn't there. He does that sometimes. Goes visiting friends and forgets to come home. I know he would've told me I was a stupid woman and to go back to sleep, but how was I supposed to go back to sleep with Tommy awake and someone screaming in the graveyard? Scared shitless I was. Still am, to tell you the truth.' She bit her lip and bowed her head, as if it was a crime to be afraid.

Lottie paused, pen mid-air; the only sound was little Tommy sucking hard on his thumb.

'You heard a scream?'

'You believe me, Guard, don't you?'

'I'm Detective Inspector Parker, and yes, Bridie, I do believe you heard something. But I don't know what. Why didn't you come in yesterday to report this?'

'Had to go to the social, didn't I? To sign on.'

'Right. What time on Monday night did you hear this screaming?'

'I just knew it. You don't believe me.' Bridie jumped up. 'The minute I said where I lived and mentioned the social. You think I'm just one of them time-wasters. Well, Missus High-and-Mighty Detective, you can think what you like. I'm educated. I got my Leaving Cert and a job. Then I got married, had Tommy and gave up work. So I had to sign on.'

'Sit down, Bridie.' Lottie waited a beat as Bridie slumped back onto the bench. 'You're reaching that conclusion about me possibly because of the way you've been treated in the past. But I do believe you.' She watched the young woman running fingers loaded with gold rings through her son's hair, biting her lip. Deciding what to say next?

'I couldn't see anything,' Bridie said eventually. 'Our windows are right up next to the wall. But the screams, they weren't that far away. Just over the other side somewhere. It was a woman. I'm sure of it. It's usually so quiet at night. Unless there's a row on the site, or ambulance sirens wailing into the hospital. But Monday night it was frosty and silent. Then I heard those screams. It was 3.15 on the clock. I remember seeing the red numbers when I got up with Tommy.'

'How long did the screams last?' Lottie had already decided that Bridie had heard teenagers acting the maggot, running through the graves for kicks and frightening the shite out of themselves in the process.

'Not long. A short burst, followed by silence again.'

'And it was definitely a woman?'

'Yeah. Are you going to go out there and take a look?'

'I'll send someone to scout around. Don't be worrying. It was probably just teenagers playing around.'

'Don't send just anyone. You go. I'd trust you to look properly. And I've heard kids there before. This was different. This was real terror.'

With a sigh, Lottie put her notebook into her bag. 'I'll see what I can do.'

'Promise me. Then I'll know.'

'Know what?'

'If you promise me you'll look yourself, I'll believe you.' Bridie's wide eyes were pleading.

'Okay, okay. I'll take a look myself. But it's now Wednesday, so I can't see what good it will do.'

'I'll feel better. And I'll know Tommy is safe. Promise?'

'I promise.' Lottie thought of crossing her fingers to cover a lie, but didn't. Bridie's sincerity had resonated with her, and she wanted to do what the young woman asked.

'There's a funeral later this morning. You'd want to get in before that.'

'I'll go as soon as I can.'

'Thank you, Missus Detective. The minute I laid eyes on you, I knew you were a lady.'

Bridie bundled up her son, and with a squeak of her leather boots, she was out the door and gone.

'Now you're a lady?' Gilly laughed.

'Could have fooled me,' Lottie said.

CHAPTER SEVEN

Lottie told Boyd to park outside the cemetery wall, under the CCTV camera. It was trained on one spot, a warning to potential car burglars to move further down the road. The old iron gates through which you could drive were locked with a clumpy chain.

She walked through the side gate, Boyd trotting beside her. The cemetery was eerily quiet.

'They believe in banshees, don't they?' Boyd said.

'Who?'

'The travellers. They believe in curses and fairies and all that shite.'

'And you don't?' Lottie walked swiftly, glancing around for any sign of a screaming woman, almost two days after Bridie McWard had heard the sound. She briefly wondered if it had anything to do with the missing Elizabeth Byrne, but dismissed that notion as ridiculous.

Halfway down the slope, she stopped as a man wearing a yellow workman's jacket stepped out from behind a tree.

'Can I help you at all?' He had a spade in one hand and shears in the other.

'Jesus, you scared me half to death,' Lottie said.

'Sorry, missus. You look lost. Bernard Fahy is the name. Cemetery caretaker.' He moved the shears under his armpit and thrust out a grubby hand. 'Are you looking for any grave in particular?'

'Detective Inspector Lottie Parker, and this is Detective Boyd.'

Lottie's hand came away covered with clay. Looking into the caretaker's yellow-hued face, she noticed that the whites of his eyes were similarly coloured. 'Have there been any disturbances round here lately?'

'Disturbances? Oh, now I get it. That nosy biddy from the traveller site was on to you, whingeing about banshees screaming in the night.' His laugh was loud and shrill, startling the birds in the bare tree above his head. They fluttered their wings and flew up as one giant black cloud into the cool blue sky. 'Bridie's as mad as old Queenie, her mother. And she's a McWard too. Into all that old witch shite. Know what I mean?'

'Did you investigate Bridie's claims about the screams?' Lottie rubbed her hands together so that she wouldn't get frostbite standing in the freezing air.

'If I was to look into everything reported by that lot living over there, I wouldn't get a single grave dug and you'd have unburied corpses in coffins lined up along with the rubbish at the main gate.'

'You're telling me you didn't investigate it?'

'Dead right I didn't. Isn't that what I just said?'

Lottie shook her head, trying to decipher his cryptic conversation.

'In the last few days, what have you been up to?' she asked.

'Dug a grave on Monday for old Mrs Green from the town centre. Ninety-one she was. The family were waiting for a grandson to come home from Australia. She'll be buried today, beside her late husband.' He pointed down the hill to a mound of clay. 'It's been quiet, to tell you the truth. But this time of year, with the freezing cold weather, you can be sure there'll be a few more kicking the bucket before the week is out.'

'You didn't notice anything out of the ordinary at all? No cider parties? Teenagers running wild through the graves?'

'In this weather? No, that carry-on is reserved for the summer. Those youngsters are at home drinking their parents' gin during the winter. Playing computer games or watching Netflix. Too cold for their young skin.'

As he tugged the shears out from under his arm and back into his hand, Lottie studied Fahy's stubbled face. Pockmarked from teenage acne, she surmised, wisps of hair snaking out around his ears from underneath a black knitted hat. His eyes were inscrutable. She couldn't read what was written in them, and she wondered if she really wanted to.

'We'll have a quick look around if you don't mind,' she said.

'Off you go.' He headed up the way they'd come.

At the bottom of the incline, Boyd said, 'I don't like the look of him.'

Lottie shrugged and glanced over at the houses in the traveller site behind the high wall. Smoke swirled up, then, as if held by an unseen force of frozen air, petered out in straight lines and back down to earth.

There was no way Bridie McWard could have seen anything over the wall in daylight, never mind in the dead of night. As she scanned the headstones in the chilly haze, she glimpsed Adam's granite resting place, on the high ground to her left.

'Isn't Adam buried up there?'

She jumped. 'Jesus, Boyd. For a minute I forgot you were here.'

'Didn't mean to scare you. But it's kind of creepy in this weather.'

'Creepy at the best of times.'

She turned left along the wall, and came to a stop beside the freshly turned clay that Fahy had pointed out. The open grave was covered with slats of timber.

'Mrs Green's new abode, I presume,' she said.

'Dermot Green.' Boyd read the inscription. 'Died September 2001. Aged eighty years. Yes, I'd say this is where she'll be going. To rest beside her late husband.'

'You'll make a good detective someday,' Lottie said with a laugh.

Boyd laughed too. The sound appeared to echo back at them, and she shivered.

Memories of the day Adam had been buried flooded her mind. His body lying in a wooden box with a gold-plated cross on top, interred forever in sacred ground. Dismissing the images, she looked at the area around the Greens' burial plot. The grass outside the kerbstones was flattened, presumably by Fahy and his workmen as they dug the grave. Lottie made her way slowly along the path, stopping at a grave three up from the Greens'.

'Boyd, look at this.' She knelt down. 'Is that blood?'

Boyd leaned over and they stared at the bead of brownish red staining the white pebbles adorning the burial plot.

'Looks like it.' He took a plastic evidence bag from his jacket pocket. 'I'll get it tested.'

'Do that.'

Standing up, she glanced all around. Some of the grass here was flattened too. It could be from the frost, or people visiting buried loved ones, or even the caretaker, she supposed. Or was it something else entirely? And why was there that stain that looked like blood within screaming distance of the traveller site?

She began to think that maybe Bridie McWard hadn't heard a banshee after all. It seemed more likely that someone had indeed screamed while running through the graveyard early on Tuesday morning.

Turning back to Boyd, she said, 'You done yet?'

'I am.'

'I don't like the feeling I'm getting. Let's have another chat with Mr Friendly.'

The caretaker's office was just inside the main gate. The windows were criss-crossed with iron cladding and the roof was shaped like one you'd find on an old country church.

'This used to be living quarters at one time,' Bernard Fahy said.

He'd divested himself of his workman's jacket and was shuffling around the small office. He wore a thin jumper under a pair of dungarees at least two sizes too big for him. His hair had probably once been blonde but had turned yellow. From cigarette smoke, Lottie suspected.

'Does anyone live here now?' She stared at the bare concrete floor, then the cracked walls.

'Not a sinner, except for the poor souls buried six feet beneath us.'

'Really?'

'Not literally.' He laughed, the same harsh sound that had earlier scared the birds.

Lottie felt her skin crawl. She looked up at the tall, thin man. It was hard to tell his age, because his skin was so weather-beaten.

'I've been caretaker here for the last fifteen years, and I could tell you a thing or two about what goes on around here. You wouldn't believe it.'

'I think I would,' Lottie said. She wasn't here for reminiscences. She wanted answers. 'If someone wanted to gain entry to the graveyard at night, is it easy?'

'The main gate is locked, unless a hearse is arriving, but the side gate is left open day and night. And anyone can hop over the wall if they've a mind to. There's a lot of illegal dumping. I work for the council and they won't listen to me about it. Did you see the mound of black bags out there? Don't suppose you can do anything?'

She shook her head. 'Sorry.' Opening her bag, she took out Elizabeth Byrne's photograph. 'Have you ever seen this young woman?'

Fahy picked up the photo and ran a dirty fingernail down Elizabeth's face. 'Pretty girl. What did she do?'

'She didn't *do* anything.' Lottie pulled the photograph from him and wiped it clear of smudges. 'We're trying to locate her.'

'You won't find her here, unless she's dead and buried,' he sniggered.

'Have you seen her?'

'You keep asking the same questions. Must be hard, training to be a guard. No, I never saw that girl before.' He picked up his jacket. 'And if you don't mind, I've Mrs Green's funeral arriving in a few minutes.'

'If you hear anything else from Bridie, or anyone else, please let me know.' Lottie handed him one of her cards.

'I will. If truth be told, she did rattle me a little with her scary stories. I was beginning to believe them myself.' He looked up at the diamond-shaped windows, lost in thought, before adding, 'You sure you don't want to look into that illegal dumping for me?'

'I'm sure.'

'If I catch who's doing it, *they* will be dead and buried,' Fahy said.

Lottie pushed Boyd out the door in front of her and strode to the gate.

'He gives me the creeps,' Boyd said.

Lottie said, 'Dead and buried. I hope not.'

CHAPTER EIGHT

Boyd started the car, checked his rear-view mirror and prepared to pull out.

'Wait a minute,' Lottie said, putting her hand on the steering wheel to stop him. 'There's the funeral cortège coming up the road. We'd better be respectful and wait until they go in.'

'You're the boss.' He switched off the engine.

She sat back and watched as Fahy unlocked the wrought-iron gates. They swung slowly inwards, and the hearse, containing a simple pine coffin adorned with a spray of lilies, passed through into the cemetery. Eight cars remained outside the gate and parked up on the opposite side of the road.

A priest in a black coat with a purple stole hanging from his shoulders alighted from the first car. He was slightly crouched, as if there was an invisible weight resting on his shoulders.

Shit, Lottie thought.

'Is that who I think it is?' Boyd said.

'Come on,' she said, ignoring the obvious. Father Joe Burke was back. 'There's only a small crowd; we can add to the numbers.'

'We have enough work to be getting on with without gatecrashing a stranger's funeral.'

'Jesus, Boyd, will you ever shut up?' Lottie banged the door on his words and followed the group of about thirty people down the hill to Mrs Green's final resting place.

'This is ridiculous, if you don't mind me saying so.' Boyd kept pace with her.

'I do mind. Keep quiet. I want to see what Mr Fahy gets paid to do.'

'He digs a grave then fills it in when the family leaves. You know that. We're wasting our time here.'

'God give me patience!' she cried. 'Go back to the car and wait for me.'

'No need to be so antsy. Now that I'm here, I might as well go with you.'

She slowed down when the hearse stopped at the end of the narrow roadway. Two undertakers opened the rear door, and the family lined up to receive the coffin. Lottie's shoulders quivered. She hadn't attended a burial since Adam's, except for the interment of her brother's bones. This was a stranger. Someone she had no connection with. She should be okay. But she wasn't.

And there was Father Joe Burke, with his fair hair cut shorter than she remembered, his fringe swept back from his forehead, and his eyes as clear as sapphires. Pulling up the hood of her jacket, she turned away. She wanted to see him, and at the same time she didn't. You're such a contradiction, she told herself. Early last year he had been her friend when things had been tough. He'd even helped her with her investigation into the murder of Susan Sullivan. But he'd left Ragmullin crippled with sorrow when he'd discovered the truth about his parentage and she'd thought she'd never see him again. Now he was back. Was that a good thing? She wasn't at all sure.

Six men, three on either side, laid the coffin down on the laths of timber that Fahy had placed across the open grave. Another man, in a workman's jacket, stood beside Fahy. They both moved to the rear of the sad family gathering.

She watched as a young man in a suit a size too small put the spray of flowers down beside the coffin, on top of the mound of clay. The scent of the lilies was evocative, and she was dragged back once more to the day she had helped lower her husband into the dead earth. Would she ever be free of the memories? They clung to her like a cold sweat.

With a sprinkling of holy water, Father Joe began the prayers. He was joined in a murmur by the small crowd. Trying to keep her focus off the priest, Lottie found herself wondering about the substance she had found on the pebbles earlier. She was sure it was blood, but it could have come from a child cutting a knee or even one of the workmen as they dug the grave.

More holy water was sprinkled, then six of the mourners, among them the only two women present, took up the leather ropes either side of the opening, rolled them round their hands, knuckles whitening, and pulled them taut. Fahy stepped forward and slid the timber supports away, and the coffin was held aloft above the gaping six-foot hole.

A scream broke from the small assembly, then one of the women let go of the rope and sank to her knees. Such grief, Lottie thought. She watched from a distance as Father Joe gripped the distraught woman's elbow and helped her upright. Fahy and his colleague hurriedly repositioned the timber laths to take the weight of the coffin again.

The woman cried out once more and Lottie pushed her way through the mourners.

'Are you okay?' she asked.

'Lottie!' the priest said. He stared at her open-mouthed, as if to ask a question, but the distressed woman began to speak.

'There's something down there.' She pointed into the grave, her face as white as the blouse peeking out at the collar of her coat.

Peering into the space, Lottie saw only clay. 'What did you see?'

Fahy shimmied in beside them. 'Probably a bird, or vermin. Freshly dug graves can attract them. Especially with an old corpse already—' He stopped as Lottie speared daggers at him with her eyes. 'Sorry,' he said.

'That's my grandfather you're talking about,' said a stout man who had wrapped his arm about the shoulders of the stricken woman.

'We'll take a break,' Father Joe said with a nod to Lottie, and shepherded the mourners out onto the path, where they huddled at the side of the hearse.

She sensed Boyd at her shoulder.

'Might be the banshee's resting place,' he said.

'Can we have a look?' she asked Fahy.

'There's nothing down there,' he said.

Lottie turned to the sobbing woman. 'What exactly did you see?'

'I'm not entirely sure. Maybe I imagined it, but when we pulled on the rope and the coffin was raised up a bit, I thought I saw what looked like skin poking out of the clay at the bottom of the grave. Human flesh. Good God! Could it be my grandad?' She shook her head wildly. 'But he's been dead fifteen years.'

'Stay right here. All of you.' Lottie marched over to Fahy, who was now standing beside the grave. 'Can you move the coffin so that I can take a look?'

'What? You're not going down there, are you?' Fahy shoved his hands deeper into his pockets.

'I want the coffin moved. Now.' The caretaker was needling her nerves like an irritating itch.

'This is outrageous,' he said.

Boyd edged in between them. 'I think you're overreacting, boss. We should let this family bury their loved one.'

She glared at him before turning back to Fahy. 'You and your colleague push this coffin out of the way. I want a quick look and then you can get on with the ceremony.'

With a theatrical sigh, Fahy called to his workmate. Between them they placed an extra piece of timber underneath the wooden casket and slid it away from the grave.

The air seemed to chill and the sky appeared to darken as Lottie leaned over the edge and peered into the opening.

'Shit,' she said. 'Boyd, get SOCOs here. And call Lynch and Kirby. Quickly.'

CHAPTER NINE

'What about my funeral?' Fahy asked, as Boyd corralled the mourners and Father Joe with the undertakers on the far side of the hearse.

Lottie squared up to him. 'Mr Fahy, it's not your funeral, it's Mrs Green's, and I want you and your colleague to join the family over there until I can get a cordon in place.'

'We have to bury her,' he said.

'And you will. But not right now. I have a strong suspicion that there's a body in that grave that shouldn't be there, so I'm asking you to move away.'

'Right so.' He grabbed his colleague by the sleeve and took out his phone. 'I'm calling my supervisor about this.'

'You can call whoever you like, just stay out of my crime scene.'

Once she was alone, Lottie stared down into the darkness. Protruding from a thin layer of soil were pink-varnished toenails.

An hour later, the serenity of Ragmullin cemetery was lacerated by a hive of action and noise. Mrs Lorraine Green's coffin had been returned to the hearse and her family members had been whisked away by the undertakers. Much as Lottie would have liked to, she didn't speak to Father Joe, but she registered his sad smile with an inclination of her head.

Eventually the crime-scene tape was in place and the main gate was closed and guarded. A line of spectators perched on the high wall as the scene of crime officers erected a tent over the gaping grave.

'Jim McGlynn is on his way,' Boyd said.

'He'll be delighted to see the pair of us.'

Boyd pulled at his chin, his eyes concerned. 'You think it's her? Our missing woman?'

'There's someone down there and it's not a corpse that's been interred for fifteen years. So, it's possible.' She looked over at the gawkers sitting on the wall. 'We need to speak with Bridie McWard again, plus Fahy and his colleague.'

'Where did they go?'

She pointed to the row of pine trees to her left, where Fahy stood smoking a cigarette. He was flanked by Detectives Larry Kirby and Maria Lynch. As Lottie neared them, Fahy sucked in hard and blew out a stream of smoke.

'I need you down at the station to make a statement,' she said.

'I saw nothing. And I did nothing either, before you go accusing me. Dug the grave on Monday and put the laths on it this morning. I saw only clay down there.'

'We need a formal statement. You're sure you didn't notice anything suspicious over the last few days?'

'I told you already. I didn't see anything.' He lit another cigarette. The smell made Lottie's empty stomach queasy.

'What's your name?' She directed her question to the plump young man with a bad case of acne standing in Fahy's shadow.

'I only started here today. I'm on a scheme.'

'What is your name? Are you deaf?' Lottie said. His teeth were yellow and his skin wan.

'I wear a hearing aid. Deaf in one ear.' He pointed to his right ear. 'But I forgot to put it in today.'

'Sorry.' Lottie positioned herself to talk into his good ear.

'His name is John Gilbey,' Kirby said, his bushy hair standing up on his head and the zip on his jacket straining across his large girth.

Lynch lounged against the wall, pale-faced. Her fair hair, usually tied up in a ponytail, streamed about her shoulders.

'You have to go to the station,' Lottie told Gilbey. 'It's a formality. Nothing to worry about.' She instructed Kirby to take the two men with him.

Lynch said, 'What do you want me to do, boss?'

'Make yourself useful. Help uniforms with the cordon at the front gate.'

As Lynch stomped off up the hill, a silver station wagon rumbled down the slope, slowed and stopped. The driver leaned out of the window.

'Well, if it isn't Inspector Morse and Sergeant Lewis. Disrupting my morning as usual.'

'Jesus, McGlynn. I didn't recognise you with your clothes on.' Lottie smirked. She'd only ever seen the head of the SOCO team in his white protective gear, hood up and mask in place. Two green eyes. That was all she knew about him. Now she could put a face to the ensemble. His craggy features told her he was aged about sixty. And he was in a foul humour, though that was nothing new.

'I'd recognise you in a blackout,' he said, mouth downturned. 'What have you dug up for me this time?'

'Not exactly dug up, though if it wasn't for a bad case of curiosity, I think she would have been interred forever.'

'And you know what curiosity did to the cat, don't you?' McGlynn let the window back up and continued down to the scene.

'Contrary arse,' Lottie said.

Within fifteen minutes, McGlynn had his team in place. They lowered a ladder into the grave, and he climbed to the bottom and stood to one side as pebbles and clay cascaded around him.

'A thin layer of clay and dirt,' he said, hunching down. He used a short-handled, long-bristled brush to carefully sweep it away, working slowly, until a foot emerged from the blackness. Toes painted in a fluorescent pink varnish. The chalky flesh looked paper thin. Brushing away the clay on the opposite side, McGlynn leaned backwards as another foot appeared.

'Can you move up to the area where a head should be?' Lottie was impatient to find out the identity of the buried person.

McGlynn continued his methodical work without reply. As he uncovered the leg, Lottie saw that it was broken, the bone sticking out.

'Tibia open shaft fracture is my initial observation,' McGlynn said. 'Broken through the skin. That's the shin bone. Signs of maggots. No flies. Not been down here long. It's been cold, with no rain, so a day, maybe two at the most.'

Lottie knelt down on the protective covering at the edge of the hole and leaned over further, praying for him to hurry up.

A second leg appeared, and as more of the body was revealed, it became evident that it was definitely a female, and that she was naked.

'No other visible wounds so far,' he muttered.

Eventually the face and hair appeared, and Lottie drew in a breath. McGlynn glanced up, emeralds dancing above the white mask. 'You see what I see, Inspector?'

'She was suffocated with the clay?'

'Even though the layer is thin, I don't think she covered herself with it. Inform the state pathologist that she is needed here.'

'I've already phoned her,' Boyd said. 'She should be here soon.'

Lottie stared down at the victim's mouth, full of clay, and the dirt-encrusted auburn hair.

'Who was the last person you saw?' she asked the lifeless body of Elizabeth Byrne.

CHAPTER TEN

Lottie left Jane Dore, the state pathologist, with McGlynn to confirm what she already knew. They were dealing with a suspicious death. She sent Lynch to find Bridie McWard so that she could be questioned again, then she and Boyd went back to the station to set up an incident team and to interview the cemetery workers.

Superintendent Corrigan was marching around the incident room when she arrived.

'You found your missing woman?'

'I believe so, sir, but we need to make a positive ID.'

'Did you inform her mother?'

'Not yet.'

'Do it soon, before the media blast it all over Twitter.'

'I intend to.'

'I need to talk to you,' Corrigan said.

Lottie followed him down the corridor and into his office.

'Sit down,' he said, and squeezed in behind his desk.

'Do you want an update, sir? I'll have a full report for a team meeting in the morning.'

'No, I won't be here then, so I'll have to leave it in your hands. In McMahon's hands, I should say. I want to tell you something.'

Oh Lord, Lottie thought. He's going to tell me he's dying and I'll be stuck with McMahon for the rest of my working days. 'Yes, sir?'

'Elizabeth Byrne. She was last seen on the train. Correct?'

'As far as we know. We only have her mother's word that she didn't arrive home.'

'It reminds me of a case I worked ten years ago. In fact, the anniversary is this week. I don't know why I'm even mentioning it, but the train bit – that's what jogged my memory. The difference then was that the young woman was never found. And now I'm wondering, could she have been buried in a grave that was awaiting a coffin?'

'Back up a bit.' Lottie tried to compute what Corrigan was saying but couldn't work it out. 'What woman?'

'Lynn O'Donnell. Aged twenty-four or twenty-five at the time. Last seen on the Dublin to Ragmullin train, but she never arrived home. Valentine's Day 2006. Pull the file if you get time. It's probably nothing to do with this murder, but no harm in knowing about it. I'm sure the media will pick up on it.'

'Thanks, sir, I'll have a look at the file. I do remember it. I was based in Athlone at the time.' She glanced at him. He was rubbing his eye again. 'And you mind yourself. I'll be checking in with you to make sure everything goes well.'

'No need for that. I'm sure McMahon will keep you busy enough.'

'I'm dreading his arrival,' she confessed.

'Stay out of his way, do a good job and he'll have no reason to complain. I'm counting on you to keep up the good name of this district.'

'I'll do my best, sir.'

'Good luck. I think you'll be needing it.'

CHAPTER ELEVEN

'Do you remember the disappearance of Lynn O'Donnell?' Lottie asked Boyd as they arrived at the home of Elizabeth Byrne.

'Yeah, that rings a bell. A long time ago now, though. Why do you ask?'

'Corrigan mentioned it. She was last seen on a train from Dublin to Ragmullin. Same as Elizabeth.'

'Does he think they might be connected?'

'Not sure. He said to have a look at the cold case file.'

'A giant stretch of the imagination, if you ask me.'

'I'll have a look anyway.' She rang the doorbell.

Elizabeth Byrne had lived with her mother in a detached red-brick house in the Greenway estate. Anna Byrne led them to the kitchen. 'I hope you have news of Elizabeth. I just boiled the kettle. Will you join me in a cup of tea? Coffee? Awful cold out there today.'

As Mrs Byrne busied herself with cups and tea bags, Lottie and Boyd sat at the table, an old-fashioned wooden affair with a red oilcloth covering it. The cooker was a cream-coloured Aga, with a saucepan simmering on top. Glancing at the clock hanging on the wall, Lottie noted that it was just over two hours since they'd discovered the body. She shivered, even though the kitchen was warm.

When Mrs Byrne turned around, Lottie noticed the lines of worry furrowed into her brow. Dressed in jeans and a pink jumper over a white cotton shirt, she wore fluffy socks on her feet. Probably belonged to Elizabeth, Lottie thought. Her heart lurched as she thought about delivering the news that would shatter this poor woman's hope forever.

'Here, let me give you a hand,' Boyd said, rising to take a jug from her hand. 'You sit and I'll make the tea.'

He knew when to switch on the charm, but Lottie was well aware that he was only putting off the inevitable. Mrs Byrne slumped onto a chair.

'Do you have any news about Elizabeth?'

'Mrs Byrne …' Lottie began.

'Call me Anna.'

'I'm so sorry, Anna … I hate to have to tell you like this, but I'm afraid the news I have is not good.' Shit, this wasn't the way to tell a mother her daughter was dead.

'Would you like a biscuit?' Anna was fussing. 'Ginger nuts. I have a packet somewhere.' She jumped up.

Lottie put a hand on the woman's arm. 'Anna. I'm sorry.'

Anna gnawed at her lip, eyes bulging with unshed tears. Her hand flew to her mouth as if trying to keep back the words she didn't want to utter.

'She's dead, isn't she?' Pulling at her sleeve now. Eyes scrunched up, avoiding Lottie's gaze.

'I'm terribly sorry.'

'Tell me.' The tears now burst forth and spilled down the woman's cheeks, around her streaming nose and over her lips. 'Tell me,' she screamed.

Lottie reached over and put her hand on Anna Byrne's. 'I'm afraid we found the body of a female earlier today.'

'No! I don't believe you. It's not my Elizabeth. She's all I have. Do you understand? It's not her.' Hysteria laced the woman's words.

'We have reason to believe it is Elizabeth. I'm so sorry.'

Anna's body rocked with convulsions, and Lottie jumped up and grabbed a glass from a cupboard. She filled it with water from the tap and held it to Anna's lips.

'Sip this. It might help.' She had delivered bad news many times before, but in the face of naked grief, she was at a loss as to the right approach to use, though if anyone should know, she should.

'Oh God. What happened to her?' A fragile calm settled in the room as Anna looked straight into Lottie's eyes.

She held the gaze. 'All we know at the moment is that the circumstances appear suspicious.'

'Was she murdered?'

'We don't yet know.'

'How did she die? This girl you found.'

'I can't say at the moment. Not until after … after the post-mortem is concluded.'

'Oh my good God!' the woman wailed.

'Can I call someone for you. A friend? Family?'

Anna ignored the question. 'Where did you find her?'

Lottie glanced to Boyd, begging for help. He shook his head slowly. 'In the cemetery,' she said.

'It can't be Elizabeth.' Anna appeared resolute in her conviction as she folded her arms and sniffed back more tears. 'She never goes there.'

'I'm sorry, Anna, I know this is hard for you, but we have reason to believe it may be your daughter. And we need you to formally confirm her identity.'

'I told you she was missing. No one believed me.' The woman's voice was almost inaudible before it rose an octave. 'You said you couldn't look for her because you had to wait forty-eight hours. Well, it's over forty-eight hours since *I* last saw her. You can start searching now.' She unfolded her arms and tore the oilcloth with her nail. Worried the hole larger and dug her finger into the wood of the table.

Lottie stared at Boyd. Come on, she pleaded silently. Time to work some more of his charm.

'Anna,' he said softly. 'We think we've found Elizabeth's body. Do you understand what I'm saying?'

She nodded, and more tears fell from her eyes.

'Please let me call someone to come and sit with you,' Lottie said.

'I'll be fine. Do you want to ask questions about Elizabeth? Go on. Ask me. Better to do it now. Then you'll know you've made a mistake.'

'We can do that another time,' Boyd said quickly.

Anna thumped the table. 'Ask me now. Before it hits me properly.'

'If you're sure?' Lottie said.

The woman nodded.

Lottie lowered her voice, speaking as softly as she could. 'Tell us about your daughter. What was she like? Her friends and—'

'I told that nice young Garda O'Donoghue everything.'

'We need to discover her last movements. Had her mood changed recently?'

'She was the same as usual. On the go. Flitting here and there. She never sits still for two minutes. Always has to be doing something. Do you have children, Inspector?'

'I do,' Lottie said. Anna's description of Elizabeth reminded her of her own Chloe. 'Three teenagers. Well, Katie is twenty now.'

'You know what it's like then. Racing in and out of the house. Changing her clothes a dozen times a day. Out at nightclubs. She goes jogging on Saturday and Sunday mornings. At Rochfort Gardens. During the week, she has to drag herself to the station for the early commuter train.'

Lottie thought this was a world removed from Katie's. 'Did she have many friends?'

'She has a few. No one close comes to mind. She hangs out with Carol O'Grady, even though I don't approve. Not that I'm a snob or anything.'

'You don't like Carol?'

Anna didn't answer the question. She said, 'Elizabeth is an only child, so it's mostly just me and her.'

'Boyfriend?' Boyd asked.

Anna was silent for a moment before she lifted her head. She looked directly at him.

'She had her heart broken a year ago. She was sure he was the one for her. All talk of getting married and looking for a mortgage and the like. No ring ever appeared, though, and then he disappeared from the scene.'

'Disappeared?' Lottie raised a quizzical eyebrow.

'Not like that. He worked in a bank in Dublin and was transferred to a Munich branch. Upped and left my girl with a shattered heart. The bastard. Sorry, I only use bad language where Matt Mullin is concerned.'

Lottie heard Boyd scribble the name in his notebook. She said, 'Did the break-up affect her badly?'

'Very. She started going out with her girlfriends every night. Even on work nights. She'd never done that before. Heartbroken, my poor pet.' Anna wiped away the tears that were dripping down her chin.

Lottie reached out and gripped her hand. 'This Matt guy, is he still in Munich?'

Anna drew back as if Lottie had pinched her. 'Do you think he could be back in town? Do you think he's involved somehow? Did that bastard kill my girl?' Anger rapidly replacing heartache.

'We don't know anything yet,' Lottie said. 'Is he originally from Ragmullin?'

'Yes. He lived on the old Dublin road. I'm sure you can find his address.'

'You gave Garda O'Donoghue a list of Elizabeth's friends. I don't recall this Matt being on it.'

'He's not a friend. I've been trying to forget about him since he dumped my girl. Last Valentine's Day. Can you believe it? She thought he was wining and dining her to present her with a diamond. Some kick in the teeth he presented her with that night.'

'That's awful,' Lottie said. 'I'll definitely contact him.'

'Do that.' Anna was dry-eyed now, glaring. Lottie realised that shock was setting in.

'Did she date anyone after Matt?'

Anna shook her head. 'No. I'd have known.'

'Could she have been dating without telling you?'

'Like I said, I'd have known.'

'Sunday night last. Did she do anything different?'

'She was the same as always.'

'But can you tell me what she did that night?' Lottie knew she appeared heartless, but she had to continue with the questions while Anna was prepared to talk.

'Let me see. Elizabeth doesn't go to mass. She stopped going since all that with Matt. So it was near one o'clock when she got up. Missed her usual run at Rochfort Gardens. She'd been in the Last Hurdle Saturday night and wasn't home until near three. I've got to the stage where I keep my mouth shut. She is twenty-five, after all. An adult, so she keeps telling me. An adult who still wants her dinner cooked and her clothes washed for her. Sometimes I feel more like a servant than a mother.'

'I know the feeling,' Lottie said, noting that Anna was still refer-ring to her daughter in the present tense. 'So on Sunday she got up at one o'clock. What did she do then?'

'We had dinner. A roast. Just the two of us. My husband, Elizabeth's dad, died eight years ago. Cancer.'

A sharp stitch screwed into Lottie's heart. Death did that to you. You never got over it; you just learned to live with it. And she was still learning. She felt Boyd staring at her and raised her head. He nodded, his knowing look.

She turned back to Anna. 'What did Elizabeth do after dinner?'

'Back up to bed she went. Said she was tired, not to disturb her. She had a hangover, so I let her be. She didn't appear downstairs again and I never heard her get up for work Monday morning. Therefore, Inspector, the last time I saw my daughter was around two o'clock on Sunday.'

'Can we see her room?' Lottie asked, thinking it was a bit odd that Anna hadn't checked on Elizabeth. Then again, she herself was guilty of the same inaction from time to time.

'First door at the top of the stairs.' Anna picked up the cups and went to the sink.

'I'll sit with you while Inspector Parker has a look,' Boyd said.

'I'll be fine. Go ahead.'

'You're sure I can't ring someone?' Boyd asked.

'Just do what you have to do.'

Lottie beckoned him to follow and they made their way up the stairs.

'Strange little family,' Lottie whispered.

'You can talk,' Boyd said.

'On first impressions, Elizabeth was a bit like you,' Lottie said to Boyd.

'How do you come to that conclusion?'

'This room screams OCD to me.'

'Maybe her mother cleaned it up.'

'I doubt it, based on what she's just told us.'

As she looked around the room, Lottie was struck by the symmetry of everything. Make-up brushes lined up in a jar by height; perfume bottles in a tidy circle; nail polish in a neat row, the colours of the rainbow. A small bottle of fluorescent pink stood at the end.

She opened the first of three drawers. Underwear, all folded. Running her hand beneath them, it came away empty. The next drawer had a hairdryer, straighteners and brushes. She placed a hairbrush in a plastic evidence bag. The last held a multitude of colourful scarves and socks.

She turned her attention to the wardrobe while Boyd rifled through the bedside cabinet. The clothes were divided neatly down the middle by an IKEA shoe-holder. One side held skirts and jackets – Elizabeth's work clothes; the other side a conglomeration of jeans, some with designer tears and holes. Beside them, a rack of long sleeved T-shirts and blouses, and a selection of Lycra running gear. The top shelf held an assortment of girlie hats, and on the floor of the wardrobe were neatly paired Nike and Adidas runners. All pristine.

'She even cleaned her runners,' Lottie said. She noticed Boyd sitting on the neatly made duvet, thumbing through a flower-covered notebook. 'What's that?'

'Love poems, by the look of it. Mr Matt Mullin broke this girl's heart.'

'Any laptop?'

'No, and no phone either. She must have had them with her.'

Lottie ran her hands under the pillows, finding only folded pyjamas. 'Gosh, I wish my girls could see this.'

'See what?'

'How they should keep their rooms.'

'Not normal, though, is it?' Boyd gestured around. 'For a twenty-five-year-old to be so fastidious.'

'Everyone is different.'

'If you say so.'

Boyd got down on his knees and peered beneath the bed.

'Anything?' Lottie asked.

'Just this.' He pulled out a red cabin-sized suitcase and unzipped it. 'Empty.'

'She hadn't been planning to run away.'

'I'm taking the notebook.'

She watched as he put it into an evidence bag. 'You know what's missing?'

'What?' He secured the flaps.

'Costume jewellery. My girls have drawers full of it.' She pointed to a small selection of silver and gold chains hanging on a plastic stand on the dressing table. 'Why did Elizabeth only have genuine jewellery? I'll ask Anna about it.'

'I think it's more important to find the ex-boyfriend.' Boyd made for the door.

Feeling the tension pushing pinpricks of annoyance up on her skin, Lottie counted to five before following him.

CHAPTER TWELVE

The box of cornflakes was in the wrong cupboard. Donal O'Donnell shook his head and opened the next cupboard. He took out the packet and got the milk from the fridge, then sat at the table and filled the bowl. Breakfast at lunchtime was becoming a habit. Picking up the spoon, he noticed it was dirty. Caked cereal dotted the handle.

'That's all I need.' His voice echoed around the empty kitchen. 'First the refrigerator packs up, then the dishwasher.' He knew things always came in threes. What would be next?

As he spooned the cereal into his mouth, ignoring the milk dripping down his chin, he realised that the third thing had already occurred. That was, if he could count the death, three weeks ago, of his wife of forty years as a thing going wrong.

Finishing his breakfast, he let the spoon fall noisily into the bowl and carried it to the sink. Then he went to the dresser and struck a match to light the candle. For ten years Maura had lit it daily. Ten years she had yearned for answers. She had always hoped. Hoped for their Lynn to walk through the door; for a guard to ring the doorbell; for someone to tell her … something. Anything.

He set his lips in a stiff line and sniffed the sob back into his throat. Poor Maura. Consigned to her grave without answers. Breast cancer, the consultant had said. Huh! Donal was one hundred per cent certain his wife had died of a broken heart.

The doorbell rang.

He laced up his shoes before going to answer it. Straightened his shoulders and unhooked the chain.

'Oh, it's you,' he said, turning away, leaving the door swinging open.

'Yes, Dad, it's me. Why aren't you at work?'

'How many times do I have to tell you, Keelan? I am not your dad. To you, I'm Donal. Right?'

It bugged the shite out of him that his daughter-in-law called him Dad. She was a nice girl, trying too hard to be even nicer. But he'd had one daughter and now he had none. No matter how hard she tried, she was just his son's wife. No one could fill the cavernous space left in his heart when his Lynn disappeared.

'I'm sorry, Donal. Do you want a lift anywhere? It's no bother. Saoirse is still at school. I can—'

'No!' He hadn't meant to shout. Easing the harshness from his tone, he said, 'I want to be left alone. Can you understand that? Lynn is gone. Maura is gone. I'm next. You can bugger off home.' Shit, he didn't want to be angry with Keelan. It wasn't her fault.

She was rinsing the bowl under the tap, her shoulders heaving. Christ, he hoped she wasn't crying. He couldn't handle any more tears. Maura's had swallowed him up. In a way, he found it peaceful now to be living in the silence of his own home without sobs shrieking through the air.

'I can do that.' He took the tea towel from her hand. When she turned around, he saw her make-up was streaked. 'Didn't mean to make you cry.'

'It's not your fault.' She was searching up her sleeve and eventually pulled out a tattered tissue. Dabbing at her mascara, she said, 'It's Cillian.'

'What's he done? Has he … has he hurt you?'

'No. Nothing like that. Not physical hurt, if you get me.'

'What do you mean? Come and sit down.'

At the table, Keelan said, 'He's different. Distant. Since Maura died. I know it's probably grief, but he wasn't particularly close to his mother. Was he?'

'Hard to say. Cillian and Finn were both close to their sister. Close in age and close … like friends. When she disappeared, it upset the whole family dynamic. You know what I mean?'

'Tell me.'

'They were only young then, early twenties. They adored Lynn and she doted on them. No fights. No hair-pulling.' He noticed Keelan returning his smile. 'I thought we were the luckiest parents in the world. But you know what? I think Maura was a little resentful of the friendship they shared. It was like they were so close, the three of them, that they shut her out. At times, it led to … I haven't a clue what to call it.'

'Jealousy? Was Maura jealous?'

'I don't rightly know. I was working long hours back then, so I wasn't home a lot. But when Lynn went missing, Maura blamed herself for not caring for the children as much as she should have. And she blamed the boys for not watching out for their sister.'

'But that's illogical. They were all adults.'

Donal slapped the table. Keelan jumped. He reached out to grab her hand, but she pulled away. He noticed a vein of fear in her eyes before they clouded over with tears.

'Silly girl. I was only trying to comfort you. I think Cillian is feeling guilty at his mother's passing. Maybe he thinks he should have been around more to reassure her. To tell her she still had two sons. But he never did. And every time he appeared at that front door, she laid into him. Blaming him. And blaming Finn.'

'He never spoke much about his mother. Always about Lynn. I can tell you, the only guilt he was consumed with was not being there for his sister when she disappeared.'

Donal stood up and put the box of cereal back into the cupboard. 'The anniversary of her disappearance is this Sunday, so tell him to call round. Tell him we need to talk. Will you do that for me?'

'Couldn't you call him yourself?' Keelan stood at the door, wrapping her scarf around her neck.

'He can make the first move,' Donal said. 'My son is lucky to have you. You know what? You look a little how I would imagine Lynn would look if she was still alive. I mean ...' He felt bile lurch from his stomach to his mouth. Not once had Maura let him speculate that their daughter might be dead. Not once in the last ten years. Never.

'I'll pass on the message,' Keelan said. 'And there's always hope.' She pulled the door closed behind her.

At the sink, Donal took the bowl from the drainer and put it in the dishwasher. He turned on the machine and listened to it, to work out if anything was amiss with the motor. He stood there for the whole forty-five-minute cycle, water filling and draining. Draining like his life had done since the day Lynn had vanished.

CHAPTER THIRTEEN

Lottie jumped out of the car at the front of the station and Boyd drove round to the yard. She was considering Anna Byrne's information that Elizabeth had suffered from psoriasis and didn't wear costume jewellery because it exacerbated the complaint, when a woman approached her. She wore a denim jacket over a grey hoodie and jeans; mid forties, Lottie thought as her progress to the steps was blocked.

'Cynthia Rhodes,' the woman said, thrusting out a hand.

Lottie kept her own in her pocket. 'Do I know you?'

'Crime correspondent with national television. I took over after my colleague was murdered.'

Lottie shuddered at the memory but dragged up her professional face. 'How can I help you, Ms Rhodes?'

'The activity at the cemetery. Can you comment on it?'

'Not at this time.'

'Ah, come on, give me a break. I'm new to the job.'

Lottie wasn't going to be taken in that easily. Not now that she recognised Rhodes. A shark with very sharp teeth who had hosted a night-time current affairs television programme a few years ago. Covering crime in the midlands appeared to be a demotion.

'What are you doing in Ragmullin?'

'My job, unlike some I could mention.' Her eyes, shrouded by a tangle of black curls, fired cold warnings to Lottie. Better watch what I say, she thought.

'I'm too busy to talk to you right now.' She made to pass by, but Cynthia held out a hand, halting her escape.

'Not so fast. I know all about you, Lottie Parker. I know about your failings in the past. I know of your husband's death and your brother's manslaughter, and I can tell you, I don't feel one bit sorry for you. If this activity at the cemetery is a murder, mark my words, I'll be walking in your footsteps, waiting for you to trip over and make a mistake.'

'Is that all?' Lottie scooted round the woman and up the steps.

'I'll be watching you. You can bet your life on it.'

'And you can bet your life I won't be watching you on television,' Lottie muttered as she charged into the reception area. She pounded in the code on the inner door.

'Hey, Inspector Parker,' the duty sergeant called out. 'You're wanted in the interview room. Detective Kirby is waiting for you there with Bernard Fahy.'

'Shit.' Lottie flew down the corridor, the door swinging shut behind her.

Kirby stood up as Lottie entered the claustrophobic interview room.

'We're almost finished here, boss. Do you want to read over my notes and ask anything further before Mr Fahy leaves?'

Tearing off her jacket, Lottie sank into a chair and indicated for Kirby to sit back down.

'I've work to be getting on with,' Fahy said. He was leaning across the table, his hands clasped as if in prayer.

'Me too,' Lottie said. 'Can you recount what you've been doing since Monday? Where you've been?'

'He has it written down.' Fahy pointed to Kirby.

Flicking through his notebook, Kirby said, 'I just need to have a word with his wife to confirm she was with him when he says she was.'

'Do you think I'd be stupid enough to bury a woman in my own graveyard?'

'Mr Fahy, I'm just trying to get the facts,' Lottie said, though she had been thinking that exact thing. She turned to Kirby. 'Does Mr Gilbey corroborate everything?'

'Gilbey only started work at the cemetery today. I took his statement and DNA and let him go.' Kirby folded his arms across his bulging stomach.

Lottie read the notes before looking up at Fahy's agitated face. 'The victim broke her leg. Was screaming as she tried to get away from her assailant. A terrified young woman running naked through your cemetery in the dead of night. How does that make you feel?'

He shook his head. 'You're making a big mistake if you think I had anything to do with it. A big mistake.'

'Are you threatening me?' She tried to keep her anger muted. Cynthia Rhodes had already said something similar about mistakes.

'I had nothing to do with it. My wife can vouch for me. I was at home every night. I was at work every day. That's all I have to say. Can I go now?'

'We'll need to take a sample of your DNA first.'

'Why?'

'To rule you in or out of our investigation.'

'I'm sure my DNA is all over the place – I dug the blasted grave.'

'All the same, will you consent to providing us with a sample?'

'Doesn't look like I have much choice in the matter.'

'Interview terminated.' Kirby stood up and sealed the DVD.

Fahy picked up his coat and headed for the door. 'Leave John Gilbey alone. He's not right up here.' He pointed to his temple with a muddy finger. 'I know your reputation, Detective Inspector, and that's the last thing I'm saying about this.'

When he had left, with Kirby in tow, Lottie sat in the humid silence of the room and rested her head in her hands. Thoughts swam in and out of focus. She could do with a Xanax. Half of one, even. She reached into her bag and searched among the till receipts, unopened bills, keys and loose change. Found a blister pack with one pill. Maybe she shouldn't take it. She needed to be alert and focused. Especially with Cynthia Rhodes on her case.

A tap on the door and Boyd entered.

'You okay?' he said.

'Do you really want me to answer that?' She palmed the pill. 'Any word from Lynch on Matt Mullin's whereabouts?'

'Not yet. What next?'

'I need to access the O'Donnell cold case file and speak with Elizabeth's friend. What was her name? The one Anna didn't seem to like.'

Boyd consulted his notebook. 'Carol O'Grady.'

'Address?'

'Will I look it up?'

'That would be a help.'

'The longer this day gets, the shorter your fuse.'

'Boyd, get the address.'

When she was alone, the bang of the door echoing like a gong in her ears, she swallowed the pill and left to find water to wash the chalky taste from her mouth.

CHAPTER FOURTEEN

Lottie looked at the house beside which Boyd had parked. St Fintan's Road backed onto the old army barracks. Most of the houses were still owned by the local authority. After her encounter with the reporter and then the cemetery caretaker, she'd held an impromptu meeting with Lynch and Kirby in the incident room. She wanted Matt Mullin found. She wanted every piece of information on Elizabeth Byrne, and she wanted Bridie McWard formally interviewed. She wanted results, goddammit.

Boyd glanced at the page in his hand and read, 'Carol O'Grady. Aged twenty-four. She has two younger brothers and lives with her mother and father.' He'd printed off her photograph from her Facebook page. There'd been information about one brother on their PULSE database.

'Let's see what she has to say about Elizabeth,' Lottie said.

Leaving the car, they walked up the short path to the red door of number 36. It was the end house in a terrace of five and looked well maintained, with sparkling clean windows.

The bell appeared broken, so Lottie knocked hard on the glass panel.

The door was opened by a young man. He was the image of the girl in the photograph. Terry, the eighteen-year-old brother they'd read about on PULSE.

'Is Carol at home?' Lottie asked.

'Who wants to know?'

She took out her ID, flashed it in front of his face and watched the complacency fade.

'My apologies,' he said, his tone streaked with sarcasm, 'I didn't know you were the pigs … I mean, the guards. Carol should be at work today but she's off sick. Will I get her for you?'

'Do that and we'll wait inside.' Lottie placed one foot inside the door, in case he slammed it shut.

'I … I'm not sure,' he stammered. 'My mates are here. We're studying. Exams. Leaving Cert. You know.'

'Shouldn't you be at school?'

'Study break.'

'We won't disturb you at all. Just get Carol for us.'

As he flew up the stairs, Lottie reckoned the open door was an invitation to enter. With Boyd behind her, she walked through the small hallway and into the kitchen. There was a scattering of bodies and a scraping of something off the table as she entered.

'No need to leave,' she said.

The three lads halted their progress at the back door, and without turning his head, one of them said, 'We were going anyway.'

'Don't forget this.' Boyd held up a microscopic bag of weed.

'Shit,' said one of the lads.

'Go on, get out,' Boyd said. 'I'll keep it safe for you.'

They kept going.

Lottie smiled. 'That's not enough to lift them two inches off the ground, never mind get them high.'

'Hey, that's mine.' Terry had come into the kitchen. He swiped at Boyd's hand but missed the bag.

'Where's Carol?' Lottie asked.

'She'll be down in a minute. Go on into the good room. Just through there.' He pointed to a glass connecting door.

In the living room, Lottie stood in front of the unlit fireplace. Boyd followed, and sat down on one of the floral-covered armchairs.

'Where's your mum and dad?' he asked.

'At work,' Terry said. 'But they'll be home after six, if you want to come back then.'

'Where do they work?' Lottie said.

'Where's your younger brother?' Boyd said.

'You ask a lot of questions.' Terry threw his hands in the air.

'It's our job,' Lottie said.

The door opened and a young woman entered, wearing a dressing gown. Small and pale. Her hair dyed blonde at the ends. Lottie thought how Chloe had wanted to get her hair styled that way. Balayage, or something weird. It cost nearly one hundred euros, so that put a halt to her gallop.

Lottie produced her ID. 'I'm Detective Inspector Parker, and this is my colleague Detective Sergeant Boyd.'

'I'm Carol. What do you want with me?' Her voice was timid.

'You're not at work today,' Lottie said without preamble. 'Where do you work?' She knew, but she wanted the girl to relax.

'Rochfort Gardens. Why do you want to know? This is the first day I've missed in two years. I don't think that warrants the council calling the guards.' She sank down on the armchair opposite Boyd. 'Are you going to tell me what this is about?'

'It's about Elizabeth Byrne,' Lottie volunteered. 'You're her friend?'

'What if I am? I doubt she's done anything wrong. She's above all that.'

'How do you and Elizabeth get on?'

'Why do you want to know?'

'Answer the question,' Boyd cut in.

'She lives on the good side of town. But we've been friends since school. Her uppity mum doesn't like it, but tough. Life isn't all sweet, is it?'

'No, I don't suppose it is,' Lottie said, sniffing the distinct scent of weed in the coldness of the room. She sat down on the sagging couch. 'When did you last see Elizabeth?'

The girl's eyes skittered around nervously. 'I call her Lizzie, by the way. Her mother rang me on Monday night, asking me the same thing. I'd like to know why you're asking these questions. You're scaring me.'

'We don't mean to scare you. We're trying to trace Elizabeth's movements and we need to backtrack to the last time she was seen.'

'Trace her movements? Is she missing or something?'

'Something like that.' Lottie didn't think the time was right to inform Carol that her friend had been found dead. They needed formal identification first.

Pulling the sides of her dressing gown together, her hands worrying each other, Carol crossed her bare legs at the ankles. Gulping, she said, 'I saw her on Saturday night. We went to the Last Hurdle. That's a nightclub. We had a few drinks here first before we went to the pub. Then to the Hurdle. Sorry, I'm messing this all up.'

'You're doing fine. Did you meet anyone? Friends?'

Carol looked from one to the other. Deciding what to say? Lottie waited her out.

'Loads of people were out, but we stuck together. Lizzie didn't even want to go to the nightclub, but I insisted. I've been trying to boost her up ever since that prick Matt dumped her. We were there until maybe two o'clock. I think. Taxi dropped me off first, then Lizzie, because she said she'd pay. I've heard nothing from her all week, but that's not unusual because she works in Dublin and commutes on the train. Long days. Sometimes we go out during the week, but not that much.'

'No texts or WhatsApp messages? Snapchat?'

'No. Nothing. Like I said, that's not unusual.'

'This boyfriend she had. What do you know about him?' Lottie folded her arms and stared at Carol.

'Matt? Couldn't stand him.'

'Really? Why?'

'The way he treated her. Leading her up the garden path, my mum said.'

'You didn't think he was ever going to put a ring on her finger, then?'

'Not in a million years. Lizzie might be a step above me, but Matt was a flight of stairs above her. The minute he got his transfer to Germany, he was out of here like Usain Bolt.'

'So he's been gone a while?'

'Almost a year. Why are you asking about Lizzie? She seemed fine on Saturday night, just a bit drunker than usual. What's happened?'

'Do you think she was over her relationship with Matt?'

'Well and truly over him. She hates him with a vengeance.'

'And Matt? Know where he might be?'

'Germany?' Carol shrugged her shoulders.

'Anyone else Elizabeth might've been interested in?'

'I'd really like to know what this is about.' Carol folded her arms and stared defiantly.

'Answer the question, please.' Lottie stood up like a military commander conducting a court-martial. Her legs had cramped on the low couch.

Carol appeared to shrink into the folds of her dressing gown. 'I don't think there's anyone in Lizzie's life. The only place she ever goes is her job in Dublin. Talk to her workmates.'

'We'll be interviewing them as soon as possible. So far, we know she was at work on Monday and caught the 17.10 train, but apparently she never arrived home. We need you to think where she might have gone Monday evening, and who she might have been with.'

'She *is* missing? Oh God. I honestly have no idea. This is so out of character for her. She doesn't even go into town without telling her mother. You'd think she was twelve the way that woman keeps a rein on her.'

'Did she hook up with anyone at the nightclub?' Boyd asked.

Carol shook her head. 'No. She wasn't with anyone. Only me.'

'Your brothers. Were they out Saturday night? Either of them got their eye on Elizabeth?'

'You must be joking me. Terry is gay, and Jake is only fourteen.'

Lottie rubbed her hands together, feeling the cold in the room. 'If you think of anything, will you let us know?'

'I will. Her mother must be out of her mind with worry. Why didn't she tell me Elizabeth was missing when she rang? I'd call over, only she hates the sight of me.'

'Now might not be a good time,' Lottie said. Official confirmation or not, she decided to give Carol the bad news. 'Carol, I'm sorry to have to tell you this, but I think you need to know that we found a body this morning. We have reason to believe it is that of Elizabeth.'

'What? What are you saying?' The girl jumped up, then collapsed back down into the chair. 'You can't be serious. Oh God, you are, aren't you?'

'I'm sorry.'

'I can't believe this. A body? Was it an accident? Where? How … Oh my God, was she murdered?'

'We're not sure what happened yet.'

Carol convulsed into sobs. 'Oh, poor Lizzie. She never hurt anyone in her life.' More sobs. 'Where did you find her?'

'I can't reveal too much at the moment. But a body was found in Ragmullin Cemetery. Would Elizabeth have any reason to be there on Monday night?'

Carol looked up with red-rimmed eyes. 'The graveyard? Lizzie never set foot inside those gates since the day of her father's funeral. She hates the place.' She seemed to realise what she'd said and corrected herself. 'Hated the place.'

'Okay. We have to leave now, but if you think of anything that might help us, please call me.'

Carol took Lottie's card. She looked so small and feeble, her pale cheeks now flushed with the exertion of crying. Lottie felt like giving her a hug.

'Are you off sick today? What's wrong with you? Nothing contagious, I hope?' She was trying to make light of the situation, but her words fell flat.

More tears flowed and Carol's knuckles turned white clutching her dressing gown.

'Hey, I'm sorry.' Lottie sat on the arm of the chair.

'I'm pregnant,' Carol sniffed. 'My mum and dad don't know. I did a test. No one knows.'

'You need to go back to bed,' Lottie said, 'and like I said, call me if you think of anything.' She squeezed the girl's shoulder in a motherly gesture.

Terry stuck his head around the door. 'Can I have my stash back?'

'Not in your lifetime,' Boyd said, patting his pocket. 'You should be glad I'm not taking you to the station. Why don't you do that study you were talking about before we interrupted you?'

'What study?' Carol asked.

'For my Leaving Cert,' Terry said, his eyes boring two holes into her.

'Oh … right,' Carol said, and turned back to Lottie. 'I'll see you out.'

At the front door, Carol said, 'Don't mind Terry. He's a grade A liar. I'm not … just in case you think … oh, you know. I told you the truth about Lizzie. I honestly don't know what happened to her. I feel awful now.'

'It's not your fault,' Lottie said.

She had to find out whose fault it was.

*

Upstairs in the bathroom, Carol threw up the little that remained in her stomach. As she gagged and heaved, Terry banged on the door.

'Have you been smoking my dope? You've been in there puking all day.'

'Fuck off, Terry.'

'Yeah, well I need to have a piss.'

'Give me a minute.'

She heard him thumping back down the stairs, banging the wall as he went, and sat back on her haunches. Her best friend Lizzie. Her only friend. Dead. Murdered? She pulled the inspector's card from her pocket. Should she have told her what Lizzie had said about feeling as though she was being watched by someone on the train last week? Surely that was just Lizzie being Lizzie. Always getting feelings about this and that. But maybe she should have said something.

Putting the card back in her pocket, Carol got up, flushed the toilet and washed her hands. She'd have a think about whether or not to call. First, she needed to put her head on her pillow, and hopefully that would stop the nausea in her stomach.

CHAPTER FIFTEEN

He walked along O'Connell Street and turned the corner into Talbot Street. Connolly station loomed up in front of him, and as he neared it, he looked up at the black bridge above his head. He felt the vibration of the Dart train as it picked up speed heading for Bray, and breathed in deeply, experiencing the sensation of movement. The sensation of the train and its sounds. He closed his eyes, standing there in the middle of the pavement, lost in a world of his youth.

'You drunk or wha'?'

The man lying in a nearby doorway held out a tattered paper cup. Begging. For drug money? Or a hostel bed for the night? He ignored him and continued towards the station. His mind was filled with expectation for the evening ahead. He was going to do it. Again.

As he waited for the light to turn green to cross the road, he felt a momentary stab of anxiety. Had he been right to leave the woman in the grave? Would her body be discovered? No, surely not. The grave had been open, waiting a burial. And he'd covered her over fully with the clay. He smiled to himself at his ingenuity. Buried in someone else's grave. He'd have to remember that option as a means of disposing of a body. But that wasn't about to happen again. She was a loss, a big loss, and now he had to take the other one. She was his last hope. And this time he wouldn't make the same mistake.

CHAPTER SIXTEEN

Cafferty's Bar was quiet when Lottie and Boyd entered shortly after 4.30. They sat in a corner and ordered tea and house special sandwiches. The television was showing a soap. A few men sat at the bar slurping soup, thumbing through the local newspapers, pints of Guinness at hand.

'After what I witnessed this morning, I hate this damn town. But you know what?' Lottie said.

'What?' Boyd sipped his tea.

'I hate it but I love it at the same time.'

'Bit like the way you feel about me then?'

'You know what?'

'You're repeating yourself now.'

'It's impossible to have a normal conversation with you.' When their sandwiches arrived, she pushed hers around on the plate until the filling squeezed out of it.

'Right, this is my serious face,' Boyd said. 'I know what you're saying, kind of. I haven't lived here long, so it's not the same for me. But I get it. Ragmullin gets under your skin. Some days you love it, and other days it's just a bitch.'

'Eloquent. As usual.' Picking at the tuna that had spilled out onto the plate, she shoved some of it into her mouth and licked her fingers.

'I'll get you a fork, shall I, or maybe you prefer eating like a baby?'

'Speaking of babies, I must have that conversation with Katie this evening.'

'And what conversation would that be?'

'About visiting Tom Rickard in New York.' Rickard blamed Lottie for the death of his son, but she had never spoken to him about it.

Boyd said, 'Let the girl go. Rickard is the baby's grandfather and it'll be good to have him in Louis' life as he grows up.'

'Why do you say that?'

'One, he's bloody loaded, and two … he's bloody loaded.'

'It's just … Oh, I don't know.'

'I think I do.'

'Enlighten me.'

'You're scared of losing Katie and your grandson to Rickard. She didn't travel in November because you were recuperating from that nasty stab wound. But now there's nothing holding her back and you're frightened he will introduce her to a world you can't afford. You're also fearful that she might not want to come home.'

'She has to come home. She only has a holiday visa.'

'Money talks in strange places, and as I said, Tom Rickard is—'

'Bloody loaded. I know. Why do I carry such fear around with me? And before you say it,' she held up her finger in warning, 'don't mention Adam. You've given me that lesson once too often.'

Boyd chewed on a piece of chicken before putting down his sandwich. She didn't like it when he thought things through too seriously. He usually came out with a long-winded notion that ultimately proved correct.

'You're right, I used to think your fear of loss stemmed from Adam's death. But now, with the revelations about your family history, I'm thinking this thing inside of you originates from your childhood.'

'Yes, Sherlock. I lost my father to a suicide that was quite possibly murder, and my brother was murdered in a hellhole of an institution. Then my husband died of cancer and I recently discovered my mother isn't in fact my biological mother. I may also have a half-sibling whom I know nothing about, and my biological mother was incarcerated … How could I be right in the head?'

'About your biological mother—'

'Shut up. You know that conversation is totally out of bounds. Just eat your sandwich like a good boy.' She really didn't want to go back there. Too many lies.

'Oh Lottie, you wouldn't like me when I'm a good boy.'

'That's enough.' She smiled, despite herself.

Boyd picked up his sandwich and she looked at the mess she'd made of her own. She still felt hungry, but the food now looked so far removed from what she'd ordered, she couldn't face eating it.

'I promised Sean I'd bring him to his hurling training tomorrow evening,' Boyd said with his mouth full. 'Hopefully we'll have this murder solved soon.'

'It's good to see him back at his hurling.'

'And once the evenings get a bit brighter, he wants to join the cycling club with me.'

She looked at him then. Really looked at his thin, finely featured face and his brown eyes with their sparkling flecks of hazel. 'You know more about my own son than I do.'

'He talks to me.'

'When? How?'

'When I take him to his training sessions. Since you were injured. Since Christmas. You know that.'

'I thought you were just giving him a lift, not interrogating him.' She felt her chest tighten with jealousy. She knew she could never be a substitute for the boy's father. But she didn't want Boyd stepping in either. 'What does he talk about?'

'Not much. If he wants to chat, to go training or cycling with me, let him.'

She bit her lip, the silence hanging between them like an invisible sword. Eventually she said, 'It's hard. Damn hard.'

'Nothing in this life is easy.'

'You can say that again. How's Grace getting on with you?' she asked, deflecting the conversation away from her own family.

'You should ask how am I getting on with her. My sister is a tough cookie. Wearing me down, in her own pleasant, unassuming way.'

'When did she arrive?'

'Sunday night. Offloaded by my mother. She's doing a media course in Dublin for four weeks and staying with me during the week until it's finished. She has to go home to Mam at weekends, but she thinks she can stay with me *forever*. Her word, not mine.'

'How old is she again?'

Boyd hesitated before saying, 'Twenty-nine, but she acts younger. She has a lot of anxiety issues.'

'I can't wait to meet her.'

'Look, Lottie, Grace is different. You mightn't like her.'

'Let me be the judge of that. I know so little about you, yet in a perverse sort of way, I know so much. You're a real conundrum, Boyd.'

After a few bites of his sandwich, he looked up at her. 'I'd like to take you out to dinner.'

'What?' Lottie spluttered, drops of tea flying out of her mouth.

'Dinner. You know, what normal people do? Go out at night. Sit in a restaurant and eat delicious food someone else has prepared. Would you like to?'

Gulping down her surprise, Lottie thought about it. It'd be nice for a change. Relieve some of her tension, especially with the murder investigation. No. It was a bad idea.

'Like a date?' she asked.

'Yeah, like a date.'

'I don't think so. No, Boyd. Sorry.'

'Think about it. Maybe tonight? I can pick you up around seven thirty.'

'No … maybe some other time. Not tonight. It's too soon.'

He'd been so good to her since all that heartache last October. A friend. And now Father Joe was back. What had made her think of him? She smiled.

'Ah, that smile. It's agreed so. Tonight. Seven thirty. Now, are you going to eat that mess you've made, before I do?'

She really should set him straight, but she hadn't the energy, so she watched him finish the food instead. When it was time to leave, she felt like she could have sat there all afternoon in the silence. But they had a murderer to find. She needed to go back to the cemetery.

CHAPTER SEVENTEEN

He bought a takeout coffee and a pastry and stood sipping and eating, looking up at the giant electronic timetable above his head. He knew that plain-clothes gardaí mingled with passengers on the concourse and armed detectives patrolled the main door. In plain sight.

Biting into the crumbling pastry, he turned and scanned the crowd. Watching. Waiting. He was impatient for her to arrive so that he could follow her and sit in the same carriage.

The digital clock clicked over. One minute closer to departure time in four minutes. He walked back to the café and dumped the coffee and paper bag into a flip-top bin inside the door. Licking his lips, he rubbed his hands together. She was late. She would miss the train. He moved towards the gate, careful not to stand under the lens of the camera.

He'd have to wait on the platform. He scanned his ticket and went to Platform 4. The train was waiting. Ready to go. There'd be no seats left. He'd have to stand. He hated standing. Come on, girl, hurry up.

A chill wind gusted from outside and up along the platform as a train entered on Platform 3 and the Belfast express shunted out on the track furthest away. And then he saw her. Desperately trying to scan her ticket. The woman behind her was trying to scan hers at the same time. Eventually they both rushed through, running on the slippery tiles. He knew they'd have to jump onto the last carriage, so he got on just before them.

As he'd thought, the carriage was full. He moved down halfway until he got to the blockage of people standing in the aisle with their technology glued to their hands. He glanced over his shoulder. Three rows down. The two of them were standing in the middle of the aisle.

The train snaked out of Dublin into the dark of the evening, heading for Ragmullin. Over the slow rhythm of the engine his mind whirled with plans. He had to ensure the other woman wasn't going to be a problem. That was Plan A. Plan B was to ensure his target didn't attempt to escape.

He smiled to himself and kept his eyes glued to the two women.

*

Grace laughed, a nervous reaction to mask her fear. She'd run too quickly. Her breath was catching in the back of her throat.

Fumbling in her pocket, she found her inhaler and, trying to keep the pulsing bodies from touching her, brought it up to her lips. As she inhaled, she felt a slight reduction in the palpitations, but the panic lingered beneath the surface of her skin.

'Are you okay?'

She looked up at Mollie, her new friend.

'I'll be fine once I get to carriage C.'

'Not a hope in hell.'

With her saliva drying up, Grace took another hit from her inhaler. 'But I *have* to sit in carriage C. It's the only way I'll get home safe.'

Mollie laughed. 'You're not *that* superstitious, are you?'

Suddenly Grace found herself in what she called freeze mode. Stock still, only her eyes moving. Slanting to the right, then to the left, then back to Mollie's grinning face. Her lips stuck together, tongue thick and throat closed. As she breathed quickly through her nose, perspiration bubbled on her forehead. She felt it drip down into her eyes and tasted the saltiness on her lips. Mollie's hand reached out and grabbed hers. No! Don't touch. But her words were lost in the drying mucus.

In, out, in, out. One, two, three, she counted in her head. No use. Ten, nine, eight. Still useless. I can't pass out, she warned herself. There was nowhere for her to fall, nowhere for her to go.

People pushed up against her as the train left the station. Her worst nightmare: physical touch. And the suffocating smell of sweat and last-minute cigarettes. Her hand tightened on the leather strap of her satchel. The numbness began to ebb. Her lips opened, and she exhaled a breath.

'A little colour is coming back to your cheeks,' Mollie said. 'You had me worried for a minute. What came over you?'

Shrugging, Grace clutched her bag tighter to her body. How could she explain to this girl, who was still a stranger, what it was like to live inside her skin? She couldn't, so she remained mute, silently praying for an opportunity to get to carriage C. Only then would she be okay.

CHAPTER EIGHTEEN

The evening sky was grey-blue. Not quite daylight and not yet night. Dusk. It'd be fully dark soon. February was being a stubbornly cold month, with very little hint of spring appearing. Lottie zipped up her hoodie and then her jacket. The wrought-iron gates were wide open to allow the forensic vehicles entry to the cemetery. Crime-scene tape hung limply across the space, guarded by two uniformed officers.

They signed in and entered the grounds. Lottie stopped to view the caretaker's office, dark and lifeless in the shadow of the trees.

'Jesus, it's cold,' Boyd said.

'Beginning to freeze. Look at that lot. Fahy mentioned illegal dumping.' Lottie scanned the heaving mass of black bags sitting on top of a yellow skip. 'They look like they're moving.' Then she spied the vermin boxes around the house. Ugh!

Boyd said, 'See there. Sacks scattered on the ground. People must drive up outside and hurl their rubbish over the wall.'

'The council need to put up more cameras,' she said. 'Have we got the surveillance footage yet?'

'Kirby's looking after it.'

'Good,' Lottie started down the slope, which was glistening silver with the evening frost. A series of halogen lights on tripods illuminated the forensic tent and cast spectral shadows on the headstones surrounding it. A colony of SOCOs were working systematically, like ants, sifting through the clay and dirt.

She walked towards the wall that backed onto the traveller site. 'How high do you think this is?'

'Must be nine or ten feet.'

'And Bridie's house is just beyond it. She says she heard a scream after three on Tuesday morning. Will you go back up there and scream?' She indicated the direction they'd come from. 'I'll see if I can hear it.'

'You're having me on?'

'I'm serious.'

'Then I'll stand here while *you* go and scream.'

'Maybe I should warn Bridie first.'

'Maybe you should warn the banshee that you intend to take her place.'

'Boyd, I need to confirm one way or the other if someone's screams could be heard the other side of the wall.'

'There are flaws to your plan. Say, if you stand right under the wall, you can be sure you'd be heard.'

Lottie swung her flashlight around the headstones, silently admitting that it had been a half-thought-out plan. But she couldn't shake the feeling that Bridie really had heard the woman's screams. Travellers were renowned for their insights and vision. And if Bridie had heard Elizabeth Byrne screaming, it could tie down time of death.

She went over to the SOCOs. McGlynn was on his knees in the bottom of the grave, brushing and scraping where the body had lain. He looked up.

'Before you even ask,' he said, 'I haven't found much for you to work with. Just flakes of skin, clay, dirt and stones.'

'Blood?' Lottie ventured, peering over the edge.

'Some. It'll be analysed.'

Lottie recalled the spot of blood she'd found on the stone from the neighbouring grave. She'd follow it up in the morning.

'If he covered her with clay, did he use his hands?' she asked.

'How would I know that?' McGlynn said.

Lottie turned to Boyd. 'We need to examine all the tools used around here.'

McGlynn's voice rose from the grave. 'I've taken care of that. You'll have the results as soon as I have them. I'm assuming you took the two workers' DNA and fingerprints.'

'Of course,' she said, hoping Kirby had done his job properly.

'Good.'

'The entire area has been fingertip-searched,' Boyd said. 'When will your work be finished here?'

McGlynn glanced up, his eyes dancing with green fire above his white mouth mask. 'It will be finished when it's finished.'

Lottie looked over at the rows of headstones, misshapen humps on the landscape. The vastness of the resting place for the dead chilled her.

'I don't think this is what the killer intended,' she said. 'It's more than likely the girl escaped from him and he followed. But why were they here in the first place? Were they having sex and it got too rough, or he was raping her and she fled? Where did they come from? He had to have a car, so where was it parked?'

Boyd said, 'We've been assuming this is the work of a man, but it could just as easily have been a woman.'

'True,' Lottie conceded. 'The victim was naked, so that implies something sexual. Hopefully the post-mortem will tell us more about that. And something might show up on the CCTV footage. If it was an accident, why not try to get her out, or call 999? Was the intention all along to kill her? I can't get my head around it. And so far, we haven't one clue. That's unthinkable.'

'Wait for the post-mortem. And the results from McGlynn.'

The embankment to their right lit up with the lights of the Sligo to Dublin train. A horn screeched into the evening air and the inky sky brightened in a V from the light.

'I've to pick up Grace,' Boyd said, and headed up the hill.

Checking the time, Lottie said, 'You've less than fifteen minutes if you want to catch the train coming in from Dublin.'

It was almost dark, and in the cone of light cast by her torch, she noticed crystals of frost on the plastic heads of imitation flowers. White granite sparkled and a blackbird cawed from a branch above her head. She tried to keep up with Boyd's long strides.

When they reached the gate, she looked over at the old office. 'We need to search in there.'

'Once SOCOs finish on site, they can move up here.'

'Did you see that?' She pulled Boyd's sleeve.

'Only thing I saw was a big fat rat crawling out of one of those bags over there.'

'Oh Jesus, let's get out of here.'

They hurried to the car. As Boyd reversed and turned it, Lottie said, 'I hope to God the camera recorded something.'

Boyd said, 'Apart from the front wall, the cemetery is wide open on three sides. The railway tracks at the end plus the traveller site; the old folk's home to one side and a housing estate on the other. Easy access.'

'Nursing home.'

'What?'

'Old folk's home is not a PC term.'

She stared over at the nursing home. A newly built block with floor-to-roof windows facing out over the cemetery. Behind it she could make out the roof of the older building, with its copper roof turned green. Why hadn't anyone heard or seen anything? Why was Elizabeth in the cemetery? Where did she go when she got off the train? If they could figure that out, they might get a direction to follow. But at the moment, they were getting nowhere.

Boyd pulled the car onto the road with a grunt. Lottie was relieved when they sped away from the place of death.

CHAPTER NINETEEN

'Do you have anything for me, Lynch?' Lottie shouted out to the main office as she flicked through her emails.

Lynch came to stand in the doorway.

'Elizabeth Byrne had very little online presence. She closed down her Twitter account a year ago, hasn't posted on Instagram in that time either. She doesn't appear to use Snapchat at all, and her postings on Facebook are sparse. She used WhatsApp.'

'Check it out. Have you contacted her Facebook friends?'

'Working my way through them.'

'Any joy with Matt Mullin?'

'The bank is to get back to me in the morning. The head of HR wasn't in and no one else would give me details.'

'Get on to that first thing.'

'Boss? This surveillance job that Kirby and myself are working on, I don't think it's getting us anywhere. Do you think it's time we abandoned it?'

They'd had problems recently with illegal bare-knuckle boxing among the traveller community. Vast amounts of money were being wagered, resulting in plenty of injuries. Lottie felt it was only a matter of time before someone died.

'What have you discovered over the last three weeks?'

'Nothing,' Lynch said.

'Just wondering if you found the McWards involved in anything underhand?'

'Don't recall seeing the name anywhere, but I can check.'

'What type of detective are you?'

'A good one,' Lynch said, folding her arms.

'Prove it to me then. I want to know where Matt Mullin is. A banker in Germany can't be that hard to find now, can he?'

Lynch sighed. 'Could I have a few days off, boss? I know it's the start of an investigation, but I really need time to—'

'No. All leave is suspended until this case is solved.'

'But—'

'No buts, Lynch. I need everyone. Is that all?'

Lynch grabbed her coat and was out the door before Lottie could call her back. It really was one of those days.

Lottie phoned the state pathologist.

'Hi, Jane. Did you get to my graveyard victim yet?'

'Sorry. A sudden backlog here. Hypothermia deaths in February are a new thing for me. I've your girl scheduled for the morning. I'll call you with a time so you can attend.'

Hanging up, Lottie went out to the main office and pulled a chair over beside Kirby's desk.

'You were a bit harsh on Lynch,' he said.

'I don't know why, but sparks fly every time we talk recently.'

'Not just recently, boss, it's been going on a long time. And not just with Lynch, if you get my meaning.'

She didn't want to talk about Lynch or Boyd. She'd never really got along with Lynch but she didn't want anyone else knowing.

'Did you interview Bridie McWard?' she said.

'Same as she told you. Heard screams around 3.15 Tuesday morning. Refuses to come in to make a formal statement. I spoke to her at the site.'

'And the footage from the camera at the cemetery. Was there anything useful on it?'

'The tech guys sent me a clip.' He pressed an icon and a grainy grey image appeared in the centre of his screen. Maximising the size, he sat back and let Lottie watch it. 'This is 3.07,' he said.

'I don't see anything.'

'There's nothing to see except for a change in the light. Hold on and I'll rewind it.' He clattered his thick fingers on a couple of keys and the image rolled once more. 'Look carefully at the road. See that? It's the lights of a car approaching, but then they disappear. I'd say he swung the car to park on the opposite side of the road, where there's no camera coverage.'

'Okay. But we can't see any people?'

'No.'

'Might just be someone dumping rubbish over the wall.'

'I don't think so.'

'Why not?'

'Because the footage confirms a vehicle was parked here for twenty-four minutes.' He fast-forwarded to 3.31. 'Look. There's a swerve of light on the road as if a car is turning.'

'And?'

'And that's it.'

'Nothing in between? No other cars?'

'Not a thing. On a Monday night, the town is dead.'

'So it looks like he drove in from town, stopped for nearly half an hour, then turned and went back towards town. Track our own traffic cams around those times and see if you can pick up the car.'

'I'll try.'

Lottie pushed the chair back and moved towards her own office. 'I want all the residents in the nursing home interviewed. Especially those with windows facing the cemetery.'

'Tonight?'

'No. Tomorrow. Did uniforms get anything useful from the housing estate?'

'Database is being compiled, but nothing worth reporting so far.'

'And the residents at the traveller site?'

'No one heard or saw anything.'

'Same old Ragmullin. Squinting windows and silent houses.'

'What?' Kirby scratched his head with the tip of a pen.

'I want an update at our incident team meeting in the morning.'

CHAPTER TWENTY

He secured a seat once passengers disembarked at Maynooth. The two women got seats also. Now they were sitting opposite him, albeit a few rows down the aisle.

How he wished he was beside her, with her soft flesh trembling beside his own. Skin on skin. Nothing more beautiful, he thought. Unless you counted the rocking motion of the train. Oh, naked flesh on flesh in tune to the motion of the train. That was an image he couldn't stop flitting behind his eyes. How beautiful would that be? The quiver of her lips as he looked down on her, the redness puckered, waiting.

For him.

For no one else.

With the answer he craved.

*

Ragmullin train station was crumbling under its age. Multiple renovations over the years had done little to enhance its appearance. The fact that it was a protected structure limited the railway company from doing anything major. Protecting it was a paradox, because it was disintegrating before twenty thousand pairs of Ragmullin eyes.

'How's it going, Jimmy? Any news?' Boyd sauntered over to the porter and leaned on the gate to the platform.

'Sure, the only news around here is the weather and late trains.' Jimmy Maguire scratched at a point on his scalp under his cap.

'I hope this one isn't late.'

'Should be in on time. Due at 18.20.'

Boyd smiled as Jimmy made a drama of checking his watch with his gloved fingers. Bright yellow, synthetic fabric. The top of his peaked-capped head only came to Boyd's shoulder, and he looked as weather-beaten as the station.

'In fifty-seven seconds, to be exact.'

'Very precise.'

'It's my job to know these things.'

Boyd stared up along the platform as he heard the train approach.

'She's a little early.' Jimmy straightened up. 'By fifteen seconds.'

Boyd ducked as a pigeon swooped from the gantry that hung over the concrete platform.

The train's hydraulic brakes hissed as it idled to a stop and the doors slid open. Boyd stood to one side to allow the passengers to pour from the carriages, rush to the gate and head for their cars in the overcrowded car park. As quickly as it had arrived, the train departed with a loud rumble along the tracks.

His sister appeared. 'Hi, Mark. You look tired. Is anything wrong?'

'No, just waiting for you. Couldn't see you for a minute.'

'I have a new friend.' Grace looked around. 'She was here a minute ago. I was going to ask if you could give her a lift.'

'Probably went on ahead,' Boyd said, thinking that Grace's new friend wanted to escape his sister's constant chatter. 'Car's outside. On double yellow lines.'

'Breaking the law again?' she said.

'I am the law,' Boyd said.

He pinged the key fob and sat into the car. Grace unwrapped her heavy knitted scarf, folded it neatly on her lap and placed her bag in the footwell, then seemed to think better of it and put it on her knee on top of her scarf.

'Shut the door,' he said. 'It's bloody freezing.'

'You always state the obvious.'

She's worse than Lottie, Boyd thought. He wondered if he had been an insanely bad person in a previous life to be condemned to inhabit the same planet as contrary women.

He swung the car around in a U-turn and nudged into the line of traffic.

'Tell me about your friend.'

'I met her on the train this morning. She told me she always gets the 17.10 home. So I decided to travel with her.'

'In your usual carriage?'

'It got a bit complicated, because she arrived later than me. I had to wait for her and then we had to stand in the wrong carriage. I had a little panic attack, but I'm fine now.'

'Are you sure you're okay?'

'Stop treating me like I'm an imbecile. I might be sixteen years younger than you, but I'm not stupid.'

The traffic lights on the bridge changed to green and Boyd gunned the car to make it through before they flipped again. They were red by the time he was on the crest of the hill, but he kept going.

'You hit it off with her, then?'

'Don't sound so surprised. I can hold conversations with people.'

'That's what worries me.'

'Are you trying to be funny?'

Boyd kicked himself. Grace didn't get jokes. She saw things as either black or white. Straight down the middle. Whatever you wanted to call it, Grace was it. 'On the spectrum' was a phrase he had often heard in the same sentence as her name. He loved his sister, but she tried his patience something terrible. He reminded himself that he'd have to be more careful with his choice of words in her presence. And he'd have to remember she was twenty-nine years old.

'Why are you driving down Main Street?' she asked.

'I'm getting a takeaway for dinner.'

'But I don't eat food made by someone else. You know that.'

'Just this once, Grace. For me? Please?'

'Mark! You have a date.'

'How do you know that?'

'I can read you so well.'

Just like Lottie, he thought, and double-parked outside the Chinese takeaway.

'Don't suppose you'll go in to get it,' he said.

'You suppose absolutely correct.'

Boyd shook his head. He was glad he was going out tonight. Then again, he wondered if it might be frying pan and fire. He hoped Lottie would be in better form than Grace. With all that had happened today, he doubted it.

CHAPTER TWENTY-ONE

The temperature had dropped to freezing. Windscreens shimmered with a fine coating of hoar frost. A constellation of stars glittered in the clear sky as the commuters exited the station, preceded by their white breath fogging the raw evening air.

Mollie felt a tap on her shoulder as the crowd rushed towards the exit.

'Hi there,' the man said.

The same man whom she had accepted a lift from yesterday evening. He'd been a perfect gentleman, dropping her off outside her apartment. He seemed really nice and sensible. She knew him to see around town but didn't know who he was. They hadn't exchanged names let alone phone numbers. And she was happy enough with that.

'I can give you a lift again,' he said. 'Thought you might want to escape your chatterbox friend.'

She sidestepped around Grace without her noticing. She was chatting with a tall, thin man. Mollie supposed it was the brother she'd heard about on the endless train journey. Feck it, she thought, she had to escape the constant nattering.

'That'd be cool. Thanks,' she said. She felt his hand on her elbow and she was propelled down the steps.

They glided on the frozen ground to the darkness at the left of the car park.

'Your friend is some talker. Never stopped to catch a breath. I'm sure your head must be mithered with her.'

'She's not too bad,' Mollie said. Why was she defending a girl she didn't even know? Why was she taking lifts from a man she didn't know, come to that? The car park was almost empty now. There was only one car parked up against the back wall to the rear of the station. She stopped. He turned to look at her.

'What's up?' he asked. He sounded normal. Not a weirdo, then.

'Thanks for rescuing me. And thanks for the lift yesterday evening, but I think I'd rather walk now. I need some fresh air.'

She stepped back. He walked into the space she had vacated.

'It's no trouble. My car's over there.' He pointed to his dark saloon, out of the range of cameras and lights. This was getting scary. That wasn't where he'd parked yesterday.

'Honestly, I'm grateful for the rescue. I might see you tomorrow?' As she turned, the hand on her elbow tightened, biting through her clothes, hurting her. 'Hey! What are you playing at?'

'I'm not playing, Mollie. That's your name, isn't it? If you walk quickly, I won't have to hurt you. Come along like a good little girl.'

'You're out of your fucking mind.' Mollie opened her mouth to scream, but in that second of hesitation, his gloved hand filled the void and a cloth was stuffed halfway into her mouth. She looked around wildly, but everyone was either in their cars queuing up to exit or rushing away up the hill, heads bent against the biting wind.

'Help.' She thought she said the word, but nothing came out of her mouth because the cloth was there. His arms circled her body, pulling her close to him. The cloth was choking her. And that smell …

'Do what you're told or you die, do you understand?'

The car lock beeped. He opened the door and pushed her inside. She cracked her head against the steering wheel and fell across the two front seats. He lifted her ankles and shoved her legs in behind her. She raised a hand to press the horn before he got in behind her, but she was too slow. He gripped her fingers and shoved her out of the way, sitting himself into the driver's seat. She lashed out. Her nails snagged on the collar of his shirt.

'Bitch,' he cried, and placed his hand back over her mouth, stuffing the cloth in further. From his pocket he took a plastic bag. She could see another cloth, just like the first one.

'You'll be sorry for trying to hurt me,' he said. 'So fucking sorry, you won't know what's happened to you. You'll beg. Beg, do you hear me? You will beg for your life and do you know what I'll do? No, I don't suppose you do, but you're sure going to find out.'

His hand thumped into her face again and he brought the second cloth to her nose. A sickly-sweet smell filled her senses as darkness fell upon her like a shower of soft rain.

CHAPTER TWENTY-TWO

'Am I in the right house?' Lottie asked as she hung her jacket on the clutter-free stair post.

The aroma of chilli and cheese drifted in waves from the kitchen. Didn't smell like microwave food. Opening the sitting room door, she was surprised to find it neat, tidy and empty. She walked to the kitchen. The table was set with matching cutlery. There was even a tablecloth that only saw the light on Christmas Day.

'What's going on here?' she said.

Standing in a line at the cupboards to her right were Sean and Chloe, with Katie holding Louis in her arms.

'Surprise!' they cried.

'But why? ... What? ... I'm stunned.'

'You could try a thank you,' Katie said.

'Thank you. I mean, this is a major shock to the system. I'll have to sit down.'

'Yes, you sit down and I'll take out the lasagne,' Chloe said. 'Do you think it's cooked, Katie?'

'Definitely. Here, Mam, you hold Louis and I'll dish up. There's chilli in it. Sean insisted, hope you don't mind. We found a jar in the cupboard.'

Lottie took Louis in her arms as they began fussing over the food. Her mind went into overdrive mode. They wanted something. Nothing for nothing in her life. What, though? Why had they gone to this much trouble? She glanced around to see if her mother was commanding the operation. She was nowhere in sight. That figured. Rose was in a lethargic mood recently, feeling unwell all the time, and Lottie was trying her best to call to her with food in the evenings.

Definitely a conspiracy. But she had no idea why, so she decided to play along.

'This is delicious,' she said when they'd finished eating. 'And it's great to sit around the table as a family. We should do it more often.' It was then she caught a look passing between Chloe and Katie.

'I'll take Louis and put on Baby TV.' Sean released the brake on the buggy and pushed it out to the hall, pulling the door behind him.

'Right, tell me what this is about,' Lottie said.

The doorbell rang.

'I'll get it,' Sean shouted from the hallway.

'Oh, shit,' Lottie said, jumping up.

Boyd stood in the doorway, a bunch of six red roses in his hand.

'I see you had dinner without me,' he said.

'Oh God, Boyd. We didn't agree anything, did we? I should have made myself clear. I'm sorry. I didn't …' Shit, she was babbling.

'Let me hang up your jacket,' Sean said.

'No, I'm disturbing a family gathering. I'll leave.'

'It's okay,' Chloe said.

'Bring Boyd into the sitting room for a minute,' Lottie told her. 'I want to have a chat with Katie.'

When they were alone, she looked at her daughter standing with a pile of plates in her hands. 'Sit down and tell me,' she said.

'Mam.' Katie put the dishes on the counter, 'I know you don't agree with me going to New York to visit Louis' grandad, but I want to go. I put it off when you were attacked, and then there was Christmas and … Wait a minute. Don't jump out of your skin yet.'

Lottie sat down again and studied her daughter's beautiful, sad face. Katie had endured so much in her twenty years that maybe it was time to allow her to live for herself. To have a life. Wasn't that what Boyd had said?

'Okay, Katie. I won't argue with you. How much money do you think you'll need?'

'That's the thing. I don't need anything. We cooked the dinner to celebrate ... to tell you ...'

'Tell me what?'

'Tom Rickard booked the tickets and put money in my bank account. Me and Louis, we're leaving for New York on Friday. I was afraid to tell you before now. Please don't stop me.'

A conflict of emotion surged through Lottie. The hairs on her arms tingled, her tongue stuck to the roof of her mouth, a knot tightened in her chest and tears bulged at the rims of her eyes.

'Say something.' Katie pleaded, widening her eyes. They were crystal clear now that her days of smoking weed with Jason Rickard were behind her. The only thing lurking there was evidence of sleepless nights.

'Which Friday?' Lottie whispered, afraid of the answer.

'This Friday.'

'What? But today is Wednesday ... You can't, it's too soon. I need to organise things ...'

'You don't have to organise anything. It's all sorted. I couldn't tell you before now, because you'd have time to think up ways of stopping me. I really want this, Mam. Please say it's okay.'

No matter what she said it'd sound wrong, so Lottie kept her mouth shut and nodded. She was suddenly enveloped in a hug. Katie didn't do hugs too often. But now she did.

'You are the best mother ever. This is an amazing opportunity for me. And I know Tom will love Louis just as much as you do.'

'How long will you be away?' Lottie croaked.

'Just for a few weeks.'

'How many is a few?'

'Three.'

'Three?'

'I really want to do this, Mam. For Louis' sake.'

'How much money did Tom send you?' Shit, why had she asked that?

Katie shifted from foot to foot. 'Five thousand euros. Can you believe it?'

'What?' Lottie stared at her daughter. 'Plus the tickets?'

Katie nodded. 'Isn't it great? I'm going into town tomorrow to buy new clothes for myself. I have to look right when I meet him again. It's so exciting. And I have to pack. You'll take me to the airport Friday morning, won't you? Love you, Mam.' She rushed from the kitchen, leaving dishes and cutlery scattered over the worktops.

Lottie had been on the verge of telling her not to forget how badly Tom had treated his son. But there was no point in dampening the happy smile on Katie's face. She stood up wearily and started to load the dishwasher.

'Let me give you a hand.' Boyd joined her and together they cleared the remnants of the meal.

'Thanks,' Lottie said when they were finished. 'You must be starving. Did you cancel the restaurant? Why don't you go on your own? I'm sorry if I gave you the wrong impression. Maybe you should—'

Her arms were gripped by his long, smooth fingers and he looked into her eyes. 'I'm fine. We'll go out tomorrow night instead. Deal?'

'I'm not sure it's a good idea.'

'Deal?'

'No deal,' she said. 'At least not until this murder is solved.'

'I can't win, can I?' Boyd released her arms and leaned against the table. 'Do you want to tell me what that was about with Katie?'

'Not really. It's enough to know she's happy. For now.'

'Are *you* happy?'

'As much as I can be. Sit down and I'll make coffee. Where'd you put the flowers? Thanks, by the way.'

'I left them in the sitting room.'

'Did you collect Grace from the station?' Lottie asked.

'Yes. She's ensconced on my sofa with a Chinese takeaway and Netflix.'

'Sounds like a little bit of heaven.'

'This here, right at this moment, is a little bit of heaven.'

As he smiled at her, Lottie thought of Katie's imminent departure. Then she remembered her mother.

'Shit, Boyd. I'm sorry.'

'What now?'

'I've to go over to Rose with her dinner. I totally forgot.'

He stood. 'You've a tough time trying to keep everything together.'

'I just need to stay focused. I'll try my best to organise things so that we can go out for a meal some night, but …'

'But you can't guarantee it?'

'I can't, so it's a maybe for now.'

'I'll take a maybe.' He smiled. 'Though like I told you before, I won't hang around forever. You know that?' He brushed his lips to her cheek.

The door burst open. Chloe came in and opened the fridge. Then banged it shut and left.

'What was that about?' Boyd asked.

'Teenagers,' Lottie said.

CHAPTER TWENTY-THREE

'Hi, darling, you're late again. Miss the train?'

Ignoring his wife, Cillian O'Donnell hung his black leather jacket on the back of a chair and bent down to whisk his five-year-old daughter, Saoirse, up into his arms.

'What've you been doing while Daddy was at work, you little minx?'

Saoirse snuggled her curly head into the crook beneath his chin and wrapped her arms and legs about his body. He welcomed the scent of peach shampoo and his daughter's soft skin. Kissing her gently on top of her head, he eased the child to the floor and she dragged him to the kitchen table, where brightly coloured pages were scattered around and brushes stuck out of a jar of water.

'You were painting,' he said. 'Did Mummy help you?'

Saoirse shook her head and stuck her bottom lip out in a scowl.

Keelan said, 'She was a naughty girl at school today, weren't you, honey? I only allowed her to paint for half an hour.'

Cillian lowered his head to the paintings, fearing Keelan would see the torment he was desperately trying to hide. He sensed his wife turn from the stove, felt her stare. She was ordinary. Just plain ordinary. Short-cropped black hair, grey eyes, and the only make-up she wore was so minimal that it was invisible. Her body had failed to regain its slender shape after Saoirse's birth, and he couldn't forgive her for not trying harder. But only in his head. He didn't dare say it out loud.

'Did you forget?' she asked.

'Forget what?'

'The meeting. Tonight. It's at nine. And you're just in the door.' She rubbed her hands dry on a tea towel and sat at the cluttered table. 'Where were you until now?'

'Work was mental. I forgot about the meeting. I'll have a shower, go to the meeting and maybe a bite of dinner before I go to bed.'

'You can't go to sleep on a full stomach. It's bad for you.' She got up and slapped the tea towel against the edge of the table.

Saoirse flinched and scrambled up onto her father's knee.

He knew Keelan had tears of anger in her eyes. She liked everything to be exactly on time, the same day after day, no break from routine. In some ways, though not all, she was a carbon copy of his brother's wife. And both women were copies of Maura, their mother. How did they manage that? He turned his attention to his daughter again.

'Here, pet, use the red. And there's a clean sheet of paper. When Daddy comes down from his shower, I want to see a lovely red steam engine.'

'But I don't know how to do that. Will Mummy help me?'

He physically shuddered at the loud grunt Keelan emitted, standing beside the sink with her back to him.

At the bookcase, he pulled out one of his many train magazines and opened it at the correct page. 'There you are now, Saoirse. Copy that one.'

'It's too advanced for a five-year-old,' Keelan said, facing the window. 'And your father wants you to call him.'

He could see her grimace reflected in the glass. He rolled his hands into fists, quelling the urge to smash them into her face, then turned away and headed for the stairs, pulling off his shirt as he went.

What the hell did his father want with him?

*

Finn O'Donnell shuffled out of his coat and hung it up on the rack inside the door. One step took him from the hallway into the small living room. Sara was in the scullery. Too small to call a kitchen, she'd said when they moved in with notions that it was only temporary. Five years was too long to live in temporary accommodation, she'd moaned every single bloody night.

'I'm not staying,' he said. 'I've to go to a meeting.'

'You always have something to go to. Can't you sit in for one night?'

He fell into his armchair without bothering to ask if there was anything to eat. He knew the answer by the whiff of alcohol coming from her breath as she squashed into the chair opposite him. He'd get a takeaway later.

The smack of the glass on the coffee table caused him to look up. Sara was round and plump. Fatty blubber. Hair unwashed, hanging about her shoulders, and she'd worn the same clothes for the last three days. God, why had he ever married her? But he knew why. His mother. Maura had forced his hand once Cillian snared Keelan. He hadn't been man enough to handle the jibes, the insinuations she flung at him day after day. Finn knew that no matter what he did, he could never be as good as his brother. Not since Lynn had disappeared. Even before she vanished. He was never good enough in Maura's eyes. And definitely not in his father's. He really should call over and see how Donal was faring. That could be tomorrow night's escape.

'What's going on in that dim brain of yours?' Sara's voice was high and squeaky, like a rat.

'Don't,' he said, standing up. 'Please don't start. I've had a bitch of a day and I'm not listening to you going on and on about shite.'

'Go to your silly meeting then. See if I care.'

As he grabbed his coat and opened the front door, he knew he didn't care either.

*

The man skulked into the collar of his coat as he drove slowly through the industrial estate then up Gaol Street. He couldn't count how many circuits of the town he'd done since he'd left the train station. He didn't want to go home yet. Maybe if he drove around a bit more she would be in bed by the time he got there.

His eyes were blinded by the tears flowing from his eyes. He hastily wiped them away with his sleeve, like a child. He was no longer a child, but he felt like one. And some days he wished he could go back there and start all over again.

CHAPTER TWENTY-FOUR

Lottie laid the plate, wrapped in a tea towel, on the table. There was no sign of her mother. 'Anyone home?' she yelled.

'I'm in here.' Rose Fitzpatrick's voice sounded weak.

Lottie went back down the hall and stood at the open door to her mother's bedroom.

'Have you been lying there all day?'

'Nothing to get up for,' Rose said, her mouth turning downwards.

With a disgruntled sigh, Lottie plumped up the pillows and straightened the duvet. Rose didn't move. Stared straight at her. Shrugging off an unwelcome feeling, Lottie took a step away and said, 'I brought over dinner. Are you hungry?'

'Not if it's a fry again.'

'It's lasagne. The kids cooked. It may be a bit hot.'

'Better than being cold like it usually is.'

'I mean spicy. I can throw it in the bin if you don't want it.'

'No need to be so sharp, missy.' Rose dug her elbows into the bed and sat up. 'I'll have it here. And a cup of tea.'

'Right so.' Lottie stomped back down the hall.

The last few months had been difficult, as she tried to come to terms with her mother's cataclysmic revelations. Their relationship had already been flawed, but now Lottie struggled to define exactly what Rose meant to her. If she wasn't her biological mother, then what was she? A liar?

She poured water into a cup with a tea bag, swirled it around with a spoon, slopped in milk, and took it to Rose along with the plate of food.

'Could you not find the tray?'

'Jesus!' Lottie said. 'You ate your food from a plate on your knee yesterday. What's changed?'

Rose was being awkward for the sake of it. To annoy her. Well, you're winning on that score, she thought. She placed the cup on the bedside cabinet and sorted the plate with a knife and fork.

Rose leaned over and sipped the tea. 'You forgot the sugar.'

'You never take sugar.'

'I do now. It might give me energy. Will you get it for me?'

Lottie bit her lip, silencing an impulsive retort. She watched Rose picking at the food. The once tall, vibrant seventy-six-year-old was now a shadow of that woman. Her hair, which used to stand to attention in short silver strands, was plastered to her skull, with white skin peeking out in places. Her head appeared to have shrunk with the rest of her body. Although Lottie tried hard, very hard, she couldn't feel any love for the woman who had raised her, and who she had thought of as her mother for forty-four years. She couldn't find forgiveness in her heart. But she knew it wasn't this woman lying here that she couldn't forgive. It was the woman Rose used to be. And it was the lie. She could never forgive the lie. Of course, she also knew that it was all her father's fault.

Returning with the sugar bowl, she said, 'You need to see a doctor.'

'I'm not changing doctors at this stage of my life. I'll wait until Dr O'Shea comes back to town.'

Lottie sighed. She had no idea when her friend Annabelle O'Shea would return to Ragmullin. She hoped it would be soon; she was running out of pills.

'I don't know how long she'll be away, and this staying in bed all day is not normal for you.'

'Not one day of my life has been normal since I married your father. So off with you. Go home and watch your children. And here.' Rose handed her the plate of food. 'I can't eat this. It's like the hide off a donkey.'

Lottie sighed. She could never win where Rose Fitzpatrick was concerned. 'Do you even know what the hide of a donkey tastes like?'

She left without waiting for an answer.

*

'You're home early,' Grace said with a smile.

'Change of plans.' Boyd took off his jacket and loosened his tie. 'What are you watching?'

'You're changing the subject.' Grace pressed a button on the remote and folded her arms as the television screen faded to black.

Boyd folded himself into his armchair, pulled off his shoes and nudged them under the coffee table in front of him.

'Would you like—' she began.

'Don't mention tea.'

'I was going to ask if you wanted a drink.'

'Yeah, great. Thanks.'

As Grace went to the kitchenette, she said, 'I can assume things didn't work out with the delightful Lottie Parker. And in case you have forgotten, I have yet to meet her.'

'You don't *have* to meet her. Anyway, her family had other things planned for this evening. I have to reschedule.'

Grace handed him a bottle of Heineken and sat down with a glass of Diet Coke for herself. 'Reschedule? I thought it was a date, not a work meeting.'

'You know what I mean.'

'You should say what you mean.'

'Don't start.'

Grace sipped her drink with a smile. Boyd couldn't help himself. He smiled too. His sister sounded so like Lottie, it was uncanny. And then in other ways she was a million miles removed from his boss.

'You are a very lonely man,' Grace said, pulling at her short brown hair.

Boyd glanced up. She was staring at him over the rim of the glass.

'Where did that come from?' he said.

'I am astute, even though everyone thinks I'm stupid.'

'You're one of the most intelligent people I know.'

'Thank you, brother dear.'

'No need to be cynical.'

'I don't do cynical.'

Boyd sighed and took a swig of his lager. He thought of the way Lottie had rushed him out of her house. No matter what she said about her mother, no matter how confused she was over her parentage, she possessed an innate sense of duty of care to Rose. Family was everything to Lottie Parker, and he despaired that he could ever be part of that family.

'You *are* lonely,' Grace said.

He raised an eyebrow. 'I am not,' he denied, a little too forcefully. 'I like my own company and my own space.'

'I won't be here for long.' Grace put her glass on the coffee table and picked up the remote control again.

'I didn't mean that the way it sounded. Sorry. Believe me, I honestly didn't mean that you're in the way. I love having you here.'

'You're an awful liar.'

'And you can't lie to save your life.'

They both laughed.

'True.' She switched on the television. 'I want to meet Lottie. You better organise it, soon.'

'Okay.'

He sipped his beer. This was only the third day of Grace staying with him; there was still three and a half more weeks to go. He wondered just how he was going to put up with his sister sharing his home.

CHAPTER TWENTY-FIVE

After the railway preservation meeting, a few of the committee members went to Cafferty's pub, and sat at a round table, pints of Guinness in front of them.

'The station will close down no matter what we do,' the chairman said. 'I'll be out of a job.'

'We have to fight to the bitter end,' Cillian O'Donnell said.

'We need television coverage,' Bernard Fahy suggested.

'I'll see if I can find out anything.' Cillian sipped his pint. He smoothed down his dark hair as the chairman waved a tired hand and headed for the door.

'Thanks for that. Goodnight, lads.'

'Maybe we could have a march on Leinster House,' Cillian said when it was just the three of them left.

'Bit cold for marching this time of year. Very few would turn up,' Bernard said.

'The weather must be good for your business then.' Cillian smirked.

'The graveyard is filling up nicely. Trying to keep the banshees away and all. And the guards.'

'What are you talking about?' Cillian sat up straight and stared at him.

'Oh go on, tell us,' Finn urged. 'Nothing like a few witches to take our minds off the railway bastards.'

'Piss off, the pair of you,' Bernard snorted. 'I'm the one who has to walk around there in the dark.'

'Doing night duty, are you?' Finn straightened his back and gave a mock salute with his dripping pint. 'Keeper of the dead.'

'You're very funny. Ha ha. But I'm not laughing. There's queer things goings on there. Wasn't I trying to get an old woman buried this morning, and this detective was snooping around because of the screams the young traveller one heard—'

'What are you on about?' Cillian said. 'What screams? What happened?'

'All serious now, aren't you? A young woman was found dead in the bottom of the grave.' Bernard put the glass to his lips and drained the black liquid in a single gulp.

'A dead woman? In a grave?' Finn said.

'Jaysus. I've heard it all now.' Cillian sipped his pint.

'Whole place is cordoned off. I can't get in. No one can.' Bernard grabbed his coat. 'I'm off home. See you next Wednesday? Same time?'

'Sure,' the brothers said.

He flattened his cap to his head, pulled on his well-worn black council jacket and headed out into the frost of the night.

'He's a real oddball,' Cillian said. 'A body in a grave? Now that's nothing new, is it?'

Finn stared into the frothy head on his pint, dreading the prospect of going home to Sara. The thought of seeing her frosty face was unappealing. If he could stay out until after eleven, then she would definitely be in bed. Clockwork. That was what she was. He was convinced that a horologist lived inside her ribcage, winding up dials linked to her brain. Time for this. Time for that. You're late for this. You're late for that. For fuck's sake!

'All right there, lads?' Darren, the barman, asked from behind the counter.

'I will be. Just as soon as I finish this,' Finn said.

'Any luck with the plans to keep the station open?' Darren asked as he polished a glass with a tea cloth.

'Ongoing,' Cillian said.

'If anyone can get them to change their minds, you can.' Darren reached up and put the glass on the shelf. 'Awful news about that young woman found murdered in the graveyard.'

'Murdered? I didn't hear that bit.' Finn pulled on his navy anorak and zipped it up. Time to face the clockwork orange once again. The thought filled his stomach with bile.

'Where are you off to?' Cillian said as the brothers left the pub together.

'Home,' Finn said.

'We need to meet with Dad this week.'

'Why?'

'It's Lynn's tenth anniversary. On Sunday.'

'I hadn't forgotten.' Finn looked up at the night sky. 'The first one without Mother. Do you think we should do a fresh appeal?'

'Not going to bring her back, is it?'

'You never know,' Finn said.

'It might send Dad over the edge. According to Keelan, he's lighting candles. She says he's in a bad way.'

'Was he ever any other? The fucking bastard.'

'Hey, keep it down. No need to tell the world.'

'You always did like to bury the truth, didn't you?' Finn pulled his collar tighter to his throat and walked away from his brother.

'You know what, Finn, you're a piece of shit,' Cillian shouted.

'And we both came from the same family.' Finn kept walking, talking over his shoulder. 'You're no angel, Cillian O'Donnell. I know you. Don't ever forget that. I know all about you.'

CHAPTER TWENTY-SIX

The mirror wasn't doing her any favours tonight. Gilly O'Donoghue wasn't used to the art of applying make-up. A scrape of lipstick was her usual fare. At least she liked the short cut of her hair. It was handy, especially when wearing her peaked garda hat.

'You'll have to do,' she told her reflection.

She was meeting her friend Mollie in Danny's Bar because Kirby had had to cancel their Wednesday-night date due to some surveillance job. She'd rung Mollie, who'd agreed to meet up tonight even though she had to be up early for the train every morning.

Gilly had been going out with Kirby for the last four months and trying to keep it quiet at work. But it was hard to hide a secret from a crew of gardaí. Kirby was at least ten years her senior. It didn't worry her. He actually looked a lot older than that, if she wanted to be totally honest with herself. Probably all the extra weight he carried around his stomach. Could she get him to go jogging with her? She'd ask him.

'I'm running a bit late,' she said to the empty bedroom. Better let Mollie know. Tapping the phone, she called her friend. It rang out. She tried again. Same result. She checked the time: 9.45 p.m. Maybe she was in the pub already and couldn't hear the phone.

Gilly grabbed her coat from the back of the door and left her flat. She hoped Mollie wouldn't be mad at her.

*

The night was dark. The stars had fled, and the frost had disappeared along with them. It was still cold, but he could feel rain in the air.

He thought about Elizabeth. Dammit, he had thought she'd never be found. Had he been careful enough? He had disposed of her phone. Taken it apart. Dropped pieces of it out of the train window and along the streets of Dublin. He'd dumped her handbag into a rubbish bin behind a pub. Was there anything else he needed to be mindful of?

Her clothes were in the skip inside the cemetery wall. That was the reason he'd been there in the first place. Thought the bitch was still in a flatline state. He'd spent ages at the lake with her, undressing her. Dunking the clothes into the water and putting them into black bin bags, ready for the skip. The guards would probably find them now, but he'd been careful. There shouldn't be any of his DNA on them.

He'd stashed her in one of the caravans at the lake until it was time to move her. He couldn't risk leaving her there. Maybe he should have done, because her escape from the car had changed everything. And directed him to his next conquest.

He smiled when he thought of the new one waiting for him. He still had her belongings. In the morning, her phone would meet the same fate as Elizabeth's, and the laptop would be suitably disposed of on the other side of the city. He'd bagged her clothes and boots, and stuffed them into a charity recycle bin outside Tesco.

All was taken care of.

He was free to play.

*

Mollie's Canal Drive apartment was in darkness. She hadn't been in the pub, and it was unlike her not to let Gilly know that she'd changed her mind about going out.

When she got no response from ringing the bell, Gilly hammered on the door. Standing on the top step, she looked around at the bleak surroundings. In the distance, she could see the lights of the town shining brighter than the solitary lamp at the corner of the block.

Careful not to slip, she made her way down the steps. That was when she remembered she had a key. Mollie had given it to her a while ago, just in case. You never knew when you might need a bed for a night. She made her way back up to the door.

Surely she was overreacting? But now she was here, she might as well check. It couldn't do any harm, other than wake Mollie up from an early slumber. Rummaging through the multitude of keys on her key ring, she tried two before the door eventually opened inwards.

Stepping inside, she fumbled along the wall for the light switch. 'Mollie? You all right?'

No one in the kitchen. Cereal was caked to a bowl in the sink. No sign of an evening meal having been cooked. Not even takeaway boxes or wrappers. Gilly made her way to the bedrooms. Both empty.

She tried Mollie's number once more. No reply.

Leaving the apartment, she pulled the door shut behind her in frustration. She was a tiny bit angry. First Kirby and then Mollie, who hadn't even had the decency to tell her she wouldn't be around. Some friend.

As she headed along the path, she wondered if perhaps Mollie had missed the last train home and was spending the night in Dublin with one of her colleagues. But wouldn't she have let her know? Wouldn't she answer her phone? Then again, she could be wrapped around a new fellow. Feck you, Mollie.

Now she had to go home and take off her damn make-up. And she hadn't even had a drink.

*

Mollie's teeth were literally clinking against each other as she tried to recall the sequence of events that had led her here. Her head was woozy and her stomach churning. She'd been drugged, she was sure of it. Her tongue felt like coarse fur was growing on it and her throat was raw.

He had seemed so nice. Offering her a lift. And she hadn't thought twice about taking him up on his offer. After all, he'd brought her home safely yesterday.

Her train companion had been a pain in the butt. Asking a million questions. Did people no longer respect the unspoken rule of commuting? The unwritten law to keep quiet? The continuous talking had caused her to jump at the chance of escape at the station and accept the offer of a lift. Stupid girl. She didn't even know him.

The smell, like sour milk or sick wafted around her. Felt like it was stuck to her face. He'd clamped the cloth against her mouth and nose, and the chemicals had hit her brain. Everything she'd ever heard about accepting lifts from strangers reverberated in her mind. But those were warnings for children. Not for a twenty-five-year-old like herself. She realised she had done the most moronic thing of her whole life.

He was here now, sitting on a chair beside the makeshift bed on which she lay. She tried to cover her nakedness, but her hands wouldn't move. Couldn't move. They were tied to her sides by the rough rope across her waist keeping her horizontal on the dark-coloured sheets. The room was too small. The walls were too close. He was too near.

'Where am I?' she asked. Her vision blurred again before refocusing in the thin light filtering through a hatch in the ceiling.

'You're safe. With me.' He laughed, and the beam from the torch in his hand bumped up and down.

'Come on, this isn't funny. Take me home.'

'Shut your mouth. There'll be time enough for talk.'

When she'd first met him, he'd appeared normal. She'd seen him around town. He was an ordinary-looking commuter taking the train home from work. Was he the reason she'd felt like eyes were following her every move over the last few days?

'I've been watching you,' he said. 'Morning and evening. But you never noticed me. I was either brilliant at concealing my stare, or you had no interest in me. Whatever the case, I can watch you now without disturbance. And you have no choice but to look at me. Just the two of us here. Nice and quiet. The way I like it.'

'You're a fucking pervert. Let me go!' She pulled at the rope, feeling it rip into her skin. But it was the connection of his hand across her cheek that stopped her struggle.

'Take that back! Say you're sorry!' he shouted.

Who the hell was this jerk? No way was she going to apologise to him. Clamping her lips shut, she closed her eyes. Be strong, she willed her bruised body.

Fingers, rough and probing, pulled her eyelids upwards. A sharp scream escaped from her throat before he clamped his other hand over her mouth again.

'Pretty mouth,' he whispered, bringing his face down to hers. 'I have to leave you alone for a while. Don't try to escape like the last bitch. She's dead and buried now, and you don't want that, do you?'

She whimpered and nodded, despite herself.

'When you learn to live by my rules, I will reward you. Little by little.'

'What do you mean?'

'You need food and water, don't you?'

'I'm not going to be here long enough for that,' she spat.

'Let's see how long it takes for that fight to desert you. And when it does, I guarantee you'll beg for the things you've taken for granted all your life.'

'You know nothing about my life.'

'True. But now that I have you here, I've plenty of time to find out, and you will tell me what I want to know.'

'Where are you going?' She tried to lean up on her elbow but flopped back down. She watched as he moved to the iron ladder leading to the opening in the ceiling. Taking the torch with him. 'No! 'Don't leave me here in the dark. Please.'

'Begging already. See, I told you so. You had no one in your life, but now you have me.'

'You're wrong there. I'm supposed to be meeting a friend. She's in the guards. And the girl I met on the train, she has a brother. They'll come looking for me.'

As soon as she'd blurted out the words, Mollie knew she had made a mistake, but she wasn't sure what it was. His eyes darkened and his face took on a ghoulish glow in the semi-darkness.

'You are alone now,' he said flatly.

She watched as he climbed the ladder and hauled himself through the hatch. When the small square door banged shut, she was plunged into darkness.

The night wrapped itself around her cold shoulders, and she cried and cried until her throat was so raw she could hardly breathe.

*

When he had everything secure, he made his way to his car and sat there thinking. He should have been more careful. He didn't know she had a friend in the guards. Damn. He crashed his fist against the steering wheel. He'd have to find out who that might be and make sure nothing pointed in his direction. But there *was* nothing. He had never come in contact with the girl before, other than giving her one lift and seeing her on the train.

The train!

Who was that gap-toothed girl? What difference did it make if she had a brother or not? What was the significance of that? He was missing something. There was definitely something that Mollie was omitting. He'd have to find out. All this was diverting his attention from getting the answer he needed. If only that bitch hadn't escaped the other night, none of this would be happening now. It was all her fault.

He hadn't even had the time to have fun with her. But this one, yes, he would savour the pleasure of taking her down. He felt the hardness pulse between his legs. She would be just the medicine he needed. And she would give him the answers.

He switched on the ignition and began the drive home.

Slowly. Very slowly.

CHAPTER TWENTY-SEVEN

Cillian crept into the semi-darkness of the room. The street light cast enough illumination to allow him to undress, fold his clothes and slip naked into bed. Keelan stirred in her sleep. He lay on his back. Stared at the dark ceiling. And he thought of the other woman in his life.

He missed her so much. It was as if someone had taken a bone from his leg and he was forever condemned to walk around in pain, limping on one side. But it's only a bone, people would say, you can still function. Yeah, so what do you know about it?

Keelan rolled over and he knew she was looking at him.

'What did you say?' she asked.

'Nothing. Go back to sleep.'

'You thinking about Lynn?'

'Go to sleep.'

'Did you go to the pub after the meeting?'

'Yes. With Finn.'

He felt her fingers then, lightly feathering the soft hair on his taut belly. Searching lower. And he couldn't help his response. Physically he was ready. But his mind was back there. Back at that time when the darkness descended and his world changed forever.

He felt her shift beneath him.

'Slow down,' she said. 'You're hurting me.'

But he couldn't slow down. His skin slid over hers, up and down, until a soft sheen of sweat built up, oiling their bodies. Maybe tonight he could banish his demons. Shut them away in the closet and lose the key. Separate his world into two distinct parts. For a while, at least.

As he grunted, teeth gritted, eyes open, he caught sight of the pile of neatly folded clothes on the chair under the window. Everything had to be in its rightful place, like a china dinner service presented as a wedding present. Too good to use, too delicate. Left at the back of the cupboard, only taken out for important people. Like the visit of a priest or the guards …

The thought frustrated his frenzy.

'You stopped at just the wrong time,' she said. 'What's up?'

'Not a lot, by the looks of things.' He lay back on the mattress, sweating, unable to perform his sexual duties.

He was angry.

She was angry.

It wasn't her fault. But he hit her anyway.

*

'What time of night do you call this?'

Finn shoved past his wife, the talking clock, and made his way down the short, narrow hallway and into the tiny spare room. She followed him.

'What's up with you, baby?'

'Don't you "baby" me,' he said. He lay fully clothed on the single bed and closed his eyes. He still had his coat on. The room was freezing. The whole damn apartment was like an igloo. He wrapped his arms around his body. 'Turn off the light.' If he stretched out his hand, he could switch it off himself. The room was that small.

'Ah, come on. Don't be like that,' she whined and sat on the side of the bed. He rolled away and faced the wall, studying the fungus of damp beneath the windowsill. He didn't need this shit. Still she rattled on. 'I miss you when you're not here. It's so cold, I could do with a bit of body warmth. Know what I mean?'

'Fuck off,' he growled.

'There's no need for that kind of language.'

'Jesus, you sound just like my mother.'

'Your mother is dead.'

'And I wish you were too. Now turn off the damn light and leave me alone.'

He couldn't talk to her when she was in this mood. When *he* was in this mood. When life was being a complete bitch to him, why did she have to be likewise?

No longer sensing his wife's presence, he sat up and pulled off his boots and clothes. Then he tugged on a T-shirt and jogging pants and slipped under the duvet. He wondered how he was going to get out of the mess he'd made of his life. They had no money, and were still renting this piss-poor two-bed apartment.

At least you have your job, Sara would say. His job. Yeah, right. Working as a clerical officer in the public service, paid just above the minimum wage. No savings, and eighty euros a week train fares.

Why couldn't *she* get a job? No use wandering down that lane, because he knew why. He didn't want to think about Sara's drinking habits now. Things were bad enough. He was thirty-four, for Christ's sake. Wasn't life supposed to be better at his age? He should never have married her, and now he was living with that mistake every single hour of his life.

CHAPTER TWENTY-EIGHT

Bridie McWard sat up in bed and stared over at her son in his cot. She kept the light on, and Spotify was churning out easy music on her iPhone. Still no sign of Paddy. Every night it was the same. Out until all hours. She hardly saw him any more.

She pulled the sheet up to her chin and folded her legs beneath her. She was too scared to lie down. Too frightened to close her eyes.

The key rattled in the lock and the front door opened. She held her breath, body frozen; her blood seemed to stop flowing. The door to the bedroom was pushed open and she looked up into the sorrowful eyes of her husband.

'I'm sorry,' he said, and sat on the bed to drag off his boots.

'That's what you say all the time.'

She didn't relax until he switched off the light and lay down on the far side of the bed, his breathing lowering into the soft snore of sleep. Only then did she slide down, unfurl her legs and close her eyes.

*

Lottie felt like she'd been run over by a ten-ton truck. The water pounded down on her as she tried to ease the stress from her mind and body. Her wound had healed well, but the pain nagged at her constantly. And a late-night cold shower wasn't doing her any favours.

She wrapped a towel around herself, smoothed moisturiser onto her skin before pulling on warm pyjamas. She swallowed two paracetamol, then remembered the wash she'd put on that morning.

Everything would be smelly and creased. Unless Katie had looked after the chore. Chances of that were slim to none.

Down in the utility room, she emptied the clothes out of the dryer and folded them into piles, then hefted the damp laundry from the washing machine into the dryer. She switched it on, turned out the light and went back up to bed.

Listening to the sounds of the house settling down and the patter of rain against the window, she thought of Katie heading off to New York with her baby. There was nothing she could do to stop her. Lottie Parker couldn't compete with Tom Rickard. She just hoped he would treat her daughter right and send her home in one piece.

Thoughts of New York reminded her of the unofficial investigation she'd conducted into the murders from last October. She'd got nowhere, but there was a link to New York, for sure. She just had to find it.

She flipped her pillow over, fluffing up the feathers, then twisted and turned, searching for a comfortable position. She thought of poor Anna Byrne, whose daughter was never coming home. Tomorrow she would set about tracking down Elizabeth's killer. And then she remembered.

'Oh no,' she groaned. 'McMahon.'

Somewhere deep in the pit of her stomach, she knew her life was just about to turn very complicated.

*

Matt Mullin paused the television screen on Elizabeth's photograph, then sat cross-legged on the floor and stared at her. Why had he let her go? Why had he put his job before love? He *had* loved her, hadn't he? And she'd loved him.

He sniffed away his tears and allowed a knot of hate to fill the void in his heart. She had caused his heart to break into tiny pieces, so many that he knew he could never put it back together. Never again.

It was going to be a long night. And still he stared at her face on the television, frozen in time. He remembered that photograph. He remembered it well. Because he had taken it. And now she had been snatched away from him.

'Oh Elizabeth,' he cried. 'What have I done?'

*

Donal O'Donnell switched out the light and went to sit at the table. He couldn't bring himself to make his way up the stairs to his lonely bed.

The flickering of the television highlighted the photograph on the sideboard. The silver frame glistened and the young woman in the picture seemed to come to life.

He stared at her beautiful face. To him she *had* been beautiful. She still was. His princess. But she'd taken Maura away from him. Not just the ten years of yearning for answers, waiting for the knock on the door, mourning without a body. No. Lynn had taken his wife from him the day she was born. It hadn't mattered that they already had two boys; now Maura had a little girl to devote herself to. And she had shut out everyone else. Smothered their daughter with overpowering emotion and attention.

The boys had suffered. He knew that then. He knew it now. But he'd done nothing to stop it. He'd gone along with Maura for fear of losing her altogether. And he'd been complicit in the treatment of his sons. It was wrong, what he and Maura had done, but he'd been powerless to stop it. Once he was in, there was no way out.

Resting his head on his folded arms, he blotted out the image of his daughter in the photograph, but in his mind's eye he could still see her, standing there in the kitchen.

'God in heaven,' he mumbled, 'forgive me. Forgive us all for what we have done.'

But Donal O'Donnell knew his soul was long past the stage of forgiveness.

*

Bridie felt Paddy leaving their bed. Heard the buzz of his electric razor and the soft thud of the door closing as he went out. He hadn't spoken a word to her. The clock flashed 3.46. She fell back into a fitful sleep.

A loud crack woke her. She sat up. Was it a tree falling down on the roof? But there was no wind and no tree. The clock said 4.25.

Jumping out of bed, she checked on her baby. Tommy was fast asleep. The first night in weeks, and now she was awake. Drawing back the curtain, her eyes met the ugly graveyard wall, but the sky above it was lit up with stars.

The door burst open. She swirled round on the ball of one foot, her mouth open in a silent scream.

A figure stood in the doorway, highlighted by the night light.

'Who ... who are you? Fuck off away.'

As Bridie made to rush to the cot, a leather-gloved fist smashed into the side of her face. She raised her arms to shield her head, but the second blow knocked her to the floor. Crouching into a ball, like Paddy had once told her to do if she was ever attacked, she cried, 'Don't touch my baby!'

A boot stamped on her back as she rolled over. When the second boot landed on her stomach, pain flashed up through her chest into her head, and something hard crashed down on her skull.

She thought she heard a voice, somewhere in the distance. What was he saying? If she concentrated, maybe he wouldn't hurt Tommy. But even as his words began to register, the blows continued to rain down in quick succession, and darkness fell.

DAY TWO

Thursday 11 February 2016

CHAPTER TWENTY-NINE

He didn't like the reflection he saw in the mirror above the washbasin. Even allowing for the fact that it was cracked, with a brown line cutting diagonally across the glass, splitting his face in two, he knew he looked bad. He leaned in closer and ran a finger under the black bags sagging beneath his tired eyes. His pupils were so dilated they appeared to be dark buttons, masking the true colour of his irises. Not a bad thing in one way, he supposed. Perhaps he could use some of her make-up to lessen the pallor, to add a highlight to otherwise chalk-white cheeks. Perhaps not.

With his teeth brushed and the scum of last night's alcohol swirling down the drain, he splashed water on his face and dried it using the only clean towel he could find. Dressing quickly, he picked up the bundle of flyers from the table and took the stapling gun from the cupboard beneath the sink.

It was 5.25 a.m., and the morning was dark and bitterly cold. Not like spring at all. A shower of rain during the night, followed by frost, had resulted in treacherous footpaths. He parked his car and started walking around town, putting up the A4-sized posters on every lamp post and pole he could find. It was a job he had done at this time every year for the last ten years. And it was one he would continue to do, though he knew there was no prospect of her ever returning. Appearances had to be maintained. And so far, he'd been doing okay on that score.

A car drove by, heading over the bridge towards the train station, lighting up the sheen of ice on the road. With his mind distracted, his hand slipped and the staple pierced the bridge of her nose, directly between her eyes.

He smirked. That felt good. Too good.

Shaking off the sensation of fire in his belly, he moved on to the next post.

CHAPTER THIRTY

Grace Boyd settled into her usual seat on the train. Waiting for Mollie, she glanced out of the window, rubbing at the frost stuck to the glass like the spines of dead animals. Mollie would want to hurry up or she'd be late. The whistle sounded. The guard waved a small green baton and the doors whooshed shut.

Maybe she'd got on a different carriage. But no. Grace had been at the station at 5.50 a.m. She had checked the clock in Boyd's car before she got out. She looked at her phone screen: 6.01.

Sighing, she tried to relax. Maybe Mollie was avoiding her. Quite possible, she thought. She'd never had any bother making friends; it was keeping them that was the unworkable trick.

She looked over at the adjacent seats. The man was there again, with his designer stubble, but his eyes looked darker, and red-rimmed. Further down the aisle she noticed another man. The reason she supposed she noticed these two was that they were both wide awake. Everyone else was already asleep.

She rocked in rhythm to the sway of the train, wishing her brain could shut off for at least five minutes. But she knew it never shut off. Not even when she was asleep.

Should she ring her brother? Now why on earth would you do that, Grace? He would say she was nuts. Maybe she was. But she didn't think so. She liked to have silent conversations with herself. They comforted her when no one else would listen.

Grace eyed the man who had sat opposite Mollie yesterday; the man who had caused her to move seats. Maybe she was sick, or had she slept in? Why hadn't she asked for her phone number?

The train stopped at Enfield and more people crowded onto it. Hadn't Mollie said she lived alone? What if she'd fallen down the stairs and no one knew? Stop! Grace didn't even know if there were any stairs in Mollie's house, so why was she thinking these thoughts?

She took her phone from her bag and kept pressing buttons until her contacts appeared. All two of them. Mark and her mother. If she told Mark, at least she would feel better.

*

Detective Inspector David McMahon was already at the station when Lottie arrived. Leaning against the door to her office, arms folded and a smug expression on his square jaw.

She shuffled out of her jacket as slowly as she could manage and hung it on the coat rack. Who the hell does he think he is? With a sigh, she decided she would be nice to him today. If he kept his mouth shut.

His initial mistake was to speak first.

'Well, if it isn't Inspector Clouseau.' He smirked and swiped his black fringe out of his eyes.

She ignored the comment, and brushed past him. Her immediate superior for the foreseeable future was a grade A shithead.

This wasn't a good start to their new working relationship. A relationship that had been soured last October when he'd been sent from Dublin to help with her investigation into a suspected drugs and murder gang. He'd tried to take over, but she'd stood her ground and come out on top in the end. That was then. Now? She'd have to work hard at being civil. God, why had she opened that bottle last night when she couldn't sleep?

'Must be too early for you,' he said. 'I thought you had a sense of humour.' He straightened his back. 'I want you in my office with an update on your current caseload. Let's say five minutes? That should give you time to wake up.'

She watched as he bent his head to leave her office. She had nothing against tall men, but giraffes gave her the shivers.

He turned back. 'And remember this. Corrigan might put up with your bullshit, but I won't.'

Collapsing onto her chair, she glared up at the ceiling. What had she done to deserve McMahon? Scrap that. She had done plenty over the years, and now it was time to prepare her army for battle.

'Boyd!' she called. Where was everyone this morning? There was no one in the office. Shit. She'd have to face the squatter alone. And keep her mouth shut. First, though, she popped in two paracetamol, hoping they'd dull her headache.

'You didn't waste much time,' she said, entering what had been up until yesterday Superintendent Corrigan's office.

'What do you mean?' McMahon looked up with an eyebrow raised in surprise.

'Getting your feet under the table.'

She swept her hand around. McMahon had moved the desk to sit under the window, and the coat rack was now in the furthest corner of the room. Was there a strategy lurking in his actions? She didn't know, but it put her on high alert. No matter how long or short his time in Ragmullin turned out to be, he was evidently intent on making his mark. She hoped she could stay out of the way of the arrow he was staking his claim with.

'Sit, Detective Inspector Parker.' He indicated the chair in front of his desk.

Much as it galled her, Lottie decided compliance was her best option. She sat down.

'Now tell me what you're working on.' He unbuttoned his suit jacket and folded his arms over a double-breasted waistcoat. A red handkerchief poked out of the breast pocket. Jesus! She suddenly missed Corrigan, with his belly carved into the grain of the desk.

'Twenty-five-year-old Elizabeth Byrne went missing on Monday evening having caught the train home from Dublin, where she worked. We found her body yesterday morning in the cemetery. We have reason to believe she was murdered.'

'I saw the skimpy report. How did she die?'

'She had a broken leg and was covered in clay at the bottom of a grave. It appears she was suffocated by the dirt. We believe she was left there to die. I'm waiting for the state pathologist to contact me with a time for the post-mortem.'

'So you don't know for sure that she was murdered?'

'I'm positive she was, sir. Just waiting for confirmation.'

'She might have fallen into a grave, breaking her leg, and in her efforts to get out, dragged clay down on top of herself. Did you think of that?'

'Yes, sir. According to Jim McGlynn, the head of the SOCO team, the amount of clay suggests someone covered her with it deliberately.'

'Hmph. What other investigations do you have on?'

'David—'

'Sir! I am your superior.'

'Don't I just know it,' Lottie muttered.

'What?'

'Thanks for reminding me. Can I speak for a moment about Elizabeth?'

'Who?'

Jesus, this was hard work. She'd rather be outside, sourcing leads. She said, 'The young woman who was murdered. Sir.'

'No wonder Superintendent Corrigan is ill in hospital. You must have worn the poor man to a shell.'

Lottie thought that Corrigan was anything but a shell, but she let it go. She filled McMahon in on the information she had compiled so far.

'Elizabeth worked in Dublin. Her mother hadn't seen her since Sunday lunchtime. The girl caught the six o'clock commuter train each morning. She was at work on Monday and was last seen getting the 17.10 train from Connolly station to Ragmullin. We have a screen grab from Connolly CCTV footage, and two commuters who swear they saw her on the train. But we have no visual of her disembarking at Ragmullin. Then we have a young woman, Bridie McWard, who heard screams from the cemetery at 3.15 on Tuesday morning. Surveillance cameras outside the cemetery gates display the shadow of a car at 3.07 a.m. with similar images twenty-four minutes later. I am treating this as confirmation that the killer drove there with the girl in his car. It is possible she escaped and he followed her. She tripped over something and fell into the open grave, breaking her leg. Her abductor then seized the opportunity to cover her with clay and smother her.'

'You have it all worked out nice and neat. Only two problems with your scenario.'

'What might they be?'

'One, you have no confirmation that she was murdered, and two, that could've been an innocent person's car.'

'I intend to find out. Sir.'

'Do that. And report back to me.'

'I have a team meeting this morning, if you wish to sit in?'

'Didn't you hear what I just said? Report to me.'

Lottie bit her tongue, stalling her reply. 'Anything else? Sir.'

'What other cases are you working on at the moment?'

'Kirby and Lynch have been carrying out a surveillance operation on the traveller community. We believe there is an underground movement of bare-knuckle fights.'

'Fights? Is that all you have to concern yourself with these days?'

'It can be very nasty. Large amounts of money are wagered. And sometimes it turns into a fight-to-the-death kind of thing.'

'Has anyone died?'

'Not yet.'

'Then let them get on with it. I've seen this kind of thing in Dublin. It's all a show of strength.'

Lottie sighed and pulled her sleeves down over her hands, trying desperately to keep herself from fidgeting. God, she needed a Xanax. 'Do you want me to tell Kirby and Lynch to back off, then?'

The suddenness of his movement caught her by surprise. She sank back into her chair as he stood and marched around the small office, coming to a stop in front of her and perching on the edge of the desk. 'I want you to do your job,' he said. 'I don't want you getting stuck in my hair.'

You have enough of it anyway, she thought. As if reading her mind, he brushed his fringe out of his eyes. Shit, she hoped she hadn't spoken aloud.

'Attend the post-mortem and determine whether you are dealing with a murder. Pull your detectives away from the traveller community and present me with a killer. Today, preferably.'

'Right so.' Did he think she was Superwoman or what? 'One other thing,' she said. 'Superintendent Corrigan asked that I look into a cold case.'

'What cold case?'

'A young woman called Lynn O'Donnell, disappeared ten years ago this week.'

'And what has that got to do with anything?'

'I haven't had time to read the file yet, but it appears she was last seen on the commuter train from Dublin. Valentine's Day.'

'Perhaps she eloped?'

'I don't know. She's never been found. I'll read the file and maybe have a chat with her family.'

'I think you've enough to be doing without burying your nose in a ten-year-old case.'

'I'll check it out anyway.'

'Find the Byrne girl's murderer. If she *was* murdered, that is. And that's an order.'

'Yes, sir.' You bollocks, she added in her head.

'You can go,' he said.

Getting up, she edged out past his outstretched legs and left the office without a word. Sometimes it was better to remain silent. Sometimes, but not always.

CHAPTER THIRTY-ONE

'Where on earth have you been?' Lottie watched Boyd fall into his chair without removing his jacket. 'I needed your support ten minutes ago.'

'Sorry. Grace has my head wrecked. I've been away from home for so long, I'd actually forgotten how much she talks. Non-stop. Never-fecking-ending. I think she's given me a migraine.'

'You don't get migraines,' Lottie scoffed.

'I have one now. I dropped her to the train station early and was at home, standing in the shower, when she rang to tell me her friend wasn't on the train.'

'I thought you said she doesn't have any friends.'

'She doesn't. This is someone she met yesterday. I'd say the poor woman is avoiding her. God forgive me, I know she's my sister, but even I'd want to avoid her.'

'Don't be so mean. I can't wait to meet her.'

'You'll take back those words once you do.'

'Some brother you are.'

Lottie pulled Kirby's chair across and sat down beside Boyd. She thought how she would love to have a brother. She'd had one once, but he'd been murdered when he was just twelve years old. Then she thought about the mysterious half-sibling she had only become aware of during her last murder investigation. The lies. Her life had been built on lies. 'McMahon is on site,' she said.

'That's all we need.'

'My sentiment exactly. He's being a pain about this murder investigation. Won't allow it to be classed as murder until the state pathologist confirms it. I've to report everything to him first. And he wants Kirby and Lynch taken off the fist-fighting investigation.'

Pulling at his chin, Boyd said, 'They haven't had much success. Maybe McMahon is right and it's time they did something new.'

'Whose side are you on?' Lottie stood up, wheeled the chair back to its rightful place and headed for her own office to get her jacket. 'I'm driving to Tullamore for the PM, and after that, we can have our team meeting. Then I'm getting on to the press office.'

'What? After our new acting superintendent told you to report to him first?'

'Starting as I mean to go on,' Lottie said, and kicked the door closed.

Jane Dore was petite and precise. In every way. She nodded as Lottie entered her sterile place of work, aptly called the Dead House.

'Been a few months since you were last here,' she said, pulling down her face mask.

'Thank God, it's been quiet,' Lottie said. 'I was beginning to think all the murderous bastards had hightailed it off to the Costa del Sol.'

'Not quite all of them.'

'What have you found?'

'I've completed the prelims. Elizabeth Byrne was a healthy twenty-five-year-old female. I'd say she looked after her body. Probably did a lot of running, based on her muscle tissue.'

'Maybe that's how she got away from her killer.'

'You're assuming she was murdered?'

'Wasn't she?'

'You'll need forensic evidence to prove it. I can only tell you about the condition of the body and the evidence collected. If you'll allow me?'

'Go ahead.' Lottie perched herself on a high stool, surrounded by white tiles and stainless-steel benches and tables. She couldn't see any bodies. Good.

'She suffered from chronic psoriasis. Her scalp, knees and elbows were badly affected. So badly, in fact, that if she was transported by car, there will be flakes of skin everywhere. Trace evidence.'

Lottie noted this in her notebook. If they ever found a car to check.

Jane continued. 'She had cuts to her right elbow and to the soles of both feet consistent with running barefoot. The hallux on her left foot was fractured – that's her big toe. Also her left leg.'

'Tibia open shaft fracture,' Lottie said.

Jane raised an eyebrow.

'McGlynn told me. Most of this is consistent with what I already know.'

'Her knuckles were bitten by her own teeth, probably from the pain when she suffered the fracture.'

'How did she die?' Lottie was impatient to get this classified as murder.

'To put it bluntly, she was buried alive.'

'That's what I thought.'

'Her assailant grabbed her round the throat from behind with his arm. No fingerprints, but we got some fibres. She fell or was pushed into the grave, and as she lay there, clay either fell down or was thrown in on top of her, smothering her. I can give you the technical details if you like.'

'No, that's fine. So it *was* murder?'

'If I'm being honest, I don't think that amount of clay could have fallen in of its own accord. She died from asphyxiation caused by the clay.'

'McGlynn said there was evidence of maggots.'

'She had an open bleeding wound, so that would be normal, seeing as she was six feet below ground.'

'Time of death?'

'Going by the cold weather, and her lividity, I would estimate she was dead thirty-two to thirty-six hours maximum when you found her.'

'So it's possible she was murdered between three and four on Tuesday morning?'

'I'd agree with that.'

'Any of the killer's trace evidence show up on the body?'

'He wore gloves. As I said, a few fibres on her neck from his coat. It's possible she was drugged. I've sent samples off for toxicology. You will know as soon as I do.'

'Sexual assault?'

'No evidence of any recent sexual activity.'

'Thanks, Jane.'

'One other thing,' the pathologist said.

Lottie waited.

'This girl suffered greatly. Her cheeks, despite the clay, were salty. She'd been crying. Find him, Lottie, before he takes someone else.'

CHAPTER THIRTY-TWO

The mornings were the longest. When Saoirse was in school. Not for the first time, Keelan O'Donnell wished she had a job. But Cillian said he wanted her at home. He was making enough money; why would she need to work when he was providing for her? She supposed he was right with regards to the money aspect, but she needed to see other human beings during the day. He'd put a stop to her art classes, told her she couldn't paint even when the other women in the group thought her work was good. Then she'd joined a choir in the Arts Centre. Mornings for two hours. He stopped that too. Crows can't sing, he'd said.

Twiddling her phone in her hand, she toyed with the idea of ringing Finn's wife, Sara. Good God, she thought. That confirmed just how lonely she was. She put her phone away. Things weren't that bad. Not yet.

She picked up her coat. She'd see if Donal was coping any better. Glancing in the hall mirror, she checked that the make-up concealed the yellow bruise taking shape on her cheek. Cillian really hadn't been himself since his mother's death.

Why was she always making excuses for him? She had no answer to her own question.

As she lashed on an extra layer of foundation, just to be safe, she caught sight of the little pink umbrella hanging on the hall stand. As long as Cillian kept his anger directed at her, Saoirse should be safe. But the second he stepped over that line, Keelan was taking her daughter, and he would never find them. Ever.

*

Lottie was away from the office no longer than an hour and a half, but on her return to base, she noted the incident boards had filled up. She looked at the list of tools that had been taken from the cemetery for examination. She was particularly interested in getting the results of the analysis from the spade that they'd discovered propped up beside the digger used to excavate the graves. It seemed to be an opportune tool with which to heap clay and dirt on top of Elizabeth.

'I've just come from the Dead House.' She stood in front of the boards, facing her team, and pointed at Elizabeth Byrne's photograph. 'This girl was asphyxiated by clay. Buried alive.' She outlined the injuries Elizabeth had suffered. 'I want to know as soon as DNA and fingerprint results come in for that spade, and also the stone we found with blood on.' She directed her gaze to Kirby. 'You took Bernard Fahy's DNA sample, didn't you?'

'Yes, and also from John Gilbey, the other man who was working there.'

'Any matches?'

'Nothing on PULSE, but we haven't yet run them against the blood and tools found at the scene.' Kirby shifted his buttocks on the narrow creaky chair.

'Did you check their alibis?'

'Fahy's wife confirms he was at home all Monday evening and that night. But wives tend to cover for their husbands. John Gilbey lives in a hostel. I'll follow up on his whereabouts for the relevant time.'

'Okay, do that. The search of the caretaker's office has yielded nothing so far. I didn't expect it would, but I've instructed SOCOs to check it out, and I'll have a nose around later on.'

'It's more likely she was in the car that stopped outside, rather than in the building,' Kirby said.

'Bring up the CCTV footage.'

Kirby tapped the laptop on his knee. Lottie flipped around one of the whiteboards and the grainy images flashed onto it.

'As you can see, there was a car, possibly the killer's, parked there for twenty-four minutes,' Kirby said.

'Our own traffic cams are being checked for the relevant times to see if we can locate the vehicle,' Lottie added.

Lynch said, 'I've assigned a uniform to that. I'll review and report to you if anything turns up.'

Lottie thought Lynch looked considerably paler than yesterday. Hopefully she wasn't coming down with a bug. They needed all the bodies they could get to cover this investigation.

She continued. 'Today, I want the residents at the nursing home interviewed, especially those with rooms facing the cemetery. And the staff. Kirby, have you the data from the house-to-house?'

'I've checked all the reports. No one saw or heard anything. It was the middle of the night, after all. Traveller site residents give the same story, except for Bridie McWard hearing the screaming.'

'Her evidence ties in with the CCTV footage and the pathologist's estimate of time of death. It gives us a time frame to work with. We can deduce that Elizabeth caught the 17.10 from Connolly station, because she was seen by two commuters on the train. They got off at Enfield. To date we've discovered no further sighting. Just the screams heard by Bridie McWard at 3.15 a.m.'

'Maybe Bridie had a nightmare,' Lynch piped up.

'It's possible, but she seemed fairly shaken when I spoke to her,' Lottie said. 'Right, I want you and Kirby to do the interviews at the nursing home. Take uniformed officers with you so that you can get it finished quickly.'

'Boss, we were on stakeout last night. Up in the Munbally estate. Need to get a bit of shut-eye,' Kirby moaned.

'Oh right. On that matter, our *acting* superintendent wants you to cease that operation.'

'But we—'

'I'm just telling you what I've been ordered.'

'Such a waste of time,' Kirby grumbled, patting his pockets. He took out an e-cigarette and jammed it into his mouth.

'You didn't have many results, did you?' Lottie said. 'Now, on to Carol O'Grady. She was Elizabeth's friend so I think we should have another word with her. See if we can find out more about Elizabeth and anyone that might have had an interest in her.'

'Carol's brother is a bit iffy,' Boyd said.

'Terry O'Grady,' Lottie said, checking her notes. 'Pull his details from PULSE, and you and I will chat with Carol. Give her a call to see if she's at home or at work.' She paused and studied the two images of Elizabeth Byrne, dead and alive. 'And Matt Mullin, the ex-boyfriend. Any luck, Lynch?'

'I've been trying to chase him up,' Lynch said, pulling at her eyelids. Just as well McMahon had halted the traveller job. Lottie needed her team awake.

'Did you try the bank again this morning?'

'They were very cagey, but at least they gave me a mobile number for him. He's not answering. I'll get back onto the bank and see what the story is.'

'Check if his family know where he is, and see if his passport has been used.'

'Will do.'

'Anything from Elizabeth's mobile phone?'

'It's inactive. Dead. I'm trying to get the service provider to determine where and when it was last used,' Boyd said.

'I'll get McMahon to organise a press release. He can make an appeal for information. We need to speak with witnesses from the Last Hurdle, where Elizabeth was Saturday night, and witnesses from the train.'

When she had allocated those jobs, she said, 'I'll call to the station again. We need to determine if she actually got off the train at Ragmullin.'

She eyed the team, all ready and eager except Kirby and Lynch.

'You two look like corpses. Go home. Get two hours' sleep, and then I want you both back here.'

She dished out more tasks and said, 'Okay, you all have jobs. Let's catch the bastard who buried this young woman alive.'

*

'Donal, I know you're in there. Open up.'

Keelan pressed the doorbell again. Peered in through the glass on the upper half of the door. No shadows. No movement. No sound. But his bicycle was parked up under the window and she knew he didn't walk anywhere. Maybe he'd phoned for a taxi.

She turned away from the door and walked down the cracked pathway, avoiding the rambling weeds encroaching from the overgrown winter lawn. Glancing over her shoulder, she looked up at the two-storey terraced house that had been Cillian's childhood home. It was the only house in the line of ten that remained inhabited. The rest were tumbling down around themselves, some with the roofs caved in and others with the bare branches of bushes growing up around the chimney stacks. Most of the windows were boarded up.

Maybe now that Maura was dead, Donal might move out. Ten years waiting for a ghost to appear while the walls crumbled around you was long enough. She would speak with Cillian about it tonight. Maybe he could get his father to see sense.

The rusted gate creaked shut behind her and she made her way under the railway bridge and back into town.

She didn't see the curtain twitch.

CHAPTER THIRTY-THREE

Kirby smiled as Garda Gilly O'Donoghue walked towards him. He was standing in the covered smoking area at the rear of the station, which doubled as a bicycle rack. He hadn't time to hide the cigar he was puffing.

'Yuck. The smell of that,' Gilly said, indicating the bin of cigarette butts.

'Want one?' Kirby offered.

'No thanks. I knew I'd find you here.'

'How so?'

'Because I was sure you hadn't fully given up smoking. Did you discover anything enlightening last night?'

'Last night?'

'You were working, so you said. You cancelled our date.'

'Sorry, babe.'

'Doesn't suit you.'

'What?'

'The American twang. Even if you could do it correctly.'

'Not making much of an impression this morning, am I?'

'Try a little harder.'

'How about this then?' He reached into the breast pocket of his jacket and handed over an envelope, smiling as Gilly's face lit up.

'Hey, this is the play I wanted to see. You're a star,' she said.

'It's for tonight,' he said.

'Can't wait. And we can go for a drink afterwards.'

Running his hand over his stubbled chin, Kirby shook his head. 'We'll see. I'm absolutely shattered.'

'What are you doing here then, if you've been working nights?'

'On my way home.'

'I'm beginning to think you have another woman.'

'You're woman enough for me.' He stubbed out the cigar and palmed the butt into his pocket. 'How was your evening with that friend of yours?'

'Mollie? She never turned up.'

'That's a bit Irish, isn't it? Being stood up twice the one night.' He grinned.

'It's not funny.' Gilly raised her eyebrows, pocketed the tickets and went to move away.

'Do I not get a good-morning kiss?' Kirby said.

'You won't even get a goodnight kiss if you keep this up.'

'Women!' Kirby said to the empty space Gilly had left in the frosty air. He was debating relighting his cigar when Lynch rounded the side of the building.

'We have a call,' she said.

'No we don't. I need some shut-eye.'

'We have to go to the traveller site. It's urgent. Come on.'

'Maybe our night-time ventures are paying off,' Kirby said, and followed her to the car.

*

Sitting at her computer, Lottie clicked into her email.

'What the hell?' The message in her inbox was from a name she recognised. She blinked and opened a drawer. Had she taken a pill this morning? She couldn't remember, but she found one anyway and gulped it down. If she wasn't careful, she thought, she'd end up as bad as she'd been a year ago.

She was about to call in Boyd but thought that maybe this was too personal. Shit, it *was* personal. Her finger hovered over the mouse. What had prompted this communication? Read it and see, she told herself. With her tongue stuck to the roof of her mouth, her legs jittering, her hand remained frozen in mid-air.

The door opened and Boyd put his head round.

'Kirby needs us at the traveller site.'

She stared at him, unseeing. Lowered her head to the computer.

'Lottie? What's up?' He walked round the side of the desk. 'You have that wild look in your eyes.'

'What look?'

'You know. After a night of drinking.'

'I haven't been drinking,' she lied.

'What has you spooked, then?'

Jerking back to life, she hit the corner tab, minimising her email. 'Nothing.'

Boyd put his hands on the desk. 'I thought you couldn't stand lies, and here you are, lying to me.'

She stood up, knocked the chair out of the way with the back of her legs and sidestepped around him. 'I said it's nothing. None of your business. Butt out. Understood?'

'Loud and clear.' Boyd stood back, bumping against the wall.

Lottie kept walking. 'What's Kirby got himself into this time?'

*

'Hello? Anyone there?'

Mollie listened. Wind? Or was it an air-conditioning unit? She wasn't sure. But there were no cars or other sounds. Where was she?

It was dark in the room, but a dim light glowed at the edge of the hatch door, high above her head, casting an eerie shadow in a V down to the centre of the floor. She could see the floor was made of timber, well-worn laths. Knots were feathered along the wood. She looked at the strip of light again and decided it wasn't daylight. It had to come from a light bulb somewhere up above the ceiling.

Her arms were still strapped to her sides, and she badly wanted to pee. Her mouth felt like the internal muscles had swelled, and her throat was constricted with gluey mucus. The hairs in her nostrils were clogged with the fusty, musty smell of the room. And to add to her discomfort, her stomach rumbled with hunger.

A psychotic thought skittered through her brain. What if he never came back? What if he wanted her to starve to death? No. He'd never have gone to this much trouble just to leave her to die. Would he? She knew absolutely nothing about him, and the more she thought about it, the less she wanted to know. She wanted to go home. Now. Before the insane freak returned.

Home. But there was no one there to miss her. She lived alone. Her mother was dead and her father lived in London. She only ever phoned him on Sundays. And today was … Thursday? Wasn't it? She wasn't at all sure. But it didn't feel like much time had passed, unless it was the effects of the drug he'd used on her.

Surely her colleagues would wonder why she hadn't phoned in to say she'd be absent. But perhaps not. You only needed a doctor's certificate if you were going to be off for longer than two days. There was the weekend to come, so they wouldn't start asking questions until Monday.

Gilly! Yes, Gilly would miss her. But how long would that take? They'd been supposed to go out for a drink, but would Gilly wonder at her not turning up? She had no idea one way or the other. All she could do was hope that someone reported her missing.

She tried to raise her head from the rock-like bed. She really needed to pee, but before she could even attempt to wriggle free, warm liquid had seeped down her legs, soaking the mattress.

And that was when she thought she heard a train.

CHAPTER THIRTY-FOUR

The mid-morning sun, casting a blinding light, had tried its best to melt the hoar frost, but in shaded areas the ground was still hazardous. Boyd parked the car inside the gate and they made their way to where Kirby was lounging against the wall of one of the twelve concrete houses. Lynch stood in front of him, fair hair hanging loose beneath a grey beanie. Both of them were obviously trying to keep themselves awake. A small mobile home was parked in the compact yard.

Kirby moved to one side and filled the space between the house and the mobile home. His blue scarf was wrapped like a noose around his neck and his nose was Christmassy red. His bushy hair looked like he'd been hit with a bolt of lightning. A crowd of onlookers huddled on the other side of the site. Women and children in the centre of a circle of angry-looking men. Their hands were shoved warily in their pockets, but Lottie knew they could strike at any time.

She sniffed the frosty air. 'Tell me about this before I walk into a minefield.'

'It looks like a domestic,' Lynch said. 'But we have to be careful. You know how these situations can be different to how they first appear.' One eyebrow rose in an arch.

Was there a question there somewhere? Sucking in a draught of cold air, Lottie realised Lynch's words were a direct reference to a previous investigation. She decided to let it lie.

'Who lives at this property?' she asked.

'Paddy and Bridie McWard,' Kirby said. 'They have a little boy, called …' He turned the page of his notebook.

'Tommy,' Lottie said.

'Bridie's taken a terrible battering,' Kirby said. 'Go in and see for yourself.'

Inside the house, Bridie was sitting on a white leather sofa. She was holding the little boy in her arms, way too tightly, unshed tears flooding her eyes.

'Jesus, Bridie, are you all right?' Lottie said, shocked. 'You need to see a doctor. The hospital or something.'

'This is your fault,' Bridie yelled.

Was it ever any other way? Lottie sat down and searched for answers in the young woman's eyes. 'Tell me what happened.'

'I told your two monkeys out there.'

'I need to hear it for myself. Did Paddy do this to you?'

A purple bruise had swelled on Bridie's jaw, and dried blood had congealed in her long hair.

'No, but those two don't believe me.' She moaned as she spoke, one hand rubbing her stomach.

The baby began to cry. Lottie thought of Louis, and her heart constricted. Bridie stuck a soother in the little boy's mouth and rocked him close to her chest, wincing with the movement.

'Tell me what happened. You know I'll believe you.' Lottie took her notebook and pen from her bag. 'Do you want Boyd there to hold little Tommy while we talk?'

'You must be joking. No one is taking my baby away.'

'I was only trying to help,' Lottie said. 'You need to clean those wounds up before they get infected.' She handed her notebook to Boyd, indicating with a nod of her head that he was to take notes.

'Do you always talk like this?' Bridie said. 'First you want my story, then you want my child, and now you want me to wash.'

Smiling a little, Lottie nodded. 'You're right. I'm all over the place today. You do what makes you comfortable. When you're ready, tell me what happened to cause those cuts and bruises.'

'Well, it wasn't Paddy, so you can get that notion right out of your head, Missus Detective.'

'Okay. If it wasn't Paddy, who was it? And where *is* Paddy?'

'There you go again. Two questions.'

'I'll shut up and listen.' Lottie set her mouth in a straight line and willed herself to keep it that way.

'At last, a bit of silence.' Bridie rocked Tommy slowly as the child's eyes closed. 'Paddy was here last night for a while. He came to bed but only stayed about an hour before he got up again and left. I don't know where he is, so don't ask me. Right?'

Lottie nodded.

Bridie went on to relate what had happened. Lottie wondered what had prompted the attack on a defenceless young woman with her baby in the room.

'Can you describe your assailant?'

'It was dark, but he was a big fucking monster.'

Lottie waited in silence as sobs broke from Bridie's throat. She was afraid to utter a word in case the young woman refused to carry on talking.

'Leather gloves. He was wearing dark leather gloves. Dressed all in black, now that I think of it. And before you ask, I didn't see his face. Jesus, Paddy will go ballistic when he sees the state of me.'

'Don't worry. Detective Kirby will have a word with him.'

'No one is to talk to Paddy. Not until I do.'

'Have you contacted him?'

'I tried his phone. He must be out of range or something.' Bridie bit her lip as tears slid down her bruised face.

Lottie put out a tentative hand and patted the young woman's knee. 'You're doing fine, Bridie,' she said soothingly. 'Can you remember anything else?'

'That monster hammered the daylights out of me. Kicked me in the stomach. Hit my head with something hard. I could feel the blood flowing. And the pain. God in heaven, it was worse than when I was giving birth to Tommy. Well, maybe not worse. As bad as.'

'Can you remember if he said anything?'

Sniffing now, Bridie said, 'That was the worst thing. He grabbed my hair and twisted it, and said, "Stay away from the guards and the graveyard, if you don't want to end up six feet under like the other one." Oh God.'

Lottie glanced at Boyd. 'What can you recall after he said that?'

'I passed out. I woke up to Tommy screaming in his cot. And every inch of me screaming in pain along with him.'

'Tommy wasn't harmed, though?'

Bridie shook her head. 'He's okay.' She stared into Lottie's eyes, pleading, 'What did he mean? Was it because I told you about the banshee? Something to do with that woman being murdered over there?'

Lottie thought for a moment. Was that the reason Bridie had been attacked? It seemed a little far-fetched. She decided to be honest. 'I don't know, but I'll get the SOCOs in here to see if your assailant left behind any DNA.'

'What's a SOCO?'

'Scene of crime officer.'

'Like the *CSI* crowd on the telly?'

'Something like that,' Lottie said. She nodded at Boyd to make the call.

'They better not leave a mess. It's taken me two hours to wash the floor in the bedroom.'

'You what?' Boyd exclaimed before Lottie could stop him.

Tommy opened his mouth and the soother fell out. He began to roar.

'Now see what you did.' Bridie glared. 'Of course I washed the floor. I couldn't be walking around sticking to all that blood. And there's someone coming to fix the door in a few minutes.'

'Leave it for now,' Lottie said. 'Our people will have a look at it. And don't worry, there'll be a uniformed officer here to keep an eye on you until Paddy returns. Can I have his number?'

'No, you can't. I wouldn't have said anything at all, only those two out there were hanging around here for the last few weeks and I knew they were pigs. *She* even gave me one of those card things with her number. I was going to say nothing to nobody, but sure I was so stressed, I rang her and told her everything before I realised what I was doing.'

'You really need stitches,' Lottie said, noticing fresh blood bubbling through Bridie's hair.

'I'll be grand. I've got plasters somewhere.'

'Can I call someone to come and sit with you?'

'I'm well able to look after myself, thank you very much.'

The irony was lost on Bridie, and Lottie felt a wave of sympathy for the young woman settle in her chest. She took out one of her own cards.

'This is my number. Call me if you remember anything else. Even the smallest detail might be important.'

Bridie took the card. 'I'm warning you lot here and now, my Paddy won't let this pass without blood being spilled. Mark my words.'

After directing the SOCOs into Bridie's house, Lottie instructed Kirby to send the two vans of gardaí who had arrived while they'd been inside back to the station.

'Did you call the riot squad too?' she said drily.

'No, but something like this has the potential to explode.'

'Let's hope not. No need to attract extra attention to Bridie. Locate Paddy McWard and find out where he's been and what he's been up to. Okay?'

'Will do.'

She noticed the houses and caravans all had cameras attached to their outside walls. 'And see if the residents will give you access to their CCTV tapes. There are more cameras here than in all of Ragmullin.'

'Probably just dummies,' Kirby offered.

'Check them out. And it's very quiet around here. Have you scared everyone away?'

'Not my fault.' Kirby slapped a chunky cigar into his mouth without lighting it.

Lowering her voice, Lottie said, 'What's up with Lynch?'

Kirby glanced over her shoulder. Lottie turned, following his gaze. Lynch was walking in small, slow circles with her phone tight to her ear.

'Trouble at home, I think. She hasn't said anything to me, but she's calling her husband every time I turn my back.'

Lottie waited for Boyd to unlock the car. She listened as a train shunted along the tracks on the embankment beyond the cemetery.

'I'm thinking this was probably the work of Elizabeth's killer. Trying to warn Bridie against talking to us,' she said, sitting into the car.

'But she'd already spoken with you,' Boyd said.

'Maybe she saw or heard something else. Something she hasn't told us.'

'I think it's more likely to be related to her own community.'

'We'll see. What do you know about Lynch's husband?'

'Not a lot, why?' he said, turning out onto the main road.

'Just fishing.' Lottie tugged the sleeves of her T-shirt down over her cold hands.

'New hobby?'

'Drive the bloody car.'

'Where to?'

'Wherever we can find Carol O'Grady.'

CHAPTER THIRTY-FIVE

Nothing was going right for Donal O'Donnell. Not today. Not any day. He had waited fifteen minutes before moving, after Keelan had almost broken his doorbell with her insistent finger.

Shuffling across his kitchen floor, he wished for a day when he could walk around without feeling the emptiness inside of him. He glanced at the radio and considered switching it on. He opened the refrigerator instead. He'd need to go out soon. The milk was two days past its best-before date, and there wasn't anything other than cereal to eat. Perhaps he should have asked Keelan to shop for a few groceries. But then he'd be admitting defeat. And Donal O'Donnell would never give in.

He found the box of matches and lit the candle in front of the photograph. Lynn's smiling face caused him to pause. Reaching out a finger, he traced the flow of her dark hair and the stud in her ear. He wondered at the light in her eyes. How could someone so young, so full of life, so beautiful just evaporate into thin air?

'My pet,' he said.

A cold finger of terror slid down his spine, knocking on each vertebra on its journey. Donal whipped around. No one. No one but himself. Only his shadow inhabited this house now.

He turned back to the photo.

'You broke your mother's heart. You broke this family.' He had no idea if he was talking to Lynn or to himself. He'd never felt more confined by the weight of his own skin. Never more fearful for his remaining family. Because he knew the evil had returned. Tearing at his hair, he screamed at the walls, 'Leave me be. Leave me be.'

A quiet stillness settled on the kitchen. To dispel it, he turned on the radio and listened to the news. There was never any mention of his Lynn. Not like when she first went missing. When evil had gripped his heart in its claws.

It was true, he thought, as he poured sour milk onto his corn-flakes, the nefarious spirits had returned. And this time he felt powerless to fight them.

CHAPTER THIRTY-SIX

The Jealous Wall, situated on two hundred acres at Rochfort Gardens, loomed up from the dip in the valley. It was fragmented and falling down. Open spaces marked where windows had never rested, and arches jutted out haphazardly. It had been constructed to resemble the wall of a ruined medieval abbey. With jealousy at its heart.

Lottie walked with Boyd down the sharp incline to the visitor centre and entered through the sliding glass doors. At the reception desk, she hit the bell.

A young woman opened the door behind the desk and stood gawking. 'Oh, it's you.'

'It is me,' Lottie said, and smiled sweetly at Carol O'Grady.

Carol scowled, her face pale and drawn, as she sat down behind the desk. 'What can I do for you?'

'I'd like to have another word with you about your friend Elizabeth. Can you join us for a cup of tea or coffee?'

'Give me a couple of minutes. The café is over there, to your right.'

The scent of freshly brewed coffee permeated the air as the two detectives made their way inside.

'Smells good,' Lottie said. 'I'll have a toasted ham and cheese croissant. And a large coffee.' She sat down on one of the sofas to wait for Carol.

'I'm paying so?' Boyd said, and turned to the counter.

'Looks like it.'

Lottie pulled off her hat and scarf and unbuttoned her jacket. Her hands were as white as a corpse and reminded her of Elizabeth's foot with its pink-painted toenails.

Boyd joined her and sat down. 'They'll bring it over.'

She looked up as a shadow fell across the small table.

Carol said, 'I really have nothing to tell you.'

'We just want to find out a little more about Elizabeth. There has to be something in her life to give us a clue as to why she was killed.'

'I don't want to get into any trouble. I need this job.' Carol's hand flew to her stomach. 'Now more than ever.'

'Sit down,' Lottie said. 'Have a cup of coffee.'

'I really can't leave the front desk.'

'You just have. Isn't there a bell if anyone calls in?'

With a nervous glance out to the foyer, Carol appeared to settle the conflict in her mind and sat down opposite Lottie as Boyd went off to order another coffee.

'Black, no sugar,' Carol called. 'I can't bear anything sweet at the moment.'

'What's it like working here?' Lottie asked.

'It's okay, I suppose. A bit far from town.'

'What did Elizabeth do in her spare time?'

'She hadn't that much spare time with all the commuting.'

'She had time to go out for drinks and clubbing, though. And you mentioned she did some running.'

'Yeah. Out here on Saturdays and Sundays. Lots of locals use the grounds for jogging. We ran together. Don't think I'll be doing too much now.'

'Exercise is good for you, especially while pregnant,' Lottie said, thinking she could do with some herself. 'Was there anyone else that Elizabeth ran with besides yourself?'

'No.'

'Anyone take an interest in her?'

'Not that I know of.'

'How many people would be here on a Saturday morning?'

'Upwards of fifty. I can check the register. Everyone who runs has to sign in. They don't have to pay, you see, but for insurance they have to sign in. I'll get the book.'

'Scare her off already?' Boyd put a tray on the table, then sat down and dished out the coffee.

Carol returned with a ledger. Lottie ran her finger down the mainly illegible signatures. 'Can you copy this for me?'

'Sure. Is this mine?' Carol took the black coffee and blew over the steaming liquid. After only one sip, she said, 'You'll have to excuse me. I need to use the bathroom,' and escaped with her hand clasped to her mouth.

Lottie said, 'When we have this copied, I want you to go through the lists. You're good at that kind of thing.' She handed the book to Boyd.

'This goes back weeks,' he said, flicking through the pages.

'All the better to make a comparison of names each week. We might find something.'

'Or not.' Boyd put the book down and shoved a large portion of croissant into his mouth.

'I thought that was mine.' Lottie rolled her eyes and drank her coffee. Another headache was taking root at the base of her skull. She couldn't shake the feeling that there was something she should be asking Carol.

CHAPTER THIRTY-SEVEN

Ragmullin train station had stood for over one hundred and fifty years, with the canal on one side and the town on the other. It was situated at the foot of an incline. At one time, it had two viable lines. One carried trains travelling to and from Galway, and the other to Sligo. But now the only remaining line was Dublin to Sligo and vice versa. Part of the old Galway track, along the route of the canal, had been rejuvenated as a cycleway.

'It's great,' Boyd explained to Lottie as they made their way towards the station entrance. 'Very safe. Great for kids. It's always busy, but the good thing is, there's no traffic.'

'Do you use it?'

'At least once a week, when I'm not working a murder investigation. This type of job saps my energy.'

'I'd imagine this type of job would whet your appetite to get out and feel the fresh air in your lungs.'

'There is that too,' he said as they climbed the steps and entered the stone vestibule.

'How are you doing?' Jimmy greeted Boyd. 'No train due in until three.'

'Ah no, I'm not looking for a train this time. Just information.'

'You've come to the right man, then.'

'I know some of our people were asking questions the other day about a young woman, Elizabeth Byrne. But we wanted to see if you've remembered anything since.'

'Oh, the poor unfortunate who went missing and was found dead in a grave. Awful stuff. Shocking. No one is safe in this town any more. No one.'

'We're trying to keep people safe by finding whoever did this,' Lottie said.

Jimmy looked up at her expectantly. She realised he hadn't a clue who she was. She held out her hand in greeting, 'Detective Inspector Lottie Parker.'

'Jimmy Maguire, head guard. Not a guard like you, but I've worked here for the last forty-odd years. Should be retired by now, but I think they've forgotten about me. I'm part of the walls now.' He tried a laugh but it dissolved into a groan.

'Do you have a good knowledge of everyone coming and going through here?'

He pushed his peaked cap back off his forehead and looked up at her.

'One time you could say that. Not now, with all the young ones commuting up and down to Dublin.'

She showed him photographs of Elizabeth. 'This is the girl we're interested in. And we got this one from your ticket office CCTV footage, Monday morning, buying her ticket. Do you recognise her? She took the six a.m. train daily. We believe she arrived back here on the 17.10 from Dublin on Monday evening. Is there any way to verify that?'

Shaking his head, squinting one eye shut, Jimmy said, 'Can't say I recognise her at all, poor soul. They all look the same to me at that age.'

'Any other cameras in place?' Lottie prompted.

'Just in the ticket office and a few in the car park.'

'We have that footage, but there was no sign of her.' Lottie looked around the cold portico where they were standing. 'None on the platform?'

'There was talk at one time of installing more cameras, but then the conversation switched to shutting the place down altogether. It'd be an awful shame if they did that. A committee was set up to try and see if we can keep it open.' He pushed out his chest and straightened his shoulders. 'I'm the chairman.'

Lottie looked at Boyd; from his expression, he seemed to be thinking the same thing. With Jimmy as chairman, the nail might already be in the station's coffin.

'No need to be looking at me like that. I'm passionate about this place. Been standing here since 1848.' Jimmy laughed. 'The station, not me, though some days it feels like it. It's a voluntary group that I set up. Numbers have dwindled away. Only about ten of us active now. More's the pity. There's safety in numbers. Better to have a crowd at your back when you're fighting a battle.'

'You're dead right there,' Lottie said, thinking of the battles she would more than likely have with McMahon while Corrigan was off.

'There are cameras on some of the trains, if you're interested.'

Lottie stepped forward. 'Definitely. Can we access the footage from last Monday?'

'Which train would that be?'

'The six a.m. from Ragmullin to Connolly and all of the evening trains that travelled back here, especially the 17.10.'

'I can tell you here and now, there are no cameras on the morning one. We use an older train for that run. Not much trouble at that hour. You'll have to ring head office for the others.'

'If you give me the details, I'll do that,' Lottie said. 'Can we have a look around while we're here?'

'Be my guest.' Jimmy tipped his cap, opened the gate, and guided them onto the platform. 'I'm around if you need to ask me anything else. God have mercy on her soul, poor lass.'

A sharp breeze cut its way along the platform as Lottie and Boyd walked from one end to the other. There was an old signal box at the far end, and on their right lay the defunct Galway line.

'What are those over there?' She pointed to a series of dilapidated buildings.

'We would have to ask Jimmy that,' Boyd said.

'They were once waiting rooms.'

Lottie jumped as the station guard walked up behind her. 'You frightened me half to death,' she said. Recovering quickly, she added, 'What are they used for now?'

'Nothing. Falling down, overrun with vermin. No one goes near them any more.' He turned around. 'If they close this station, everything will end up in the same state. Our heritage consigned to oblivion by the swish of a pen in some fancy Dublin office.'

'I don't think it will close,' Boyd said.

Jimmy gave him a look as if to say: what would you know about it?

'Well, if this young woman was taken from the train, what do you think that will do to my commuters?'

'We have no evidence she was taken from the train,' Lottie said. 'Or do you know something you're not telling us?'

'I take offence at that remark, so if you won't be minding, I'd like you to move on, because this area is out of bounds. Health and safety. You know the score.'

She took the hint, but not before giving Jimmy a good stare, which he duly returned.

'Were you working here when Lynn O'Donnell disappeared?' she asked.

'What if I was?'

'No need to get defensive. I'm reviewing her case.' Lottie noticed Boyd's eyes questioning her. Feck him. 'Do you remember it?'

'It was a long time ago.'

'Ten years.'

'That's a long time.'

'For someone who's been here for forty?' Lottie said. 'Not that long at all.'

'You need to check your files, because I can't recall it.' He turned to face the disused tracks.

'I will. And I'll be back.'

As she walked back along the platform, Lottie said, 'He knows something.'

'I suspect that as well,' Boyd said.

'We better keep him on our radar.'

'I think he's keeping us on his,' Boyd said, nodding his head to the side.

Maguire was watching them from the old waiting room door. As they left, she could feel his eyes still on her, and she was sorry they'd decided to walk rather than driving. Even as she reached the bridge at the top of the hill, Lottie felt she was being watched.

*

The woman pulled her car into the line of traffic, keeping an eye on the two detectives walking up the hill. She toyed with the notion of returning to the train station to see what they'd found out, but she believed her time would be better utilised by keeping tabs on Lottie Parker.

Because she knew that wherever the detective inspector trod, she always left a murky footprint in her wake. She would make a mistake, that was certain.

And Cynthia Rhodes would be there to swoop in for the kill.

CHAPTER THIRTY-EIGHT

Lottie squared her shoulders against the cold and walked with Boyd up Main Street. She stopped at a pole and tore off the piece of paper. 'Someone's been putting up flyers looking for information on Lynn O'Donnell.'

'They appear every year,' Boyd said. 'Your current workload already includes a murder, so don't go off on a tangent.'

'There's another one,' she said. 'I'm definitely going to read the cold case file.'

'Lottie!'

'Not on work time; my own time.'

'You don't have any "own" time, I know what you're like. Just drop it.'

'Boyd, would you ever piss off?'

She wouldn't drop it. Not without having a peek at the file first. Superintendent Corrigan would want her to. Just in case there was the possibility of a link to the murder of Elizabeth Byrne.

She walked on ahead of Boyd, wondering why she was so touchy. Perhaps she hadn't taken two pills after all. She was losing track.

The incident room was buzzing. The phones were hopping.

'What's going on?' Lottie said.

Kirby had a phone cradled between his chin and shoulder. 'McMahon made a statement to the media asking for the public's help in tracing the last movements of Elizabeth Byrne.'

'I thought this was my investigation,' Lottie said, hands on hips.

'Something might come of it,' Boyd said.

'He probably ballsed it up and every crank in the town will be phoning in.' She sat on a chair facing the incident board. 'Any luck with the cameras on the trains?'

Boyd said, 'Head office say they only keep the footage for two days, then it's recorded over. But they'll see what they can find.'

'Probably a dead end. Any good news, Kirby?'

He hung up the call and consulted a file. 'The service provider says Elizabeth's phone was last active in the Ragmullin area. They can't give a definite location yet. And it hasn't transmitted a signal since 6.30 Monday evening.'

'The killer has probably dismantled and destroyed it.' Lottie continued to stare at the meagre information on the board. 'Any news on Bridie McWard?'

'Nope.'

'Did she go to hospital for treatment?'

'Refused.'

Lottie turned to Lynch, who was keeping her head down. 'Anything on Matt Mullin?'

Lynch exchanged a glance with Kirby and shrugged her shoulders. 'I'm working on it.'

'What the hell is wrong with you all? I want answers, not dawdling over nonsense phone calls. Get focused on proper work.' She paused to take a breath. 'Shit, I need a coffee.'

She made for the kitchen with Boyd following. Pouring water from the kettle into two mugs, she took one and sipped. Boyd took the other.

'You must have put two spoons of coffee in it,' he said.

'That's mine. Take this one. I need to be alert.'

McMahon walked by, did a double take and came back.

'This area is out of bounds. Use the canteen.'

Lottie lifted her mug to her lips and sipped slowly. 'Says who?'

'Says me. This place is breaking every health and safety regulation.'

'We've used it for the last three years.'

'You have a brand spanking new canteen and that's where you take your breaks. Anyway, I don't agree with this constant stream of tea-making.'

'It's coffee.'

'Are you being smart with me?'

Lottie shook her head, sniffed her mug. 'A bit strong, but it's definitely coffee.'

McMahon puffed out his chest. 'This kitchen will be dismantled before the day is out.'

He took himself off down the corridor. Lottie shook her head and opened her mouth to speak.

'Don't say a word,' Boyd warned.

'Two words then. Complete bollocks.'

She stormed back to her office, slopping coffee everywhere.

The phone rang. McGlynn.

'I've something you'll want to see,' he said. 'In the yard.'

'On my way.' She pulled on her jacket and headed outside.

The yard had been cleared of all vehicles and a tent erected over the skip from the cemetery. A second area for the examination of the rubbish was also covered. Three SOCOs were working their way through the sacks, one by one, as they removed them from the skip.

'It was six of one and half a dozen of the other,' McGlynn explained. 'At least doing it here, we're away from the media circus and the public gawkers.'

'What did you find? Besides rubbish?'

'As you can see, it's mainly domestic waste. People too mean, or too poor, to pay their bin charges must have used the skip as a personal dump. But I have one sack over here that you will certainly be interested in.'

Lottie followed him to the corner of the tent. The smell was worse than anything she had smelled at the Dead House. Rotting detritus. Scraps of waste food, wrappers and everything you were liable to find in a kitchen bin.

'Jesus,' she said. 'This is a horrible job.'

'Give me a decomposing body any day,' McGlynn said. 'Here we are.'

On a fold-out table covered with Teflon, Lottie saw what had made McGlynn so animated.

A black leather jacket. Grey hoodie. Blue checked shirt. Blue jeans. A pair of ankle-length black leather boots. White fluffy socks, pink bra and white knickers.

She went to touch the jacket.

'Wait.' McGlynn handed her a pair of nitrile gloves.

Lottie stared at the clothing. 'These are hers. They have to be. No one would throw out a good leather jacket.'

'Not unless it had come from someone they'd killed or were about to kill.'

'Check for DNA, trace evidence—'

'I know my job, Detective Inspector.'

'No handbag?'

'Not so far.'

'Can I photograph these? I need to show them to her mother for identification purposes.'

'They were all wet.'

'Wet?'

'As if they'd been dunked in a bath of water. I'll test them.'

'Thanks. From the CCTV images, I'm sure Elizabeth was wearing a jacket and jeans similar to these. Good work.'

'Just doing my job. I'll bag these and get them analysed.'

'Let me know as—'

'Yeah, yeah. I'll let you know as soon as I do.'

'He surely left DNA somewhere on the clothes.' Lottie put her feet up on top of her waste-paper basket as she shouted from her office out to the general area.

'This has the markings of an abduction that was well thought out,' Boyd said.

'Do you think he intentionally let her run through the cemetery?'

'Anything is possible.'

'Wish we had some idea of what we're dealing with. Hell, we aren't even sure where she was taken from. There are those unaccounted hours from six in the evening to three in the morning.' Lottie dropped her feet. 'Lynch! I need to know where Matt Mullin is.'

'I've asked for a check on his passport,' Lynch shouted back.

'What did the bank say?'

'They let him go before Christmas.'

'What?' Lottie jumped up and rushed out of her office. 'He has to be at home.'

'There was no answer yesterday.'

'Check again.'

'But I need to—'

'Now. Kirby will go with you.' Lottie turned to Boyd, eyeing his meticulously tidy desk. 'Did you find anything of interest on the list of runners from Rochfort Gardens?'

'Nothing to report. I copied the pages and scanned all the names into the computer, but nothing jumps out at me.'

'Did she run every weekend?'

'These records go back to the week after Christmas. The only day she missed was last Sunday.'

'Dying with a hangover, according to her mother.' Leaning over his shoulder, she squinted at the list on the screen. 'Is it the same crowd every weekend?'

'More or less. I'll collate them into some sort of order.'

'When you've finished that, we'll have to interview each and every person on the list.'

'What about the nursing home interviews?'

'I asked either Lynch or Kirby to do it.' She glanced at the empty desks. 'Shit, I've just sent them looking for Mullin.'

'I checked the uniforms' report from the nursing home. No one heard or saw anything.'

'I'll go over there myself. I want to have a look around anyway.'

'Will I go with you?'

'You keep at that list of runners. I'll grab a sandwich and head over. Then I'll check in with Elizabeth's mother about the clothes.'

'Are you coming back here afterwards?'

'What are you now? My mother?'

'Sorry, just asking.'

Lottie sighed. She'd no idea why Boyd was getting on her nerves today, but he was. 'I'll be going home. Katie is heading off tomorrow and I've to help her pack. I don't want to even think about it.'

'She'll be grand.'

'So you say.' She glanced at the time. 'And don't forget to pick up Grace from the station.'

'As if I'd forget that,' he said.

CHAPTER THIRTY-NINE

The sandwich was well and truly stuck in her gullet. Shouldn't eat onions, Lottie told herself. God, she'd love a drink. Alcohol. Just to give her a moment of relaxation. One. Only one.

Tonight. Later. Maybe.

'I'm not sure how we can help you.' Peadar Kane, the nursing home manager, led her into his office. He was tall and thin, with a line of hair covering a bald head.

'This is a lovely building. You must enjoy working here.' Lottie didn't do small talk, but as the residents and staff had already been interviewed, she honestly didn't know what she was after.

'Much nicer than the old home, anyway.'

'Is that building still used?'

'No. Health and safety.'

'Health and safety, the bane of my life,' Lottie said, thinking of McMahon and her makeshift canteen.

'Can't be too careful where older people are concerned. They're not as able-bodied as us.'

'I agree.' She wondered how her mother was doing today. Better, she hoped. 'Do you have a Mrs McWard here?'

'Queenie? Yes. Second floor. Do you want to see her?'

'Yes. And I'd like to have a look around.'

'Be my guest. I have a meeting in a few minutes, so I'll give you a visitor's pass then you'll have access to all areas.'

'That'd be brilliant.'

Once she had the pass, and Queenie's room number, he walked her out of the office. A man approached them. His skin was grey, and his eyes were so dark they could only be filled with sadness.

'Ah, Donal. I'm glad you made it in,' Kane said. 'I've been worried about you. Take a seat in my office and I'll be with you in a second.'

The man bowed his head and shuffled into the warm office.

'Poor Donal. He's been a porter at the home since God was a boy. His wife died a few weeks ago and I need to have a word with him to see when he's coming back to work.'

'Don't let me delay you.'

'If there's anything else I can do for you, let me know.'

Kane followed his employee into the office and Lottie headed off on her tour of the facility. She wondered idly if Rose would like it here. But as quickly as the thought entered her head, she dismissed it. Rose Fitzpatrick would die rather than move into a nursing home.

*

Gilly O'Donoghue handed over the reins to Dan, who was late arriving for his reception desk duty. She picked up her bag and headed for the door, glad that her shift was ended. She'd have to rush home to eat, shower and slap on make-up before the play. Just as she had her coat on, Boyd came rushing down the corridor.

'Hey, Gilly, before you leave, can I have a word?'

'In a bit of a rush this evening. What's it about?'

'I'm not entirely sure. Just a hunch that you might have seen something.' He showed her the copied pages from the Rochfort Gardens sign-in book. 'I notice you go running here.'

'I do. When I'm not on duty. Why?'

'I found your name on a list. Did you know Elizabeth Byrne?'

'The girl who was murdered? No. Why?'

'She ran at Rochfort Gardens every weekend. Just thought you might have seen her, or someone acting suspiciously around her.'

'I saw her photograph on the incident board, but I didn't recognise her. Do you want me to do some undercover work for you?'

'We're trying to contact everyone on the list, and then I think Lottie wants us to interview the remaining people on Saturday morning before their run, so your help would be appreciated with that.'

'Not undercover then?' She would have liked a little detective work. It might help with her aim to become a sergeant.

Boyd shook his head. 'Though if you can remember anything that struck you as being out of the ordinary, let me know.'

'Long shot, isn't it?'

'I'd take any shot that hit the target at this stage.'

As Boyd walked away, Gilly thought of Mollie, who also went running at weekends. She pressed the speed dial on her phone. Nothing. Not even a voice recording. Where was she? She thought of calling round on her way home. Glancing at the clock, she reckoned she was stuck for time as it was. She'd call after Kirby picked her up for their date.

*

She was staring at him again. Carriage C, last seat. He'd watched her get on with her nosy head glancing all around her. Who was she looking for? Surely not the prize he had won yesterday?

He debated sitting beside her. Making conversation. Just to see what he could find out from her. But then he decided life was too short to put himself through such misery. Instead, he focused his mind on visiting his prize later. He ran through the checklist in his brain. The laptop and phone had been disposed of. As had her clothes and bag. Scattered all over Dublin. No way of tracing anything back to her. Or, more importantly, to him.

Allowing a smile of contentment to widen on his face, he immediately dropped it. The little bitch with her piercing eyes was screwing nine-inch nails through him. You better not make a nuisance of yourself, he thought, or I know just the place for you, where no one will ever find you again.

She was annoying him so much, even the rhythm of the train picking up speed couldn't dispel the disturbing feeling of unease hunching his shoulders into each other, bone on bone. He'd have to waste the journey thinking of ways to get rid of her, rather than ways to play with his new toy. You will be sorry, bitch, he vowed silently.

*

Even though the building was new, the distinct scent of age lingered. Lottie could smell it but couldn't identify it. The rooms were bright and airy and most of the residents seemed contented with their lot.

She took the lift to the top floor and stood at the giant window. The evening was darkening, but she could still see directly into the cemetery from her vantage point.

She stared down to where Elizabeth's body had been discovered. The hole was gaping, uncovered, still awaiting the interment of Mrs Green. An image of Father Joe flashed through her mind and her finger slid to the screen of her phone. She'd love to have a chat with him. But that would be a mistake. They'd both suffered too much pain from their respective families in the past, and she was bad enough now without resurrecting that again.

'It's not a pretty sight,' a voice said from behind her.

She turned around on the ball of her foot. The man she'd seen a little earlier outside Kane's office moved up beside her.

'It's a dark evening,' Lottie ventured.

'All those poor souls buried out there.'

'I'm sorry about your wife. Were you married long?'

'Too long.' He put a heavy hand on Lottie's shoulder blade before heading back the way he had come.

Pain shot along her spine and up to her neck. His hand had landed on the exact spot where she'd suffered the knife wound. But it was the icy tone of his voice that had caused her the most discomfort. A chill trickled down her back as she watched him walk away.

She shook herself. Too long in this job, she thought. Even an old man she didn't know was giving her the shivers.

CHAPTER FORTY

Matt Mullin's family home was situated on the old Dublin road on the outskirts of Ragmullin. It was a large two-storey affair, with red brick showing signs of damp along the corners of the house and under the windowsills. A narrow avenue led to the front door. The land behind the house had been cleared of trees and was being excavated. Trucks and diggers appeared to be winding down their work for the day.

Lynch pressed the doorbell, half hoping Mrs Mullin wouldn't be in. She was freezing and wanted to get home.

'What's going on there?' Kirby asked.

'Building a new school.' She leaned on the doorbell again.

'Great spot to dump a body.'

'Will you shut up?'

'That girl who disappeared ten years ago,' Kirby said, taking a drag on his cigar before quenching it between thick fingers. 'She could be buried somewhere like that. It was a forest at one time.'

'And you think the builders will suddenly find her body?'

'It's possible.'

She noticed Kirby hiding the cigar butt in the inside pocket of his jacket as the door opened. A woman in her fifties, with an oblong face of fine bones, high forehead and piercing eyes, checked their ID cards.

'You said on the phone that this is about my son.' She twisted her blonde hair and let it fall over one shoulder. Lynch thought it was for effect rather than from anxiety.

'Yes, it is. Can we come in?'

Mrs Mullin turned and headed down a wide hallway. Lynch took in the expensive decor.

'Nice place.'

'We purchased it five years ago. Came on the market after the banking crisis.'

She led them into a living area with two floor-to-ceiling windows. The light in the room was dimmed by the shadow of a large tree outside. She switched on a lamp. 'Sit, please.'

Lynch and Kirby took up positions on armchairs opposite the woman.

'We've been trying to trace Matt but have had no luck so far,' Lynch began. 'Do you know where he might be or how we can get in touch with him?'

'Of course I do.'

'Is he here?' Closing her notebook, Lynch shoved her pen into the knot of her ponytail. 'We thought he was working in Germany, but his bank informed us that he was let go before Christmas. He hasn't returned our calls. I'd like to speak with him.'

'I'm afraid that is out of the question.'

'But it's imperative to our investigation that we confirm a few details with him.'

'What investigation might that be?'

Lynch noted the warning look in Kirby's eyes. This had to be handled tactfully.

'That's something I need to discuss with Matt,' she said. 'Can you confirm whether he's at home at the moment?'

'He's unwell. If you can't discuss it with me, I'm afraid I have nothing further to say.' Mrs Mullin stood up, buttoning her cardigan. Her jeans had a designer look about them.

Lynch remained seated, looking up at the tall woman. 'If he is here, I'm sure he won't mind giving us two minutes. Just to rule him out of our investigation.'

'Since you won't even tell me what the investigation relates to, I can't help.' The narrow face clamped shut.

'It relates to a murder,' Lynch blurted.

Mrs Mullin sat down again. 'Whose murder might that be, and why do you think my son needs to be ruled out of it?'

Lynch sighed. This was seriously hard work. 'The murder of Elizabeth Byrne.'

'I heard about that. Poor girl. But it has absolutely nothing to do with Matt. They split up a year ago. She broke his heart.'

Raising an eyebrow at Kirby, Lynch said, 'We were informed that it was Matt who broke it off with Elizabeth.'

'You were misinformed.'

'So it was Elizabeth who ended the relationship?'

'Correct. On Valentine's Day. How could she have been so cruel?'

'And that's when he went off to Munich?' Lynch had her notebook out again.

'She drove my boy away from me. I'll never forgive her for that.'

'Mrs Mullin, where is Matt?' Lynch had had enough.

'If you wish to speak with him, you may get a court order, a subpoena or whatever you call it.'

'Can't he make the decision himself?'

'I'll show you out.' Mrs Mullin got up and walked to the door.

Kirby cocked his head sideways at Lynch. 'What will we do?' he mouthed.

'Can I use your bathroom before we leave?' Lynch moved to the door. 'I'm really dying to go.'

'That old ploy doesn't wash with me. I'd prefer it if you just fucked off.'

The profanity emanating from such a prim-and-proper mouth caught Lynch off guard. 'What?'

'I'd like you both to leave my home.'

'Tell Matt to call into the station,' Lynch said. 'We need to have that word with him.'

The door closed on her words.

Sitting into the car, Lynch kept her eyes firmly focused on the upstairs windows. Kirby started the engine and drove down the avenue.

'You were a bit cranky back there,' he said.

'I'm pregnant.'

'Piss off! You can't be.'

'I am.'

'Jesus, Lynch. Pregnant?' Kirby checked his pocket for his cigar. 'Well, it's no excuse and you know it. The boss will fry you if Mrs Mullin makes a complaint.'

'Complaint about what? She was the one making the fuss and not answering one bloody question. She isn't going to make a complaint. She doesn't want the attention.'

'Why do you say that?'

'Because we need to speak with her son.'

'He could be anywhere.'

'He was there, I'm sure of it. Now why do you suppose he wouldn't come down and tell us where he was on Monday night?'

'You're imagining things, Lynch.' Kirby slammed his half-smoked cigar between his lips. 'I don't think there was anyone else in that house.'

They drove through the town in silence. As he turned up Main Street, Kirby muttered, 'Pregnant? Jesus, Lynch how did that happen?'

'How do you think?' She got out of the car and left him shaking his head.

✱

Bridie's eye was swollen and almost closed up, but baby Tommy was fast asleep in his cot at last. She stood at the window of their tiny house and looked out at the concrete wall.

That poor murdered girl; it had to have been her screams she'd heard the other night. Maybe she should have called the guards at the time. But what could they have done? The poor thing was dead by then. So why was there someone out there who didn't want Bridie saying anything? The body had already been found at that stage. Was her attacker the man who had killed the Byrne girl, or had he come to shut her up about something else entirely?

Paddy.

It must be to do with Paddy. And why wouldn't he answer his phone?

She picked up her iPhone in its glitter case and called again. Still no answer. She left another message for him to contact her immediately.

That was all she could do for now.

CHAPTER FORTY-ONE

After asking a nurse whether she could speak to Queenie McWard, Lottie found herself sitting by the old woman's bed.

She looked frail, with a pair of thin-framed spectacles perched on her nose, a long gold chain holding them in place. Grey hair, nicely permed, framed her face like a painting. Her wraith-like hands, clutched at her chest, held rosary beads intertwined on her fingers. And her lips were moving rapidly and silently.

'Mrs McWard?' Lottie said. There was no response, though the lips increased their movement. 'Can I have a chat?'

The old woman's eyes flew open and the spectacles fell from her face to her chest, the rosary beads slipping from her fingers.

'Now I've lost my place. I can't remember if that was my fifth Hail Mary or my sixth.' A pair of dark brown eyes cut into Lottie. 'What do you want?'

Queenie's mouth was devoid of teeth and Lottie noticed a set of dentures resting in a glass on the bedside cabinet.

'I'm sorry to disturb you, but I was passing by and thought I'd say hello.' She crossed her fingers.

'That's a lie. Tell me why you're here, young one, and let me get back to my prayers.'

'I was talking to your daughter.'

'Which one?'

'Bridie.'

'What has that husband of hers done now? Hope he didn't beat her. Wouldn't surprise me, though, seeing as his father is a third cousin of my husband, God rest his thieving soul.'

'Ah, I wondered at you and Bridie having the same surname.'

'Wonder no longer, young one.'

'Bridie thought she heard a banshee the other night. Turns out it was the screams of a girl we later found murdered.'

'Then it was the banshee for sure. Heralding the death of the one you speak of. You lot don't believe in the banshee, but my people do. Why are you pestering me?'

'You heard a banshee once before.'

'Says who?'

'Bridie mentioned it.'

'I heard many a banshee in my day. Every time I hear her, someone in the family dies. It's a warning. To be on your guard. She can shriek and keen for nights on end. Never saw one, but my great-grandmother did. Now that wasn't today or yesterday, was it?'

'I don't suppose it was,' Lottie said. She was wasting her time here, like she'd been told once too often. She had to get home and help Katie pack. So much to do.

Queenie was still talking.

'Then there was the time that young woman went missing. Last seen getting off the train. Long time ago. Must be ten years if it's a day. I heard the banshee for seven nights in a row back then. And they never found her.' She paused, placed her spectacles back on her nose and stared at Lottie. 'Don't be looking at me as if you don't believe me. Like I said, they never found her. She was just … gone. Vanished. Disappeared. Mark my words, she's as dead as those buried out there in that graveyard.'

'The anniversary of her disappearance is this weekend.'

'Is it?'

Lottie recalled the flyer she'd found in town. She had it rolled up in her pocket. Taking it out, she flattened it and showed it to the old woman.

'Aye, that's her that went missing all them years ago. Never found. But the banshee found her.'

I'd better read the cold case file, Lottie thought.

CHAPTER FORTY-TWO

Boyd sat with the engine idling, watching the commuters exit the station. Why had no one noticed Elizabeth Byrne on Monday evening? Where had she been from the time she got off the train until her screams were heard at 3.15 the next morning? She didn't go home. She didn't go to her friend Carol's house. So where? The only obvious conclusion he could reach was that she was taken after she got off the train on her walk home, and held by her abductor until he killed her.

He waved to Grace. She hurried to the car. When she had her seat belt secured and her bag on her lap, she turned to him.

'Mark, I want you to find my friend. She's missing.'

'She's not your friend and she's not missing.'

'You're not much of a detective, are you?'

'What do you mean?'

'You won't take me seriously.'

'Grace, you don't even know the girl's name. You know nothing about her. And we have no reports of anyone missing. Let's go. We need to eat. You must be starving.'

'I was. Now I'm not.'

'I'm going to cook something nice. You might change your mind.'

'Mollie,' Grace said.

'What?'

'Her name is Mollie.'

*

Mollie still had no idea where she was or what day it was, and now she almost felt like she didn't know *who* she was.

The darkness was propelling her swiftly into madness. No shadows. No sounds apart from her own breathing. Even the strip of light seemed to have vanished. Her brain conjured up her worst fears. Fear of the unknown. Fear of what might be around her. Fear of what was going to happen to her. She tried to dredge up stuff she'd learned on a mindfulness course she'd attended at work. Live in the moment. That was what it professed. A load of bullshit. She certainly did not want to live in this moment. No way. Not a second longer.

With a drought in her eyes, she had no tears to shed. A sweeping gush of anger washed over her. Why had he taken her? What was it about her that had made her a target? Was this her own fault?

Her father had that knack. Making her feel guilty about everything and anything. Spilled milk, mucky boots, her mother's bad moods. Yes, they were all Mollie's fault. One of the reasons she'd refused to move to London was to escape the condemnation that followed every single thing she did. And when her mother died, yes, that was her fault too. If you'd been here, Mollie, she'd still be alive. How did you expect me to care for her on my own? It's all your fault.

Guilty as charged.

But no. She was not going to fall for those mind games. She had to get out of here. And the only way she was going to do that was if she was strong and kept her mind alert. She would have to play the bastard at his own game. Shifting uncomfortably on the bed, she wondered what that game might be.

She had to figure it out before it was too late. Because she knew that there was no one to miss her out there. No one at all.

CHAPTER FORTY-THREE

'This house is like an ice box,' Lottie said, as she banged the front door behind her. 'Sean? Chloe? Katie?'

She dropped the Lynn O'Donnell file on the table and went to check the boiler in the utility room. The switch was on, but there was no heat. Had it run out of oil? Opening the back door, she glanced out at the darkness. She turned on the exterior light.

Sean slouched into the kitchen. 'What's all the shouting about?'

'Will you put on a pair of shoes and check the oil tank?'

She watched as he climbed up on the concrete wall surrounding the tank and plunged in the measuring rod. He brought it back and she examined it.

'Quarter full,' she said. 'So why is the boiler not working?'

'Turn it off and back on again,' Sean said. 'That's what I do with my computer.'

She tried it. The boiler blasted into life.

Sean smiled. 'Works every time.'

Emptying the washing machine, she piled the laundry into the dryer. Back in the kitchen, she searched the refrigerator for something to cook.

'Mam?' Katie's voice echoed down the stairs. 'Can you give me a hand with this case?'

'In a minute. Just figuring out dinner.' Taking a tray of mince from the fridge, she found a packet of pasta and began to cook.

'I'll have to eat later,' Sean said. 'Boyd is taking me training.'

'Shit, I forgot about that. I'll be up in a minute, Katie.'

Glancing at the file on the table, Lottie knew it had been a mistake to bring it home. She'd try to grab an hour to go through it at some stage.

The doorbell chimed and Sean belted down the stairs to reach it first. Boyd stepped into the hall. 'Well, bud, are you ready?'

'Give me two minutes. Mam's in the kitchen.'

Lottie turned from the stove. 'I'm glad you're taking him.'

'It's no problem. I see you brought work home with you.' She paused, wooden spoon in hand, as he flicked open the file cover. 'I thought you had enough work without this.'

'I want to have a read of it.' Why was she explaining herself to him? 'I went to the nursing home and met Queenie McWard. Don't laugh, but she claims she heard a banshee the night this Lynn O'Donnell went missing. Won't do any harm to have a look at the file.' She knew she was babbling. Shut up, Parker.

'I know you, Lottie, and I don't think you should get stuck into something that will suck the life out of you.'

'I won't.'

He grunted.

'I've to drive Katie to the airport in the morning. I'll be in the office by nine.' She turned to the cooker and stirred the mince vigorously, defences raised. 'Make excuses for me if McMahon asks.'

Her phone vibrated on the table. Boyd picked it up. Snatching it from him, she saw the caller ID and switched it off.

'I saw that,' he said. 'What's he ringing you for?'

'How would I know? I didn't answer it.'

'Why not?'

'Boyd, would you ever—'

'Ready when you are.' Sean arrived with his gear bag on his back and a hurley stick in his hand.

'See you later,' Lottie said, as the door closed.

'Mam!' Katie shouted. 'Chloe is melting my head.'

'Coming.' Lottie gave a final stir, lowered the heat and made her way up the stairs.

Why had Father Joe been ringing her? Should she ring back? No, he would call again if it was something urgent. Probably only wondering when he could inter Mrs Green. She had quite enough problems without Father Joe.

*

Canal Drive was dark and gloomy as Kirby joined Gilly at the top of the steps to Mollie's apartment. She pressed hard on the bell. No answer. She got out her keys.

'We're going to miss the start of the play,' Kirby said.

'It'll just take a minute.' She turned the key and entered the flat. 'Mollie? It's only me.'

'Come on, this is invasion of privacy.' Kirby edged back down the steps.

'She gave me a key!'

'We have five minutes to get to the Arts Centre or they won't let us in once the play has started.'

'Will you shut up about the stupid play?'

'You're the one that wanted to see it.'

'Come here. Look at this,' Gilly said.

He followed her into the tiny kitchen. 'Doesn't like washing up after herself.'

'Everything's exactly as it was last night. She hasn't been here since yesterday morning.'

'She works in Dublin, you say?'

'Yes. And I'm going to ring her office tomorrow morning to find out what the hell is up.'

'Do that. Now, can we leave?'

Before she followed him out, Gilly tried Mollie's phone once more. It was dead.

'This is not like Mollie at all.'

She was talking to fresh air.

*

Lottie left Katie arguing with Chloe over the ownership of a pair of jeans. Turning the key in the door of Rose's house she said, 'Mother, I brought you dinner.'

'You're stretching that description a little,' Rose said. She was sitting on a chair by the stove. 'Do you know what time it is?'

'I do, and I've been busy.'

'You're always busy.' Rose sniffed. 'Hope it's not that spicy stuff again.'

'Mince and pasta, sorry. I've been helping Katie to pack.'

'Why didn't you ask me to help?'

'You haven't been well.' Lottie put the plate on the table and removed the tea towel. The food looked pretty miserable. She knew criticism would follow. She began making tea.

'I'm not dead. Yet.' Rose shuffled over to the table. 'I could have given my granddaughter a hand if any of you had bothered to ask. And when is she getting that child baptised? He's still in a state of sin until that is done, and it's dangerous to be flying off with sin on your soul.'

The last three and a half months had turned Rose from a raging matriarch into a bitter tyrant. At times, it felt like four years since she had confessed to a lifetime of lies.

Lottie made a cup of tea, battling to keep her temper under control and her tongue silent. No matter what she said, it wouldn't be the right thing.

'Put in three sugars. I think my levels are low.'

'Too much sugar will keep you awake at night.'

'That's my problem, isn't it?'

'Yes, it is.' She put the mug on the table.

'You should have used a teapot. It stews better that way. In my day, we didn't have tea bags.'

'Are you going to eat that or offer it up?' Lottie stood with her back to the stove.

'Hard to do it with an audience, even if it was edible.' Rose put down her knife and fork and sipped the tea. 'You only put in one sugar.'

'That's enough for you.'

Rose turned in her chair, facing Lottie. 'Don't tell me what's enough for me in my own house. I live here, not you.' She pushed the plate into the centre of the table and folded her arms.

Lottie placed her hands on the table and leaned down towards her mother. She could have sworn she heard something physically snap in her brain.

'And I'm glad I *don't* live here, because you know what? My life was a misery when I did, and I hope I never have to live here ever again.'

She picked up her jacket and ran from the house. Definitely the wrong thing to say. But now that it was said, she couldn't take it back.

CHAPTER FORTY-FOUR

Finn O'Donnell could smell the whiskey on her breath from where she sat eyeing him over the rim of the glass. He was too close, but the room was so small he had nowhere else to go.

'Good day at work, was it?' she said.

'It was fine.' He shook out the newspaper and raised it to his face to keep her out of his line of vision. She was nattering on about someone or other. Doing his head in. He folded the paper and stood up.

'I'm going out.'

'Where?'

'I think I'll pop over to Dad's. See how he's doing.'

'You haven't visited him in ages. Not since the day of your mother's funeral, in fact.'

'All the more reason to go now, isn't it?'

'Do you know what time it is? I don't see why you can't—'

Did he heck know what time it was. Every fifteen minutes she reminded him. He didn't wait for the end of her stupid lecture. He was out the door, down the steps and walking.

*

Cillian looked up as his wife announced that dinner was ready.

'Saoirse, put your toys away,' he said, and closed the cover on his iPad.

'In a minute, Daddy.' The little girl dug into the page with her red crayon.

'I told you to put that stuff away,' he snapped. He didn't enjoy it when he was like this with his daughter. But he couldn't help himself this evening.

'Hey, that's enough. She's okay for a minute or two.' Keelan stood in the doorway. 'Why don't you help me set the table?'

'Oh, that's priceless, so it is.' He flung the iPad to the coffee table. It teetered on the edge, slipped to the ground with a crash. 'Now see what you made me do!'

He jumped up and snatched the tablet from the floor, ran his finger over the crack on the screen and slammed it back down. He reached the kitchen in two strides.

Keelan backed up against the counter. 'That … that was your own fault. Don't go blaming me.'

'Oh, so everything is my fault now.' He took a plate from the stack on the counter and threw it on the ground. 'I can tell you, *that* was my fault. And this.' He threw down another one. Waited for effect and flung another.

'Cillian. Stop. You're scaring Saoirse.'

The red mist that had descended lifted as he noticed his daughter poking her head around the doorway.

'Why did you do that, Daddy?'

She sounded just like Keelan. Accusing. Without a thought for what he was doing, he swept the remaining crockery off the counter, then marched through the splinters and grabbed his jacket. He'd leave before he created any real damage. Mortal damage. No, he wouldn't be the cause of that ever again.

*

Paddy couldn't console her. No matter what he did, she shivered and cried.

'Bridie, you need to get stitches. The wound is still bleeding.' He sat beside her on their white couch. 'Here, let me hold Tommy. You go on to bed. I'll feed him and put him down.'

She clutched the boy tighter to her chest, her tears dampening his hair. 'No. You can fuck off. You snuck out in the night and left us here all alone. Some arsehole comes in and beats the shite out of me, and what do you do? Nothing. That's all you're good for, Paddy McWard. Nothing. So fuck off.'

He stood up. What was a man to do? He couldn't bear to see her crying.

'Keep the door locked. I have my key,' he said, and left Bridie alone again in their tiny, immaculate house.

CHAPTER FORTY-FIVE

Cafferty's Bar was lively for a Thursday night. Beer taps with frosted lights teased the punters. Multiple television sets were showing the dying minutes of a football match.

Kirby ordered a pint and a glass of wine. Gilly sat in the nook furthest from the football activity.

'Bit loud, isn't it?' she said.

'Adds to the atmosphere,' he said.

'Depends on what atmosphere you're expecting.'

The barman arrived with the drinks and Kirby handed over a tenner. 'Keep the change.'

'Play was good. Thanks for bringing me,' Gilly said. 'I thought you might be working tonight.'

'New super called it all off. Tend to agree with him, too. We were getting nowhere. I prefer working on the murder investigation.'

'Boyd was asking me about that this evening. You know I go running at weekends out at Rochfort Gardens? Elizabeth Byrne did too. He asked if I knew her or saw anyone acting suspiciously.'

'And did you?'

'No. The only ones acting suspiciously are the old farts sucking in their bellies trying to look thirty years younger.' She blushed, hoping Kirby didn't think she meant him. 'That's where I first met Mollie.'

Kirby stalled his pint halfway to his mouth. 'The same Mollie you think has disappeared off the face of the earth?'

'One and the same.'

'That's interesting.'

'At last.'

'I'm only saying it's interesting. I'm not making a drama out of it.'

'But she always lets me know if she has to cancel a run or any-thing. It's a bit out of character, that's all.'

'Give her another ring.'

'I've tried countless times. Her phone's dead now.'

'Did you check if her passport is in her apartment?'

'No, but I think it's unlikely she went off on a holiday. Then again, her father lives in London.'

'There you are. Mystery solved.'

'I'll chase it up tomorrow.'

'Great. Now, let's chill and talk about the play.'

'Maybe we should tell Boyd.'

'Tomorrow.'

'What about now?'

'You're not going to relax, are you?'

'Nope.'

Kirby lifted his pint. 'Drink up so.'

*

Boyd returned to his apartment, tired from the hurling training and still wondering why Father Joe was ringing Lottie. He was heading for the shower when he remembered Grace. She was sitting on the couch watching television.

'How are you, little sis?' he shouted from the bedroom. Where had he put the clean towels?

The sound of the television disappeared. He looked up. Grace was standing at the door, staring at him. Accusingly?

'I really want you to listen to me, Mark. I'm worried about the girl I met on the train yesterday morning. You know me. I get a feeling that tells me when something isn't right. Like with you. I sense your loneliness.'

'So?' He pulled out a towel.

'You and I both know you're a lonely middle-aged man.'

'Hey, go easy on the middle-aged bit.'

'You know exactly what I mean.'

'I'm going to have a shower.'

'Will you listen to me? I definitely feel something has happened to Mollie.'

'Grace, she might have had a day off work. Maybe she decided to get a different train.'

'I told you, I know!' Grace stamped her foot. Then, as if realising what she had done, she retreated to the living area and sat down on the couch. 'No one ever listens to me. I'm telling you, if anything has happened to her, at least I warned you.'

'Righto, I'll remember that, but you're being irrational. I'm having my shower now. Is that okay with you? And don't blare the television too loud. I don't want the neighbours complaining.' He was finding it hard to treat his sister as a twenty-nine-year-old adult.

'What neighbours? Do you even know who lives next door? Mark Boyd, you need to get a life.'

With Grace's words ringing in his ears, he slammed the bathroom door, ripped off his sweaty clothes and turned the shower to cold. He needed to cool down in more ways than one. How was he going to last another three weeks with her here? At least she'd be going back to Mam for the weekend. He hoped so, anyway.

As the water chilled his skin, he switched the dial to hot and thought about his life. The years were getting away from him, and what did he have to show for them? Just an estranged wife whom he had yet to divorce. A sister who was getting on his wick. A mother who barely spoke to him. A woman he loved who wouldn't even go out to dinner with him.

Nothing.

Nothing worth talking about, anyway. Nothing to leave to a child. He didn't even have a child. No one to love. His sister, who hadn't been in the town a week, could read the emptiness hollowing out his very heart.

He slapped his hand against the tiles and lifted his face to the pulsing water. If he was a man prone to shedding tears, he would have cried. But it hadn't reached that stage yet. Not quite.

When he switched off the shower, he could hear Grace talking in the bedroom.

'Mark, there's a phone call for you.'

Maybe it was Lottie, he thought, wrapping a towel around his waist. He hoped he had a clean shirt.

By the time he got to the phone, Kirby had hung up. Whatever he wanted could wait until morning. Boyd pulled on a sweatshirt and jogging pants.

'You hungry?'

'Do not try to soft-soap me,' Grace said.

'I think I'll muster up a sandwich. Want one?'

She turned around. 'There are two things I want from you, and a sandwich at this hour of the night is not one of them.'

'Shoot so.' He leaned his damp hair back against the cool upholstery.

'Shoot?'

'What are the two things you want?'

'To meet Lottie Parker, and for you to find out where my friend Mollie is.'

He sat forward in the chair and clenched his hands between his long legs. 'Okay. I'll organise for you to meet Lottie. Happy?'

'And Mollie?'

'I'll do a search on her address tomorrow. What's her surname?'

Grace bit her lip.

'Please tell me you know her full name?'

'Just Mollie. She lives in Ragmullin and works in Dublin.'

'That's not enough.' He shook his head and reached out a hand to her.

'Try? For me?' She gripped his hand so tightly, Boyd thought his fingers must surely be crushed.

'You're asking a lot. A first name and the train she normally takes? But because your smile is so sweet, I'll try.'

He watched as Grace flopped back on the couch, a contented grin spreading across her face. Getting up to make his sandwich, he thought about Elizabeth Byrne. He shook himself. This business with Mollie was probably nothing more than Grace getting caught up in the imaginary world that he remembered her having in childhood.

Searching the refrigerator for sandwich fillings, he noticed there was absolutely nothing to eat.

'Grace, have you been raiding the fridge?'

'You need to shop for two, you know.'

She hadn't answered his question. Bread and butter would have to do until tomorrow.

The doorbell rang.

CHAPTER FORTY-SIX

The hatch opened and light filled the room. Mollie squeezed her eyes closed against the glare.

'The smell of you.' His voice echoed through the enclosed space.

Her eyes flew open. She slowly moved her head but could still see very little. She needed to orientate herself. It seemed to be a cellar, like one she'd seen in a film. Or some sort of underground bunker. The walls were padded with thick foil, a wrapped pipe snaking up one corner; there was a small square table squashed into the opposite corner, and a short ladder led to the hatch in the ceiling.

Directing her gaze back to him, she said, 'The smell is not my fault.' Her voice was weak from screaming earlier, even though she knew it had been a fruitless exercise.

'I'm going to release your arms. On one condition.'

'What's that?'

'Make a wrong move and I'll leave you here to rot.'

'I'll do what you say.'

'Ah, you've lost your fight.'

Mollie knew she would have to acquiesce to his demands. The knife he was using to cut her bonds was short and sharp. Could she grab it? Not now, when the pain in her released wrists was screaming at her.

'Thank you,' she said, rubbing her wrists.

'There's a bucket there. Use it.'

'I don't need to go. Not now.'

She studied him. Unable to determine his height because he was bent over under the low ceiling, she tried to see his face. The bone structure. The eyes. His features scrunched up suddenly like a squeezed lemon and he sneered at her.

'You pissed yourself. You smell like a dirty cat.'

'What day is it?' she asked tentatively. She knew it'd be wrong to anger him even more.

The slap was quick and fierce. She fell back on the bed, cracking her head against the iron frame.

'Don't speak unless I say so. You hear me?'

She nodded and bit her bottom lip, trying desperately not to cry. With him leaning over her, she couldn't get a decent look at the room again. She needed a good idea of the layout, for when he left her alone. But maybe he'd tie her up again. Maybe he wanted to kill her. She began to cry, the tears that had dried up during the day flowing once more.

'And don't fucking cry. I can't stand whingers.'

'Sorry.' She rubbed her wrists again, trying to get the blood to circulate.

He pulled her by the arms until she was sitting upright. A finger streaked a line down the bones in her jaw, travelled along her throat and caressed the crevice between neck and shoulder blade. She used every inch of willpower not to recoil from his touch. She had to understand what he wanted. Surely he wouldn't have gone to all the trouble of drugging her and hauling her into this cavern if he was going to kill her? Would he?

And then she saw the bones.

CHAPTER FORTY-SEVEN

Boyd watched Kirby jostling down the narrow hallway with Gilly O'Donoghue behind him.

'This better be important,' he said when they were all seated, with Grace sitting on a chair in the kitchenette watching them. Why couldn't she go to bed? He introduced her and waited to see what Kirby had to say.

'You tell him,' Kirby said.

Gilly tapped her phone and handed it to Boyd.

'Well, that's you at the Jealous Wall. And who's that with you?' Boyd pointed at the photograph.

'She's the reason Gilly dragged me across town to see you.' Kirby grunted and folded his arms.

'I know her through my weekend running,' Gilly said. 'Remember you asked me earlier this evening about Elizabeth Byrne?'

'Yeah.'

'That's Mollie Hunter. We met last year. Joined up for running at the same time. We started going for a drink the odd evening. I think I'm the closest she has to a best friend. Her family moved to London a few years ago.' She glanced at Kirby. 'The thing is, I can't make contact with her.'

'Her name is Mollie?' Grace said.

Boyd looked away from his sister's wide eyes and open mouth, the expression saying, 'I told you so'. Shaking his head, he said, 'Does she commute to work on the train?'

Gilly leaned forward in the armchair. 'She does. And so did Elizabeth Byrne.'

Boyd sighed, getting the insinuation. 'That's a stretch of the imagination. Have you checked out Mollie's home?'

'She gave me her spare key a while back. I've been to her apartment and it looks like the last time she was there was Wednesday morning. Breakfast dishes were in the sink. No coat or handbag lying around.'

'How do you know it was Wednesday?'

'I phoned her Tuesday. We agreed to meet up for a drink Wednesday night. But she didn't turn up and I called to her home.'

'She could have just been out,' Boyd suggested.

'We checked it earlier this evening too,' Kirby said.

Boyd stood. 'I'll do something about it in the morning.'

'Elizabeth Byrne disappeared after getting the train home,' Gilly pointed out.

'You don't know Mollie got on the train. She could be in Dublin,' Kirby said.

'What if she's in the hands of Elizabeth's murderer?'

'Murderer?'

Boyd swung around to see Grace with her hand clasped to her mouth. 'Grace, why don't you go to bed?'

'Tell them what I told you,' she insisted.

Boyd sighed and sat back down. 'According to Grace—'

She interrupted him. 'Mollie sat beside me yesterday morning on the train and we began talking. Then we got the train home together, the 17.10 from Connolly … and now she has vanished.'

Boyd said, 'I'll talk to Lottie tomorrow. We'll see if we can locate Mollie and establish if there is any connection to Elizabeth.'

He watched Gilly linking Kirby's arm as they left.

When Grace had gone to bed and he was alone, the shroud of loneliness settled on his shoulders once more.

CHAPTER FORTY-EIGHT

Two teenagers crept out of a mobile home and made their way hand in hand down the dark lake road away from the caravan park. He carried a bottle of vodka and she a bottle of Captain Morgan. They drank as they walked, and the more they drank, the more closely entwined they became.

At a cut in the trees, he dragged her by the hand off the road.

'Hey, the branches are snagging my hair.'

'I'll snag your hair in a minute, gorgeous.'

She laughed and allowed him to lead her. They were bent in two, giggling and squealing.

'Ah, Shane, this is too much. I think I'm going to be sick.' She threw the bottle of rum into the undergrowth.

'It's not too bad here. You can see the moon.'

'I can only see trees. This place is scary. It's too dark.'

He pulled her to the ground.

'Shane, it's wet. My jeans …'

His mouth covered hers in a kiss and a smell assaulted her nostrils. Shoving him off, she sat upright.

'Shane! You're rotten. Did you fart?'

'Would you ever shut … You're right. What the hell is that smell?'

She dragged her phone out of her jeans pocket and unlocked it. The light from the screen shone on his face, casting eerie shadows. She swung the phone around.

'There's something over there.'

'Fuck's sake, Jen.' He pulled out his own phone and pressed the flashlight app. 'Oh my God. It's … it's a …'

Jen screamed.

They jumped up and ran, crashing through the forest of briars and bushes.

*

His darn dog wouldn't stop barking. Where was he? Bob Mulligan switched on his flashlight and followed through the undergrowth in the direction the dog had run. Living by Ladystown lake had seemed like an idyllic dream come true for him. Peace, stillness and silence. A stark contrast to city life and all that brought with it. The isolation got to him, though. Days on end, hour after hour. Ticking away with only himself and Mutt. Until youngsters got up to their tricks, drinking and screaming. And tonight they were at it again.

He came out the other side of the clearing with still no sign of Mutt. He stood and listened. The barking had stopped. The screaming had ceased too. The lake was calm, dappled with silver from the moonlight. Stars were shimmering in a constellation against the black sky.

A yelp from his right.

Rustling in the bushes.

Two teenagers ran straight into him.

The girl screamed and pointed behind her. 'In there. It's horrible.'

'Calm down,' Mulligan said. 'What's going on? Did this lad hurt you? Did he do something to you?'

'No! No,' she gasped. 'Don't go in there. Call the guards. Oh God, I'm going to be sick.'

She took off. The young lad shrugged his shoulders and followed her.

Using his stick, Bob tore away at the frozen undergrowth. The clearing was dim, with only the shadowy illumination from the celestial orb in the night sky.

'Hey, boy, what's got you so excited there?'

As he approached, the smell caused him to gag. The dog turned round, tail wagging, something unidentifiable hanging from his jaws.

'Dear God in heaven!' Bob fumbled his phone out of his pocket and grabbed Mutt's collar.

CHAPTER FORTY-NINE

The large suitcase was packed and Katie's rucksack remained open for last-minute essentials.

Lottie sat on the edge of her daughter's bed and watched her sleep. She turned to the cot. Listened to little Louis breathing. Like she used to do when her own children were babies. Her and Adam. Shushing each other, trying to hear the breaths, to see the little chests rising and falling, before dropping back on their pillows with relief. She supposed every mother on the planet did that at some time in her life, and though her faith had been tested too many times, she prayed that her daughter and grandson would be safe on their travels.

At last she tiptoed out of the room and down to the kitchen. Tiredness chewed sharp bites into her bones as she sat at the table. The cold case file appeared to be tempting her to open it, with its thick sheaf of papers sticking out haphazardly from between the covers. But her shoulder screamed for a painkiller and she remembered the weight of the man's hand on her injury. Thoughts of the nursing home brought her to the argument with her mother.

Rose had always been confrontational, sometimes with good reason, but now she was being plain obstructive. I'm only trying to help, Lottie thought, though she was aware that she was doing it reluctantly. She should have kept her mouth shut. The things she'd said were hurtful. She'd meant them to be at the time. But now? Now she was sorry. Her feelings for Rose were so confused, she couldn't bear to fathom out a solution. Not tonight, in any case. She knew she was a past master at burying emotional turmoil deep beneath the mundanity of everyday life.

She found a box of paracetamol and swallowed two with a glass of water, then popped a third to be sure the pain would ease enough to allow her a few hours' slumber. She needed a drink. Just one.

She found the vodka at the back of the cupboard, where she'd hidden it, and poured a double measure. The first mouthful made her gag, the second went down more smoothly, and by the third, her head felt lighter.

She glanced at the file. Maybe a few minutes buried in the old case would help her sleep.

As she opened the cover, her phone rang. She jumped up as the vibration filled the kitchen. When she ended the call, she rang Boyd. It was going to be a long night.

CHAPTER FIFTY

It was gone midnight as Lottie drove with Boyd down the narrow road to Barren Point on the shores of Ladystown lake.

Ladystown was the largest lake bordering Ragmullin. Whereas Lough Cullion was the water source for the town, Ladystown had treated sewage pumped into its depths daily. It was still good for fishing, so Adam had told her years ago.

'Where am I going?' she asked.

'Sharp left,' Boyd said. 'Mind that tree. Jesus. You should have let me drive.'

'I've to be on my way to the airport at six, so it's best I have my own transport.' She hoped he couldn't smell the alcohol on her breath.

'What about me?'

'There's the squad car.'

She parked haphazardly and jumped out. She took her protective suit from the boot and dragged it over her clothes, then got a torch and headed towards a uniformed officer standing beside a crime-scene tape. A man with a dog was there too.

'Who are you?' she asked.

'Bob Mulligan.'

'You're the man who discovered the body?'

'To be honest, I think two teenagers stumbled on it before Mutt here. Don't know how much damage he did to it.'

'Did he dismember it?' She was anxious to see the scene, assess the situation and maybe catch some sleep before she had to be back on the road.

'He had part of a hand in his mouth. I got it out. You'll need to be taking my DNA because I touched it. Isn't that the right procedure?'

'Yes, sir.'

'It can't have been there long.'

'What do you mean?'

'The body. It must have been dumped in the last week. Mutt and I have been away, over in Galway, and he'd have sniffed it out if it had been there before that.'

'Where do you live?'

Mulligan pointed to a light shimmering through the trees. 'Over there.'

'Do you know where these teenagers went?'

'They might be staying at the caravan park.'

'Wrong time of year for holidaymakers.' She instructed two guards to check. 'Mr Mulligan, please stay here. I'm going in to have a look.' She turned to the uniforms. 'Anyone got a torch stronger than this? And call in reinforcements. We need to find the teenagers.'

With an industrial-sized torch in her hand and Boyd behind her, she made her way through the bushes in a crouch, frozen leaves crunching underfoot, until the clearing opened up in front of her.

Though she'd seen a fair number of bodies, her stomach heaved and her skin bumped and crawled. Under the glare of the artificial light, the blue-black body seemed to be heaving too.

'Jesus, Boyd. Tell me what I'm looking at.'

He joined her. 'I hope that isn't Mollie Hunter.'

Lottie took a step back and looked up at him. 'Who?'

'I don't think it can be. This body is too decomposed. She only went missing yesterday evening, if she even is missing.' Boyd was shaking his head.

'What on earth are you on about? Who is Mollie Hunter?' She stepped into his space.

'A young woman who may or may not have disappeared. Gilly O'Donoghue is her friend and she can't locate her. Could be nothing.'

She felt her mouth hanging open and quickly said, 'And when were you going to inform me about this? Jesus, Boyd, sometimes, you know … sometimes I just want to … Oh, I don't know!'

'Why don't we see what we have before you hang me out to dry?'

'Don't touch a thing until the scene is fully cordoned off. Did you contact Kirby and Lynch?'

'Neither of them is answering. McGlynn said to secure the site and he'll be here in the morning.'

'Get a tent erected over the body. And I want those teenagers found.'

As Boyd went off to make more phone calls, Lottie stood at the side of a tree with the light of her torch directed on the body.

'Who are you?' she whispered, then screamed as a rat ran out from beneath the remains.

DAY THREE

Friday 12 February 2016

CHAPTER FIFTY-ONE

After the train left Enfield station, Grace realised that the man who had eyed her suspiciously yesterday did not appear to be on the train. Maybe he didn't have to go to Dublin on Fridays, or perhaps he was seated in a different carriage. Was she in the wrong one? She twisted to look at the sign above the door. C. Relief.

The carriage heated up from the extra body warmth as people crowded on. The smell of perfume and hastily sprayed deodorant filled her senses. She avoided breathing in too deeply or her allergies would play up.

Where was Mollie? And where was the man she had seen talking to her at Ragmullin station on Wednesday evening?

It was then that she remembered she hadn't told anyone about him. She must tell Mark. She looked in her bag for her bulky Nokia, but couldn't find it. She'd charged it last night and with all the fussing had forgotten to put it in her bag this morning. Damnation, she thought, she had no way of contacting him. He was expecting her to be heading straight to Galway from Dublin this evening, and she had forgotten to tell him that she'd changed her plans. Late last night she had phoned her mother to say she would be staying in Ragmullin for the weekend. She'd just have to take a taxi to Mark's place this evening.

A knot of anxiety twisted in her stomach. She never forgot things. Her life had to be ordered, otherwise she couldn't cope. Deep breaths. She found her inhaler. At least she had that. A few puffs and the shaking in her hands ceased. Her throat was still clogged. Another puff and she put the inhaler back in her bag. Searched for her anxiety pills. She'd forgotten those too. With all the talk of Mollie, her mind was not as focused as it should be.

Feeling annoyed with herself, she looked up, and that was when she saw him. Sitting at the other end of the carriage. Staring. As she slipped her bag onto her knee, goose bumps popped up along her arms. Her first thought was that she wished she could call Mark. The second was that she had to find Mollie.

CHAPTER FIFTY-TWO

At the gates to the airport security area, Katie held out an envelope.

'What's this?' Lottie said.

'I only spent about a hundred euros. I want you to have the rest.' Katie pressed the envelope into her hand. 'I withdrew it from the bank. For you.'

'But you need spending money. You'll be going shopping. Oh Katie, you have to go to Woodbury Common. We were there when you were little. Do you remember?'

'Don't worry about me. I kept a little, and I won't be doing much shopping. Tom says he wants to spend time with his grandson, and of course with me.'

'I can't take this.'

'You can. Treat yourself, and Chloe wants that balayage so badly, and I'm sure Sean could do with new training gear or something. Spend it. Don't feel guilty thinking it's Tom Rickard's money. It's my gift to you for being the best mother ever. You've put up with all the shit I've thrown at you since Dad died; for once, let me do something for you.'

Lottie nodded. 'You have to see the Empire State Building, and don't forget Central Park.' Her voice cracked, and she pushed away memories of her trips to New York with Adam. The time they went on their own, before the children were born. She'd suffered severe vertigo at the top of the Empire State, couldn't look out over the edge of the viewing gantry. Adam had had to practically carry her down in the elevator.

She hugged little Louis, kissed his hair and fingers and nose, inhaling his baby smell, before Chloe took him for her own hugs.

Katie enveloped Lottie in her arms. 'Don't be worrying about me, Mam. I'm only going for three weeks. Love you.'

'Love you too.'

After hugging Chloe, Katie moved to her brother. Tall, awkward Sean hesitated for a moment, then smothered his sister in a bear hug, and suddenly they were all crying, tears of happiness for Katie and loneliness for themselves.

'Ah, guys, come on,' Katie said, taking Louis back and strapping him into his stroller, 'I'll have to do my mascara again.' She fixed the baby bag on the handles and hoisted her rucksack onto her shoulder.

'Drama queen,' Chloe said.

'Look who's talking.' Sean nudged her.

Normal service has resumed, Lottie thought.

As she turned to head for the car park with Chloe and Sean by her side, she felt a hollowness lined with a tinge of fear etch into a corner of her heart. It would not dislodge until her family were all back together, whenever that might be.

She was already late for the team meeting by the time she'd dropped Chloe and Sean at school and returned home to pick up the cold case file. She'd read most of it after returning from the lake last night, managing about an hour's sleep before she had to get up for the airport. Exhaustion gnawed her bones, which didn't bode well for the remainder of the day. Outside the incident room, she swallowed half a Xanax and hoped for the best.

McMahon was at the front of the room, commanding the team meeting, when she blustered in the door.

'At last you decide to grace us with your presence,' he said, gripping his chin with his thumb and index finger.

Lottie glared at Boyd. Had he not made up some plausible excuse for her absence?

'I'm here now,' she said.

Dredging up her confidence, with a buzz in her head from the pill, she marched through the gathered detectives and uniformed officers, stealing a glance at the incident boards. A shadowy photograph of the body found in the woods by the lake had been added.

'So you are,' McMahon said. 'And my arrival in this district has been met with not one but two murders. I'm beginning to believe the media when they say Ragmullin is a nightmare town.'

'And what media would that be?' Lottie asked, trying to gather her thoughts.

McMahon glared. 'I had a visit from the television crime correspondent, Cynthia Rhodes. I believe you've met her. She paints a very dim picture of this town.'

'She must be a damn bad artist then.' Lottie banged her bag onto the floor and bundled her jacket on top of it.

Kirby snickered, and Lottie couldn't help the smile that spread across her face.

'As senior investigating officer, I'll take over here,' she said.

She waited until McMahon had stepped to one side with a smirk on his face. What was that all about? Pointing to the first photograph on the board, she began.

'Elizabeth Byrne. Last physical sighting was on Monday, when she clocked out of her office at 16.00 hours. We have CCTV image from Connolly station placing her there at 17.00. The train departed at 17.10 and arrived in Ragmullin at 18.20. Her body was found on Wednesday morning in the cemetery as a funeral was about to take place. You have the times and details of the relevant interviews. One lead we have is from Bridie McWard, who lives on the traveller site. She claims to have heard screaming at 3.15 a.m. on Tuesday.

The post-mortem findings agree that this was the approximate time of death. Bridie has subsequently been the subject of an attack in her home. Unclear if it is connected or not, but a verbal threat was made during the assault.'

She paused to direct her thoughts back to the murder. 'Elizabeth was more than likely chased through the cemetery, then fell into the grave, breaking her leg, if it hadn't been already broken. She was buried alive. Perhaps the killer hoped she would be entombed with a coffin placed over her that day, Tuesday. As it was, the funeral was delayed until Wednesday, as the deceased's grandson had to fly home from Australia. This meant the loose clay dispersed slightly in the intervening time, leaving part of the body exposed.'

'Do you think any of the Green family was involved?' McMahon asked.

Lottie had forgotten he was still there.

'Kirby, you conducted those interviews.' She turned to the detective. 'What did you come up with?'

'All in the clear. Everything checks out. Also, after the media appeal for information by Acting Superintendent McMahon, I scrutinised the statements of those who came forward having attended the Last Hurdle nightclub on Saturday night and also those who were on the Monday evening train. No one saw anything out of the ordinary. No one remembers Elizabeth, or at least nothing stands out as suspicious. A few commuters said she was a regular on the train but don't recall anything unusual about Monday.'

'Okay. Go back over the station CCTV. Originally we were only looking for Elizabeth. This time check for anyone who might be acting in a suspicious way, anyone who might already be on PULSE.'

'Will do,' Kirby said.

'The only lead we have is a bundle of clothes found in refuse sacks in the cemetery skip. It is possible the killer dumped them there the same night Elizabeth was murdered. CCTV places a car there for twenty-four minutes. Mrs Byrne has confirmed that this clothing belongs to her daughter. Jim McGlynn says the garments were wet. Are the results of his tests back yet?'

'Not yet,' Kirby said.

'Do Elizabeth's colleagues check out?'

'They can all account for their movements and Elizabeth didn't stay with any of them.' Kirby shuffled a sheaf of papers back into a file.

'The question we have to ask ourselves is this. Where was Elizabeth from the last positive sighting at 17.00 until Bridie heard the screams at 3.15 the following morning? Was she taken from the train at Ragmullin? Or did she get off it safely and was subsequently abducted on her walk home? She doesn't own a car. Have we checked all the town CCTV footage? Businesses along her usual route?'

'All checked and no sign of her,' Kirby said.

'Taxis?'

'No taxi driver recalls her.'

'The ex-boyfriend. Matt Mullin. Did Lynch find him?' Where was Lynch this morning? She couldn't see her in the assembled group.

'Called to his house yesterday,' Kirby said. 'Met with his mother. She was uncooperative to say the least.'

'Why?'

'Refuses to talk without a warrant.'

'So what is she hiding?'

'Matt,' Kirby said. 'He was let go by the bank before Christmas, so he has to be at home.'

'Confirm he's back in town, by whatever means you can. We need to locate him as soon as possible to establish where he was on Monday night. Get his photograph circulated to the media.'

'Bit soon for that,' McMahon interjected.

'He is our *only* suspect,' Lottie emphasised. Why did he have to interrupt her train of thought? 'We can say he's needed to assist our ongoing inquiry.' She folded one arm and rested her other elbow on it, hand under her chin. Thinking. She added, 'Elizabeth's phone hasn't been found. Hound the service provider.'

Boyd said, 'I'm working on it.'

'We have to assume she was on that train. So, what happened to her when the train pulled up in Ragmullin? Come on, guys. That's what we need to discover.'

A muffled murmur rippled through the room.

'Anything else?' Lottie asked.

Kirby piped up. 'The assault on Bridie McWard. SOCOs have finished at her home. They've collected DNA and fibres. We need to speak with her husband, Paddy, to eliminate him from that inquiry.'

McMahon reared up. 'Where is he?'

'Don't know, sir.'

'Find him. Get the registration of his van or car circulated. I don't think Ragmullin is that big a place that you can't find him. Enough of this time-wasting.'

'It's big enough if you don't want to be found,' Lottie said. She noticed that Boyd had his hand tentatively raised. 'Yes, Boyd.'

'We have to consider the possibility that there's also another young woman missing.'

'Who?' Lottie asked.

'Mollie Hunter,' Boyd said. 'I mentioned her to you last night.'

Shit, so he did. 'Is she on the missing persons database?'

'No, not yet. She lives alone in an apartment at Canal Drive. She's a friend of Gilly's. Garda O'Donoghue,' he added for McMahon's benefit. 'Gilly spoke to Mollie on the phone on Tuesday but hasn't been able to contact her since. She has a key to the apartment and checked it twice. No sign of the girl. And this is the interesting bit.

She gets the six o'clock train every morning to her job in Dublin and then the 17.10 home.'

'Have you contacted her employer?' Lottie said.

'Not yet. I only heard about this last night.'

McMahon stepped forward. 'There's no point in flying off on a tangent and—'

'I think we need to follow it up, sir,' Lottie interjected. 'At least to establish that she's not missing.' She noted Kirby was keeping his head studiously stuck in his laptop.

McMahon raised his voice two octaves. 'Why hasn't her family reported this?'

'They're in London, so I think we need to act—' Boyd began.

'She hasn't been reported missing,' McMahon interrupted. 'You have enough to keep you busy with the murder, haven't you, Detective Inspector?'

Lottie was going to fight him but felt if anyone looked crooked at her she might cry – she was that tired, and still emotional over Katie leaving.

'Now what's the story with this body that was found last night?' McMahon pointed to the photograph on the board. 'Could this be your missing Mollie?' He cocked his head at Boyd.

Lottie spoke before Boyd could rise to the provocation. 'We don't know who it is yet. Bob Mulligan, who lives out at Ladystown lake, discovered the body around midnight. Well, his dog did, though that was after two teenagers had already tripped over it.'

'Can you explain what you're talking about?' McMahon swiped his fringe back off his forehead.

Lottie thought she could see a line of pimples pulsing on his furrowed brow as she explained about the situation at the lake.

'I have yet to formally interview Mr Mulligan, but he claims the body can't have been there longer than a week.'

'And how would he know that?'

'He was in Galway from Friday, the fifth, until last night. The dog was with him. He claims the animal would have sniffed it out if it had been there before then.'

'Have you checked his alibi? He could be involved and is trying to put you off his scent. Or the dog's scent.' McMahon laughed.

Lottie ignored him. 'I've to interview the two teenagers this morning. They were in shock last night. They're staying in a mobile home at the caravan park.'

'In this weather?' Kirby piped up.

'They're young, and perhaps squatting. But I'm not concerned about that. The body is still *in situ*. The state pathologist will be there soon, and SOCOs are already at the scene.'

'Follow it up, then.'

Lottie held her breath, counted to five and exhaled slowly. He was going to crack her up. 'Yes, sir.'

'And this Elizabeth Byrne murder. You've told us everything you haven't got; what *have* you got?'

'We spoke to her friend Carol O'Grady. She says Elizabeth went running at Rochfort Gardens every weekend. We have a list of those who participated and are working our way through it. If nothing worthwhile turns up in the meantime, I'll go out there tomorrow and follow up with anyone we haven't made contact with.'

'What good will that do?' McMahon said.

Jesus Christ, she thought. Why doesn't he just fuck off back to Dublin?

'One of them might hold a clue as to what happened. Maybe saw someone acting suspiciously.'

'Could she have been stalked?'

'It's a possibility.'

'I'll tag along then. Tomorrow? Fine. I want to get to know the locality.'

'You do?'

'Of course.'

'Right so.' Holy Jesus, this was going to get worse before it got better.

'And don't waste time on this missing girl who hasn't been reported missing.'

Lottie counted to five again. 'Any further updates, team?'

'John Gilbey is living in a hostel on Kennedy Street,' Kirby said. 'I'm going up there to interview him again after this meeting. And as I mentioned before, Bernard Fahy's wife says he was with her all Monday night.'

'Hmph,' grunted McMahon. 'I'd rattle that alibi good and hard if I were you.'

'I will, sir.'

'I don't think Fahy is involved,' Lottie said.

'No stone and all that,' McMahon said. 'Right. Get to it, everyone. And DI Parker, I want a word. Now. Outside.'

She watched him nod to the team and march out of the incident room. She stayed where she was until he stuck his head back around the door.

'When I say now, I mean now.'

'You better go,' Boyd advised. 'Before he drags you out by the heels.'

McMahon was pacing up and down the corridor.

'Listen here, Parker, I'm getting distinct vibes that you don't want me involved in these investigations.'

'I …' Lottie clamped her mouth shut. Safer.

'Superintendent Corrigan may have let you run your own one-woman show, but I don't intend to.'

'With all due respect, *sir*, that is untrue. I have a great team in Boyd, Kirby and Lynch.'

'And where is Detective Lynch this morning?'

'Out sick, as far as I know.' She didn't know, but she intended to find out.

'Is everyone in this damn place on sick leave?'

'Only Superintendent Corrigan and Detective Lynch. Sir.'

'You've a smart mouth as well as everything else.' He coiled his large frame and leaned in towards her. 'You have all those men and women in there and you sideline them with the mundane jobs. Glory-hunting, are you?'

Lottie laughed. 'That is one thing I cannot be accused of.'

He seemed to consider that before saying, 'I'm watching you, Parker. Every chip you thought you had on your shoulder is going to be a fully fledged chunk of timber if not a fucking tree by the time I'm finished here. And the shadow you're going to see following you, let me tell you, will be me.'

'Is that all?' Lottie clasped her hands into tight fists, just in case she lashed out at him.

She watched as he strode off down the corridor. This was serious. Kind of. Feck him.

She felt a presence at her shoulder and shivered. What had he said about shadows?

'What did he have to say for himself?' Boyd said.

'Get the car and I'll tell you on the way out to the lake. Do you know where Lynch is?'

CHAPTER FIFTY-THREE

The lake was a mirror of the sky, silver grey, with the shadows of the clouds rolling across it like steam from an old train engine. On the ground, at the base of the trees, white snowdrops had eased through the hard earth. Birds were singing. A flap of wings and one surged through the branches and soared up into the sky. A sharp wind blew in off the lake, and Lottie zipped her jacket to her throat and hauled the white protective clothing over it.

The area leading to the body had been marked out with tape, and she followed it through the undergrowth with Boyd close behind her. In places, greenery was struggling to bloom against the weather. Overhead, branches dipped and snagged her hair. She pulled up the hood and placed a mask over her mouth before entering the crime scene.

A loud squawk caused her to look upwards. A magpie, black-and-white plumage plumped and ready for flight, observed her as she marched through the inner cordon.

'One for sorrow,' Boyd said, quoting the old saying.

Entering the tent, she looked around the small space and approached McGlynn.

'Have you taken impressions of the footprints?' she asked.

'Everyone and their dog, literally I may add, has tramped around this crime scene.'

'And those branches out there? Perfect for snagging fibres and hair.'

'It'll be done,' he said grumpily.

'Any sign of Jane?' she asked.

'On her way. She was finishing up the paperwork on Elizabeth Byrne. I think she might have some DNA results too.'

'Great. I could do with a break. Anything on the clothes from the skip?'

'If you didn't keep calling me out to dead bodies, I might get to spend some time in my lab.'

'That's a no, then?'

'Yes, it's a no.'

Inching closer to the bloated naked body, Lottie felt, rather than saw, McGlynn's warning eyes.

'I wouldn't go any further,' he said. 'I need the pathologist to have a look at her first.'

'It's a female, then?'

'Yes. But she's been doused with bleach, and vermin have had a good nibble. I'll know more when I get to the lab.'

'How long has she been here?'

'Maybe three or four days. However, she has been deceased longer than that. How long, I don't know.'

'Jane will be able to make the call on time of death,' Lottie said.

'Someone taking my name in vain?' Jane Dore appeared in her protective suit. What she lacked in height, all of five foot nothing, she made up for with her professional and no-nonsense behaviour. 'Good morning, all. Make way.'

Lottie watched with admiration as the pathologist immediately got to work, visually assessing the body, then asking McGlynn to turn it slightly before holding up her hand to halt him.

'Did you move the body?'

'Waiting for you,' he said.

'Turn it so.'

As McGlynn and a technician began to move the body, Jane said, 'Carefully.'

'Of course,' he said.

Lottie smiled wryly. He didn't talk to Jane the way he talked to her. Pecking order sprang to mind.

'No visible sign of wounds,' the pathologist said.

'How did she die, then?' Lottie said.

'I don't make assumptions, as you know. But I'd say foul play is highly likely in some form, given that the body seems to have been washed in bleach.'

'That looks like the remnants of a refuse sack,' Lottie said pointing to two strips of black plastic on the ground.

'Bag it all,' Jane instructed McGlynn. 'She may have been wrapped in it. You might get trace evidence.'

'Good,' Lottie said. 'You'll prioritise this, Jane?'

'I will.'

'What age group are we looking at?'

'Early to mid thirties, I'd say.'

'Thanks.'

Lottie left the tent with Boyd.

'You were fairly quiet in there,' she said.

'You were putting enough feet in it for both of us,' he said, and made off down the trail.

What the hell was eating him? she wondered.

At the outer cordon, they tore off the protective clothing and bagged it.

'Mulligan next on your list?' Boyd said.

'Yes.'

She decided to let him stew in whatever mood he was in. She had enough worries without Boyd. And then she wondered how Katie was doing on her flight. 'Dear God, keep them safe,' she muttered.

CHAPTER FIFTY-FOUR

The bones. Tiny chips of them lying on the narrow table. And the smallest skull. She should have asked him. Were they real? Had they been left there to frighten her into submission? She didn't know, but she supposed she didn't want to find out either. Best to pretend they were made of plastic. A toy. Yes. No. They were real. Very real.

Sitting on the side of the bed, she took a sip of water from the plastic bottle he'd left her. And still she stared. Why would there be the bones of a child down here? Unburied. Or had they been buried and then excavated? Fear trawled her skin, pricking away like bites from hungry ants. And the odour. The room was filled with it. Like ammonia, or bleach. What had he been cleaning before he'd brought her here? Whatever it was, he hadn't done a very good job. She could smell the underlying scent. Like rotting meat. Like the dead mouse she'd found behind a skirting board once. Much as she feared and detested vermin, she hoped that was what she was now smelling, masked beneath the acidic fumes.

She was weak and tired but knew she wouldn't sleep. Not with those bones over there. On display. Taunting her.

Was she to suffer a similar fate?

No way. She was stronger than this. She wouldn't meet the same fate as … Her throat snagged and she gulped. Were the child's bones challenging her?

*

A picket fence surrounded Bob Mulligan's home. The prefab house sat in a dip half a mile from the lake shore and about the same from where the body had been found. It was obvious to Lottie that it had been constructed long before more stringent planning laws had been introduced. Then again, maybe Bob Mulligan operated outside the law.

A wire run housed a few hens devoid of most of their feathers, and the dog was tied up with a gnawed rope on a concrete square.

Mulligan brought them into the house and they sat at a table cluttered with the remains of breakfast. No tea was offered, which pleased Lottie. She didn't fancy drinking out of the brown-rimmed mugs.

'How long have you lived here, Mr Mulligan?' she began.

'Thirty years or thereabouts. Inherited from my granny.'

'What do you work at?'

'Retired. I just fish the lake now.'

'It seems very isolated.'

'It's what I like. Me and the animals are happy. Wasn't always so. There was a time, must be fifteen, if not twenty years back, when the travellers threatened to take over with their caravans. But the council moved them to a site in town.'

'Really? Why were they out here?'

'There's that caravan park down the other side of the lake. For holidaymakers, you know. I think the travellers thought they could set up their own park over this side. I didn't have an issue with them, but they had no running water or toilets.'

'That was a long time ago,' Lottie said. 'Has anything other than that ever disturbed you out here?'

'Boy racers from time to time. Lovers in cars with steamed-up windows at night. Other than that, it's nice and quiet.'

'How often do you walk through that particular area where you found the body?' Lottie said, folding her arms.

'I'm not a suspect, am I? I had nothing to do with it.'

'Can you answer the question?' Boyd said.

'I usually walk on the road along the lake, but last night there were those youngsters mucking about. They found the body first. It was the young girl's scream that alerted Mutt. He got the scent and took off. So I followed him.'

'When were you there before last night?' Boyd asked.

'Like I told you already, it was more than a week ago. You can ring my friend in Galway. I went over there Friday last, the fifth.'

'And before that, you were here all the time?'

Lottie watched as Mulligan shuffled on his chair.

'Yes. Doesn't mean I killed anyone.'

'We're just exploring everything until we get the time of death.'

'Was she murdered, do you think?'

'Why would you say that?'

He pointed to the newspaper on the table. The front page carried a report on the murder of Elizabeth Byrne.'

'"Buried in someone else's grave",' Lottie read. 'We'll check with your friend. And I need details of your movements for the last couple of weeks.'

'I'll write it out for you.'

'You can make a formal statement at the station, and give a DNA sample. Sometime today suit you?'

'That's grand.'

'Here's my card. Let me know if you think of anything else that might help us. I'm leaving a uniformed officer at your gate while the forensic examination of the scene is ongoing.'

'So I'm under house arrest?'

'It's for your own safety,' Lottie lied.

*

Before they got to interview the teenagers, McGlynn sent word for them to come back on site.

'We found this.' He pointed downwards while one of his team stood to one side.

Lottie peered at a piece of upturned earth. 'Someone was digging?'

'Attempting to.'

'The intention may have been to bury the body, but with all the frost, the ground was too hard.'

'So they stripped off the plastic wrapping and left her to the wildlife and the elements.' McGlynn placed a marker beside the hole. 'Hoping that if she was ever found, it would be just a bundle of bones.'

'No sign of a shovel?'

'No.'

'Tyre tracks?'

'None of those either. He probably parked on the road and carried the body over his shoulder. He came in as far as he could before the forest closed over entirely.'

'Has to be a local.'

'Why?'

'To know the area, the lie of the land.'

Boyd said, 'Or he could be from out of town and uses the caravan park.'

'The manager needs to be interviewed.'

'We're trying to make contact with him.'

'And get a list of everyone who has used the park in recent months.'

'You'd have to be mad to live there in this weather,' Boyd said with a shrug.

As they made their way to the car, Lottie said, 'Do you think the person who killed Elizabeth is responsible for this?'

'Hard to know. Wouldn't you think that if he buried Elizabeth in a grave, he'd do the same with this one?'

'That's what I'm thinking. So maybe he tried to dispose of this victim before Elizabeth. And if we agree with Mulligan's hypothesis that his dog would have found her if she'd been here earlier, the body had to have been dumped this week.'

CHAPTER FIFTY-FIVE

In the incident room, Lottie pinned up another grainy photograph of the body found at the lake, then returned to her own office.

They'd learned nothing new from Shane Timmons or Jen O'Reilly, the two terrified teenagers who had escaped Dublin for a few days to make out in the caravan belonging to Shane's mother.

'Okay, so this body cannot be that of Mollie Hunter, who may or may not be missing. She's aged twenty-five, and it's likely that the body is that of a woman in her mid thirties. She's been dead perhaps a week.' Lottie sat down at her desk. Boyd lounged at the door.

'I'll get someone to go through the national missing persons database, because I don't think anyone local fits that description,' he said.

'We might have her DNA later.'

'In any case, I'll check with Mollie's employer and colleagues to see if they have any notion where she might be.'

'Get Lynch to go through the database.' Lottie strained her neck to see around Boyd. 'Where is she?'

'She called in sick.'

'Shit. We're too busy for anyone to be off.'

'Why don't you give her a call?'

'I don't think so. She might see it as harassment.'

'Is that ugly word rearing its head again?'

'You know what happened before, Boyd. I don't want to go there again.'

Kirby appeared. 'We found Paddy McWard. Do you want to interview him?'

'What grounds did you bring him in on?'

'I didn't bring him in.' Kirby flustered around with a file of papers in his hand. 'He turned up demanding to speak to whoever is in charge. So that's either you or McMahon. Will I get the super to do it, then?'

Lottie stood up.

'The less he's involved in, the better. Which interview room is he in?'

Paddy McWard was standing against the wall, arms by his sides, suppressed rage filling the air. He was wearing a T-shirt, though it was freezing out, and he had a sleeve of coloured tattoos on one arm and a Celtic cross on the other. His voluminous black hair was neatly combed and his hard-blue eyes held a challenge. Lottie was struck by how handsome he looked despite his simmering temper.

She knew from the file she'd read that he was six foot three, thirty-six years old and had two arrests for disturbing the peace. Neither had resulted in a court appearance but both had been logged on PULSE.

'Mr McWard. What brings you here?'

'*You* do.'

'What can I do for you?'

'You can find the bastard who beat the shit out of my wife.'

'Sit down, please.' Lottie didn't like the air of intimidation exuding from him.

'I want to stand. You sit if you like.'

'Mr McWard, this is my interview room. I can bring in a couple of uniforms if you wish.' Lottie smiled sweetly and directed him to the chair on the opposite side of the table.

When he had reluctantly seated himself, she sat down too. He smelled of aftershave and his clothes were fresh. She had dealt with many members of the travelling community during her years in the force, and she knew they were basically good people trying to live their lives the way they wanted and protect their heritage and culture. Like any community, there were always troublemakers, giving everyone a bad name.

'So, Mr McWard, where've you been all week? We've been looking for you.' She folded her arms and rested back in her chair. The effect made him lean forward.

'What are you on about? I came here to talk to you, Missus Detective. You don't be going on about shite, asking me the questions.'

'Your wife was assaulted and you were nowhere to be found. Obviously we want to speak to you about it.'

'And I want to talk to *you* about it.'

'Go ahead.'

'What are you doing to find the bastard who did it? Tell me that.'

'We've carried out forensic analysis of the scene and interviewed everyone on the site, and—'

'This wasn't my own people. This was an outsider.'

'How did they gain access?'

'Through the front gate.'

'I noticed that all the homes, and even the caravans, have cameras. No one was willing to part with their tapes. That's not very helpful.' Lottie had garnered this information from Kirby's investigation.

'There was nothing to see. I checked them out. I want justice for my Bridie. She's a nervous wreck since the attack.'

'Why do you think she was so viciously assaulted?'

'What do you mean by that?' He leaned away from her, eyes wary.

'Are you involved in anything that could have made your wife a target?'

He shoved back the chair and stood up, towering over her.

'This has nothing to do with me.'

Lottie remained seated, unmoving. 'Where were you Monday night and Tuesday morning, Mr McWard?'

'None of your business.' He sat down again.

'You're aware that we found a young woman's body in the cemetery. Your wife heard her screaming. But you weren't at home. So where were you?'

'It's none of your business where I was. You've no right to be asking me these questions.'

'Will you consent to a DNA test?'

'A what? Are you out of your mind?' He slapped the table.

'Can you account for your whereabouts every day and night for the last week?' Lottie kept her voice soft and even.

'This is harassment.' He grimaced, then his lips curled in a smirk. 'Ah, I know. Because I'm a traveller, you think you can harass me.'

'Everyone is being asked the same questions. But you interest me because you don't seem to be very forthcoming with information. Are you going to tell me where you've been and what you've been doing?'

'No, I am not. And if you're not bothered to get off your bony arse and do something about the bollocks who beat my wife, I'll do it myself.'

He hurled the chair back against the wall and strode to the door.

'Mr McWard?' Lottie mustered up her calmest voice. As he turned with his hand on the handle, she said, 'I'll be watching you.'

He flung the door open and stormed out.

Boyd poked his head in.

'Cynthia Rhodes wants a comment from you.'

'Tell her to piss off.'

CHAPTER FIFTY-SIX

Lottie walked out to the reception area, opened the door to the left of the desk and switched on the light. It was a mirror image of the interview room she'd just left, only smaller. Used mainly for applicants filling up forms. It just about held two people, uncomfortably.

'I'm very busy, as you can imagine,' she said, sitting down and folding her arms.

'I won't take up much of your time. Thank you for agreeing to talk to me.' Cynthia Rhodes pulled out a chair.

'I haven't agreed to anything. Just ticking a box.' Once she'd said the words, Lottie knew she'd succeeded in ruffling Cynthia's journalistic feathers. Paddy McWard's fault. She had yet to digest the interview and identify the source of his anger.

'Will I sit?' Cynthia asked, placing her phone on the tiny desk and opening the recording app. She pushed her black-rimmed spectacles up her nose.

'Two minutes. That's all I can spare.'

'I want to do a feature for the weekend news.'

'Feature on what?'

'The tenth anniversary of the disappearance of Lynn O'Donnell.'

Lottie whistled out a sigh.

'I wasn't based in Ragmullin at that time.' She was determined to say as little as possible.

'Could I speak with Superintendent Corrigan, then? I believe he was the SIO back then.'

'He's on sick leave at the moment.' Come on, Lottie wanted to say, you know that already. Wasting precious time. She had two bodies and a potential missing person to deal with. 'However, we do need media help in seeking information from the public about the last movements of Elizabeth Byrne. That's the young woman we found murdered in—'

'I got the press release and I'm well aware of your current work-load,' Cynthia said.

Lottie raised her eyebrows. 'My workload? What's that got to do with you?'

'I had a chat with David.'

David who? Shit. McMahon! Lottie crushed her nails into her hands. 'Maybe *David* can help you with the ten-year-old case then.'

'He said to talk to you.'

'Did he now?' The meddling bastard.

Cynthia was still talking. 'I want to see if Ragmullin gardaí missed something at the time. Especially now that I've discovered that Elizabeth Byrne vanished from a train. Same as Lynn O'Donnell.'

Lottie sighed with relief. At least Cynthia had no inkling about the possible disappearance of Mollie Hunter, also last seen on a train.

'And then there's Mollie Hunter,' Cynthia said with a smile that verged on being sly.

'For Christ's sake,' Lottie exclaimed. 'For your information, we have no missing person report on Mollie Hunter. You've been misinformed.' She stood up and opened the door.

'Shut the door for a moment.'

'What?'

'I said shut—'

'I heard you,' Lottie said, 'and I think it's time you left. When the press office has information to share publicly, I will make sure you are included on the email list.'

'I'm already on the email list. But don't you think it a bit uncanny that almost exactly ten years after Lynn vanished, suddenly you have the murder of a young woman of similar age, and another missing? All disappeared after getting the evening train from Dublin to Ragmullin. Maybe the killer is back on the trail again. Stalking and killing young women. That could spark panic among commuters. To the detriment of a train station already under threat.'

Closing her eyes, Lottie counted to three and opened them again, hoping Cynthia had scuttled out the door. No such luck.

'If you start spreading malicious rumours, causing panic in Ragmullin, I will hold you responsible.'

'I don't mind causing panic if in the process I help save the life of some other unsuspecting young woman. Do you have anything to add?'

'About what?'

'The O'Donnell case?'

'Listen here, Ms Rhodes, you and I both know that the chances of finding Lynn O'Donnell are virtually non-existent. For all we know, the girl was murdered back then and her body dumped in the Dublin mountains. If that is the case, she'll never be found, unless by accident. So please don't go raising the hopes of that poor family when you know there is none.'

'Anything else?'

'Get out.'

'Oh, I'm leaving, but remember, Detective Inspector Parker, your past will catch up with you in the end.'

Lottie stood, open-mouthed. 'What the hell do you mean by that?'

'I think you know right well. The apple doesn't fall far from the tree.'

CHAPTER FIFTY-SEVEN

Lottie pounded into her office and banged the door shut. She kicked off her boots, swung her feet up on the table and opened the Lynn O'Donnell file. As if she hadn't enough to be doing! Cynthia Rhodes had crawled under her skin and was scratching like vermin trying to suck blood from her veins. She didn't even know the woman and already she hated her.

Before starting on the file, she rooted around in a drawer for a pill. She needed something to slow down her angry heart. Something to ward off the demons of her past. What had Cynthia meant? Was she referring to the fact that Peter Fitzpatrick, Lottie's dad, had been a bent guard? Did she think Lottie was the same? Surely not. Or was it to do with her biological mother? But no one knew about her. Did they? She found a pill and swallowed it dry, gagging at the chalky aftertaste. Was she turning into a replica of her addict mother? God, she hoped not.

Her memory of the file's contents was hazy, the result of a combination of things from last night, including vodka. Shit. She sensed another headache. God help anyone who came in the door.

She focused her eyes on the photograph stapled to the inside cover. Auburn hair, curled around the shoulders. Sky-blue eyes full of life. Lips turned slightly upward in a mischievous smile. Lynn O'Donnell appeared younger than her twenty-five years, and Lottie wondered if it was a photograph taken some time before she vanished.

The file made for sombre reading. The last sighting of the young woman had been on the 5 p.m. Dublin to Ragmullin train. Jimmy Maguire, the station porter, had given a statement saying he came across her after she had disembarked. She had dropped her handbag and he helped her pick up her belongings. After that ... nothing. She simply vanished. There were no CCTV cameras around the station ten years ago, and very few in the town, and even after an intensive investigation the gardaí still had nothing to go on. Lottie could see plenty of areas that hadn't been explored at the time. Things that would be done differently today.

Superintendent Corrigan had written copious amounts of notes at the back of the file. As she scanned them, she remembered the cases of other young women who had disappeared over the years. Some of them had been found. Murdered. But there were still too many unaccounted for. Too many families without answers. Like the O'Donnells.

If there was a remote likelihood that the current cases were linked to Lynn, then Jimmy Maguire would have to be interviewed again. The O'Donnell family members were listed. Maybe she'd have a word with them also.

And as she reached for the phone, an uneasy shiver warned her that Mollie Hunter needed to be found soon.

Before she could lift the phone, it rang.

Jane Dore.

Lottie robed up and joined Jane in the mortuary.

'Thanks for doing this so quickly, Jane,' she said.

'Slow day.' The pathologist opened a file on her computer. 'I have the prelims. A woman in her mid thirties. Extremely undernourished. Verging on malnutrition, I'd say. As you saw, her head had been shaved, but the follicles tell me her hair had turned grey. Blue eyes, and even though you wouldn't think to look at her now, she was Caucasian.

'She'd been wrapped in some kind of plastic, possibly heavy-duty bin bags. With that and decomposition, it's difficult to pin down time of death. Plus, the use of bleach on the body doesn't help. But the presence of flies and maggots in this cold weather makes me think she's been dead at least a week. Possibly longer. And she may have been held indoors, somewhere warm. Too many unknown variables, I'm afraid. I've further analysis to do, so I may know more later today.'

'Okay.'

'I've taken samples of her DNA, which you should run through the national missing persons database. It might be the only means of identification.'

'Did you do toxicology screens?'

'Yes. On my initial analysis they came up negative, but I've sent them off for more detailed tests.'

'Can you tell me how she died?'

'As I said before, no visible wounds, apart from the obvious vermin activity. The body had been outdoors for around a week. You know I hate making assumptions until I've completed all the tests, but I'm inclined to go with natural causes.'

Lottie widened her eyes. 'But she was wrapped in plastic and dumped in the woods.'

'That suggests foul play after death. At the moment, I can only say that cause of death is inconclusive.'

'Anything else?' Lottie said. 'I'm grasping at fast-disappearing straws now.'

'She'd given birth.'

'Recently?

'No, I'd say five to ten years ago, if not more.' Jane busied herself with a sheaf of paper.

'Any hope of DNA?'

'For the baby? No, but if you find the child, I may be able to match it to the mother.'

'Thanks, Jane.'

'I'll let you have the full report as soon as.'

'And you'll call me if you find anything else?'

'I will.'

Lottie was at the door when Jane said, 'Oh, one other thing.'

Lottie turned around.

'Almost forgot, as I was saving this bit for last. I found a silver Claddagh ring embedded in the junction between the oesophagus and the stomach.'

'What?'

'You heard me. It had been lodged there for some time. Perhaps she swallowed it or it was forced down her throat. But she never passed it.'

'That's terrible. Any inscription?'

'I'll photograph it and send it to you.'

Lottie left Jane to her Dead House. On the drive back to Ragmullin, she wondered who this mystery victim was, and how someone who might have died of natural causes came to be left out in the woods by the lake. And why had she swallowed a ring? Where was her child? Alive or dead? Then another thought struck her. Why had the victim's head been shaved?

CHAPTER FIFTY-EIGHT

Grace's course finished early. As she left the building, she looked around her. She could feel eyes on her back. She leaned against the wall, letting the rushing crowds file past, then took a deep breath and sniffed away her fear.

She had thought of nothing all day but Mollie. Irrational behaviour was foreign to her. She was a creature of habit. Now she wanted to help a girl she hardly knew. If only she could be brave, if only she could shed her anxiety for a few hours, maybe she could confront the man she'd seen on the train. Would she be able to do that? No, of course not. Yes, Grace, you can. You will.

Shouldering her bag, she tied her scarf around her neck with shaking hands. She really needed her anxiety medication. Taking her first step away from the building, making herself as small as possible to avoid contact with people, she headed for the station. If he was on the train, she was going to approach him. And get him to tell her where he'd taken Mollie.

She headed down Talbot Street, turning her head every few seconds.

Checking.

*

On her return from the Dead House, Lottie bumped into Detective Maria Lynch.

'Sorry about this morning, boss,' Lynch said.

'Not feeling well?' Lottie said. 'Come into my office.'

'I'm a bit nauseous. Mainly in the mornings,' Lynch said when she was seated.

'You're pregnant?'

'I am. I'm thirty-five. I already have two young children and I didn't want any more, and—'

'Congratulations.'

'Thanks.'

'I'm genuinely pleased for you.' Lottie caught the glimmer of something in Lynch's eye. 'You're not happy about it?'

'It wasn't planned. I'm still getting used to the idea. The reason I'm telling you this early is that I may miss a few mornings, but I'll work later in the evenings to make up for it.'

'Don't worry about that.'

'I don't want any preferential treatment. No desk duty.'

'Me? Give preferential treatment? You should know me by now.'

Lynch laughed and the tension eased out of the room. 'Now that the surveillance job has been abandoned, I'll have more energy.'

'Great. Your first priority is to get Matt Mullin in for interview. Can you work on that?'

'Will do. Thanks, boss.'

When Lynch was gone, Lottie felt relieved. She thought it might be the effects of the pill she'd taken earlier, or maybe it was just that she could knock Lynch off the list of people out to get her.

She had just closed the door to try to get a few minutes' peace when there was a knock and Gilly O'Donoghue walked in.

'What's up?' Lottie said, noticing the young woman's pallor. Surely she wasn't pregnant too?

'I want to officially report Mollie Hunter as a missing person.'

'I agree with you, but tell me what's changed.'

'I contacted her office. She works in the Department of Social Welfare on Townsend Street in Dublin. Her line manager says she very rarely misses work. If she has to take a day's sick leave, she always rings in. She hadn't booked any annual leave, so he was particularly worried when he heard she hasn't been seen since Wednesday.'

'Did he confirm she was feeling okay when she finished work on Wednesday? Have you spoken to her colleagues?'

'Not in person. But her manager rang me back and said no one has heard from her. He thinks it's odd.'

'In light of the murder of Elizabeth Byrne, go ahead and file the report. Establish Mollie's last known movements. Talk to anyone who saw her at the station.' This was counteracting McMahon's direct order. Another collision course in the making.

Gilly said, 'I've already put up a personal Facebook appeal, so I'll do an official call-out too. And I'll have a word with Boyd's sister, Grace. She travelled on the train with Mollie on Wednesday.'

'Do that, and keep me up to date on your progress. We need to find Mollie.' As the door shut on Gilly, Lottie whispered, 'Alive.'

CHAPTER FIFTY-NINE

Lottie gathered the team in the incident room for an impromptu meeting and filled them in on the post-mortem details from the victim found at the lake.

'We need to find a match for her. Kirby, run her DNA through the national database. See what turns up.'

'Will do.' Kirby scribbled on his growing to-do list.

She pinned up a photograph and pointed to it. 'This is a silver Claddagh ring. It was found by the state pathologist in the victim's intestines. Take copies of it. See if you can find out where it came from.'

'Jaysus,' Kirby said.

'It might be a clue to who she was. I can't see any engravings on it, so it may be a lost cause. All the same, we're good at fighting lost causes around here.'

A whisper of laughter before Boyd said, 'It's a symbol of love.'

'What is?'

'The Claddagh. My father gave one to my mother as an engagement ring. It can mean that you're spoken for. It's a traditional ring but nowadays it's mass-produced.'

'That's not much help to us, but bear its significance in mind.' Lottie studied the picture before continuing. 'This victim had a child some years ago. We're looking for a thirty-five-year-old mother. Someone has to be missing her. Her child? Her husband or partner? The man who gave her the ring, perhaps?'

'Someone local?' Boyd piped up.

'The only missing persons we've had in the last couple of weeks are Elizabeth Byrne and now Mollie Hunter,' Lottie said. 'We know Elizabeth is dead and we have her body, but Mollie's age doesn't fit this body and as far as we know she had no children. Therefore it is someone else.

'Mollie Hunter is now officially classed as a missing person. Garda O'Donoghue is organising an appeal for sightings, and we need to track her phone and trace her last movements. See if anything in her life overlaps with Elizabeth Byrne's. It can't be a coincidence that both women were last seen at Ragmullin station. Boyd, you get whatever CCTV footage is available from the station for Wednesday.'

'I'll do my best.'

Lottie patrolled the perimeter of the incident room. 'I don't believe in coincidences, so we need to find Mollie before she ends up like Elizabeth in someone else's grave.'

'Should we warn rail passengers?' Boyd asked.

Lottie cringed, thinking of Cynthia Rhodes' threat. 'I know you're worried for Grace's safety, but I don't think that's warranted at the moment.'

'It's not just Grace I'm worried about.'

'As it stands, we don't know where Elizabeth was actually abducted from. It could have been on her walk home. But we'll put uniforms on the platform this evening. Then we have the weekend to make headway before the Monday commute begins again. All leave is cancelled. Who was taking a second look at Monday's CCTV from the station?'

Kirby raised his hand. 'I was. It's very blurred. No one jumps out at me as recognisable.'

'Check it again.' She pointed to Matt Mullin's photo on the board. 'He is a wanted man. Find him.' Pausing in front of Kirby, she said, 'Any word on John Gilbey?'

'The gravedigger? I interviewed him again and he's in the clear.'

Lottie stopped in front of the incident board. 'Who has the list of names of those who run at Rochfort Gardens?'

'I have it.' Boyd waved it.

'Is Mollie Hunter on there?'

She tapped her foot, waiting as Boyd traced his finger down the list.

'I think this signature is hers.'

'Show me.' Lottie took the page and squinted at it. 'I thought I asked for someone to type this up. Jesus, I can't read it. Whereabouts is her name?'

Boyd pointed to it.

'You're right.' She glanced up at him. 'Has any progress been made with contacting the people on the list?'

'We haven't addresses for all of them.' Boyd dropped his gaze. 'So it's a bit difficult.'

'I don't want to hear about difficult. I want answers.'

'We started on it, but now we have this new body and—'

'Allocate the list to a uniform. Get Gilly O'Donoghue to do it. Which reminds me, Gilly wants to have a word with Grace to see what she remembers about meeting Mollie on the train.'

'I'm not bringing my sister into this.'

'Make some arrangement with her.' Lottie let out an exasperated sigh. 'Do I have to think for you now?'

'Just as well you can't.' Boyd folded up the list and marched out of the room.

*

He was staring at her. Standing there leaning against the door of carriage C. Beads of sweat appeared on her forehead, and her hands were slick and clammy. She took deep breaths, but in the end, she had to use her inhaler. Thank God she had that with her. At least when she got back to Mark's place she could grab her pills and maybe sleep for a bit. That sounded like heaven. She put her inhaler back in her bag, and when she looked up, he was standing in front of her.

'I think you should sit down,' he said. 'You don't look very well.'

She hadn't noticed him moving. Hadn't noticed the train stopping at Maynooth. Hadn't noticed there were now plenty of seats available.

'I … I'm okay,' she stammered.

'Sit,' he commanded.

She was sure he could see her heart hammering against her chest. Lowering herself onto the seat behind her, she perched on the edge, clutching her bag on her knee. The woman beside her was asleep, head resting against the window, earphones in, oblivious.

He sat down opposite her. Grace held her breath. He leaned over the narrow excuse for a table and said, 'Don't be afraid of me. I can help you.'

Her eyes widened and her mouth seized up. 'What do you mean?'

'I saw you this morning. And yesterday. Looking for your friend.'

She didn't have to ask what he meant. She knew.

'Mollie,' he said. 'She's in a spot of bother. I think she would be happy to see you, even though she told me not to tell anyone.'

As he continued to stare at her, Grace felt her chest tighten and scoured her bag for her inhaler once again. 'Where is she?'

'If you promise not to make a fuss, I'll contact her and find out if she wants to see you.'

Mark wouldn't be at the station to pick her up. What was she going to do? Go with the man and find Mollie, or scream blue murder? Maybe for once in her life she could be brave. She took a quick puff of air and let the thought take root in her anxiety-ridden brain. She would go with him and find Mollie.

'Okay,' she whispered.

CHAPTER SIXTY

'Are you not supposed to be at the train station?' Lottie checked the time on her phone. 'To pick up Grace?'

'She's heading home to Galway for the weekend.'

'You'll get a break so,' she said. 'Gosh, this day feels as long as a week. I need a coffee. Join me?'

She grabbed her mug and made her way to the makeshift kitchen. Katie should be in New York by now. Still no word. She'd give her an hour, then she was going to ring to make sure they were okay.

'What the hell?' she said. 'Who stole my kitchen?'

The corner was bare, except for pipes with insulating tape around copper nozzles sticking out of the wall.

'McMahon,' Boyd said, stifling a snigger.

'It's not funny.' Lottie turned on her heel and stormed back down the corridor.

'Here, give me your mug,' Boyd said. 'I'll get you some from the canteen.'

'Don't bother. I'm going home.' She went to get her jacket.

Kirby piped up, 'You know what you both need?'

'I know you're going to tell us,' Boyd said, sitting down at his desk.

'A couple of pints.'

'I'm not going drinking with you, Kirby, not on your life.'

'You can come too, boss, and you, Lynch.' Kirby twirled an unlit cigar between his fingers.

'Sorry, I'm not drinking,' Lynch said, keeping her gaze studiously focused on her computer screen.

'Never known you to turn down a drink from Kirby before; not that he offers too often,' Boyd said.

'I'm going home,' Lottie said. 'It's been a long day and I've to be at Rochfort Gardens early in the morning to check out those runners. And you lot better be here bright and early.'

'I might be a bit late,' Lynch offered.

'No worries.' Lottie dragged her jacket over her shoulders and picked up her bag.

Boyd followed her out to the corridor. 'Fancy a bite to eat?'

'I'm starving, but I've a family to feed.'

'Another time maybe?'

'Whenever that may be.' Lottie let the door close behind her.

✳

When the train stopped at Ragmullin station, Grace walked meekly at his side through the throng on the platform. She noticed the uniformed gardaí patrolling up and down and thought of screaming out, but dismissed the notion. She wanted to see Mollie, didn't she? Mark would be proud of her if he could see how brave she was being. Even though he still thought of her as his little sister, she was almost thirty. Time for her to stand on her own two feet.

He had her elbow in a vice. Every muscle in her body blared at the physical contact. She tried to shrug off his hand but he held firm.

At the rear of the station, he opened a car door. 'Won't be long now.'

'What won't be long?' She stalled, uncertainty eroding her earlier bravado.

'Until you see your friend.'

'I thought you had to ring her first,' Grace said.

'I'm sure she won't mind.'

She sat into the car. 'Where are we going?'

'Only a couple of miles along the road. Mollie's nice and comfy and I'm sure you'll both have a great chat.'

Grace clipped on her seat belt and stared out of the window at the street lights vanishing as he drove out of town. She bit her lip and tightened her fingers around the strap of her bag. Maybe this wasn't such a good idea, her inner voice warned. Too late now.

*

Matt Mullin parked his car around the back of the house. He could see his mother in the kitchen preparing a dinner he didn't want to eat. She mustn't have heard him pull up; she didn't look out the window.

It was no good. He couldn't handle going inside. She'd question him about work. No, I haven't got a new job, Mother. He switched the ignition back on and drove slowly around the house and down the avenue.

He missed Elizabeth. Why had things gone so wrong? It was all her fault. Why had she cut him off? Changed her number, closed down her social media accounts. He couldn't find out what she was up to. But then, just before Christmas, she was back on Facebook. She was reaching out to him. She wanted him home. He'd been sure that was the reason for her going back online.

And then it had all fallen apart again.

He was such a fool. He gripped the steering wheel so hard, his knuckles were in danger of piercing the skin. And he was driving too fast. He slowed down. No point in attracting unwanted attention.

At the Dublin bridge he waited for the lights to change. He looked at the town nestled below him and the canal flowing beneath the bridge. Should he abandon his car and jump into the murky water?

The light flicked to green and he dismissed the thought.

*

Keelan had put Saoirse to bed early, read her a story and then tidied the kitchen before Cillian arrived home. The row started over nothing.

'You spend more time fussing over Saoirse than me.' Cillian kicked off his shoes and put his feet up on the coffee table.

'And you spend more time giving out about your brother than looking out for him.'

'What's that supposed to mean?'

'Have you not noticed how down he is lately?'

'Down? And how would you know that?'

'I saw him wandering around town. He seems … depressed.'

'Our sister vanished off the face of the earth and it tore our family apart.' He dropped his feet from the table and leaned over with his hands dangling between his legs.

'I know that. I've lived through it with you for the last five years.' Every year it was the same. The week before and the week after the fourteenth of February. And she knew the roses he presented her with annually were really in memory of the sister he had lost.

'Yeah, but you don't know what it did to me, to my family, at the time.'

She placed Saoirse's train book, which Cillian had bought her, back on the shelf and turned to him. 'That's because you won't speak to me about it. You just bottle it all up. Then every so often the cork explodes from the bottle and I have to suffer your temper.'

'I said I was sorry about the plates. Did you buy a new set?'

'I'm not talking about the damn plates. I'm talking about you and me. The way you treat me. It's not right, Cillian. I think you need help.'

He shot up from the chair and grabbed her by the arm. 'Don't you dare say that. First you say my brother is depressed, then you lay all the blame on me.'

'You're hurting me.' She tried to wriggle out of his grasp. He tightened his grip, his fingers digging into her skin, right through to the bone of her arm.

'Hurting? I can hurt you a lot more. Would you like that?'

'Stop!' She snapped his fingers away from her skin one by one. She knew it was anger that drove her strength. He stood looking at her slack-jawed.

She said, 'I've lived with the ghost of your sister haunting me every day since I met you. I thought by now you would have exorcised her spirit. But it gets worse. Every fucking year it gets worse. I've just about had enough of it. Do you get me?'

And then the tears started. She didn't want to cry. She knew it would incense him further. Clenching her fists to keep from lashing out at him, from tearing her nails into his pathetic face, she turned away. Took out the train book and began ripping out the pages, one by one. She had no idea why she was doing it, taking a rise out of him, when he could explode at any minute.

His phone rang, and when he hung up, he said, 'I'm going out.'

She watched him pulling on his shoes. 'Where?' He didn't answer. Helplessly she said, 'Take your coat.'

At the door, he spun round. 'You sound more like my mother every day,' he snarled.

The slam of the door woke Saoirse, and as Keelan rushed to her daughter's room, she wondered if she now possessed the strength to leave Cillian O'Donnell once and for all.

CHAPTER SIXTY-ONE

The house was unnaturally quiet when Lottie arrived home. Then she remembered that Katie and little Louis were in New York. She pushed the buggy out of the way and wheeled it into the sitting room, glad Katie had the light stroller with her.

'Sean?' she called up the stairs. 'Will you fold up this buggy, please? And where is Chloe?'

Without waiting for a reply, she went to the kitchen and began pulling things from the refrigerator to prepare dinner.

'Can we get takeaway?' Chloe said, walking in behind her.

'I've to cook something for your granny, so I may as well cook for us all.' Lottie turned to find Chloe lounging against the kitchen door, pulling at her sleeves.

'What's up?'

'Nothing. We're on mid-term next week, and with Katie and Louis away I was wondering maybe we could go somewhere for a few days.'

'I'm in the middle of a murder investigation. I can't just up and leave.'

'It's always about you, isn't it?'

'Sorry, Chloe, I didn't mean—'

'Forget it.'

'I'm sorry.' She was talking to fresh air.

Sean shouted from the sitting room, 'I haven't a clue how this thing folds up. I'll just push it in behind the couch.'

Her phone rang. 'Yes, Mother?'

'I roasted a chicken for myself. There's some left over if you want it.'

'No, it's fine. We're getting a takeaway.'

She hung up before her mother could lecture her about the importance of healthy eating for the development of teenagers' brains. At least Rose seemed to be on the mend.

Chloe appeared at the door. 'Will I ring for food, then?'

'Yeah, do.'

But Lottie didn't feel like takeaway. She felt like going out. Somewhere she could get a drink without Chloe finding out.

She rang Boyd.

CHAPTER SIXTY-TWO

The three men were sitting in the kitchen. The doorbell pierced the silence. Donal got up to answer it.

Cillian eyed his brother across the table. Finn dropped his head and Cillian smiled. He always did have the upper hand where his brother was concerned. His father returned with a woman behind him. Cropped curly hair and black-rimmed spectacles. She was about forty years old. Not much to look at, he thought.

'This is Cynthia Rhodes. She's from the telly,' Donal said.

'Hi, I'm pleased to meet you all.' She shook hands and sat down uninvited.

With the four of them seated around the table, Cillian said, 'Are you going to tell us what this is about?'

'I don't like dredging up sad memories, but I want to do a feature for the news on the tenth anniversary of Lynn's disappearance. It might rekindle an interest in her case.'

'I'm not so sure,' Donal said.

'Do you mind if I record this.' She placed her phone on the table, with its recording app open.

'I do mind,' Cillian said, folding his arms. She took a notebook out of her bag. 'And you can put that away too.'

'Okay.' She put her bag on the floor. 'I've seen the posters around town. I thought you would like some more publicity.'

Finn spoke up. 'Depends on what you mean by publicity.'

Donal said, 'We miss Lynn so much. And my wife Maura … she died …'

Cillian sighed. He hoped his old man wasn't going to start blubbering. He'd seen enough tears to last him forever.

'I'm sorry for your loss,' Cynthia said. 'Maybe something will turn up if I do a particularly good feature? Like *Crimecall*.'

Cillian grunted. 'The authorities seem to think no body, no crime. But we've been without our sister for the last ten years, so in my mind that is a crime.'

'I agree,' Cynthia said.

'Then why are you talking to us?' Cillian said. 'Talk to the guards. See what they can tell you.'

'I tried, but they're very tight-lipped about it. I thought with the murder of a young woman last seen on the train, they would see the similarity to Lynn's disappearance.'

'I heard that. Awful it was,' Donal said.

'So, can you tell me anything that might help jog someone's memory?'

Donal stood up and busied himself folding the newspaper. 'You know the facts. My daughter worked in the civil service in Dublin. Commuted every day. And on the fourteenth of February 2006, she got the train home as usual, only she never arrived. That morning was the last time any of us laid eyes on her.'

'And you boys, when did you last see your sister?'

Cillian observed the reporter taking notes surreptitiously in the notebook on her knee. Does she think I can't see her? 'We all lived at home then. Lynn got up for the early train. There was only the one early train back then. Me and Finn, we saw her the night before, when we were going to bed. Isn't that right?'

Finn grunted, head still bowed. Cillian kicked him under the table. 'That's right,' he said.

Standing up, Cillian said, 'I think the only place you'll get all the information is from the guards. But we'd appreciate it if you could do a new appeal for information.'

He watched as she flattened one of the posters out on the table. 'This phone number, is it one of yours? Can I publicise it?'

'It's a dedicated number. For information. Not that it does much good. Hasn't rung in ten years.' Cillian looked at his father, who by now had the newspaper folded into a small square.

'Aye, that's right,' Donal said.

'Maybe my news feature will throw up some new suspects for the gardaí.'

'They never had any suspects in the first place,' Donal said. 'I'll see you out now, Ms Rhodes.'

After she'd left the house, the three O'Donnell men eyed each other. They knew there was one prime suspect who had never come under garda suspicion. They should have said something back then, but they'd never allow the family to suffer that indignity. Never.

＊

Carol lay on her side on her bed. Nausea wended its way up from her stomach and settled at the back of her throat. How had she let this happen? She was a fool. She should have told the guards that Elizabeth knew about her pregnancy and the fact that she was much further on than she had intimated.

She figured she had to talk to him soon. To the father of this child growing in her womb. He had been so nice, hadn't he? After all that had gone before. So understanding of her frustrations with her home life, her gay brother and her dumbass job. Yes, he had been nice to her. But not at the time.

Bloody hell, she thought, it's a freaking mess.

Her phone lay on the pillow beside her. She'd opened his contact details. Saved under a made-up name, just in case. You can never be careful enough, he'd said. Yeah, she knew he was married. But he had a right to know. Hadn't he?

Another wave of nausea released itself from her throat and she retched into the bowl she'd placed beside her bed.

How long was this going to last? As a cold sweat broke out on her forehead, she shut off the contact and locked her phone. Not now. She was too sick.

*

The traveller site was lit up like Christmas Eve. Paddy McWard parked his Jeep and had a good look around before entering his home.

His dinner was on a plate in the microwave and Bridie was sitting on the couch with Tommy on her knee.

'How's Tommy?' he said.

'My face is very painful, thank you for asking.' Bridie was sulking.

He sat beside her and took his son in his arms. He kissed Tommy's sweet-smelling hair, and the baby nuzzled into his chest. 'I'm sorry I haven't been here for you recently.'

'Why is that, Paddy? Why haven't you been here? Where have you been? Or am I not allowed to ask?'

'Please don't ask and I won't have to lie to you.'

'Like that, is it?' She shuffled away from him but he could see her eyes were on Tommy.

'I'm not going to hurt our son, nor you, for that matter,' he said. She was biting her lip. He knew this was a sign that she was desperately trying not to cry. 'And don't start bawling. I want you to believe that beating you got had nothing to do with me.'

'I'm sure it had something to do with whatever you're involved in. Why else have the guards been swarming around this place for the last few weeks like flies on a shite?'

'They're looking for scapegoats. Someone to blame for every fight or burglary in town. And I can tell you here and now, it has nothing to do with me.'

She inched back closer to him. 'But why would someone break in and beat me up?'

'I don't know. But I'm going to find out.' He could almost feel the heat blazing from her eyes. 'What?'

'If it's nothing to do with you, then it's because someone thinks I saw something at the graveyard. The night that poor girl was murdered.'

He handed the baby over to her and stood up. 'You leave it to me. I've got two of my cousins keeping an eye on this place, and you're not to go anywhere without bringing one or both of them with you.'

'But I did nothing wrong. It's not fair.'

'Listen here, this town is a very dangerous place at the minute, so I don't want you wandering around on your own. I can't afford to lose you too.' He pressed the code on the microwave and watched the plate turn under the light.

'How is your mother?' he asked. He had to change the subject.

'What do you mean, *you too*?' she said from behind him.

He could smell the expensive perfume he'd bought for her. He wanted to tell her everything was going to be okay. But he didn't know how to, and anyway, he couldn't tell her something he didn't believe himself.

*

They sat in a corner in Cafferty's, nursing pints of Guinness and suffering each other.

'The old man is losing it,' Cillian said.

'I reckon *you're* losing it,' Finn said.

'You can talk. I think I've just gone off my pint. Don't know why I even agreed to come here with you.'

'You know why. You wanted to escape the old man's trip into madness with Lynn's anniversary coming up.'

'He was always mad. Lynn vanishing didn't make him any worse.'

'Maybe not, but Mother did.'

'Don't mention her.' Cillian sipped his pint. The bile rising from his stomach soured the taste in his mouth.

'She adored Lynn.'

'We all did. Me more than anyone.' Cillian shrugged his chin down to his chest. He didn't want to be having this conversation. Least of all with a brother he despised.

'You're the lucky one in all of this. You have Keelan and Saoirse.'

Cillian shot his brother a look that he knew could make milk turn. 'Never, ever talk about my wife and daughter. You made your own bed. Go home and lie in it.'

Finn's jaw crunched up and down as if he was trying to speak but the words were locked in his throat.

After downing his pint in two swallows, Cillian made for the door. 'I don't know how you do it, but every time I have to spend even a minute in your company, I get the urge to kill someone.'

Outside, he stood for a full three minutes in the cold before he could put one foot in front of the other. The collision course that had been mapped out in black and white for them since the day they were born was now flashing in front of his eyes in high definition.

As the chilly air cut through his sweater, he cursed the stubbornness that had made him leave home without his jacket. He didn't want to return to Keelan. Not just yet. There was someone he would much rather be with.

He made his decision and headed for his car.

CHAPTER SIXTY-THREE

'I remember the last time we were in that restaurant.' Boyd sipped a glass of red wine.

They'd had an exquisite Indian meal and had returned to Boyd's apartment. Lottie didn't need any coercion to come in for a nightcap. Three glasses of wine in the restaurant had done nothing to assuage her thirst. She craved a bottle.

She smiled. 'It was snowing so hard it was a virtual whiteout.'

'And you had to pour me into my car and drive me home. Father Joe was sniffing around you back then.'

'That is such a vulgar comment, Boyd. He was just being a friend.'

'There are friends and … there are friends.'

'Are you sure you didn't have a second bottle of wine while I was eating?'

'Just the one.'

'Liar,' she laughed, feeling more relaxed than she should. 'Do you miss having Grace's company?'

'Nope. What's it like at yours without Katie and Louis?'

'Quiet.'

'And that's a good thing, isn't it?'

'I miss them already. I know, I know. But Chloe's being a drama queen. She wants us to go away for a few days next week because she and Sean have a mid-term break. And I put my big foot in it by using work as an excuse.'

'Knowing you as well as I do, I'd have thought you'd use lack of finance as an excuse.'

Lottie sighed. 'I couldn't play that card. Katie gave me some money before she left.'

'Katie? Where did she get it?' Boyd paused, and opened his mouth in shock. 'Tom Rickard?'

'Yes, and I'm not spending any of his dirty money.'

'I'd spend it.'

'I didn't think you'd be like that.' She sipped her wine, trying to make it last a bit longer, while eyeing the bottle on the table.

'Then again, maybe I'd just burn it,' he said.

'No you wouldn't, and I won't either. Katie will need it when she gets home.'

'How is she getting on?' Boyd rose from the couch and poured himself another glass. She held out her glass and he got the bottle of white for her.

'She sent me a text to let me know they'd arrived safely. I sent back a ton of messages but she hasn't replied yet.'

'Give the girl a chance.'

'Maybe I should call her ...'

'Don't you dare. Let her have a few weeks without you interfering.' He sat down beside her. She noticed he was closer than he had been a moment ago. She drained her glass and poured herself another. Shit, she'd better slow down.

'That's twice in the space of a few minutes you've insulted me.' She shifted to her left and was met by the arm of the couch. She knew he was smirking.

'You fancied him, didn't you?' he said.

'Who?'

'Father Joe.'

'If you keep that up, I'm going home right now.'

'I apologise.'

She felt herself slowly unwind and studied him from the corner of her eye. 'You don't look at all sorry. Actually, you look a bit pale. Are you feeling okay?'

He reached out a hand and caressed her cheek. 'I'm not feeling myself at all.'

'You're such a messer.'

But she didn't spurn his advance. A tingle of anticipation curled around the pit of her stomach, and she welcomed it. Or was it just the wine? If he kisses me now, she thought, I'll end up in his bed.

The clink of his glass on the coffee table jolted her. He took hers and put it down too, then his hand returned to her cheek. She turned to face him.

'Will I put on some soft music?' he asked.

'Soft music? Boyd, you don't even know what soft music is.'

'Can I kiss you, then?' he whispered.

'I thought you'd never ask.'

'That's the corniest line I ever heard.'

'Are you refusing—'

His lips on hers was answer enough.

*

Grace's eyes flew open. She was shivering uncontrollably. Her skin felt like it had been flayed with a knife. When her chest constricted and the pain shot around her back, she was sure she was having a heart attack. But it was just her anxiety. She couldn't have a panic attack. Not now.

The ground beneath her was damp. Through a boarded-up window, she could make out a weak stream of moonlight. Her breath quickened. This was bad. Very bad. With her hands bound to her sides, she had no way of finding her inhaler. Another few hours like this and she was sure she would die. He hadn't brought her to Mollie. She had no idea where he'd brought her after he clamped the soaked cloth to her mouth in the car.

How had she been so gullible? Maybe everyone was right. Maybe she was stupid. And now, trussed up like a piece of meat ready for the oven, she had no way to prove them wrong.

CHAPTER SIXTY-FOUR

Bridie McWard cuddled Tommy to her chest, wrapping the duvet tighter around them both. She had no idea what was eating Paddy the last few weeks. He was like a different man. Hardly ever at home. Angry when he was. Banging and shouting, upsetting Tommy. He was definitely up to something, but she was too afraid to ask. As she smoothed her baby's hair, she realised that whatever Paddy was up to, she really didn't want to know.

When Tommy fell asleep, she lifted him into his cot and returned to bed. Her head still ached from the thumping she'd got. Paddy had been so mad about that too. Maybe he was out trying to chase down her attacker.

As she settled herself in the empty bed, she felt the house shake with a violent bang. Tommy screamed in his cot. Bridie shot upwards, jumped out of bed and grabbed the baby.

Opening the bedroom door, she was flung backwards by a gust of wind. The noise deafened her and the light blinded her. She smelled something in the air, right before she felt the heat.

'No!' she screamed and tried to slam the door shut, but the flames had taken hold of the flimsy wood and she was driven back into her room, chased by the fire.

'Paddy!' she cried as she curled into a corner, shielding her screaming baby. 'Help me. Someone help me.'

The flames rushed along the synthetic carpet, tracking her foot-prints until they lapped like scalding waves at her feet. She screamed until the smoke took her voice away and the noxious gases clogged her lungs.

As she buried her face in her son's hair, folding herself into the corner, she thought she heard the sound of the banshee. And in her final moments, she understood that those screams of foreboding had not been for the girl in the cemetery. They'd been for her and her beautiful little boy.

CHAPTER SIXTY-FIVE

The street light filtering through the slatted wooden blinds was the only illumination in an otherwise dark room. Lottie raised herself on her elbow and glanced around. Where was she? What time was it? God, her head! God, Boyd!

She sat up suddenly, her head spinning, and looked at him lying in the bed beside her. His face was shrouded in darkness except for the horizontal lines of light cast from the blinds. He groaned and opened his eyes.

'Hello, gorgeous,' he said. 'What are you smiling at?'

She lay back down and curled away from him.

'Was my lovemaking that bad?' he said.

'It was sublime, but I have to apologise. I'm so out of practice.'

'You know the saying. Practice makes perfect.'

'Don't ruin the moment with your smartarse comments.'

'You're usually the one with the smart arse—'

'See. I told you. It's ruined now.'

'Let me unruin it.'

'You're talking pure shite.'

'I'll shut up so,' he said, and pulled her beneath him.

She felt the weight of his body and the freshness of his kiss. Her mind told her to stop, to go home, but her body rebelled. Her head was dizzy. From alcohol? Shit. How much had she actually had to drink? Too much.

'You're making my ears ring,' he said softly, his lips moving down her neck towards her nakedness.

'It's my phone!' She shoved him to one side and bolted out of the bed. 'Where's my phone? What time is it? Boyd! Turn on a light.'

'Hold on a minute.'

The room filled with a dim glow as he switched on a lamp. Lottie scrambled around on the floor. Her phone was still ringing. She realised it was out in the living area. Pulling a sheet from the bed, she wrapped it around herself and found her bag beside the couch. The ringing stopped.

'Shit. It might've been Katie. I hope she's okay.'

'Will you stop panicking.'

Glancing back at him silhouetted at the door, she almost abandoned her search for the phone. Almost.

As her fingers found the device, it began to ring again.

'Ah, for feck's sake,' she said, glancing at the caller ID. 'It's only Kirby.'

'I'll wring his neck when I see him. Don't answer it.'

Lottie put the phone to her ear.

CHAPTER SIXTY-SIX

Boyd drove in silence. Lottie didn't know what to feel, so she just numbed herself into nothingness and let the memories of the evening slip uneasily over her like a shroud. No good was going to come of this, she could feel it in her blood.

Kirby was standing at the entrance to the site. Two trucks were there, fire personnel hosing down the dying blaze.

Jumping from the car almost before Boyd had brought it to a halt, she said, 'I can't believe this, Kirby. I hope Bridie and her family aren't in there.'

'We've evacuated all the residents but there's no sign of the McWards.'

'Has no one seen them? Where is everyone? Can I talk to them?'

'They've been taken to the nursing home around the corner. The staff there are providing blankets and hot tea. Everyone's in shock. The faces on the poor kids. This is bad, boss, very bad.'

'You think the McWards are in there?'

'No idea yet. But they're not among the residents escorted out. I was here almost as soon as the fire crews.'

'How did you manage that?'

'I've a couple of informants who live here. One of them gave me a call. Myself and two uniforms helped everyone to escape while the fire crews got to work.'

'So either the McWards weren't at home or they were in that …' She took a step forward and was halted by the chief fire officer.

'Sorry, but you'll have to wait until it's safe to enter. There are caravans and gas cylinders around. Everything is combustible in this heat.'

Lottie nodded and turned to Boyd. He gripped her elbow to lead her away. She shrugged off his concern.

'Take me back to get my car and then return here to Kirby. Erect a crime-scene cordon until we establish what the hell happened. Contact me if you find the McWards and call as soon as it's safe to enter the site.'

The chief fire officer overheard her. 'It'll be morning before we can deem it safe.'

'All the same,' Lottie said. 'Kirby and Boyd, you coordinate the uniforms and then interview the survivors. I want to know where the McWards are, if they're not already dead.'

Even though it was after three a.m., the lights were still on in her house. Lottie went into the kitchen, but it was empty. She automatically took clothes, mostly belonging to Louis, from the washing machine and filled the dryer. Still only the one text from Katie. Maybe Chloe had heard from her.

At the top of the stairs, she noticed light filtering out from under Sean's door. She stuck her head inside. He didn't hear her. A massive set of headphones covered his ears and he was gesticulating wildly at a screen with a remote control. Opening her mouth to tell him to get into bed, she stopped and decided to let him off for one night. There was no school for a week. He'd be grand.

Outside Chloe's door, she hesitated. Her daughter was probably asleep and she didn't want to wake her, but a nerve tingled at the base of her skull, so she opened the door.

Chloe was lying in bed, propped up with pillows, her face lit by the screen of the phone in her hand. The creak of the door had alerted her and she jumped, dropping her phone. The room was plunged into darkness. Lottie flicked on the light switch.

'I thought you were out for the night,' Chloe said. 'Working. Or something. Oh, or maybe you were *fucking Boyd.*'

'Chloe!' Lottie reeled back on her heels from the venom in her daughter's voice. How the hell was she going to handle this? Carefully. Very carefully. 'We just went for a meal.'

'A very long meal, including alcohol from what I can smell.'

'Chloe, there's no need for that.'

'I think there's every need. You've been drinking. Jesus, have we to go through all this again?'

'Please. I only had the one glass.' Why was she explaining? But she knew her drinking had caused her children suffering in the past. Dear God, she didn't want to go back there again.

'Drinking with Boyd?' Chloe curled up her lip. 'And I thought he was nice. Just shows what I know.'

'It's nothing to do with him.' Lottie let her arms fall limply by her sides. Nothing good could come of sleeping with Boyd. The fire was a warning. Leave him alone, she told herself, or you'll succeed in dragging him down to your level. She had no idea how to explain things to her seventeen-year-old daughter, so she didn't even try.

She said, 'I have to work again in the morning, but ring me any time you want to talk. Please.'

Chloe pulled the duvet to her chin and eyed her. 'So how was Boyd in bed?'

'Goodnight, Chloe.' Lottie switched off the light.

*

He had left the light on. His 'treat'. Then he'd sat on the small wooden chair, staring at her. She had no idea how long he stayed there before he rose and slowly traced a line down her body with his finger. She shuddered and cringed, but he had tied her down and she couldn't fight back.

She must have passed out, because when she awoke, he was gone and she was untied. The light was still on and the first thing her eyes focused on were the bones. Laid out on the bench in the form of a skeleton. Fear obstructed her throat and congested her lungs.

Finding the bottle of water and the sandwich he'd left for her, she wondered if she should ration them in case he didn't come back. But he would be back. She knew that as surely as she knew the bones on the bench were human. She knew it from the pain he'd left between her legs. Bile swirled in her stomach.

Closing her eyes, she sucked in a deep breath of stagnant air. When she opened them again, she scanned her surroundings. Then she noticed something she hadn't spotted before. Paintings. Tiny watercolours. Pinned to the wall behind her.

She got up from the bed and gingerly tested the floor with her bare feet. It was cold to the touch. She felt weak from being cooped up. Two steps and she was beside the wall where they hung, faded and grey. Screwing up her eyes, she tried to make out the initials in the corner of one of them. But they were smudged. Even the subject matter was hard to decipher. Once more her eyes were drawn downwards to the bones that had haunted her all day.

Bones that were so small they could only belong to a baby.

DAY FOUR

Saturday 13 February 2016

CHAPTER SIXTY-SEVEN

The fire trucks were lined up on the main road and traffic was being diverted. Lottie walked onto the site. The smell of smoke and soot choked the air. Lynch and Garda Gilly O'Donoghue had replaced Boyd and Kirby. Lynch looked worse than yesterday. Lottie was glad she didn't have to face Boyd. The vodka she'd downed after her confrontation with Chloe was lodged in the pit of her stomach. The pill hadn't helped either. No, she didn't want to see Boyd.

She looked up to find Paddy McWard running at her like a bull at a matador. Tears streamed down his face, smeared by his blackened hands.

'This is your fault. Your fucking fault, you pigs.'

'Mr McWard, Paddy, I'm sorry ...' Lottie reached out to him but he swiped her hand away. He'd been nowhere to be found last night. How the hell had he accessed the site?

He kept ranting. 'Don't you dare say you're sorry. Don't even begin to talk to me. Pigs poking around brings nothing but trouble. My wife and my son. Dead. Mark my words, you'll pay for this.' He spat at Lottie's feet, then turned swiftly and stormed back to the smouldering remains of his home.

She couldn't bring herself to move until she felt a hand on her arm. Boyd.

'I thought you'd gone home?' She buried her chin in the collar of her jacket and her hands deep in her pockets.

'Couldn't sleep. Decided I'd be better employed back here.' He dropped his hand.

Had he sidestepped away from her? Shit, her imagination was in overdrive. She turned her attention to the SOCOs. McGlynn and his team were moving about at the periphery of the site, waiting for the fire chief to give them the go-ahead.

'What in God's name happened here, Boyd?' she said.

'Revenge? For something Paddy was involved in?'

'Or for Bridie talking to us?'

'But she didn't tell us anything that could point us to Elizabeth's killer, and the body was found by accident. Don't go blaming yourself for this.'

'A mother and baby. Burned to death in their own home. I can't get my head around it.'

'Don't even try until we have all the facts.'

'She was only a kid herself.' Lottie found herself thinking of Katie and Louis and the text she'd got earlier from her daughter, full of the joys.

The fire chief eventually gave the SOCOs the nod, and they began their work.

'Is Jane Dore on the way?' Lottie asked McGlynn.

'We have to locate the bodies first.'

'We're not even sure anyone was at home,' Boyd said with a shrug.

'The husband says they were here and no one else has seen them since yesterday around five.' McGlynn consulted soot-smeared notes. 'I'm fairly certain we will find the remains.'

Lottie moved away, unable to witness the sight of Paddy kneeling on the wet ground outside the inner cordon, keening. She thought of the young woman who had come to the station and had then suffered an assault in her own home. Bridie, so beautiful, articulate and intelligent. Was Paddy correct in his assessment? Had his wife made herself a target by speaking to the guards? She hoped not, otherwise they'd have a whole new scenario to consider.

She turned to Boyd. 'It must be something Paddy's involved in. And if that's the case, much as I hate to say it, we need to hand it over to another team.'

'Don't go making any assumptions yet. McMahon will have his say on it.'

'Oh no. I'd forgotten we have to pick him up before we head to Rochfort Gardens.'

She instructed Lynch to keep Paddy McWard in her sight at all times and to notify her if McGlynn had anything to report. 'And then find Matt Mullin. I'm sick of waiting for him to crawl out from under a stone when all the time he could be behind this … this … catastrophe.'

She shoved her hands into her pockets in exasperation. Or for fear that she might hit someone?

As they made their way out, the hoses were being rolled up and the fire crews were packing away their equipment. A train rumbled and slowed down on the tracks behind the site, making its way into town.

'Still no sign of Mollie Hunter?' Lottie asked.

Boyd shook his head and walked ahead. 'And I've yet to get Wednesday evening's CCTV footage from the train station. Shit.'

It was going to be another one of those days.

CHAPTER SIXTY-EIGHT

Boyd parked the car, and they made their way down the narrow incline to the visitor centre.

McMahon stopped them before they entered through the sliding glass doors. 'So that's the Jealous Wall.'

'It is.' Lottie hoped she wasn't going to have to give him a lesson in local history.

'I read up about it last night,' he said.

'Thank God for small mercies,' Lottie said.

'What?'

'You found it interesting?' She tried to cover for herself.

'A folly, built like a ruined abbey by an earl in the seventeen hundreds. He was insanely jealous and wanted to keep his brother from spying on his wife. Then he imprisoned her in the manor house.' McMahon looked around. 'Where is that located?'

'Up the hill. It's not too far if you want to take a look.' Maybe he would bugger off and leave them on their own.

'Another time.' McMahon pushed on ahead.

Lottie sighed and followed him inside. A deafening cacophony emanated from the main concourse area.

'How many do you reckon are here?' Lottie whispered to Boyd as she tried to calculate a quick head count.

'About fifty,' Boyd said.

'Are they mad? It must be minus two and they're about to go running,' McMahon said.

There was a murmur of dissenting voices.

'Quiet, please.'

Did he think he was a schoolteacher? Lottie moved up beside him.

'Most of you have already spoken on the phone with my team,' she said, 'but I have a list of fourteen people with whom we haven't made contact. The rest of you are free to head on out for your run. I really appreciate your help in finding anyone who can give us information about the murder of Elizabeth Byrne and the disappearance of Mollie Hunter.'

She took the list back from McMahon and called out the fourteen names. Other runners shuffled out of the way as they made their way forward.

'I only count twelve,' Boyd said.

'Let's get started,' McMahon said, commandeering a table and chairs.

A blast of cold air spread through the high-ceilinged area as the door opened to let the rest of the runners escape.

It didn't take long to interview the twelve. Elizabeth was known by several of them to say hello to, but no one had noticed anything out of the ordinary or anyone acting suspiciously around her. The same was true of Mollie. Lottie looked down at the two names remaining on the list, then glanced up at Boyd.

'See the two who haven't turned up this morning?'

He nodded. 'Do you think they're related to …?'

'I'm sure of it.' She gathered her interview notes and looked around for McMahon. 'Where's the super?'

'Gone to have a snoop around the big house.'

'We haven't time for this.'

'We better go find him.'

'Or maybe abandon him to his fate.'

'Now, Lottie, you can't be like that.'

She hauled on her jacket and shoved the papers into her bag. 'I can, but I don't feel like facing the consequences of his temper.'

Reaching the door, she heard her name being called. Carol came out from behind the desk.

'I was wondering if you found anything helpful? You know, from your interviews.'

'There are two people on the list who don't seem to be here today. Maybe you know them.'

'Who?' Carol wrapped her hands tight around her midriff as if fighting off a bitter wind.

'Cillian and Finn O'Donnell,' Lottie said.

The colour drained from the pregnant girl's face. Boyd reached out a hand to steady her.

'What is it?' he asked.

She shook her head and turned away. Lottie followed.

'Hey, what's up? Do you know them? They're related to the girl who went missing ten years ago, aren't they?'

Carol stopped and turned slowly. Her face was wet with tears, her lips pursed tightly. As if she couldn't trust herself to speak, she nodded, then held her hand to her mouth and ran towards the toilets.

'Being pregnant must be a bitch,' Boyd said.

'And what would you know about it?' Lottie stepped outside, letting the door slide back in his face. She didn't want to be around Boyd today. The tenderness of his caresses was too fresh and too raw, and too wrong.

✳

David McMahon parked in front of the apartment he'd been lucky enough to rent short-term at a knockdown price. On the outskirts of Ragmullin, it was surrounded by trees. Secluded. Anonymous. Great.

He smiled when he saw the car pull in behind him. Stepping out, he leaned back and waited for the occupant to join him.

'Cynthia. What a pleasant surprise.'

'You're such a liar, McMahon.'

'Have you any news for me?'

'I was about to ask you that.' She tried a coy look but he wasn't buying it. He knew what she was like.

'You want to know about the fire?' he said.

'And anything else you can fill me in on.' She took out a pack of mints and offered him one. He shook his head and waited. 'Look, David, I'm digging as much and as quickly as I can. But so far no one will say anything about her.'

'Try Detective Maria Lynch. I get the feeling they're not the best of friends.'

'Right. The fire? Tell me.'

'Not much to tell. Two dead. Mother and her baby. House gutted. All the signs of an arson attack. Have you got anything juicy for me to sink my teeth into?'

'Nothing so far. I told you I'm doing a piece on the missing O'Donnell girl.'

'So you did. An appeal for information?'

'More like a biopic of the effects on Lynn's family. I get the feeling her disappearance ripped them apart.'

'And you intend to rip them wider still?'

'No. This is a human interest piece.' She smiled slyly. 'I'm not all bad, you know.'

'Oh, I think you are.'

He pushed himself away from his BMW, wetted a finger and rubbed away a piece of dirt from the door. Then he walked towards his apartment. Lottie Parker had made a fool of him last October. He was still smarting from the rebuff he'd suffered and he wanted revenge. He wanted her face in a mire, with his shoe on the back of her neck, holding her down.

'Hey, David?' Cynthia called. 'I need something soon. I'm back in Dublin on Monday.'

'Quid pro quo.'

'Not asking me in for a coffee?' she said.

'I've already had some.'

He disappeared into the apartment wondering if Cynthia Rhodes was worth his trouble.

CHAPTER SIXTY-NINE

On Lottie's return from Rochfort Gardens, she found Jane Dore seated in her office.

'Jane! Why are you here?'

'I've just left the scene of that awful fire.'

Slumping onto her chair, Lottie said, 'You found a body?'

'Two. What's left of them.'

'Oh God, this is too much.' Lottie pulled at her hair. 'Any hope of identification?'

'DNA, possibly. An adult female and a child.'

'Bridie McWard and her baby.' Trailing her hands up and down her arms, Lottie tried to rub away the feeling of hopelessness.

'Their remains are on the way to the Dead House. I'll know more later.' Jane leaned over the desk, her petite hands joined together. 'What's going on in Ragmullin, Lottie?'

Catching the pathologist's eye, Lottie shook her head. 'I wish I knew. Any evidence of foul play?'

'The fire was started maliciously.'

Lottie flicked through a file on her desk. 'It was reported by a neighbour almost immediately. How could it burn so quickly?'

'McGlynn can fill you in on the details, but it was a fabricated house. Went up like tissue paper.'

'They hadn't a chance.'

'Did you know the victims?'

'I met Bridic a couple of times. I think she heard Elizabeth Byrne's screams the night she was murdered. And she was assaulted in her home the other night.'

Pushing her spectacles up on her nose, Jane said, 'I have some more information on Elizabeth's murder. I emailed it to you early this morning. You may not have accessed it yet. The clothes found in the skip have trace evidence of water.'

'Yes, I knew that.'

'It's a match for water found in Ladystown lake.'

'Where we found the unidentified body. Why was Elizabeth there? How did she get out there?'

'Maybe it was just her clothes. The killer may have dunked the clothes to get rid of evidence of fibres or cells.'

'Christ, this gets weirder by the minute. Had Elizabeth's body any evidence of being in the water?'

'No. And regarding toxicology, I found trace samples of chloroform. Just minute amounts, but it was there.'

'I'm going to string up the bastard when I find him.' Lottie shot up from her chair, pacing the small office before sitting on the edge of the desk. 'And the body at the lake?'

'As you may have noticed, the fingernails were bitten down to the quick. But I found traces of paint embedded in places.'

'Paint? What type of paint?'

'I don't know. I've sent samples for analysis.' Jane stood up. 'Did you find a match for her in missing persons?'

'We checked back a couple of weeks. There's no one. Only Mollie Hunter, and she was around up to Wednesday as far as we can determine. Plus she doesn't fit the age profile.'

'Did you cross-reference on the national database? Run the DNA?'

Lottie shot her a look. 'Of course.' But had they? She needed to double-check.

'A thirty-five-year-old woman, a mother, deceased at least a week and no one has missed her? I don't buy that, Lottie, and I don't think you should either.'

'But you said she died of natural causes.'

'Her heart stopped beating, that's the only natural thing about it. She was malnourished. No food in her system. No drugs. No clothes. No hair. Washed in bleach. Evidence of plastic sacks in the vicinity of the body. No shoes either. No indication that she walked to that location and lay down to die. Who brought her there? That's one of the questions you need to be asking.'

'And who was she?'

Jane stood at the door.

'You need to find out, Lottie. Before someone else ends up dead or missing from Ragmullin.'

While she was still assessing what Jane had told her, her phone rang. Unidentified mobile number. She answered. It was McMahon.

'Sir?'

'Keep me up to date on all your investigations. You can get me on this number.'

'I will.' *Not*, she added silently.

'Might be no harm having a chat with the O'Donnell family. I've heard that Cynthia Rhodes is doing a feature on them. She's already spoken to them, if I'm correct. Bring yourself up to speed.'

'But sir, I've too much—'

'Do it, Parker.'

'And fuck you too,' she said, when she was sure the call was disconnected.

She had enough reason to speak with the O'Donnells without trying to find out what the journalist was up to.

She flicked through the old file for the phone number.

'Boyd! Get your coat on.'

CHAPTER SEVENTY

After the detectives had left, Carol felt even worse. The nausea continued unabated, and she called her manager and went home.

She switched on her electric blanket and curled into bed, glad that her mother and father were in town doing the weekly grocery shopping. Wrapping her arms around her stomach, she tried to suppress her queasiness. How long would this last? Three months? Longer? She couldn't handle much more.

She'd have to tell him. Soon. Before it was too late. She missed having Lizzie to talk to. If she was here, she would know what to do. That thought offered her no comfort. Her friend was dead. A quiver of fear tensed her muscles. She hadn't told the guards that she also knew Mollie Hunter. Not a friend really, but Mollie had happened to be there that night. The night he had … Anyway, Mollie had helped and now she was missing.

Was this all because of her? Surely it couldn't be.

But as she lay miserably in her bed, Carol couldn't help feeling that it had everything to do with her.

*

Wind battered the walls of wherever she was being kept. Grace tried to take short, even breaths, but they came out as strangled gasps. Her eyes were gummy and a rash irritated her skin. It felt like someone had pulled a heavy sack over her head and abandoned her.

Trying to drag herself upright was impossible. She lay there, dampness seeping into her pores, ropes cutting into her flesh and her heart thumping in her ears.

It was useless to fight it. Her situation was hopeless. Mark thought she was in Galway and her mother thought she was with Mark. She was at the mercy of the man who'd brought her here.

A wave of nausea crept up her throat and she struggled not to vomit. She knew that if she did, she would choke to death.

CHAPTER SEVENTY-ONE

The terrace of houses was surrounded by a stone wall with a door cut into the brickwork. Behind it, a path led to a set of steps up to the front door.

Pushing the creaking wooden door inwards, Lottie studied the two-storey house. Most of the pebble-dash had eroded over time, leaving bare cracked concrete to face the elements. A bush, branches bare, peeked out at the side of the chimney, while a satellite dish hung lopsided from a trail of wires on the other side.

'Bit dilapidated for habitation, don't you think?' she said.

'Donal O'Donnell lives alone. Maybe he hasn't the money to relocate to somewhere, let's say, more upmarket.' Boyd quenched his cigarette and doubled up in a fit of coughing.

'You okay?' she said.

'Think I've a bit of a cold.'

'Keep it to yourself. It sounds more than *a bit*. My mother swears by honey and lemon.'

'Your mother doesn't swear.'

'Piss off, Boyd.'

She pressed the doorbell and waited, blowing hot breath into her cupped hands. The door opened.

'Donal O'Donnell?' she said.

'Yes. You must be Detective Inspector Parker. Come to the kitchen.'

He turned and made his way down the dark, narrow hall. Lottie raised an eyebrow at Boyd. He shook his head as if to say, what?

But she'd recognised the man. From the nursing home. He'd been waiting to see Kane and then, up at the glass window, he'd placed a hand on her injured shoulder. She shivered.

'You must be getting a cold now,' Boyd whispered in her ear. She pulled away from him.

The O'Donnell brothers were seated at a table. The kitchen was dull and dusty and Lottie tried to pinpoint the sour smell. The floor had either been washed with a dirty mop or it hadn't been washed in months.

'Thanks for agreeing to speak with us,' she said, and introduced Boyd. With the five of them in the small room, she began to feel claustrophobic. They all shook hands and sat down.

'Is this about our sister?' Cillian O'Donnell was tall and sleek. His black hair was brushed back behind his ears and his leather jacket covered what looked like a blue lambswool sweater, with the collar of a white shirt tight to his neck. When he'd stood to shake her hand, she noticed he was wearing jeans with the requisite tattered designer cuts at the knees.

His brother, on the other hand, had an unkempt appearance, more in line with the look of their father. His sweater sported holes in the sleeves and she was sure they were not there by design. His face was unshaven and his hair unwashed and scraggy.

She struggled to remember the question.

O'Donnell senior said, 'My daughter. Are you here to tell us something about her?'

'No, I'm sorry, I've no news on Lynn's disappearance. We're investigating the murder of a young woman. Her body was found on Tuesday morning in Ragmullin cemetery.'

Cillian shot out of his chair. 'You got us here on false pretences. We thought you had word about Lynn.'

Finn said, 'We know nothing about any murder.'

Lottie thought he'd had his nose broken at some stage in his life; the bone was crooked. His eyes were dark spots of intensity.

'Please sit down and I'll explain,' she said.

'Yes, explain yourself or I'm going to ask you both to leave,' Donal said, nodding his head, agreeing with his own statement.

He appeared to have sunk into himself. He was probably once tall and striking, but a sense of loss pressed on his shoulders like a boulder, weighing him down. A striped shirt hung loose about his skeletal body, and his jaw bones almost jutted out through paper-thin skin. She noticed he continuously screwed his hands into each other, as if the motion could lessen the pain chewing up his heart.

'First of all, I want to thank you, Cillian and Finn, for agreeing to meet us here with your father. It speeds things up greatly,' she said. 'The reason we wish to speak with you is that your names turned up on a list of people who jog around Rochfort Gardens at weekends.'

'But I thought you said the girl was found dead in the graveyard?' Cillian said. Was he taking on the role of spokesperson?

'That's true,' Lottie said. 'But we're talking to anyone who might have known her. One line of inquiry is that she was stalked, perhaps while jogging.'

'Well, you're not pinning anything on my boys,' Donal said, unfurling his hands to slap the table. 'We have enough grief in this family without you dropping more like dog shit on our doorstep.'

'I understand, Mr O'Donnell. We're merely trying to build up a picture of the deceased.'

'You'd do better to find out what happened to my daughter. Her mother went to her grave without any answers and I fear the same will happen to me.'

'Now, Dad, don't go all melancholic,' Cillian said. He twisted in his chair and faced Lottie. 'You're right, Inspector. Finn and I run most weekends. Not together. We just happen to be there at the same time.'

Placing a photograph of Elizabeth on the table, Lottie watched for their reactions. Finn folded his arms after a quick glance, but Cillian pulled it towards him and studied it.

'I'm sorry, I don't know her.' He pushed the photo back across the table.

'You sure? Take a closer look.' Boyd leaned in and shoved the photo back again.

'I told you, I've no idea who she is. There must be fifty or sixty people out there on a weekend. I go to run, not to admire the women. I'm a happily married man.'

'Me too,' Finn piped up. Was he destined to always be in his older brother's shadow?

Lottie took out another photo. 'Mollie Hunter. She is missing. Also took part in the weekend runs. Recognise her?'

Both men shook their heads. Remained silent. No other discernible reaction.

'If that's all?' Donal rose from his chair, gingerly. He looked so wan, Lottie thought the man might be sick at any minute.

'I'd love a cup of coffee, if you have it?' she said. Why on earth had she said that?

Donal mumbled, 'I've no groceries in. I was writing a list for Keelan. My daughter-in-law.' He remained standing.

Lottie knew when she was being dismissed. She'd have to talk to the brothers individually. Not give them an opportunity to band together. But they had nothing to hide, had they? As she stood, she caught sight of the photograph on the dresser, a candle burning in front of it.

'It's a decade now, isn't it?' she said.

'Ten years tomorrow.' Donal picked up the frame and ran a finger down the face in the picture. 'My pet never came home.'

'She wasn't in any kind of trouble at the time, was she? Any rows at home?'

'What are you accusing me of?' Donal slammed the photo down. The candle flickered and extinguished itself.

'Nothing at all. I read the file and wondered if Lynn had maybe wanted to disappear. Make a new life for herself away from Ragmullin.'

'Why would you even think that?' Cillian now, standing beside his father. 'What brings you to that conclusion?

'It's not a conclusion, just an observation.' Lottie eyed Boyd for support, but of course he hadn't read the file. 'Had she a boyfriend?'

'Boyfriend?' Finn said, still seated at the table, his eyes dancing balls of intensity. 'Did someone say something? Did you find out something that you didn't tell us?'

'No, no. There is no mention of it in the file. I just thought a beautiful young woman like Lynn might have been in a relationship.'

The temperature in the room appeared to have dropped at least ten degrees, and Lottie had an immediate urge to look through the rest of the house. Not just to escape the closeness of the three men, but to see if some clue had been overlooked ten years ago.

Back then, five adults had lived in this small house. Three men and two women. What had it been like? Cramped and full of hormones. Had they sat around this very table to eat meals as a close, happy family? Or was the tension she felt now even worse back then. Strings pulled so taut that eventually one snapped?

Donal said, 'My daughter could have had any man in the world. Lads were knocking down my front door wanting to bring her out. But no. Lynn was a career woman. She wanted to work her way up the ladder, to the very top. And she wasn't going to be held back by some snot-nosed Ragmullin tosser.'

'Someone from Dublin, maybe? A lad at her office?'

'My girl's life was dissected by you lot. The only thing left unknown by the end of the investigation was her whereabouts.'

Lottie gazed over Donal's shoulder at his two sons. They were standing on opposite sides of the table, glaring.

'And neither of you ever saw Elizabeth Byrne or Mollie Hunter out running?'

'Can't remember everyone we see,' Cillian said.

'Is that a no?'

'It's all you're getting. I'll see you out, Inspector.'

CHAPTER SEVENTY-TWO

Back at the office, Lottie threw her jacket on the back of a chair. 'I can't figure out whether those three men are just losers in need of sympathy or they're hiding something.'

Kirby raised his head. 'What three men?'

'The two O'Donnell brothers and their father.'

'The family of the girl that's been missing for years?'

'Ten.'

'Right.' Kirby stood and licked his fingers before attempting to calm the bush that was his hair.

'What's up?' Lottie folded her arms, thinking she could do with a ten-minute nap. The chances of that were zero.

'I've a bad feeling about Paddy McWard.'

'We're not in the business of feelings, Kirby. Facts and evidence.'

'You go by your gut, don't you?'

She couldn't argue with that. 'Go on.'

'We, Lynch and I, had been carrying out surveillance on the travelling community for the last few weeks.' He hesitated.

'Jesus, Kirby, spit it out.' She hauled herself out of the chair and headed for her office, beckoning him to follow and shut the door. 'What's bothering you?'

'I've gone back over our notes. I know we did most of our work in the housing estates, but we also covered the traveller site. He hasn't been around any night. I don't know where he goes. But my informant tells me no one else has a clue either.'

'Someone knows.'

'I get that. But he has a wife and young child …'

'Had a wife and child.' Lottie felt a shiver rattling her spine. 'Do you think he killed them?'

'No. Well I'm not sure, but I'm wondering if he was involved in something that went haywire, or he double-crossed someone and this was a revenge attack. A warning to him.'

'Some bloody warning.' She mulled it over. 'Bring him in for questioning. He may or may not have killed his family, but he's guilty of something or other.'

Kirby opened the door before closing it again. 'Lynch is gone home again. Not feeling well. She said to tell you.'

'That's fine. Let me know when McWard is here. And I'm still waiting for someone to locate Matt Mullin!'

'His photo is on social media and we've put out an alert for him.' Kirby scooted out the door.

Once she was alone, Lottie tried to get a handle on McWard. Checking PULSE, she once again scrutinised the entries under his name. Disturbing the peace. A few petty misdemeanours. Then something caught her eye. Something she had missed when she'd checked yesterday. Surely it couldn't mean anything. Then again …

She tugged the sleeves of her sweater and studied the screen. Maybe McWard had some questions to answer besides the obvious one of why his home had been burned to the ground and his family annihilated.

Boyd stopped her at the door.

'I've been going through Elizabeth's notebook.'

'The one you took from her room?'

He nodded and pointed to a page. Lottie looked over his shoulder at the words written in multicoloured gel pens, surrounded with hearts and stars.

'A bit childish for a twenty-five-year-old.'

'The notebook was from years ago. When she was a lot younger. But … here, read it.' He handed it over. 'Look at the name.' He sat back on the edge of his desk and folded his arms.

Scanning down the page, Lottie concluded it was a diary entry. 'She must have been about fifteen when this was written. It's just about school. And exams and stuff. I can't see any name … Jesus, Boyd!'

'Not Jesus, no.'

'Bridie McWard. Was she in Elizabeth's class in school? She told me she finished her Leaving Cert.'

'So, was Elizabeth a friend or a foe?'

'What's up?' Kirby asked.

'I'll read it out.' Lottie squinted at the pink writing. '"Today Bridie McWard got an A for her history essay. I'm so pleased for her. Not."'

'Not what?' Kirby asked, sticking an unlit cigar butt between his lips.

Lottie looked over the edge of the notebook at him and cocked her head to one side. 'She either means she wasn't pleased or she was going to write something else and never finished the sentence.' She flipped over to the next page. It was full of colourful doodles. The following page had a poem. She read aloud, '"He is so near, yet so far, I cannot ever go there. It is taboo. I am forever lost to his undying love. And he can never be mine."'

'That's a bit deep for a fifteen-year-old,' Boyd said.

'Unrequited love, or someone she fancied but was already taken?'

'Could be anything, but it can't possibly have anything to do with her murder. Can it?'

'But there is a connection to Bridie McWard, who is also dead. Has Paddy arrived yet?' she asked Kirby.

He lifted the phone. 'I'll check. And there's still no sign of Matt Mullin or Mollie Hunter, boss.'

'I'm going to have a quick look around Mollie's flat,' Lottie said. 'When I come back, I want McWard in the interview room, waiting to be questioned. Boyd, you come with me.'

She'd got the key from Gilly, and now she stood in Mollie Hunter's tiny kitchenette. Cereal had caked to a rock on the bottom of the breakfast bowl, and a spoon was similarly congealed.

'Not much to see,' Boyd shouted from the bedroom.

'Why didn't she share with someone?' Lottie asked, even though she thought she'd only been thinking it. 'I'm sure the rent around here is high.'

The building shook and a window rattled.

'What the hell ...?'

She pierced the wooden blind with her fingers. A train hissed along the tracks. She could see into the carriages as they sped by. It was possible the people on the train could see right back in at her.

Extracting her fingers, she let the wooden slats settle.

'No diaries.' Boyd's voice echoed from the other room.

'Young people nowadays don't write in diaries. Everything is on their phones, Facebook and ... That reminds me ...' She stood at the door and watched Boyd systematically going through the drawers of the dressing table.

'Reminds you of what?'

'Elizabeth and Mollie's phones. Not a peep from them.'

'Probably in the bottom of the canal.' With gloved fingers, Boyd held up a plastic bag with a red thong inside. 'What is this?'

Lottie shook her head and turned away. 'Sometimes you disgust me, Boyd.'

'No, I'm serious. I know it's a thong. But it doesn't match any other item of underwear in the drawer. Everything is practical and clean. This is not clean and it's the only one. And it's in a plastic bag! If she had underwear for special occasions, don't you think she'd have more than one, even a matching set?'

Returning to the room, Lottie held out an evidence bag and Boyd dropped the bag with the thong into it.

'Maybe it isn't hers,' she said.

'If it isn't hers, why is it here?'

'We'll ask her if we find her.'

'When we find her.'

'Okay, Mr Positivity. When we find her.'

Inside the front door, a line of hooks held jackets and coats. Lottie went through all the pockets and checked the soles of the shoes and boots.

'Anything?' Boyd asked, coming up behind her.

'Not even a tissue.'

'That's what struck me. Her neatness. Everything in order, in its proper place. The only items left unwashed are the cereal bowl and spoon, presumably because she might have been rushing. And the red thong.'

'Still doesn't tell us anything,' Lottie said, then added, 'But Elizabeth was fastidiously neat too. Two similar personalities?'

'What did you make of Bridie McWard?' Boyd asked.

Lottie closed her eyes, recalled the shining table and white leather sofa. 'She was a neat freak also.'

'Not like your kids then.'

'Not like my kids at all. Does it mean anything?'

'I don't think so.'

'But I think something links these three women, and we'd better find out what, because it might give us an answer.'

'Do you think Mollie is dead?'

Lottie shook her head. 'My anxiety levels are at a status red warning level, but I sincerely hope she isn't dead.'

CHAPTER SEVENTY-THREE

Lottie placed the evidence bag on the desk.

'What is that?' Gilly O'Donoghue said, her eyes widening in shock.

'You know what it is. Why did Mollie have it?'

Gilly turned up her nose. 'How would I know what kind of underwear she likes? We're not that close.'

'It was the only one. No other similar types of underwear. And it was in that plastic freezer bag. Don't you think that's odd?'

Gilly shrugged her shoulders helplessly.

Lottie persisted. 'Why did she give you the key?'

'She lives alone. Her family are in London. I believe I'm her only friend.'

'Did you have any sense that she was in danger? Feared anyone?'

'No. Not at all.'

'Then why the need to give you a key? That puzzles me.' Lottie tapped Mollie's name into PULSE. It came up blank. 'She hasn't even got a parking ticket.'

'She hasn't got a car.'

'When did she give you the key?'

Gilly thought for a moment, brushed her hair behind her ears. 'We'd been friends a good few months, but I think it was sometime before Christmas. Let me think.' She screwed her knuckles into her brow. 'It was mid December. I was pissed at Kirby because he was working on that stakeout thing. Mollie and I went for drinks and on to a nightclub. She asked if I'd hold onto her spare key in case she ever got locked out or I wanted a bed. I didn't think it odd. I just said, sure.'

'And she gave it to you that night?'

'Yes. We shared a taxi. Dropped her off first, then me. Nothing out of the ordinary. A few drinks, a dance and then home.'

'She had no other friends? No boyfriend?'

Gilly shook her head. 'Not that I know of.'

'Did she know Elizabeth Byrne or Bridie McWard?'

'Sorry, boss, I have no idea.'

'What did you talk about? When you were out?'

Gilly smiled. 'Mainly it was just me giving out about Kirby.'

'That's an—' Lottie clamped her mouth shut before her words hurt the young woman in front of her.

'An odd match?' Gilly laughed. 'You were going to say that and you'd be right. He is a lot older than me, but you know what? We click. I like him. And he's good fun to be with, so I don't care what people say behind my back.'

Lottie returned Gilly's smile and felt a motherly instinct take root. She really liked the young guard. Kirby was branded a lovable rogue, so she could understand how Gilly would be attracted to him.

'I admire you,' Lottie said. 'You're a great worker and I appreciate your help on this case. You'll make a good detective some day soon.'

A smile split Gilly's face. God love her, Lottie thought.

'Thanks,' Gilly said. 'That means a lot to me.'

'You've spoken to Mollie's family?'

'Her dad. He hasn't seen her since Christmas. From what I can gather, they're not in regular communication.'

'Have another word with him. See if you can find out anything, anything that might point us in the right direction.'

'Will do. Straight away.'

When Gilly left, the office felt darker. Lottie wondered what everyone was saying behind *her* back. About her and Boyd. She was not about to give them any reason to talk. Last night was a mistake. A nice one, but a mistake.

Kirby waved at her from the outside office.

She would have to get that glass replaced and a full wooden door installed.

Then she realised he was calling her.

'McWard is here,' he said.

After sending off the red thong for analysis, Lottie made her way to the interview room with Boyd.

'I'm sincerely sorry for your loss,' she said as she sat down in front of Paddy McWard. His jacket was flung across the table. He was wearing jeans and a short-sleeved black T-shirt.

'What are you doing about it, eh? Persecuting me won't help find the bastard who murdered my wife and son.'

'Do you want a solicitor present?' Lottie nodded at Boyd to switch on the recording equipment. 'I've some questions for you and I want you to be clear that you can have a solicitor present if you—'

'I don't want no poxy solicitor.' He folded his bare tattooed arms and leaned back in the chair. 'Get on with it.'

'Right then.' Lottie flicked to the page in her notebook with times and dates given to her by Kirby. 'Where were you last night?'

He unfolded his arms so quickly, she blinked at the sound of the smack he gave the table.

'I'm telling you here and now, you're wasting my time and yours if you think I could do something so … so horrible as to burn my family alive.'

'Just answer the question,' Boyd said.

With a sigh, McWard appeared to relent. 'I was away.'

'Come on now. I need more.' Lottie was pissed off. So far this morning, they had achieved nothing except for a red thong that probably had absolutely feck all to do with anything.

Tugging at his hair, McWard bit his trembling lip. Jesus, don't cry, she thought.

'I don't want to tell you if I don't have to. Where I was or what I was doing has nothing to do with the fire. Take my word for it.'

'I'm sorry, but that's not enough. I need to know.'

He rubbed his hand over his nose and sniffed. Dear God, the big man was sobbing.

'I loved her. Bridie. In my own way. But she never believed that. When Tommy was born, she locked me out. Not with a key turned in the door, but out of her heart. I'm a good bit older than her. And it was hard for me to be … you know … a loving husband. And the baby, little Tommy, he cried a lot. I couldn't hack it. So I escaped. Every night. I'd drive around for hours and come back in the morning or sometimes in the afternoon, and then I'd disappear again.'

'That's a load of bollocks,' Boyd said.

'It's the truth.'

Lottie didn't know whether to believe him or not. 'Give us an idea of where you drove to last night.'

'Like I said, around.'

Lottie sighed. 'You can make this a lot easier if you just tell us. Otherwise I'll have to keep you here until I can verify that you were nowhere near your home last night when it was torched.'

'You're sure it was arson, then?'

'Yes.'

'Bastards. I knew it. Just knew it.'

'What did you know?' Lottie said.

'They couldn't leave me alone.' He was twisting his hands into knots, his face screwed up. She couldn't determine if it was rage or sorrow causing him to buckle.

'Who are you talking about, Paddy?'

'You wouldn't understand.' He looked up at her, his dark eyes piercing through her. They were unreadable. He intrigued her; not in the same way as the usual criminals who sat across from her, but as a man. She had to physically stop herself reaching out to touch his hand, to tell him it was going to be okay.

'Try us,' Boyd snapped.

'If you're not arresting me, I'm going home.' McWard paused, before crumbling with the realisation that he had no home to go to.

'Did you know Elizabeth Byrne?' Lottie asked.

'Who?' A line of confusion knitted his brow before his hair fell in a black crest over it.

'The woman who was murdered next door to your home. In the cemetery.'

'No, I did not know her.'

'Did Bridie know her?'

'I don't know.' The big man folded up into himself, fingers crunching into his eyes.

There was a knock on the door and Kirby beckoned Lottie outside.

She switched off the recording device. 'Give me a minute. Would you like a coffee?'

McWard recovered some composure and dropped his hands. 'Two minutes. I'm not waiting any longer than that.' The thick tattooed arms were folded once again as he stared at a point on the wall above her head.

Out in the corridor, Lottie took the sheet of paper from Kirby's hand.

'DNA result?' she questioned.

'We found a match on the system.'

'But this sample is from …' She glanced at the name at the top of the page. 'This can't be … It doesn't make sense.'

'It doesn't make sense, for sure, but it's been checked twice.'

'Shit, Kirby. This is … I don't know. What is it?'

'Weird?'

'Yeah. Weird will do for now.'

CHAPTER SEVENTY-FOUR

They let McWard go. They had nothing to hold him on. But he was issued with a warning not to disappear again.

'I think it's a mistake letting him off like that,' Boyd said. He sat down, crossing one leg over his knee, making himself comfortable in her office.

'I don't think he killed his family. I've sent uniforms to shadow him. He's too distraught to do anything.' She showed him the page Kirby had given her. 'We have something more urgent on our hands than Paddy McWard. The body at the lake.'

'What the hell?' Boyd dropped his leg to the floor. 'Lynn O'Donnell? But she disappeared a decade ago.'

'And now she's turned up dead.'

'But that body at the lake … it was a woman in her thirties. It can't be Lynn O'Donnell. She was only twenty-five.'

'When she went missing, she was twenty-five then. But this DNA result means she was alive, Boyd. All those years, she was alive!'

'Shit. Where was she all that time?'

'I don't know, but we better find out before her brothers do.' She made her way across the small office, but her arm was pulled back as she opened the door. Boyd was standing into her space, right beside her, and staring into her eyes as she turned around. 'What?' she said.

'Sit down for a minute. You need to think this out clearly. Before McMahon gets on your case.'

Breathing out, Lottie put a hand on his arm. 'You're right. Get Kirby in here too. Then we'll try to regroup.'

She walked away from him and slumped down at her desk. She opened the cold case file. Unclipped the photograph, held it up to the light. 'Where were you?'

'Lottie?'

She dropped the photo. 'The implications of this are huge. Corrigan was the lead detective at the time. Everyone thought Lynn was dead. Only her family believed she could still be alive. The way her body was when she was found can only mean one thing.'

'What?'

'She was held somewhere against her will. Her poor father. How am I going to tell him?' She pursed her lips and gulped. This was a right mess. She'd put a hole through the cuff of her sleeve, she'd poked it so hard with her finger.

'First things first,' Boyd said. 'How are you going to tell Superintendent McMahon?'

'Tell me what?' The voice boomed as the door was opened.

'Oh, shit.' Lottie covered her face with her hands.

'Well at least the media can't blame you for this, Parker.' McMahon had convened them all in the incident room.

'As a force, we failed this girl,' Lottie said.

'Now is not the time for that kind of post-mortem,' McMahon paraded up and down at the front of the room. 'Concentrate. Review the file. Look at the evidence from the body.'

'Ten years, though,' Lottie said. 'Was she at the lake all that time?'

McMahon seemed to consider this. 'Question the geezer who reported the body, and the caravan park manager. You lot missed something.'

Lottie nodded and said, 'Prick' under her breath.

'Heard you,' Boyd whispered.

She looked up at McMahon. 'The state pathologist confirmed that Elizabeth Byrne's clothes were washed in water that came from Ladystown lake. Could her murder and Lynn O'Donnell's disappearance be linked?' As she said the words, she thought how stupid they sounded.

'There's a whole decade separating the two events,' he said.

'But only a few days separating the discovery of their bodies.'

'Who else lives at that location? I want everyone interviewed.'

'We already did that,' Kirby said.

'Do it again, because this time you're looking for somewhere this woman lived for ten years,' McMahon yelled. 'Ten fucking years under your snotty noses.'

'Hey, there's no need to abuse my detectives.' Lottie marched up to him. 'None of us here worked that original case. Superintendent Corrigan was in charge.'

'As you may know, he had surgery yesterday. There's no point bothering him with this.'

'How is he?' Lottie said.

McMahon chewed his bottom lip. 'I don't know. Perhaps you could give Mrs Corrigan a call? When you get time, that is. Don't mention this cock-up.'

'What? Right, sir, but—'

'Was there something you wanted to add?'

'Is there any chance of extra support from another division?'

'Where is Detective Lynch?'

'She's ill at the moment.'

'I'll see what I can do. In the meantime, get uniforms up to speed. Involve every last detective that works at this station. I want answers. Do you hear?'

Nods were accompanied by a blinding silence.

'Am I talking to myself? I want answers and I want them now, and the only way you're going to get them, you dozy lot, is by action. Get out of here.'

'We need to inform the O'Donnells,' Lottie said. 'Before the media get wind of it.'

'Do it. Because I can guarantee that once the media find out, they will push us into a full-on force ten gale.'

CHAPTER SEVENTY-FIVE

'Back so soon?' Donal O'Donnell led the two detectives into his home.

'Are your sons around?'

'They left shortly after you.'

'Do you think you could ask them to come back again?'

Donal appeared to shudder as he lowered himself onto a chair. 'This is it then. The bad news I've dreaded every day since my little woman went missing. You can tell me. I'll tell the boys.'

Two watery eyes stared up at her and Lottie tried not to avert her own. She was about to crush any remaining hope from the bones of Donal O'Donnell. The kettle whistled and steam rose behind him.

'Better switch that off, love. It'll keep boiling for another two minutes if you don't.'

'Do you want a cup of something?'

'No. I'm okay. Sit down.'

She hated breaking bad news to anyone. But this … this was going to kill the old man. 'You're right, Mr O'Donnell, I do have bad news.'

'Well you're hardly here to tell me I won the lottery, are you?'

'No, I'm not. It's about your Lynn.'

He began refolding the newspaper along the creases where he had folded it previously. 'What about my girl. You find her? I'm guessing she's not alive, or she'd be skipping in the door behind you.'

'I'm so sorry.'

'Don't be sorry. You didn't know her. She was my baby. Now I can finally grieve for her.'

'Are you sure you're okay?'

'Holy God!' The old man stood up suddenly and stretched his arms out wide, like he was welcoming the son of God down on top of him. Or ridding himself of Lucifer, the devil. Lottie had to stop herself squirming. 'The evil that stalks this land is living right here,' he shouted. 'Under this very roof.'

'Hey, steady on,' Boyd said.

'Sit down, please,' Lottie said.

'Piss off, the pair of you.'

'Do you want to know about Lynn?' Lottie asked.

'She's dead. What else can you tell me to ease my pain? Her bones are bare and naked of life. That's all that's left after all this time. I don't need you to tell me. I know.'

'That's not exactly the case,' Lottie said slowly. 'You see, Mr O'Donnell, the thing is, we believe your daughter was alive up to at least two weeks ago.'

The transformation was instantaneous. Donal O'Donnell fell to the floor. A loud wail shattered the silence left in the wake of Lottie's words. Then it was quiet.

*

Matt Mullin eyed his mother from under his long lashes. She had her arms folded, leaning against his open bedroom door.

'I can't cover for you any longer, Matt. They know you're here. Please, tell me what you've done. I might be able to help you.'

He closed his eyes and curled into the wall, like he used to do when he was nine. 'I don't want to talk about it.'

'If you won't talk to me, call your therapist. Are you taking your medication?'

'Go away. I want to sleep.'

'You were out all night. Where were you?'

Her voice screeched through his skull like chalk on a board.

'Will you shut up with the questions. My head is ready to burst.'

'Did you do something bad, Matt?'

He blew out a breath, opened his eyes and sat up in bed. A pungent sourness swarmed about him. Was it coming from his body, or from her? Cradling the pillow to his chest, he looked over at the woman who'd given birth to him; who had loved and tended to him all his life. And he hated every bone in her body. She was a stranger. All he'd ever wanted was Elizabeth and she hadn't wanted him.

Throwing the pillow to the floor, he pulled on his shoes and walked by his mother, nudging her angrily with his shoulder as he passed.

'Matt? Matt! Where are you going?'

Her voice trailed behind him as he ran from the house.

*

Grace tried to blink, but her eyes were still glued shut. She couldn't move.

Where was she? She tried to remember.

The train. The man.

She tried to scream, but her lips felt like they were taped shut. She wanted to cry, but no tears could escape. She wanted to shout, but her words were snared deep in her chest.

She grappled against her restraints and struggled with her reality as she drifted back to the darkness.

CHAPTER SEVENTY-SIX

A magpie eyed Lottie from a bare branch of a tree before extending its wings and flying off.

She was standing on the step waiting for Boyd to finish his cigarette. She dared not ask for a drag. Too many bad habits already. 'They're taking their time.'

'It's not gone five minutes since you phoned them. Patience.'

'I haven't time for patience. We have a mountain of work and this—'

'You want a drag?' He held out the cigarette. 'Calm your nerves?'

She declined the offer with a lie. 'My nerves are very calm. I just want to get over to the nursing home to have a chat with Queenie McWard.'

'Why do you need to do that? She's already been notified of the deaths.'

'I'm not rightly sure, but I want to establish if there was a connection between Elizabeth and Bridie. The notebook. Remember?'

'But what does it matter? It's not going to solve anything even if they did sit beside each other at school.'

'You never know.'

'Here's the cavalry.' Boyd threw down the cigarette and ground it out with the heel of his shoe. The sky had darkened and the air held the impending threat of rain.

They waited as four people came through the wooden door in the outer wall.

'You know he has a bad heart?' one of the brothers said. Cillian. The clean-cut one.

'Your father is in shock,' Lottie said. 'Otherwise he's fine.'

'Fine? Ha, you need to go back to fucking garda school.' That was the untidy one.

'Calm down, Finn.' A dainty little woman in a pink sweater spoke. Her eyes were red-rimmed. From crying, Lottie wondered, or something else?

'Are you his wife?' Lottie asked, nodding towards Finn.

'No, I'm Cillian's wife, Keelan. Sara there is Finn's wife.' She pointed to the overweight woman with hair streeling around the shoulders of a black woollen coat.

'Jesus, this is a right mess,' Cillian snapped.

Lottie recalled thinking the exact same thing earlier that morning. 'Let's go inside and see what needs to be done.'

The family shuffled through the narrow door and down the short hallway. As Lottie followed with Boyd, she noticed that Keelan had held back.

'Are you okay?'

'There are some things you need to know,' Keelan said quietly. 'But I can't talk now. This is my number, please give me a call.'

Lottie took the piece of paper from her and slid it into the pocket of her jeans. Keelan looked up with tired eyes and mouthed a thank you.

'What was that about?' Boyd asked once the woman was out of earshot.

'I have absolutely no idea.'

'Nothing new there so.'

'Shut up, Boyd.'

*

She had seen one photograph of Lynn on display in the kitchen, but as Lottie entered the living room, she walked into a shrine.

The wall in front of her was covered with photos of the dead woman. All framed, with dust gathering in the corners. She assumed the late Mrs O'Donnell, Donal's wife, had once kept them pristine and dust-free. But the room appeared not to have been used in months, if not years. The furniture was dated, floral and grimy. The fireplace was empty and a two-bar electric heater blazed from a corner after Cillian plugged it in. The smell of burning dust smothered the air in the room.

She tried to imagine how it might have been at one time. Filled with the happiness of children laughing and playing, or watching the battered old television on the corner table. But no, she didn't get that image. A shiver scurried up her spine and rested on the crest of the bones between her shoulder blades.

A hideous brown wallpaper with faded flowers was just about visible behind the multitude of photographs, and a pair of thick velour curtains hung over lacy nets yellow with age and smoke. The carpet was threadbare, so she knew the space had been well used, but she felt like it was a Dickensian room. Dark, dank and dusty.

And then it struck her. Among the photos hanging before her, she could not see one of the two boys, or of the boys with their sister. Odd. She scratched her head trying to figure it out.

The seven adults crowded into the small space and Lottie stood with her back to the mantel beside Boyd. Donal sat in an armchair, while his sons squeezed onto the sofa, bookended by their wives. Lottie was glad no tea had been offered or they'd have to ferry it in on a rota. There was hardly room to raise an elbow.

'Spit it out,' Finn said, his words laced with bitterness.

'We found a body on Thursday night. Out on Barren Point at Ladystown lake.'

'Thursday! And you're only telling us now?' Finn tried to stand up but was wedged between his wife and his brother.

'The body was that of a female in her mid thirties,' Lottie continued, trying to keep her tone sympathetic. 'We found nothing on it to allow us to make a visual identification. It was only this morning that her DNA was matched to a woman on the missing persons list.'

'DNA? What DNA?'

'Shut up, Finn.' Cillian nudged his brother in the chest with his elbow. 'Let her speak. You can ask your questions later.'

Thank God, Lottie thought. Someone talking sense at last.

'Without the DNA match, we had no reason to believe the body was that of Lynn. As you know, ten years missing usually means that the person is deceased.'

'She's deceased now,' Donal muttered.

'But it can't be Lynn,' Cillian said. 'She was only twenty-five. You say this woman was in her thirties.'

'I'm sorry but it is Lynn. We believe she was held somewhere for the last ten years.'

'Where? Where was our Lynn?' Finn said.

'We're trying to find that out.'

'Was she murdered?' He continued with his questions despite the daggers Cillian was throwing at him with his eyes.

'There's no evidence of murder. Not from the preliminary post-mortem results. It's possible she died of natural causes.'

'Nothing natural about being out at Barren Point on a cold February night.' Donal was pulling at his chin.

'It's early days yet—'

'It's a decade too late, that's what it is.'

'Mr O'Donnell, we're doing our best to get answers.'

'You didn't do your best back then; how can we believe you now?'

Lottie sighed and glanced at Boyd for help.

He straightened his back. 'The body was washed in bleach and wrapped in black bin bags, which were then ripped open, leaving her body exposed to the weather and wildlife.'

Jesus, Boyd, Lottie thought, there was no need to be so blunt. But she didn't blame him. The family were not displaying the emotions she would have expected. The overriding emotion in the room, the one she felt more forcefully than any other, was resentment; maybe anger. That usually came a couple of days later. After shock and sorrow. There was something else too. An underlying sensation that she couldn't identify. Not yet. Later, maybe.

'You're a bad bastard,' Finn shouted.

Freeing himself from the constraints of the bodies on the couch, he lunged at Boyd. His fist connected before Lottie could get her hands out of her pockets. As she moved, Cillian grabbed his brother in an armlock and wrestled him to the floor.

'Shut your mouth,' he snarled. 'You're an eejit. Assaulting a guard. What do you think you're doing?'

'I'm going to kill the fucker.'

'Boys! Shut up!' Donal stood and put a foot on Finn's back. 'You're a disgrace to your sister's memory. And to your poor mother.'

When Lottie glanced Boyd's way, he was rubbing his cheek and eye socket, glaring at the men on the floor. She placed a hand on his arm and held him back. Things were bad enough without him retaliating.

'Did Lynn have a baby?' Lottie asked.

Finn got to his feet.

She scanned the men's faces. All three registered varying degrees of the same expression. Horror.

At last, Donal spoke. 'Not that I know of. Why?'

'We suspect she had given birth.'

'One way to keep warm, I suppose,' Lottie said.

'I can think of better ways,' Boyd murmured.

She caught his grin and blushed uneasily as she consulted the typed list of names Gilly had provided. 'Anyone ever say you have a one-track mind?'

McMahon was standing at the reception desk hitting the bell. Carol O'Grady appeared from the back office. McMahon slapped his ID on the counter.

'I'd like to have a word with the joggers before they go outside. Through here?' He turned on his heel and made for the inner doorway.

'Hey, come back. I don't think that's allowed.' Carol lifted the phone on the desk. 'I need to contact my manager.'

'Already agreed.' McMahon snatched the list out of Lottie's hand. She did her best to keep her mouth shut, and just about succeeded.

The scent of freshly brewed coffee permeated the air as they made their way through the assembled heaving masses of luminous Lycra.

Boyd headed for the door on the opposite side of the large open-plan area. It led to the vast expanse of grounds. He blocked the exit as McMahon attempted to make himself heard.

'Ladies and gentlemen! Just a minute, please. Can I have your attention?'

Gradually the noise descended to a hum of mutterings before silence reigned.

'Thank you,' he said.

Lottie seethed. This was her gig, but she had a feeling McMahon was going to fuck it all up.

'My name is Superintendent McMahon and I have a list of people here with whom my detectives would like to have a few words. Detective Inspector Parker will call out your names, and we'd ask you to wait behind to speak to us.'

'This just gets worse,' he said. 'Is there a child out there some-where?'

'I intend to find out,' Lottie said. 'One final thing.' She opened the flap on her bag and took out a piece of paper. 'This was found … on the body. Do you recognise it?'

'What's that?' Donal said. 'Where did you get it? I don't under-stand.'

'It's a photograph of a sterling silver Claddagh ring. Does it mean anything to you?'

The O'Donnells remained tight-lipped, shaking their heads. A dead loss to pursue it now, but Lottie knew it meant something to them. Their faces told that story.

'Look, you're all in shock,' she said, though that wasn't the word she wanted to use. 'We'll call back later. Give you time to get your heads around this awful news. Let me know if you remember anything about the ring. Make some tea and talk to each other.'

'Tea? Tea, she says,' Finn said, his voice coming to life. 'I know what I'd like to do with a pot of boiling tea. And drinking it isn't on my agenda.'

The naked anger in his words stunned Lottie. She had to get out, and quickly. Otherwise she, not Boyd, would be the one lashing out.

CHAPTER SEVENTY-SEVEN

It had started to drizzle while they'd been inside, and the temperature had risen a little.

'I'm going to see Queenie McWard,' Lottie said. 'I'll drop you at the office. Find out what else Kirby has dug up.' She crossed the road to the car park.

'I need a doctor.' Boyd was still rubbing his cheek.

'You won't die. But if you really feel you need one …'

'That lunatic should be locked up.'

'I'll lock you up if you don't shut up.' She unlocked the car. 'Get a grip.'

Boyd stared at her across the roof. 'What's eating you?'

'Something was off in there. Did you feel it?'

'Unsettling.'

'I can't put my finger on it. But it'll come to me.'

'Right. Why did you tell them that Lynn had had a child? That's a bit of a conundrum, isn't it?'

'I wanted to see their reaction.'

She started the car and headed up under the bridge, past the train station. The traffic lights were red. The wipers swished across the windscreen, dragging scum with them, making visibility problematic.

'Those brothers were straining at the leash,' she said. 'It's like they can't stand each other.'

'Most siblings are the same.'

'I loved my brother.'

'He died when you were four. How can you remember that far back? He probably pulled your pigtails and you hated him for it.'

'How'd you know I had—'

'Just saying.'

'Well don't.'

She glanced at Boyd. His head was resting back on the seat, eyes closed, the red mark pulsing on his cheek. She wanted to reach out, to feel the tenderness of last night, but now was a different time. Now it was work. And that was the way it had to stay. Professional. Gripping the steering wheel, leaning over it, trying to see through the film of grease, she waited for the green light. She couldn't start a relationship with Boyd. No way.

'Hate,' she said.

'What?'

'That's what it was.'

'I'm a bit lost.' Boyd ran his fingers over his cheek and winced.

'The tension in that room. Among the O'Donnell family. It was more than anger. It was pure hatred.'

Raindrops trickled down the window. The cemetery looked drab and grey in the distance. Lottie went up in the elevator, then made her way along the corridor to Queenie McWard's room.

The old lady was half sitting up in bed, twiddling her rosary beads. She appeared to have aged thirty years.

'Saw the fire last night. It was one of the *teachíns*.'

'*Teachín?*'

'That's Irish for a little house. Did you not go to school? My Bridie did. Learned a lot. Got a job. Did she tell you that?' Tears rested in the hard crevices of the old woman's face. It was lined like a delta waiting for the tide to come in. 'Until that good-for-nothing proposed marriage. That was all fine, but he was suffering from a broken heart.'

'You mean Paddy?'

'Yes, Paddy. Good-for-nothing, that's what he is. Did I say that already?'

'I'm sorry to have to ask questions at this sad time, Queenie, but have you any idea why someone would want to burn down their home?'

'And murder my daughter and grandson? We are outcasts in this town …'

'I don't think that's true at all. As long as I can remember, there's been a traveller community in Ragmullin. Of course, there are the usual public order offences, but you get that everywhere and—'

'Prejudice. That's what's rife. Always has been and always will be. That's the reason the *teachín* was burned.'

Lottie sighed and stared at the ceiling.

'Don't be rolling your eyes, young lady. I may be old but I'm not blind. Not yet.'

'I was just thinking. This may have nothing to do with prejudice. I think it might be related to something Paddy's involved in.'

'Paddy's always involved in something or other. But when he married my Bridie, he promised me he was going to be good. I thought he was doing okay for himself and my girl.'

'Doing what?'

'This and that.'

'Queenie, I need to know if he was into dodgy dealings; something that brought the wrath of someone down on his family.'

The old woman tucked an elbow beneath her birdlike frame and tried to raise herself up in the bed. The scent of lavender wafted from the sheets as Lottie leaned over to assist. A hand of bones with a ring on each finger pushed her away. 'Don't need your help.'

Once she was sitting, Queenie squinted over the rim of her spectacles. 'Boxing. That's what he was into.'

'Bare-knuckle fights?' Lottie thought of Kirby and Lynch, trying to get to the root of the activity.

'Nothing illegal, so he said. Travelled the country to boxing clubs. Training young lads.'

That might account for his absences, Lottie thought.

'My Bridie was in here crying like a baby more days than I care to count. Always about him. Her Paddy. She hadn't a clue what he was up to. So I sent for him. Came in here like a lamb to slaughter, he did. I had my say and he had his.' She clamped her lips together.

'And? He told you he was teaching boys to box?'

'He did. Boys *and* girls nowadays.'

'But he was disappearing all night.'

'I know. Told me that sometimes he had to stay over. If it ran late. That's what he said.'

Lottie wondered *where* he stayed over. And why hadn't he told her all this? If it was an innocent activity, surely he wouldn't have been reticent in divulging it. She knew it was unusual for members of the travelling community to be unfaithful, but that was what she was thinking now. She'd have to get Paddy to reveal all, otherwise he was looking at a charge of manslaughter, if not murder.

'He didn't do it, if that's what you're thinking. Not this time, anyway.'

'What's that supposed to mean?'

'Don't get stroppy with me, young lady. I'm just telling it as I see it. Like I said, I'm not blind yet.'

'I'm under a lot of pressure. What with the fire, the murder in the cemetery, a young woman missing after getting the train home, and the body at the lake, it's all—'

'Missing after getting the train? That's what happened to the young lass years ago.'

'I'm talking about Mollie Hunter. She's been missing since Wednesday.'

Queenie slipped down in the bed, appearing to shrink in size as the sheet covered her bony frame.

'What is it?' Lottie asked, alarmed.

'History repeating itself. That's what it is,' the old woman croaked.

'I don't follow you.' Lottie wanted to escape out of the ward. Away from the smell of old people. Away from the creaking bones of Queenie McWard.

The old woman grabbed Lottie's hand. She almost shrieked at the swiftness of the movement.

'That girl was no good. No good for any relation of mine. But that wasn't the real story. They thought *he* was no good for her.' Queenie folded up in a fit of coughing. Foam gathered at the corner of her mouth and a bony ring-clad hand pulled at her lips.

Lottie pressed the call button for a nurse.

Medical staff filled the room, pushing Lottie to one side, and she watched as they worked vigorously on the little old woman.

'Please don't die, Queenie,' she whispered.

She had so many more questions, but it looked like she wouldn't be able to ask them. Not today.

She was moving towards the door when it dawned on her. She glanced back towards the scrum of medical staff. The silver Claddagh ring amid the gold bands on the skeletal hand.

She left the room. Left the hum of machines and the shouts of nurses and doctors. Left Queenie McWard to her fate.

Sitting in her car outside the nursing home, Lottie felt the rusting wheels of her brain begin to turn. Picking up speed. It was there. Within her grasp. She just had to think. Her phone rang.

'This better be good, Boyd, because you've interrupted my thoughts. I was getting somewhere, and now it's gone.'

'You need to get to Carol O'Grady's house now. I'll see you there.'

CHAPTER SEVENTY-EIGHT

They'd received no response from ringing the bell which appeared broken, and now Lottie was banging on Carol O'Grady's door.

Boyd's eye was beginning to yellow and bruise as a result of the whack he'd taken.

The door opened.

'Terry?' The young man's eyes were sunk in his head. Was he drunk, or high? At this hour of the day?

'Who wants to know?'

'I met you the other day. DI Lottie Parker and DS Boyd. Do you remember?'

'Nah.'

'We want to speak with Carol.'

'She's at work. Ma and Da are in town.'

'I think she's here.' Lottie ducked under the teenager's arm.

'You can't do that,' Terry and Boyd said together.

'I just did.' Lottie stood at the foot of the stairs and shouted up. 'Carol. I want to have a word.'

Footsteps sounded on the landing and Carol appeared. 'What's with all the hammering? I'm trying to sleep.'

Lottie beckoned the young woman down the stairs. 'Would you put the kettle on, Terry?'

'I'm going out.' He bundled past Boyd and down the path.

'You might need a coat,' Lottie shouted after him.

'Fuck the coat.'

Lottie and Boyd followed Carol into the sitting room.

'How are you feeling?'

'Sick as a dog. Had to leave work early.'

'Pregnancy can do that, you know.'

'Shh. Keep your voice down.' Carol swung her head in the direction of the door leading to the kitchen.

'Don't worry. Terry said your parents are in town.'

'What does he know? He's been drinking down the tracks since last night.'

'We want to ask you about Mollie Hunter.' Lottie had had enough of time-wasting for one day.

Carol crossed her arms and tugged at the elbows of her sweater. She pursed her lips tightly shut.

'You know her, don't you?'

'I suppose.'

'No suppose about it. Care to tell us?'

'Not really.'

'I haven't got all day, Carol. I know you're sick, but I'll drag your arse down to the station and put you in a puke-smelling cell and you can vomit your guts up all night. It doesn't really bother me. So tell me.'

'She ... she was nice to me.'

'For God's sake. Why did we find an item of your underwear in a plastic bag in Mollie Hunter's flat?'

'What?'

'We fast-tracked a sample of DNA. Your DNA is a match.'

'Match for what? How did you have my DNA?'

'You were arrested with Terry three years ago. Possession of cannabis.'

'The charge was dropped.'

'It was, but your DNA is on file.'

Carol appeared to shrivel up. She sniffed back tears and looked as though she might be sick.

'Tell me,' Lottie said.

'I was raped. There. Now I've said it.' She pulled tighter on her sleeves.

Lottie turned to Boyd. He shrugged. They hadn't considered this scenario at all.

'Tell me, please, Carol.' She spoke more gently.

'It happened near her place. She came along. She was all right, so she was, even though I didn't know her. She found me in a heap on the side of the lane that runs down between two blocks of flats. She brought me into her home. Wanted to call the guards. But I was in shock. Didn't know what I was doing or saying. I must've said not to call anyone.' She sniffed and rubbed the back of her hand beneath her nose.

Lottie widened her eyes at Boyd.

'Who did it, Carol? When?'

'Oh, for Christ's sake. It doesn't matter now. It was over two months ago.'

'Did you recognise him? Someone you knew?'

'I … I'm not sure. I thought he seemed familiar. His voice was gruff, angry. I think he was drunk. I don't know.'

'And the thong. Why had Mollie got it?'

'She took my clothes that night. I was wet and grubby. I was a mess. She said she had a friend in the guards. I got hysterical and said I wanted no guards. She told me if I changed my mind I could talk to this friend. I made her promise not to tell anyone. I don't think she did but she must've kept my clothes for evidence or something. I honestly don't know.' Carol curled into herself, gulping back huge sobs.

Lottie eased back into the armchair, realising she had been coiled, ready to spring forward.

'This man … this excuse for a man who did this to you, is he the father of the child you're carrying?'

Carol shrugged. 'I'm not sure.'

'Were you in a relationship with someone else at the time?'

A nod.

'Who?'

She shook her head. 'Not saying.'

'Who else knows about the attack?'

'No one.'

'Did Elizabeth know?'

Carol bit her lip, tears coursing down her cheeks. 'Yeah. I told Lizzie.'

'So, two young women who knew that you'd been raped. One is dead – murdered – and the other is missing, quite possibly also murdered. And you didn't think it important enough to tell us? Jesus Christ, where are your brains?'

Lottie felt Boyd touch her arm, restraining her. She let his hand rest. He was right. She was angry with the girl for withholding information, but she was suffering enough. Dear God, she thought for what seemed like the tenth time that day, what a mess.

'You have to report this, Carol.'

'No, I don't. It was just an accident. He didn't mean it. He's a good man.'

'What do you mean?' Lottie reached out and grabbed Carol's hand as the truth dawned on her. 'It *is* someone you know.'

'I didn't say that. Stop putting words in my mouth.'

'I'm sorry. I have to advise you to do the right thing.'

'I'm telling no one. End of. You can go now, before my parents get home.'

Thinking over the girl's words, Lottie said, 'Have you been threatened? By this man?'

Another sniff and a shake of her head.

'Is he married?'

A shrug of shoulders. 'I'm not saying.'

'Are you still in a relationship with him?'

'He thinks so.'

'Does he know you're pregnant?'

'No.' Her eyes, the pupils deep black, glared with terror. 'Don't say a word about any of this. Please. I'm begging you.'

Lottie sighed. 'I'm so sorry this happened to you, Carol, but people will notice you're pregnant eventually.'

'I'm not ready to tell anyone else. The only two people who knew about the rape are … are …' She pulled her legs beneath her and lay in a foetal position on the couch, weeping.

'Give me your brother's number. I'll get him to come back and sit with you.'

'No!' Carol let out a strangled cry. 'Just go. Please. Leave me alone.'

'I'll have to make a report on this, you know that.' Lottie felt sorry for the girl, but she knew she had to do her job too. 'When you're ready, come to the station. There will be trained people available to talk to you. In the meantime, I'll get a liaison officer to stay with you.'

'No fucking way.'

'It's for your own safety. Now give me Terry's number.'

CHAPTER SEVENTY-NINE

Anna Byrne opened the door and led them inside.

'We're sorry to intrude, but we need to ask a few questions.' Lottie remained standing with Boyd while Anna slumped down on a chair. Her grief was palpable.

'Ask away.'

'Did Elizabeth ever talk about a Mollie Hunter?'

'No, I don't recall that name. She only ever said she was going out to meet Carol O'Grady.'

'You're sure?'

'I can't be sure about anything these days.'

'What about Matt Mullin? We have reason to believe he hasn't been in Munich since Christmas. Did he make any contact with Elizabeth?'

Anna stood. 'I'll put the kettle on.' She was wearing the same clothes as the other day and looked like she had cried non-stop since then.

'We haven't time for tea. Talk to me, please, Anna.'

'I've heard nothing from Matt.' Anna sat back down. 'I don't know if he'd been in contact with Elizabeth. Did you find her phone?'

'There's no trace of it.' Lottie sat down beside the distraught mother. 'I know you've no time for Carol, but is there anything we need to be aware of?'

'Like what?'

'Something she may have got Elizabeth involved in?'

'That tramp. Is it her fault my girl is dead?'

'I'm not saying that at all.' Lottie tilted her head to one side, directing Boyd to work his charm.

'Mrs Byrne,' he said, 'Anna. We're finding very little to lead us to Elizabeth's killer. We think Carol might be a link. A tenuous one, but a link nonetheless. Can you think of anything that was out of the ordinary?'

'Everything was out of the ordinary with that one.'

'Please,' Lottie pleaded.

Anna folded her arms, pulling at the sleeve of her cardigan with her fingers, nails bitten to the quick.

'She was never round here, if that's what you mean. But Elizabeth was always calling round to her. More so in recent weeks. Since Christmas. I've no idea what it was about. Elizabeth never said, but I suspect it was to do with a man. You know what young people are like at that age.'

'I do,' Lottie said.

'Maybe Matt was back in town or something. I don't know.'

'Can we look through Elizabeth's things again? If you don't mind.'

'Your forensic guys have been all over them, but go ahead. Don't take anything without telling me first, though.'

Lottie was glad to escape the sorrow permeating the kitchen walls. Elizabeth's bedroom looked the same as they'd left it.

'What are you hoping to find?' Boyd asked.

'Something to indicate Matt Mullin was in contact with her.'

'But we didn't find anything first time, and neither did SOCOs.'

'We didn't know what we were looking for then.'

'We don't know what we're ...' Boyd began. Lottie threw him a warning look. He continued, 'I suppose I'll know it when I see it.'

He brushed by her, and her skin tingled with the touch of his hand as he passed. The slightest connection, but she felt it. Her chest constricted with anxiety. A pill would help, but there was no way she could sneak one. She willed concentration into her brain. Clues to the fate of Mollie Hunter might be somewhere in this room. They had to be thorough.

'Was there anything in her notebook to give us a hint?' she asked.

'Not unless she was writing in some sort of code.'

After searching the room carefully, Lottie ran her hand through the necklaces hanging on the plastic stand on the dresser. She paused, her fingers snagged in a silver chain.

'Boyd, look at this.' She held up the chain with a ring attached. 'Was this here all the time?'

'Must have been. Ask Anna.'

'Ask me what?' Anna stood at the doorway, clenching and unclenching her fists. Lottie didn't know if it was from anger or a gesture of helplessness.

'Is this Elizabeth's?' She held up the chain and ring, anticipation prickling her skin.

'I've never seen it before.' Anna took a step into the room. 'Are you finished here?'

With a glance at Boyd, Lottie nodded. 'I need to take this.'

'I don't think it belonged to Elizabeth, so you can have it.'

Sliding the jewellery into an evidence bag, Lottie smiled sadly and left the room.

CHAPTER EIGHTY

The day, if it was still the same day, seemed interminable. Boredom had replaced fear. And the bones, the baby bones, mocked her, lying there on the table as if they expected her to do something.

But what could she do? She was locked up. She had no means of escape. She still had no idea why he'd taken her. But she was sure she had been his target. Not opportune. No. He had sought her out and snatched her. Why?

She'd studied the paintings on the wall, trying to find a clue to who had painted them. To the person who had previously inhabited this prison. Or were the paintings a message? Maybe that was it. Kneeling on the end of the bed, she looked at them, really looked at them. And that was when she saw it. Painted in the tiniest of black letters, along the body of a crooked steam engine, it was there. Hidden in plain sight.

A name.

But it meant absolutely nothing to her.

*

At the office, Boyd plonked two mugs of coffee on Lottie's desk, having first put down coasters.

'Where did you get those?' She opened her eyes wide with amazement.

'The mats? My drawer. You never told me what Queenie said.'

'That feels like two days ago.' She tapped her computer keyboard. 'Wait until I log in here. I want to find a picture of Paddy McWard.'

'Why?'

'To see if he wears any rings.'

She clattered at the keyboard.

'I know we found a ring attached to a chain at Elizabeth's house and a ring in the unidentified female from the lake, but what has McWard got to do with it?'

'Boyd, drink your coffee and shut up for a minute. I'm trying to get my head back in gear.' She brought up a set of photographs and zoomed in on one.

'Is that a recent picture?' Boyd asked.

'It's a few years old. When he was arrested for car theft ... There. See his hands?' She turned the screen so that he could see what she was looking at.

'No rings.'

'Right.'

'Right what?'

'Most of the traveller community wear jewellery. Thick gold chains, rings and all that shite. But he has no rings.'

'And that proves what?'

'Hold on a minute.' She zoomed the cursor up McWard's arm. 'Jesus, Boyd. Look at that tattoo.'

He stretched across the desk, squinting. 'It's a Celtic cross.'

'Up further. Just below the hem of his sleeve. It's a Claddagh.'

'So it is. So what?'

Lottie thumped a key and the screen turned to black. 'I don't know.'

'What's brought this on?'

'Queenie said that Paddy had a broken heart. We can assume Elizabeth was in school with Bridie. And we've just found a Claddagh ring on a chain in her room. What if there was a love triangle and Paddy was mixed up somehow?'

'And he killed Elizabeth and then his wife? Oh, and I suppose you think he also abducted Lynn O'Donnell and kept her hidden for ten years? And Mollie Hunter too, just for good measure. You need more coffee, Lottie, your brain is dead.'

'My brain is on fire. I need to talk to McWard again.'

She brought two squad cars and Kirby, along with Boyd, for protection. There was no knowing how this was going to pan out. She had a lot of unconnected lines of thought but she knew that somewhere in the maze the answer was waiting to be found. And currently, Matt Mullin aside, all paths were leading her to Paddy McWard.

Crime-scene tape circled the remains of the McWard house. Paddy was at his cousin's mobile home. He stood at the door. No invitation to enter. If that's the way you want it, Lottie thought. We'll do this in front of your relations and neighbours.

'Your mother-in-law passed away an hour ago, Paddy.'

'Good.'

'Good?'

'At least she won't have to mourn her daughter and grandson.'

A pang of fear pierced Lottie's heart as she thought of Katie and Louis so far away from her. She better ring Chloe to make sure she and Sean were okay. As soon as she finished here.

'Did you know Elizabeth Byrne?'

'No.'

'Mollie Hunter?'

'What's this about?'

'Answer the question.'

'Never heard of her.'

Lottie played her trump card. 'What about Lynn O'Donnell?'

'No.'

But his face told the lie. Eyes shrouded over, pupils dilated to black crescents beneath their lids, and the light spilling from the bulb outside the caravan cast a yellow hue on his rapidly tensing skin.

'Come with us, Paddy. We need to have a word down at the station.'

'Again? How many times have I been there and each time it's been a waste of time. So no. You either arrest me or be gone. I've done nothing.'

'We need to speak to you with regards to the arson attack on your home.' She watched as his fists curled. 'We can do this the hard way.'

She took a set of handcuffs from her pocket and pointed to the two squad cars with their flashing lights at the gate.

'This is the last time.' He relented and pushed by her, heading for the nearest car.

Lottie could have sworn there were tears in his eyes.

CHAPTER EIGHTY-ONE

They followed the two squad cars back to the station, and Lottie jumped out at the front steps. She wanted to be inside when McWard was brought in.

Even though it had started to spill rain, she began pulling off her coat as she ran up the steps.

'Inspector Parker! A word, please.'

Lottie turned to see the reporter, Cynthia Rhodes, complete with a cameraman behind her. A feeling of déjà vu flashed before her eyes. This wasn't going to turn out well.

'What do you want, Cynthia?'

'I believe two complaints have been made against you today. Care to comment?'

'What complaints?'

'I've had a call from a Mrs O'Grady. She says you upset her daughter unnecessarily. Wants to highlight garda insensitivity. The girl's best friend was found murdered and all that.'

'That's a load of bull.' Shut up, Lottie, she chided herself. But she knew it was too late.

Rhodes was in full swing. 'And the O'Donnell family. I've a complaint from them also. DI Parker, can I have a comment about the discovery of Lynn O'Donnell's body two days ago?'

'No, you can't.'

'Why did it take so long to inform her family?'

'None of your business.'

'I think it is the nation's business, Inspector. Was she badly decomposed? Was that the reason for the delay?'

'Why don't you piss off back to Dublin?'

Shit!

Paddy McWard had been taken to a cell by the time Lottie got inside, because there was someone in both interview rooms. She rushed upstairs to find Lynch standing in the middle of the office, wet and bedraggled-looking.

'What now?' Lottie snapped, rolling her coat into a ball and kicking it beneath her desk. Her T-shirt was sopping and her jeans were stuck to her legs. Fuck it, she thought. But she couldn't get Cynthia Rhodes out of her head. She was in deep shit if that toerag excuse for a journalist broadcast … What exactly had she said? She sank into the nearest chair and held her head in her hands.

'Would you like a coffee? A Diet Coke? I've a can in my bag.'

'I thought you were off sick.'

'I'm okay now, boss. This can wait.'

Lottie looked up at her detective. 'I'm sorry. What was it you wanted to say?'

'Matt Mullin. He was with his mother all along.'

'The shite.'

'He's depressed. Actually, he's in a fairly bad way. He's in the interview room.'

'Now?'

'Yeah.'

'Shit.' Running her hand under her nose, Lottie blocked a sneeze.

'You need to go home and change,' Lynch said. 'Did you eat today?'

'Did I eat? You know what? I honestly don't know. I'll be down in five minutes. You stay with him until I get there.'

When Lynch retreated, Lottie searched her pockets for a tissue and found the slip of paper with the phone number Keelan O'Donnell had given her. What could that be about? No time now. She'd call her later. Stuffing it back into her pocket, she squeezed out her dripping hair and figured Matt Mullin would have to take her the way she was.

CHAPTER EIGHTY-TWO

The man in front of her didn't look anything like his photograph. For a start, he looked much older. Despite black rings beneath red-rimmed eyes, there was a certain smugness to his demeanour. Well, Mr Mullin, we'll see how long that lasts.

Without preamble, Lottie placed Elizabeth's photograph in front of him. The death-mask one. He recoiled instantly. That worked nicely, she thought.

'Was breaking up with Elizabeth a recipe for murder?' she said.

'What are you talking about? I never laid a hand on her.'

'Expect me to believe that? Mr Mullin, I'm in no mood for games. I've had a bitch of a day. Start talking.'

'Talk? About what? I didn't kill Elizabeth. I loved her. I miss her so much. I can't believe she's dead.'

Lottie showed him a photograph of the chain and ring she'd found.

He looked up at her with a raised eyebrow. 'Was that Elizabeth's?'

'Was it Elizabeth's?' Lottie mocked. 'You gave it to her, didn't you?'

'Honest to God, I never did. I never saw it before.'

'You think I'm going to believe that?'

'It's the truth.' He bared his teeth, gnawing his bottom lip.

'When did you last see her? And don't tell me it was a year ago, because guess what? I won't believe it.'

He sighed. Considering. 'I found the break-up hard. Once I was in Germany, I knew I'd made a mistake. But she wouldn't listen to me. Blocked my number. Wouldn't talk. It made me ill.'

Was this guy for real? Lottie rolled her eyes and felt Lynch nudge her knee.

'Go on.'

'I got so depressed, I couldn't work and came home to Mum.'

'A thirty-five-year-old banker, jacking in his job and running home to Mummy. Priceless.'

'You're a bit of a bitch, aren't you?'

'Ah, now I'm getting to hear the real Matt Mullin. So you came home. When?'

'Early December.'

'And you met Elizabeth?'

'No. I told you, she wouldn't meet or talk or anything. So I started following her. On the train.'

Lottie let out a low whistle. *Stalker* popped into her mind, quickly followed by *murderer*.

'Did she see you?'

'Probably. But she ignored me. Some days she was sitting beside that other girl.'

'What other girl?'

'The one that's missing. Mollie Hunter.'

Lottie sat up straight. 'You saw Elizabeth sitting on the train with Mollie Hunter?'

'Yeah. Not every day, though. Not like they were friends, just companions.'

'So you killed Elizabeth and then abducted Mollie.'

'I did not.' He looked wildly around the room. 'Am I entitled to a solicitor?'

'If you want one. Might make you look like you have something to hide, though.'

'That's bollocks and you know it.'

'Did you follow Elizabeth out at Rochfort Gardens?'

'I don't know what you're talking about.'

'Running. Jogging. At weekends.'

'No. I didn't. Just on the train.'

'And what did you do all day in Dublin while she was at work?'

'Walked around. Had a coffee at the station and waited.'

'Tell me more.'

'There's nothing to tell. Elizabeth didn't show up on the train on Tuesday or Wednesday and then I heard what happened to her. On the news. Oh God, I can't believe it.' He began to sob.

'What did you do on those days when Elizabeth wasn't on the train?'

'I … I tried to talk to that Mollie girl. But she wouldn't engage with me. Moved off to sit with some nervy young one.'

Wheels clicked in Lottie's brain. Grace!

Could this idiot be telling the truth? She looked to Lynch for some idea of what the detective was thinking, but Lynch was staring at the wall, her face a dreadful shade of grey. That was all she needed, for her detective to puke on a suspect.

Matt stood up, 'I want my solicitor now. Or let me go.'

She really didn't have anything to hold him on. She needed evidence.

'Will you consent to giving a sample of DNA?'

'Get a warrant.'

Christ, he wasn't going to make life any easier for her. 'Okay, I will. You can go, but I want you back here at ten in the morning. With or without your solicitor. Are you agreeable to that?'

He shrugged and left.

'I think I'll join you for that coffee now, Lynch.'

In the hallway, she met Boyd, running.

'Oh, Boyd. The very man. Can you call your mother and get Grace on the phone? She might have seen that Mullin fellow on the train with Mollie.'

'Lottie. The canteen. Now.' He was breathless.

'That's where I'm headed. I'm badly in need of a coffee.'

He was shaking his head. 'You might need something stronger after you see this.'

The canteen had a wall-mounted television, which was usually muted with subtitles. Now, the sound was turned up.

Lottie sat down on one of the new red plastic chairs, open-mouthed.

'This is Cynthia Rhodes reporting from Ragmullin, in the midlands. A town that has seen its fair share of tragedy and murder over the last few years. But now locals are accusing the local Garda Síochána of incompetence.'

'What the hell? Bitch!' Lottie jumped up, rage spiking in her chest.

'The most tragic event to strike the town of Ragmullin concerns the O'Donnell family, who just a few weeks ago buried their wife and mother. Maura O'Donnell battled cancer, but those who knew her say she died of a broken heart. She went to her grave not knowing where her daughter, Lynn O'Donnell, vanished to ten years ago. The gardaí believed Lynn to be dead, possibly buried at an unidentified location in the Dublin mountains, information I got from a detective inspector at Ragmullin garda station.'

'Liar. She's misquoting me.'

'You said that? Out loud?' Boyd asked.

'Kind of.'

'God, Lottie, wait till McMahon finds out.'

'I know.' McMahon's voice boomed out behind her.

'Creep,' Lottie muttered. He had an annoying habit of appearing out of nowhere, silent and sneaky. Or perhaps it was her suspicious mind at work.

'Shh.' Boyd turned the sound up further.

'Turn it down,' Lottie shrieked. 'We can read the subtitles.'

'Turn it up. I want to hear it so I can decide on damage control.' McMahon pulled out a chair, and the plastic squeaked as he sat.

Cynthia was standing outside Donal O'Donnell's home.

'Yesterday I interviewed this heartbroken family. They asked me to highlight the ineptitude of the gardaí and to appeal for information on Lynn's whereabouts. Sadly, I learned today that the body of Ms O'Donnell has been found. And not in the Dublin mountains, but at Ladystown lake, just a few short miles outside Ragmullin.'

A photograph of Lynn appeared on the left-hand side of the screen, with the right-hand side showing the road leading to Barren Point.

'What is more disturbing, my sources tell me that Lynn O'Donnell had not been dead for ten years. She was alive up until a week or two ago. That begs the question, how did local gardaí fail in their efforts to find this beautiful young woman? And where has she been for the last decade? Was she free all that time, or was she the victim of an abduction, held against her will? A short while ago, I attempted to speak with Detective Inspector Parker of Ragmullin garda station.'

The screen cut to the steps of the station, rain spilling down in sheets and Rhodes standing with her microphone in hand. Lottie appeared from the right running up the steps, pulling her coat off.

'Turn it off,' she cried. 'I know where this is leading.'

'What did you say to her?' Boyd whispered. 'Oh God, I hope it isn't anything they can crucify you with.'

'I can't watch this.' She bolted out of her chair, but paused at the door, waiting for the humiliation she was about to suffer on national television.

Cynthia's voice boomed through the canteen. 'DI Parker, can I have a comment about the discovery of Lynn O'Donnell's body two days ago?'

'No, you can't.'

'Why did it take so long to inform her family?'

'None of your business.'

Lottie cringed. Shit, this was worse than she'd feared. She saw McMahon turn his head to face her. Was that a sly smirk snaking across his face?

'I think it is the nation's business, Inspector. Was she badly decomposed? Was that the reason for the delay?'

'Why don't you piss off back to Dublin.'

The image showed Lottie shoving her way past Rhodes. Then the shot returned to a bemused-looking, very damp Cynthia.

'And that is DI Parker, who is heading up two murder investigations and the case of Mollie Hunter, who has been missing since Wednesday.'

Lottie groaned. 'Jesus, if you're going to hang me out to dry, at least get your fucking facts right.'

'What facts?' McMahon rose from his chair as Boyd muted the television.

'Lynn wasn't murdered, she died of natural causes.'

'That, Inspector, is beside the point. Where was she for ten years? If she was being held captive somewhere, don't you think that was a contributing factor to her death?'

'Yeah, well, what do you know?' She leaned back against the door frame and closed her eyes. The day couldn't get any worse, could it?

'My office.' McMahon stormed past her, leaving a trail of sickly aftershave in his wake.

'Will you come with me, Boyd?' she said.

'I think you've dug your own grave on this one, Lottie.'

'Okay. A favour, though, before I throw myself under McMahon's bus. I need you with me while I interview Paddy McWard.'

CHAPTER EIGHTY-THREE

McWard said he didn't want a solicitor. As Lottie slumped onto a chair, Boyd set up the recording equipment and read out the procedures.

'Get on with it,' McWard said.

'Tell me about your Claddagh tattoo,' Lottie said.

'What?'

'Show it to me.'

He shrugged and held out his arm.

'When did you get that done?'

'Maybe ten years ago. I can't remember.'

'Why that symbol?'

'I liked it. Going to arrest me for it?'

'You don't wear any rings?'

'I don't.'

'Not even a wedding ring?'

'Not a crime. I broke it, if you want to know.'

'Really?'

'My hand swelled up after a fight. Had to get the ring cut off. Satisfied?'

'Not really. Did you know Lynn O'Donnell?'

'I told you already. I didn't know her.'

'I don't believe you.'

He shrugged again.

It was time to play what she thought was her trump card. The photo of the ring Jane Dore had taken from Lynn O'Donnell's intestine. Her own gut was telling her McWard was involved, but she had no concrete evidence to link him to anything at the moment. Placing the photocopy face down on the table, she waited. Then, slowly, keeping her eyes on his face, she turned it over.

No change in expression.

'So?' he said. 'It's a Claddagh ring. What's it got to do with me?'

'Would you like to know where we found it?'

'Not particularly, but I guess you're going to tell me. Pig.'

'Did you just call me a pig?'

'Oink.'

'For God's sake, stop being childish,' Lottie said. Under the table, she felt Boyd kick her leg. She turned to look at him. A slight shake of his head, warning her to back off. Not on your life.

'This ring was recovered two days ago from the body of a woman who was found dead.'

'Like I said. Nothing to do with me.'

'She went missing ten years ago tomorrow.'

Lottie braced herself for more insults. But instead there was a suffocating silence as McWard's face drained of colour and turned ghost white.

Biting the inside of his cheek, he pulled the photograph towards him and stared. A sob strangled in his throat. 'Lynn?'

Lottie glanced at Boyd. What? He *did* know her.

She gave a little cough. 'Yes, we found the ring inside the body of Lynn O'Donnell.'

He pushed away the photo and folded his arms. 'I know nothing about any Lynn.'

'You're not a great liar, Paddy. You've just said her name. You knew her. Admit it.'

His silence hung in the air like a delicate cobweb. Lottie felt like a fly about to pounce on a spider.

'Paddy. Talk to me, for Christ's sake.'

His eyes were shrouded as he lowered his head. 'I've just lost my wife and my son. And you think I had something to do with that girl? You are the lowest form of scum on the earth.'

'But you knew Lynn O'Donnell. Did you abduct her? Hide her away for ten years and then leave her to die?'

'You're mad, do you know that?'

'Left her to rot out at the lake?'

'I did not.'

Lottie sighed. She had nothing on Paddy McWard. Not a single thing, yet her bones itched with the feeling that he was involved.

'All those days and nights you spend away from home. Where do you go?'

'This again?'

'Yup. I'll find out eventually, so you may as well tell me.'

He folded his arms, put them on the table and laid his head on top of them. 'I must be due a break.' His voice was muffled.

With her own shoulders sagging in defeat, Lottie asked Boyd to terminate the interview.

'As you have no home at the moment, we'll provide you with a nice sterile cell for the night. Give you time to decide to tell us the truth.'

'Bare-knuckle boxing.'

'What?' She nodded to Boyd to continue the recording. She'd seen this on PULSE. He'd been arrested for it eight years ago, but the charges were dropped. Was this all he was guilty of? She needed to find out.

McWard raised his head listlessly. 'I used to be involved in underground bare-knuckle fights. Lost a lot of money. Nearly lost my life.'

'Go on.'

'I had a younger brother who … who died from a kick to the head at one of those fights seven years ago. That changed me.'

'How?'

'Now I try to stop them. I travel the country hunting them down. I try and talk sense into the young lads. Anyone who'll listen, I take them to legit boxing clubs. I even train some of them myself. That's all I've been doing. Nothing suspicious. Just trying to make up for the loss of my brother.'

Was this what Queenie had meant by his broken heart? Glancing sideways at Boyd, Lottie raised a questioning eyebrow before returning her gaze to McWard.

'Can you prove this?'

'I can bring you to some of the clubs. The lads might talk to you. But the illegal stuff, I can't let you in on that. Sure, even your own pigs couldn't uncover anything about them.'

Lottie took a deep breath and expelled it slowly. 'I think you're telling me the truth, but not the whole truth.'

'You've nothing to hold me on. I'm not going to flee, I've funerals to organise. I'll come back tomorrow.'

'You're going nowhere until you tell me the truth. About everything, Paddy.'

Maybe it was the use of his first name that did it, but Lottie watched in wonder as his fingers gripped the image of the ring.

'I loved her so much,' he whispered.

Her breath caught at the back of her throat and her mouth opened without any words escaping.

'My Lynn. I can't believe she's dead. I always thought she'd be found. I searched and searched. We were so in love. But it could never be. Not with that arsehole family of hers. Once they found out, we were finished.'

'Found out what?'

'That we were meeting. That we were lovers.' He looked up at the ceiling, cleared his throat. 'Bridie was only fourteen when I was betrothed to her. I didn't love her. But that was the way of my people. I'd already met Lynn by then, when I went to Dublin to sort out some welfare stuff at the head office. That was where she worked. She had such a happy smile. I was in love from that first day. And the odd thing was, she felt it too.'

'You had a relationship with Lynn O'Donnell?' Lottie said, incredulous.

'Don't look so shocked. Love happens. I gave her that ring. To show her my loyalty and love.'

'You're sure it's the same one?'

'If you let me see it, I'll know.'

Lottie didn't know if that was a good idea. Was he lying?

'What I can't understand is that your name never appeared anywhere in the original investigation. Why is that?'

'Her family didn't want to suffer the indignity of the whole country knowing their beloved girl was making out with a traveller. The shame of it.' He curled his lip in distaste. 'I hate them. Every last one of them. It's their fault Lynn went missing.'

'I think it's your fault.'

'Maybe you're right there.'

'Where did you keep her for the last ten years, Paddy?'

His eyes, blacker than she'd noticed before, stabbed her with a look of hatred. 'I didn't take her and I didn't keep her anywhere. I want my solicitor. I'm not saying another word.'

With exhaustion eating its way into the core of her being, Lottie wound up the interview, then made arrangements for Paddy's detention to be extended overnight. They needed to run more DNA tests. She hoped that maybe tomorrow she could extract the whole truth from him and, in doing so, find Mollie Hunter.

*

McMahon's mood had soured considerably in the half-hour she'd left him to stew.

'I thought I told you I wanted to see you immediately. Where the hell were you?'

'I had an interview to conduct. McWard was on a time limit.'

'I'm your superior officer. I come first.'

'Yes, sir.' Too late now, she thought. She'd already relegated him behind Paddy McWard. And there was no way she was telling him about the possible breakthrough in the case of Lynn O'Donnell. He could find out for himself when they filed for an extension of detention time.

'Sit. That debacle of a television interview. What were you thinking?'

'I wasn't thinking, obviously.'

'None of that smart mouth in here.' He slammed his fist on the empty desk.

Lottie slipped down on the chair, hoping it might make her disappear. She was so tired; she couldn't remember the last time she'd slept. She needed to get home.

'I'm exhausted, sir. Can't we do this tomorrow?'

'There's no tomorrow where you're concerned. You're suspended, pending an inquiry into your attitude and behaviour.'

Shit!

'Don't I get a warning first? You can't just suspend me. You have to follow procedure.' She shot forward in the chair, reached out a hand. She didn't do pleading, but she was doing it now.

'And did *you*?' he said.

'What?

'Follow procedure?'

'That was different. Rhodes hijacked me. I wasn't prepared for—'

'You have to be prepared at all times. Someone in your position knows that.'

'I forgot. I was—'

'Exhausted? No excuse.'

She threw up her hands. 'I've nothing else to offer.'

'Get out, Parker. You're a disgrace to the force.'

She couldn't help rolling her eyes. Incensing him further. Wrong move, Lottie.

He rose from his chair, slow and panther-like. She didn't blink. Wouldn't give him the satisfaction. Remaining seated, she folded her arms.

'Do you know, as bad as that display was on national television, it gave me a quiet moment of satisfaction. Because, Parker, you are nothing but trouble, and I'm making it my one and only aim to have you dismissed from the force.'

'We'll see about that, shall we?' She rose languidly and strolled out of his office.

Hearing the door slam behind her, she stopped and sighed, raising her eyes to the ceiling, then looked around for Boyd. He was nowhere to be seen.

She grabbed her coat and keys and walked out without a backwards glance.

CHAPTER EIGHTY-FOUR

Chloe cooked dinner. Oven chips and burgers. Lottie wolfed down the food and helped her stack the dishwasher.

'Granny was here earlier,' Chloe said.

'The miraculous recovery.'

'She said she was fed up with your cooking. I don't think she's sick any longer. I helped her tidy up here a bit. She even got the hoover out. Insulted me and Sean in the process.'

'She's definitely better,' Lottie laughed.

Chloe smiled, and Lottie felt the tiredness in her bones ease a little. She pulled her daughter into a hug. Sean strolled into the kitchen but quickly turned on his heel with a 'Yuck!'

'Would you mind if Boyd came over for a while?'

'Work stuff?' Chloe asked.

'Not really.' Lottie released her, then closed the dishwasher door and pressed the button.

'I don't care.'

And before she could reply, the girl had left the room, slamming the door on her way out.

She rang Boyd. They had things to discuss, and it wasn't work-related.

'What are you dressing up for?' Chloe plonked herself down on Lottie's bed. 'It's only Boyd.'

'What about this?' Lottie asked, holding out a cream blouse.

'Try the blue dress.' Chloe folded her arms.

Lottie held it up to her chest. 'I don't think it fits me any more.'

'That's because you've gone to skin and bone. You need to eat.'

'I do eat.'

'Junk food. You're wearing yourself to the bone again.'

'Again?' She pulled the blue dress on over her long grey T-shirt.

'Every time you have a murder case, you forget about yourself. That's too big for you.'

'Any other suggestions?'

'Your jeans and a clean shirt if you can find one.'

'Chloe, don't be so mean.'

'It's only Boyd, for Christ's sake. Not Johnny Depp.'

'I want to look … different from my normal look.'

'Sounds serious.'

'You're right, it's only Boyd.' Lottie pulled two shirts off hangers. 'Which one?'

'The green one.'

'That doesn't go with my eyes.'

'The white one then.'

'What's the matter, Chloe?' Lottie threw the clothes on the floor and sat beside her daughter. She held her hand. 'Boy trouble?'

'Not my boy trouble. Your man trouble.'

'I don't have man trouble.'

'That's the problem. Boyd, well, he's your friend. You can't go on a date with him.'

'For the last time, it's not a date.'

'Why is he down in the sitting room with another bunch of flowers then?'

'He's just being Boyd.' Lottie bit her lip. She hadn't a clue how to handle this awkwardness with her daughter.

'I know you slept with him last night. This is going to end in tears.'

'Hey.' She gripped Chloe's hand tightly. 'I just have things to discuss with him. It's nothing serious.'

'Yeah, but he's your friend. And you're going to ruin that friendship, just like you ruin everything. I miss Dad!'

'Wait a minute …'

But Chloe had fled.

Flopping back on the bed, Lottie stared at a water stain on the ceiling and wondered where she was going wrong.

CHAPTER EIGHTY-FIVE

In the end, she rushed Boyd out the door and drove over to his apartment behind him.

As usual, the place was clean and quiet. She sat beside him on the couch and sipped a glass of white wine. They had agreed to no work talk.

'Do you miss Grace being around for the weekend?'

'No. I've been on my own for so long, I find it hard to share my space. Anyway, she'll be back tomorrow.'

'No hope for me then,' she laughed. The illicit wine was relaxing her. A little.

'There is always hope for you, Lottie Parker.' He clinked his glass to hers and the hazel in his eyes sparkled with the light. 'I enjoyed having you here last night. In my bed. Our lovemaking.'

'I was only here a couple of hours.' She turned her head to him. How was she going to handle this without ruining their friendship?

'You're beautiful, but you don't realise it.'

'Will you stop!'

'I thought I'd go mental all day, restraining myself.'

'What do you mean?'

'Trying to keep my hands off you and my expression neutral.'

She smiled awkwardly. 'McMahon didn't remain neutral. He's preparing my walking papers. I don't know what I'm going to do.'

'He can't suspend you without consulting the chief super, so don't worry about it.'

'I have to worry about it. I need my job. It's the only thing keeping me half sane.'

'You have your children. They're brilliant kids. I love Sean.'

'Chloe is an enigma, though. If only I could fathom out how her brain works.'

'Problems there?'

'She thinks I'm going to ruin a good friendship.'

'And are you?'

'I ruin everything, according to her.'

'No you don't. She's just a teenager. Afraid she's going to lose her mum.'

'It's more than that, Boyd. I fear for her. She says she misses her dad.'

'Of course she does. Sean too.' He leaned over for the bottle and refilled his glass. 'Another?'

'I shouldn't be drinking at all. I've got to drive home.' As he drew away, she said, 'Well, maybe half a glass.'

They reclined in the silence, their legs touching, her head on his shoulder. She felt that if she sat here long enough, the hassles of her life might just disappear, if only for an hour.

'Do you ever crave sex?' he said.

'Jesus, Boyd. Where did that come from?'

He pointed to the pit of his abs. 'Here. Somewhere down here.'

Lottie stood up and walked to the window. 'That's an odd question.'

He said nothing.

She flicked a slat in the wooden blind, cutting the scene outside in half. She didn't want to turn around. To see him sitting there, hands resting just above the buckle of his belt. His fingers long and lonely. His hair short and damp. And his eyes. Questioning.

'I don't think about it,' she said.

'You must do.'

'Do you?'

'Not as often as you might think,' Boyd said.

She heard him standing up, the glass clinking on the table, the rustle of his trousers, the pad of his feet on the carpet. She sensed his closeness as he stood behind her.

'Do you love me, Lottie?'

That made her take a step away from him. She turned to stare. Side-on, he was even more handsome, because she couldn't see his sticking-out ears.

How to answer him without hurting him. Without hurting herself. Did she love Boyd? Adam had been the only man in her life, all her life, until he got that bastard cancer and died on her. Boyd had always been on hand when she felt her life rug being snatched from beneath her feet. Yes, she'd slept in his bed after bouts of drinking, but last night had felt different. And that was what scared her the most.

As he slowly turned to face her, her breath caught in the back of her throat at the sight of the sadness lurking in the corners of his eyes. She wanted to reach out and touch his cheek, to hold his hand, to tell him what she knew was deep within her heart. But then she might lose him too. Wasn't it safer to keep plodding along, playing the game? But how long could she do that without succumbing to her true feelings? And would Boyd even be around when she faced up to what she knew was the truth?

'This is never going to work,' she said. 'I have to go home.'

He broke away from her.

She left him standing at the window, picked up her coat and bag, and let herself out of his apartment into the loneliness of the night.

CHAPTER EIGHTY-SIX

It was almost midnight and the house was creaking in silence when she returned home. She automatically sorted the laundry, then put on a wash and placed the damp clothes in the dryer. Upstairs was chilly. She pulled Adam's old fishing jumper out of a drawer and dragged it on over her pyjamas.

Before getting into bed, she checked on Chloe, who was fast asleep. Sean was in bed, headphones on, watching a movie on his laptop. He winked at her when she blew him a kiss and her heart leaped with love as she closed the door.

She fell into bed. She needed sleep to extinguish all thoughts of the problems she now faced with Boyd and her job. She'd worry about murders, missing girls and McMahon tomorrow.

*

Boyd had finished the bottle of wine by the time his mother rang him wondering if Grace needed a new anxiety pill prescription for next week.

Grace? His stomach lurched.

His mother thought Grace was with him. He thought Grace was with his mother. But it turned out she was in neither place. And she wasn't answering her phone. Where the hell was she?

He'd last seen her yesterday morning when he'd dropped her at the train station. Images of Elizabeth Byrne's naked body in the pit of a grave surfaced, and his heart pounded a triple beat in his chest.

As he went into the bedroom, his breathing accelerated and he clutched his chest. He fell back on the bed, his arm dangling. His fingers touched something. Grace's phone, on the floor, her little bottle of anxiety pills lying beside it.

Lottie. He should ring Lottie.

Pain shot up his arm and flew to his chest, and his breath died in his lungs as darkness washed over his eyes.

*

Smoke. She could smell smoke. Fuck!

Lottie threw back the duvet and sat bolt upright. Flicking on the lamp, she jumped out of bed and opened the door. The landing was filled with thick black smoke. Beyond it, at the bottom of the stairs, flames licked upwards. She grabbed her phone and ran into Chloe's room, hauling the girl out of bed, then did the same to Sean.

'What's going on, Mum?' Sean was bleary-eyed, headphones around his neck.

'Oh God. No! The house is on fire,' Chloe screamed at the top of the stairs.

Lottie pushed her children behind her, her body convulsing in shakes, and with her arm across her nose and mouth placed one foot on the top step.

'No, Mum!' Chloe shouted. 'The smoke. It'll kill you.'

'What are we going to do?' Sean cried.

She descended two steps before smoke threatened to overwhelm her. She ran back up. 'We need to get out of a window.'

'My room.' Chloe turned and ran, Sean behind her. 'I've got out this way before.'

'Wait!' Lottie cried. 'Wet towels. We need wet towels.' All her composure and training evaporated as her lungs clogged with fumes. Was this how Bridie McWard had felt in her dying moments? No,

Lottie wasn't going to let that happen to her family. She quickly followed them into Chloe's room and punched the door shut behind her.

Chloe had opened the window and was sitting out on the ledge. 'You need to jump onto the shed roof. It's not far.'

Staring out, Lottie saw the garden lit up with bright orange flames, smoke billowing from her kitchen. Had some bastard torched the house? She had no time to worry about her possessions burning before her eyes. She had to get her family to safety.

Sean had his phone to his ear, shouting out their address. She hadn't even thought of ringing the emergency services. Focus, Lottie, focus.

'Come on!' Chloe cried, holding out her hand.

Lottie didn't need to give her tall son a leg-up onto the windowsill, but she did anyway, then watched as Chloe jumped onto the shed roof, quickly followed by Sean.

The white paint on the bedroom door was peeling from the heat. Tendrils of black smoke eased through the cracks in the jamb and the bottom of the door. Her breath was almost spent by the time she escaped out the window. Without even worrying about falling and breaking her neck, she leaped down to the roof of the shed. The children had already shimmied down the grassy bank behind it and were huddled together when she joined them.

Arms wrapped around each other, they stared up at their burning home. The wail of sirens pierced the night sky, competing with the crackling and whistling of the flames.

Gone. Lost.

She had lost everything.

And then she heard the soft sobs of her children.

*

The cold and wet had eaten into her bones. She couldn't open her eyes, no matter how she tried. The voices in her head came and went, trickling away like froth on a wave.

Her body shook incessantly, her lips trembled and her teeth ground against each other. Who was she?

Grace. That was her name. What had happened? The man on the train. Had he brought her here? Where?

And a name flitted into her consciousness. Mollie. She hadn't found Mollie. Would anyone find her?

*

Wrapping the thin blanket around her shoulders, Mollie lay back on the bed and wished she had the means to turn off the light. It was blinding her. Keeping her awake. There was no night or day in this place. Only long, unending hours.

She had no notion of when he had last been with her. It seemed like an eternity. Had he forgotten about her? Had he left her here to die? Would she end up like the bones on the table? Rotted bare of all flesh. Unburied and unblessed.

Surely someone had missed her by now?

Her throat was raw from screaming and her eyes had dried up like gravel had taken root behind them. And she was hungry and thirsty. She had nothing left.

She turned onto her side.

No one was coming.

She was alone.

She would never be found.

There was nothing she could do.

She was going to die.

Alone.

DAY FIVE

Sunday 14 February 2016

CHAPTER EIGHTY-SEVEN

Lottie awoke to a soft light filtering through thin cotton curtains. She shot up in the bed. Where the hell was she?

Looking around the room, it all came crashing back to her. Her throat was clogged with a taste like the aftermath of smoking one too many cigarettes, and she smelled of smoke.

She hadn't slept in this room since she'd married Adam, but now memories of her childhood flowed about her like a waterfall. As a child, she'd felt safe here, but now she was like an interloper. A giant in a miniature world. Not nostalgia, just sadness. She didn't belong here. The only place she could truly call home was now a smouldering mound of ash.

All her memories of her husband and their life together had gone with the house. Disintegrated to ash. Tugging Adam's sweater to her body, she realised it was the only thing of meaning she had left of him.

The door opened. Lottie hastily wiped the tears from her face and watched her mother place a mug of coffee on the bedside locker.

Rose Fitzpatrick looked healthier than she had in months. Hair washed and standing to attention. Clothes sharply ironed. A mask of yellow still lingered on her skin and her eyes held that sorrowful, dry look you often saw in people who had grieved so long they'd no tears left to shed. Still, it was as if last night's fire had acted as a catalyst for Rose, causing her to take on the role of Lazarus and rise from the dead.

In that instant, Lottie realised how much she wanted her mother to take control of things. Not that she was going to let it get out of hand. But for now, she was glad of it. Maybe some day soon they might be able to deal with the complexities of their past.

'Chloe and Sean? Are they okay?' she asked.

'Still asleep, poor pets. Awful thing to happen to anyone.'

'Thanks,' Lottie said.

'For what?'

'Taking us in.'

'Don't be acting the lady now, Lottie Parker. Taking you in? Isn't that what a mother is for? Looking after her family.'

Somewhere in that statement there was a slight on Lottie's ability to care for her own family, but she let it pass. Slurped the coffee, trying to kick-start her brain.

'I need to go down to the house. Get some clothes.' She sensed her mother's stare. 'What?'

'There's nothing left. You know that.'

'I didn't …' She quickly swallowed a mouthful of coffee, to mask the sob gaining traction in her throat.

'You need to think, Lottie, long and hard. You and my grand-children are welcome to stay here. I know you won't want to do that for very long, but in the meantime, can we at least be civil to each other? Do you think you can manage that?'

Lottie held her tongue. It wasn't her that was always throwing out snide remarks. Or was it?

'Okay. Thank you.'

Rose nodded and left the room, closing the door with a soft thud.

'What am I going to do?' Lottie cried at the four walls.

She needed air. Shit, she needed clothes.

And then her phone beeped with a message.

CHAPTER EIGHTY-EIGHT

Last night, once he'd got over his panic attack, Boyd had scoured the town. Grace was nowhere to be found. He'd rounded up Kirby, Lynch and Gilly to start phoning. Store Street garda station, Garda HQ. The rail company. Anyone and everyone. Someone must know where she was.

It was fruitless. He knew that. Look at Mollie Hunter. No sighting of her since Wednesday. And Grace had been on that train with her. So where was she?

When he'd heard about the fire at Lottie's house, he'd rushed there to see what he could do to help, and had made sure she and the children were safely ensconced at her mother's. Now SOCOs were sifting through the embers for clues to what had happened. Had Lottie and her family become the target of whoever had murdered Bridie McWard and her child? The only variable in that synopsis was that Paddy McWard had been detained in a cell all night.

Boyd paced the incident room. He needed to get into his car and do something. Go somewhere. But where?

Right now, he could do with some of Lottie's gut instinct.

Right now, he could do with Lottie by his side, full stop.

CHAPTER EIGHTY-NINE

Standing at the corner by the caretaker's office, Lottie looked down the hill at the small gathering. Father Joe was sprinkling holy water from a narrow hand-held brass bucket. She wanted to walk away from this intimate activity, from the tranquillity of the morning after the mayhem of the last twelve hours, but she'd been drawn here and now she couldn't move her feet.

She shuffled her hands up the sleeves of her mother's coat for warmth and bit her lip as the mourners passed by, arms linked, heads bowed. She felt awkward in Rose's boots, trousers and shirt. All too big, hanging off her body, but beggars can't be choosers, Rose had said. Gilly had come over with stuff she thought might fit Chloe and said she'd bring her to town later to buy clothes for Sean. A squad car with two officers was parked outside Rose's house with orders to keep watch.

Father Joe stopped when he saw her. His face wore a tormented expression, like the look you'd see imprinted on the faces of people who'd suffered tragedy in their lives. That look. Lottie knew exactly what Father Joe Burke had suffered. The loss of a mother he never knew. A mother whom he'd been taken from against her will. And then her murder. Too much suffering for one man.

'Hello again,' she said.

He smiled, and she noticed that single act could still light up his face, though now it was full of sadness. The blonde hair that used to fall into his once-mischievous blue eyes was gone, replaced by a tightly shorn head. Was it a form of self-flagellation? Was he divesting himself of who he thought he was? She knew that feeling well.

He moved into her space, placed a hand lightly on her elbow, and she bit harder into her lip.

'You got my text,' he stated. 'Are you okay? The children?'

She shrugged. 'I suppose so.'

'You need to talk to someone, Lottie. Will you come up to the house for a chat?'

'I've things to sort,' she said, feeling foolish for having come.

'Let's walk then.'

She felt his arm link hers and allowed herself to be led.

Halfway down the hill, she felt dizzy and they sat on a steel bench.

'It's all a bit mad,' she said, watching Bernard Fahy filling in Mrs Green's grave.

'Isn't it always?'

She laughed sadly. 'You'll be having a few more funerals in the coming days. I was with Queenie McWard just before she died.'

'Very sad.'

The sun glinted off the copper roof of the old nursing home nestled behind the new building. 'Do you ever visit the residents in the home?'

'Sometimes. But I only came back just before Christmas.'

'Thought you were gone for good.'

'I had a change of heart. This is where I belong.'

'I thought I did too. Belonged. Now I'm not so sure.'

'You're in shock, Lottie. It was an awful thing to happen.'

'The fire?'

'Yes. Are there other things?'

'Plenty. I think I'll be suspended from my job. One daughter hates me; the other's flown to New York to stay with her son's grandfather for a while. Sean is Sean, and my mother ... That's a story for another day.'

'What about Boyd?'

'What about him?' And as she said the words, Lottie felt a longing in her heart. She wanted to speak with him. Knowing Boyd, he was giving her space. 'I like Boyd.'

'I think you need a comforting arm around you. And not just a priestly one.'

'You are so good, Joe. I'm sorry for all the things that happened to you.'

'Not your fault. I'm working my way through the pain.'

'So am I. But now I might have no job.' She found herself explaining to him how her investigations had led to her being in danger of suspension.

'I've been following the news. Do you think the current cases are linked to Lynn O'Donnell?'

'I'm beginning to think so.'

'I was thinking that maybe Mollie Hunter is being held where Lynn was held for ten years,' he said.

'It's possible. But we have no clue where that might be.'

'Go back to when it all started. Today, ten years ago.'

Lottie shivered as a bird flapped its wings above her head to the sound of a train slowing down on the tracks as it headed for the station. 'You always were good at detective work.'

He smiled.

The train blasted its horn and disappeared from view.

CHAPTER NINETY

After she left Father Joe at the cemetery, Lottie went into town and grabbed a coffee, then walked slowly up Main Street, ignoring the shop windows full of red hearts. She found herself at the train station without really knowing that was where she'd been headed.

She doubted Jimmy Maguire would be around on Sunday morning, and it was half an hour since she'd heard the Sligo train. But as she stood in the portico, just outside the ticket office, she saw his capped head approaching.

'The lovely Detective Inspector Parker.'

'I wanted to have a word with you.'

He directed her towards the ticket office. 'There's a vending machine inside if you'd like a hot drink.'

'No thanks. I've just had a coffee.'

She sat on the wooden bench outside the door and felt the cold wind whistle around her ears. She nestled her chin into the wool of her mother's coat as he joined her.

'What did you want to ask me? I can't remember anything else about those two lassies. Terrible. One murdered and the other missing. Shocking business.'

'This is about Lynn O'Donnell.'

His face paled and he bit the inside of his cheek. 'What about her?'

'Did you know her?'

'No.'

'Did you see her the day she disappeared?'

'I'm presuming you read up on the case, so you know I saw her that evening when she got off the train.'

'She dropped her bag on the platform.'

'I helped her pick up her belongings. That's the last I saw of her.'

'Did you know her before then?'

He seemed to digest that, perhaps wondering if it was a trick question. But she was throwing out a line, hoping something might bite.

'I knew her a little. Knew her brothers. They were avid train watchers. Obsessed with trains, those boys were. Still are. Both are on the railway preservation committee.'

Lottie filed away that snippet. 'How did Lynn seem that day?'

'Ah, sure it was a long time ago.'

'Try to remember.'

He closed his eyes. 'Flustered. She dropped her bag, didn't she?' He opened one eye and squinted at Lottie.

'Was there any reason for that? Did she see someone or something to make her flustered?'

He closed his eyes again. Imagining that day ten years ago?

'The platform was packed,' he said. 'Busy. Not as many trains running back then. There were more people crowded onto the few that were operating. All the men were flitting about with bunches of roses. Probably got them cheap on Moore Street.'

'After you helped her repack her handbag,' Lottie probed, 'did you notice where she went?'

'What did I say in the report?'

'I want to know what you can remember.'

He sighed and looked up at pigeons nesting on a rafter. 'My memory is not as good as it used to be.'

'I'm sure it's just fine.'

He smiled at the compliment.

'She was red-faced. Embarrassed? I don't know. She rushed through that gate from the platform and went outside. Most of the crowd had dispersed by then. I flagged the train on its way and closed the gate. I remember standing on the steps there, thinking I was almost finished for the day. That was the last train. And ...'

'And what?'

'I never said anything before.' He clasped his hands tightly, as if the gesture might keep his tongue quiet.

Lottie placed a hand on his arm. 'You can tell me.'

'I ... I couldn't tell anyone. You see a small fire started. I think it blurred my memory. The old waiting rooms round the back. It was beginning to blaze. I never told anyone. It was my responsibility. I was terrified of losing my job.'

'What was your responsibility?

'Keeping the place clean and free of rubbish.'

Lottie sighed. He was trekking off on a tangent. 'Jimmy, you were telling me about Lynn O'Donnell?'

'There's nothing to tell.'

'Was it a big fire?'

'I thought so at first. But I put it out quick enough.'

'How did it start?'

'A build-up of rubbish caught light at the side of the building.' He wrung his hands together, his lips quivering. 'I never reported it as it was my job on the line. Can you understand that?'

She could, but she said, 'What aren't you telling me?'

'I couldn't say anything back then. And I can't now.'

'We found her body. Lynn. Did you know that? We think someone abducted her that day and hid her away for ten years until she died. Can you imagine anything worse? Was your job worth the heartache that family had to go through?'

'He said nothing either. So it wasn't all my fault.'

'Who are you talking about?' Lottie sat up straight. This was certainly new.

'He helped me. To put out the fire. I couldn't say anything or he might have dropped me in the shit, you know.'

'Jimmy, you have to tell me what you mean.'

He stood up, pushed his cap back and scratched his forehead. He had his back to her, and his voice was so low she had to stand up to hear him.

'You see, he was with her, collecting her or something. They were in the car. I think he saw the flames starting around the same time I did, because he came to help me. When we got it quenched with the extinguishers, I shook his hand to thank him and asked him to say nothing to no one, and he said …'

'Go on, Jimmy.'

'He said, I expect the same from you. Then he joined her in the car.'

'Jesus!' Lottie felt a tingle of anticipation catching fire in her belly. This had not appeared anywhere in Lynn O'Donnell's file. 'Who? Who was it?'

He looked back at her, his eyes half closed with sadness.

'Her brother.'

Lottie gulped down her surprise.

'Which one, Jimmy? Tell me! Which brother?'

CHAPTER NINETY-ONE

'Carol?' Terry's voice echoed up the stairs.

If he wakes Mum and Dad, I'm going to kill him, she thought as she jumped out of bed. The contents of her stomach rose to her mouth. Grabbing a tissue, she threw up in the bowl beside the bed. When would it ever stop?

'Carol, get down here.'

'I'm coming, you moron.' Maybe it was a delivery of flowers for Valentine's Day. That would be great. Maybe he was leaving his wife.

'What's all the racket?'

Now her dad was awake.

'It's for me. Go back to sleep, Dad. It's Sunday,' she said.

At the bottom of the stairs, Terry stood with the door open. 'Someone wants to talk to you.'

'You!' Carol said, her jaw dropping almost to her chest. 'What are you doing here?'

'We need to talk,' the man said, and turned away. 'I'm parked around the corner.'

'Give me five minutes. I better get dressed.'

*

The office was in uproar when Lottie entered. Desks were littered with mugs of coffee and half-eaten croissants, crumbs everywhere. People eating on the go.

'What's going on?' she asked, stretching her arms out, imploring an answer from her animated team.

'What are you doing here?' Boyd jumped up from his desk and dragged her into her office. 'Jesus, Lottie, you look a sight. You should be at home in bed.'

'I don't have a home, never mind a bed.'

'And didn't McMahon suspend you?'

'He only thinks he did. I don't care about him. Anyway, the chief super won't want to get rid of me. Someone tried to murder my family last night. That's all I care about. As soon as McGlynn has the evidence, I'm going to swing for the bastard who did it. So tell me, what's all this about?' She slammed the table, immediately wincing with pain. Her own news would have to wait until she found out what was going on.

'Your hand, it's hurt.'

She held up her bandaged left hand. 'So it is, Sherlock. I didn't realise how quickly flames could climb stairs.'

'At least you got some clothes, even if they are a bit vintage.'

She studied Boyd's haggard face. 'You look awful. What's going on?'

'It's Grace. She's missing.'

'What? Tell me.'

He explained about his mother's phone call, and all they'd done so far without finding a trace of his sister.

'She'll be fine. Don't fret.' Lottie didn't believe her own words.

Boyd's breaths came in short puffs as he said, 'She can't be fine. Her phone and medication are at my place and I'm sure she's wherever Mollie Hunter is. And if Mollie is already dead, then I'll never see Grace again.'

'One step at a time, Boyd. Breathe before you have a panic attack.'

'Had one already. Passed out.'

'See a doctor. Get checked out.'

'Look who's talking. I'll be fine. Once I find Grace.'

'Have you followed the protocol for a missing person?'

'Yes, and more. I asked McMahon to talk to the media. In the light of all that's happened this last week, he agreed.'

'Okay. If Grace is linked to the current cases, we need to retrace our steps on Mollie Hunter's disappearance and maybe that way we'll find your sister. Agree?'

'I suppose so. Are Chloe and Sean okay?'

'They're with my mother. Gilly is there. They're fine.'

'You should be with them.'

'I know. But I'll be like a hen on an egg if we don't find Grace, so I'm better off here. My kids know me well; they understand.'

'McWard is still refusing to say anything,' he said. 'We have him for another few hours and then it's either charge or release.'

'Forget McWard for the moment. I made a discovery earlier. It might throw new light on our investigation. The day Lynn O'Donnell vanished, there was a fire in the old waiting rooms over on the disused platform.'

'What's that got to do with her disappearance?'

'When I gave him a nudge, Jimmy Maguire remembered that a man met her that evening at the station.'

'Paddy McWard?'

'Nope. Her brother.'

*

Carol pulled the collar of her coat tight to her neck and settled into the passenger seat of his car. She shoved her hands into her pockets defiantly.

'You have some nerve coming round to my house. My brother will kill you.'

'I'll kill the little shit first. Fucking dope head.'

'What do you want? I don't see any flowers, so that's not a good start.'

'I can give you something much better than flowers. I missed you. Just wanted to see you.'

'And risk my dad seeing you? What is this really about, Cillian?' She twisted in the seat to get a good look at him. He appeared strained, his hands tense on the steering wheel. His eyes were rimmed with black circles. But he still looked stunningly handsome.

'Let's go for a drive,' he said. 'I know a quiet spot at the lake.' He turned on the ignition without waiting for her reply. 'There's something important I need to tell you.'

Fuck it, thought Carol, she could do with a hug. She slipped her hand out of her pocket and caressed his leg as he drove out of the estate, down the road and on towards the lake.

CHAPTER NINETY-TWO

Lottie watched as Boyd digested the information.

'Okay, so we don't know which brother it was,' he said. 'Maguire won't tell and he says he's never raised it with whichever one it was over the last ten years. That doesn't make sense.'

'Dealing with covering up for the fire tainted his judgement. So he says. I was lucky to get that much out of him.'

'And there's no mention in the file of either brother meeting her that day?'

'Not a dicky bird.'

'We better get them in.'

'Wait, Boyd. There may be no connection to Lynn's case but if we do that, and he's the one who's taken Mollie and Grace, he might never tell us where they are. We need a strategy.'

He let out a sigh. His hands were trembling and sweat bubbled on his brow. She reached over but he folded his arms.

He said, 'We've searched the town high up and low down for Mollie, without a result.'

'What about Rochfort Gardens? That's where the girls ran.'

'There are acres out there.'

'Exactly. And an old house and all those ridiculous follies.'

Boyd got on the phone and organised a search team and the garda helicopter.

'Where else?' he said as he hung up.

'The train station and surrounding areas have already been searched. Including the old buildings. So that's out.'

'What about that terrace of dilapidated houses where Donal O'Donnell lives?'

'Another possibility,' she said.

Boyd lifted the phone to organize that search.

'Just a minute.' Lottie halted him. He was moving too fast. They needed to think. 'We don't want to spook anyone. Maybe we should get Donal out of there first.'

'How can we do that without causing suspicion?'

'I'll say we have new evidence on Lynn and need him to identify something.'

'He might've been in on it.'

She paused. She hadn't considered that.

'Makes sense. A family thing. Hiding the possibility that Lynn got pregnant with a traveller.'

Once she'd said the words, Lottie realised something.

'Shit, Boyd. What happened to her baby?'

CHAPTER NINETY-THREE

When Donal O'Donnell refused to come to the station. Lottie decided to go to him.

In the car, her phone rang.

'Is that Inspector Lottie Parker?'

'Yes. Who's this?'

'Keelan. Keelan O'Donnell.'

'What can I do for you?'

'You never contacted me.'

'Sorry. Things are hectic.' And that was putting it mildly, Lottie thought. 'What's up?'

'It's Cillian. I don't know where he is. And …'

'And?'

'Things are bad at home. Very bad, the last few months. That's why I wanted to talk to you. I think he's up to something.'

'Something?' Lottie rolled her eyes over at Boyd. 'Like what?'

'I think he's seeing someone else. Look, the reason … I'm scared, Inspector. He's become a bit violent. I'm terrified he'll do something to me, to Saoirse.'

'Keelan, I'm on my way to your father-in-law's place. Why don't you meet me there?'

The television was on, the sound muted. The candle on the dresser in front of Lynn's photograph remained unlit. Donal sat at the table with his hands clenched in fists. Opposite him, Lottie sat with Boyd.

'Mr O'Donnell. Donal. Can you tell us about the day Lynn disappeared?'

'Jesus. Now you've found her body, all you have are questions. It's all in the file. I'm sure it's a big fat file. You can't miss it.' He pulled the newspaper towards him and began to fold it.

'We have new information.'

'You have her body.'

'We believe Lynn got off the train this day ten years ago and was met by her brother. Did she come home? Did something happen? A family row because she was in love with a traveller? Something like that, huh?'

The paper-folding exercise halted, his hand in the air. 'What makes you say that?'

'Remember I told you about the ring the pathologist found inside Lynn's body?'

'What about it?'

'It was given to Lynn by Paddy McWard.'

His lip curled up to his nose. 'That piece of scum. I wouldn't let him near my sons, never mind my daughter.'

'But he *was* near your daughter. According to Paddy, they were in love. Probably would've run off together to get married if someone hadn't stopped that happening.'

She recoiled as Donal spat on the kitchen floor. 'He wasn't near my girl.'

Deciding offence was the best option, she said, 'I have reason to believe one of her brothers picked her up from the train. Did they come back here? A big row broke out. Then what?'

'Fuck off, devil woman. Talking evil in my house. I won't have it.'

The doorbell chimed.

'I'll get it,' Boyd said, and escaped.

He returned a few seconds later followed by Keelan and a little girl.

'Hey, Dad, what's going on?'

'I'm not your dad! What do you want?'

Lottie noticed Keelan shrinking back and her daughter cowering behind her legs.

'I'm … I'm looking for Cillian.'

'He's not here. You can bugger off.'

Lottie interjected. 'Sit down, Keelan.' The woman was so scared, she might as well have had the word FEAR written in bold letters on her face.

'I'll just let Saoirse play in the living room.'

When she returned, she sat at the end of the table.

Lottie said, 'Donal, this is serious. Please tell us what happened this day ten years ago.'

The lids of his watery eyes rose slightly before he looked down at his hands and shook his head.

'It was bad. Evil. My girl brought a curse on this family. Cavorting with the likes of them, living in caravans with their spells and curses. Can you imagine how my poor Maura would have felt if she'd found out about it? Devastated she'd have been.'

'Was Lynn planning on telling her mother?' Lottie said.

'She told Cillian. He was always her favourite. She never got on with Finn. Think the lad was mighty jealous of his brother. But that's beside the point. Cillian knew she intended to tell all that day, it being Valentine's, and she'd planned to meet the tinker fellow.' He paused as if the word caused his mouth to dry up. 'I was just in from work when the boys sat me down. She stood there.' He pointed to the dresser. 'Stood there like a hussy and told me she was pregnant.'

'Where was your wife?'

'She was still at work. We worked hard for our kids. Day and night. And that's how the girl repaid us. Slut. That's what she was. A fucking slut.'

'There's no need to speak ill of your daughter like that.' Keelan hugged her arms to her chest, her features incredulous.

'Please continue, Donal,' Lottie said. She didn't want him to clam up, or they might never find out what had happened; might never find Grace and Mollie. That is, if they were linked at all.

Donal eyed her before continuing. 'You've no idea what it was like. I nearly died, right where I was sitting. That's the kind of shock it was. But when she said who she'd been whoring around with, I lost it. Jumped up and hit her smack in the face. She fell back and Cillian caught her. He started shouting at me, and Finn stood there with his mouth open like the big eejit he was and always will be.'

'And then?'

'And then I stormed out of the house. Went to the pub. Must have drunk ten pints, and when I got home, there was no Lynn.'

'What had happened? What did your sons say?'

'Cillian said Lynn had run off. He told me he'd driven round to the site, where that yoke lived, but she wasn't there and the tinker hadn't a clue.'

'And did you believe him, that she'd run off?'

'What else could I believe? That he'd killed her and hidden her body? That's what I believed for the last ten years. That's why I never mentioned the McWard fellow. There was enough disgrace hanging like a noose around my family without that.'

'And your wife. What did you tell Maura?'

'Finn told her that Lynn never came home. And that's what we stuck to. That's the story we told all those years. He covered up for Cillian, like brothers do.'

'But Lynn wasn't dead. Where was she?'

'I've no idea. I convinced myself she was dead since that day, and now she is.'

'Where's Cillian now?' Lottie turned to Keelan.

'I don't know. He was out half the night. Like he is most of the time.' Keelan paused, struggling to get the words out. 'We had another blazing row this morning and he stormed off. But he said something that frightened me.'

'What did he say?'

'He told me I was a jealous bitch. Then he said that jealousy took his sister from him and got her killed, and if I didn't shut up, he'd kill me.'

'Any idea where he goes at night?' Boyd asked.

Lottie glanced at his anxious face, etched with concern for his sister. 'Keelan, do you know where he might have kept Lynn hidden all these years? Where he might be keeping Mollie Hunter and possibly Grace Boyd?'

'Oh God. You don't think … He couldn't. Not Cillian.' Keelan stood up, her hands pulling at her hair.

'Please think,' Lottie said. She turned to Donal. 'Is there anywhere your sons went to when they were younger? Someplace no one would think of looking?'

'All the houses beside us are empty, ten if not eleven years. Maura wouldn't let us move in case Lynn came home and couldn't find us.'

'Okay. I want you to come to the station. We'll organise a search.'

'I'm going nowhere,' Donal said.

'Mr O'Donnell, you've been complicit in covering up a crime. You're coming with us.'

'You'll have to handcuff me.'

'I will.' Boyd pulled a set from his pocket and clicked them open.

'Wait a minute,' Lottie said. She turned to Keelan. 'We need to get Finn and his wife into protective custody. Are they at home?'

'I imagine so.'

Lottie phoned Kirby to get there straight away with a squad car. She left Boyd with Donal and ushered Keelan into the sitting room to collect Saoirse. The room exuded misery and loss.

'Inspector?' Keelan said.

Lottie looked at her.

'I don't think my Cillian could do that to his sister. He loved her.'

'Love can do strange things to people,' Lottie said.

CHAPTER NINETY-FOUR

The car windows were fogged up from their lovemaking. Carol straightened her clothes, glad that her nausea seemed to have waned. She ran a finger down Cillian's face. 'You look sad.'

'I love you, Carol,' he said. 'I know a horrible thing happened to you. But I need to know if the baby you're carrying is mine or from the bastard who raped you.'

Carol turned away. Why was he saying this? It was him, wasn't it? She couldn't tell him that she knew he was her rapist. That he'd got drunk and followed her and attacked her that night. She'd been fairly drunk too, so what would that make her? Complicit? The only thing keeping her going was the fact that it could only be Cillian's baby. She hadn't had sex with anyone else. How could she convince him?

She wanted to be angry at him, but her heart was filled with love. And sorrow for her dead friend. Lizzie, who had held onto the chain and ring she'd pulled from her rapist's neck. The same one that Cillian had always worn but no longer did. Oh, why could she not remember more? Why had she been drinking so much that night?

'Answer me,' he said, leaning over her, his mouth so close she was swallowing his words. 'I'll tear him apart with my bare hands. Who was the bollocks who did it to you?'

'I'm not sure.'

'But you have an idea?'

'Yes.'

'Tell me.' His face was hard and his eyes darker than she'd ever noticed before.

'First I need to know that you're going to leave your wife,' she blurted, clasping her fingers into each other.

He pulled away from her and she felt a cold void spring up between them. And something else. Something that was consuming the cramped space in the car.

And then she knew.

It was her own fear.

*

Kirby took Keelan, Saoirse and Donal to the garda station. Donal was raving and shouting about evil spirits, so Lottie told Kirby to call a doctor. She was in enough trouble without being the cause of a suspect dying.

'I need to find Grace,' Boyd said as they finished searching the old man's house.

'The search team are working their way through the terrace. So far we have nothing.'

'Where could he keep a girl hidden for ten years? Never mind the why.'

'There must be a clue in this house. This is the last place we know where Lynn was.'

'You'd think she'd be safe in her own home.'

'A house with a demented father and two brothers oozing hormones, and God knows what the mother was like. Then Lynn brings home news that in Donal's mind was the ultimate taboo. Pregnant by a traveller. Prejudice is an awful thing, Boyd.'

'So is keeping a young woman hidden for ten years. Do you think when Lynn died he went over the edge and took Elizabeth to replace her?'

'That's what I suspect. Then Elizabeth escapes, and he kills her and has to find another replacement. Where the hell did he keep them?'

Lottie entered Donal's small bedroom again. It was suffused with such a thick, fusty smell that she felt she could touch it if she put out her hand. She didn't dare. Beside the bed was a small bookcase, folders sticking out haphazardly.

'I already looked there,' Boyd said. 'Seems to be old work stuff. Mainly relates to the nursing home.'

'That's where he works.'

'The boys worked with him for a while. I saw invoices. Donal was a cute fucker. Billed the health board for his sons doing a bit of painting.'

'Where did you see that?'

Boyd tugged a black A4 ring binder from the shelf and two others slipped to the floor.

'Jesus, leave them there,' Lottie said as he bent to tidy up. 'Which page? Show me.'

He leaned over her shoulder and flipped through. 'There. Fixing up a boiler room and painting some corridor or other. February 2001.'

'This relates to the old nursing home. It closed down maybe a year after that. Could that be it?'

'What?'

'I think it might be where he kept Elizabeth.' Lottie made for the door.

'Jesus, that's a long shot,' Boyd shouted.

She kept running.

*

'Carol, you have to tell me what you suspect. I can't promise you anything until I know.'

She looked out the window at the ripples roughing up the lake. 'You used to wear a ring on a chain round your neck. But you don't wear it any more. Why?'

'I don't know what that's got to do with anything. But to satisfy you, I'll tell you.' He turned around to face her. 'I had a row with my brother one night. I can't even remember the exact thing we fought over. Something to do with the railway preservation committee, I think. But fight we did. Down and dirty. Like we used to when we were kids. He pulled the chain off me. It got lost. Searched the ground for it when he was gone. Never found it. Are you saying the rapist had it?'

'You don't know where it might be?'

'No and I don't care any more. It was a Claddagh ring. Lynn had one just like it … when she vanished. I bought a similar one and wore it around my neck to remind me of her.'

Carol twisted away from the window and faced him.

'The night I was attacked, my rapist was wearing one exactly like it. I pulled it from his neck.'

'What?' The realisation of what she was saying began to dawn on him. 'You thought it was me. All these weeks, you still met up with me, thinking I might have attacked and raped you. How could you?'

She shrugged. 'I just did. The ring was yours. I was sure of it. I gave it to a friend to mind for me, in case I ever reported the rape and needed evidence.'

'You what? Jesus, Carol. I could never …' He stopped. 'I don't think I could … you know, be violent like that. But I've been so stressed recently, I'm not myself. I actually hit Keelan one night, and another evening I broke every plate in the house.'

Tears streamed down his cheeks. She reached up and wiped them. 'I'm sorry. I love you and didn't want to believe it was you.'

'I don't really blame you.'

'Cillian.' Her voice dropped to a whisper. 'The man who attacked me, could it have been, you know, your brother?'

'Finn? No!' he cried.

She watched him and saw his expression changing.

'Oh God,' she said.

Banging his head against the steering wheel, Cillian wailed at the waters rising on the lake.

And in that moment, Carol feared for her life and that of the baby growing in her womb.

CHAPTER NINETY-FIVE

The door of the hatch opened and his legs appeared, climbing down the ladder. Why hadn't she thought of whacking him before? A day or two ago, when she still had the strength? But now hunger gnawed at her stomach like a rat, and she could hardly move.

When he jumped off the last rung onto the floor, she saw he held scissors in one hand, and a battery-powered razor in the other.

'Time for a haircut,' he said. 'Or maybe you'd like to tell me where you hid it first?'

'Hid what?'

'Oh, don't go all coy on me, pretty girl. I know you were friends with that slut. Took her in the night she was attacked. Didn't I tell you? I did that to her. She was some fighter. A terrible vixen.'

Was he talking about the girl who was raped? What was her name? Carol O'Grady? But Mollie hardly knew her. 'What am I supposed to have hidden?'

'So that's the way you want to play it? I thought a few days of confinement might loosen your tongue, but it seems I have to use brutal measures. Poor old Lynn. She didn't like getting her head shaved. But I had to do it. The creepy-crawly lice would've torn her scalp to shreds in this place. See, I'm not all bad.'

Before she realised what he was doing, he had pulled her upright by her hair. Gripped it in a tight knot around his fingers and sliced through with the scissors. She watched helplessly as it fell to the ground at her bare feet.

'No!'

The buzz of the razor drowned out her sobs as it sliced close to her scalp, shaving her hair clean from her head. It nicked a spot that had erupted over the last day, and blood seeped down her forehead into her eyes.

'What do you want?' she cried.

'The silver chain with the ring. The one your raped friend gave you to mind.'

'I don't know what you're talking about.' She honestly hadn't a clue.

'Come on. I'm not stupid. She either gave it to that Elizabeth bitch or she gave it to you. That cow died before I could get the information from her, so I'm back to thinking you must have it. Now where the fuck is it?'

Mollie crumpled in a heap on the floor in the midst of her shorn hair and tried to remember. She had Carol's clothes. Nothing else. No chain. No ring. But he wasn't going to believe that. As he hunkered down to continue shaving, she knew she had to come up with a plan. And mighty quick. Otherwise she'd end up fermenting beside the bones on the table.

CHAPTER NINETY-SIX

On the way, Boyd checked in with the other search teams. Still ongoing at Rochfort Gardens, but nothing had been found. Yet. As they drove towards the old nursing home, Kirby came on the radio.

'Dropped the O'Donnells at the station. Heading to pick up Finn and Sara, then I'm going to join the search at the Ladystown caravan park.'

Boyd clicked him off.

'They'll find her,' Lottie said. 'Are you okay?'

'I will be once this is all over.'

He drove up to the front of the old home and parked. Lottie got out of the car and walked between two buildings leaning in over her until she came to the oldest structure.

'It dates back to the famine,' she said as Boyd joined her.

'I thought Lynch was our local history fanatic.'

She pointed to a plaque above the black timber door. 'Says it right there.' Pushing against the door, she found it was firmly closed. 'Let's have a look further back.'

Rusting oil tanks and odds and ends of machinery were lined up against the ancient wall behind which the current nursing home was housed. She continued walking to her right, with Boyd by her side. They turned another corner and stopped. A car was parked haphazardly.

'Who owns that, then?' Boyd asked, taking out his phone.

'My bet is Cillian O'Donnell. Check the registration.'

He was already on the phone as she made her way past the car and behind a mound of rubble to the side of another building.

'Is that a boiler house?' she said.

'I'd say so but look at the chimney.' He pointed upwards. 'There must have been an incinerator here.'

To the rear, a door. Lottie nudged it with the knuckles of her good hand and it swung inwards. She raised her eyebrows at Boyd.

'That's a stroke of good luck,' he said.

'You always can read my mind. Pull on gloves, just in case this leads to anything.'

They moved inside.

'I think you're right, Boyd. This was an incinerator. You go that way and I'll take this side.'

They spent five minutes looking, searching and listening. Nothing.

'There's a car out back, so someone must be here,' Lottie said.

'Maybe he's avoiding parking charges at the nursing home. Just dropped the car there and headed off.'

She ignored him and opened the door to the oven-like structure built into a brick chimney breast. Leaned over the edge and peered in.

'Holy fuck, Boyd. There's a hatch built into the floor.'

CHAPTER NINETY-SEVEN

Was that a voice?

Sounded like one. Up high.

He was so busy scalping her bald, he mustn't have heard it. She was sure someone was there above them. Someone with him? Or help for her? She had to distract him.

'The bones,' she said. 'Where did they come from?'

'Why do you want to know?'

'They scare me a little.'

'I can scare you a whole lot more than bones.'

'I'm not afraid of you.' The hope that rescue might be close gave her a smidgen of courage.

He let go of her head and sat back on the floor. She twisted round and faced him.

'Who do you think I'm going to tell, locked up here?' she said.

'You have a smart mouth on you, for a pretty girl.'

'Oh, don't bother telling me. I don't want to know.'

He stared at her, chewing the inside of his cheek. Weighing it up. Was she getting to him? She hoped so.

'They belong to a baby,' he said.

'Whose baby? And who was Lynn that you mentioned?'

'Now you want to chat. I don't have time for this.' He raised the scissors.

'I'll tell you where the chain and ring are if you tell me about her.' Mollie had no idea where she was getting the strength from, but deep down she knew this might be her last chance. If she kept him talking, whoever was up above might hear them.

'You playing games with me?'

'No.'

'My nutjob of a wife does that to me.'

'I'm sorry about that,' she lied, trying to be convincing with her sympathy.

'The bones. That was my sister's baby. Lynn was pregnant when I took her. Took her away from her loving brother. She always had more time for him. He was always getting me into trouble. Blaming me for things. She was the star of our family show and everyone doted on her, and I was left out. The middle child, that was me. Left behind.' He set his mouth in a grim line and Mollie saw his fingers whiten as they clenched the scissors.

'That's awful,' she soothed and wondered if she could grab the scissors.

'Not fair,' he said. 'She came home that day, the whore, and announced in front of my excuse for a father and my brother that she was pregnant with a tinker's child. I knew she was finished then. The golden girl was tarnished and I saw my chance. I took her for myself.'

'How did you manage that?' Keep talking, Mollie prayed. Silence from above. Was it a good or a bad sign? As long as she could keep him talking, there was hope.

'The old man stormed off to the pub, my brother was broken before my eyes, and Mother was due home. I knew I'd be blamed, because, sweetheart, I got blamed for everything. Lynn fled the house, scared shitless. I followed her. Picked her up. Sweet-talked her. Told her a pack of lies and brought her here.'

'Was this place always here?'

'This place is a stroke of genius on my part.'

'You must be very clever.'

'I think I am actually.' He smirked. 'I held her upstairs in the old incinerator room, but over a few weeks I built a false bottom in the chamber with an entrance down here. All this is part of the original boiler house. I helped renovate it one summer. I blocked off the door and put in the hatch and steps. Yes, I am very clever. Anyone who decided to search was never going to find her. And they never did. I finally had something my brother couldn't have. I had her to myself.'

'What happened to her … baby?' Mollie couldn't help her eyes being drawn to the stark whiteness of the tiny bones.

'He was born dead, the little bastard. I left him upstairs to rot. Thought of burying him. But it was a better idea to leave his bones out for her to see every day of her miserable life.'

Mollie felt sick to her stomach. The mental torture that poor girl must have suffered. 'Where is she now?'

'Who?'

She noticed his eyes glazing over, a film of insanity shrouding the whites, the pupils dark rings of hate. She struggled to keep her voice even.

'Your sister.'

'She died. It was such fun, every year, watching them all wallowing in grief, wondering where she was.' He laughed, a strange, screechy sound. 'They never told a living soul about the traveller. She had this ring. A Claddagh or something. Swallowed it, she did. Stupid bitch. Don't know if it got stuck in her gullet, poisoned her or what, but when I told her that Mother had died without ever finding out she was still alive, it was like Lynn couldn't hack it any longer. Or maybe it was because I was busy with the funeral, relations and all that shite. It went on for a week, the wake, the funeral, the afters. I forgot to come with food and water. So maybe she starved. I don't really care. I was left with the bother of getting rid of her body.'

'You could have left her here,' Mollie ventured. 'With her baby.'

'I wasn't able for the smell. And I wanted to have this space free in case I needed it. And I did.'

Mollie was afraid to ask, but she got the words out, 'What did you do with her body?'

'Doused her in bleach, wrapped her up in bin bags and dumped her out at the lake for the rats and wild birds to feast on. But some teenage trash found her before she was eaten to the bone. So, pretty girl, I'm done with talking. Your turn. Tell me, where is the chain with the ring?'

*

Lottie held a finger to her lips. 'Shh. I hear voices. There's someone down there.'

Boyd leaned into the cavernous space with her. 'You're right. I'm going down.'

'No, you need to call for backup. And have a good look around outside. There might be another way in. This building is next to the boiler house. Have a look there. But do it quietly.'

'I'm not leaving you alone.'

'Why not?'

'Because it might be my sister down there and you'll do something stupid.'

'I won't. I'll just guard this door. Go. Make the call.'

She watched him reluctantly leave, then put her ear to the wooden hatch in the oven floor. The sound was muffled, but she could make out some of the words. She switched her phone to record and pushed it over the widest gap in the timber that she could find.

She had been listening for about five minutes, with no sign of Boyd returning, when she heard the scream.

Without further thought, she slid her phone away, pulled the hatch door open and jumped down.

CHAPTER NINETY-EIGHT

Lottie hit the floor with a thud, having missed most of the rungs on the ladder.

'Drop your weapon, Finn. Step away from Mollie.'

Two sets of wild eyes gaped back at her, Mollie's with terror and Finn's with confusion. The air was filled with the scent of claustrophobic fear. It dripped down the walls and rested like a sheen on the skin of the naked girl.

She was on her knees, her head haphazardly shaven. He stood behind her, one arm around her waist, pulling her into his body, the other about her neck. A pair of scissors in his hand was pointing directly at her eye.

'Stay there,' he growled. 'I'll do her, I swear I will.'

'That's not a good move.' Still on the floor, Lottie tried to see something in her vicinity that she could use as a weapon. She had no bag and no gun, but Mollie was in danger and she had to do something. Where the hell was Boyd?

'Oh, I think it is a good move. I outsmarted the lot of you.'

A noise above them caused Lottie to look up. But it wasn't Boyd. It was Cillian O'Donnell. Where the hell had he come from? This was not good.

A wild laugh broke from Finn. 'Now we can play happy families, dear brother.'

Cillian stepped off the ladder, then reached down and pulled Lottie to her feet. Shit, she thought. The two of them are involved in this together. Where the fuck was Boyd?

'It's okay, Finn, I have the guard now,' he said. 'Put down the scissors. You don't want another murder on your head, do you?'

'Another murder? What are you talking about.'

'We can do this together. Me and you. Like old times.'

Lottie felt the hairs on her arms sizzle. How was she going to take down the two of them? Mollie looked in no shape to help. Boyd better be quick.

'Yes, Finn,' she said. 'Put down the scissors.'

'Shut her up,' Finn shouted.

'I have her. No need to shout,' Cillian said, and Lottie felt his arm loop around her neck.

Finn snarled. 'What do you care? You never thought about me before; you're not going to change now.'

'But I do care,' Cillian said. 'I want to help you. Like you helped me with Lynn.'

'What do you mean?' The hand holding the scissors wavered.

Mollie was as still as a statue, only her eyes giving away that she was alive. Darting from Cillian to Lottie, pleading for help. Lottie scanned the room once again for a weapon. The space was so confined, they were virtually on top of each other, but at the same time Finn seemed to be miles from her reach.

'You took her away, didn't you?' Cillian said. 'Before she could disgrace our family. You saved us a shitload of heartache, bro.'

Was he inverting the truth, trying to get Finn to believe he was the good guy in all this? Smart move if that was the case. But maybe it was a ploy. With exhaustion and the effects of the last twenty-four hours, Lottie felt her gut instinct had deserted her. She couldn't read the situation. She needed Boyd.

'You really think so?' Finn said, his hand falling lower. It was now at Mollie's neck. She still hadn't moved.

'Sure. And that traveller,' Cillian said, 'he got what he deserved.'

'He sure did. I burned his hovel to the ground. Now he's got nothing. Living there all that time, laughing at us, and he never knew how close he was to Lynn. I thought that was funny.'

'Finn?' Cillian said.

'Yeah, bro?'

'You took Lynn, I can understand that. But Carol. Why'd you have to take her from me too?'

'What're you talking about?' Finn said, his brow tightening in two straight lines.

Yeah, what are you talking about? Lottie thought.

'You raped her. Why?'

With her body pressed to Cillian's, his arm still around her neck, Lottie sensed the tears streaming down his face. She glanced down at his other hand, to see if he held a weapon, but saw nothing. She had to hear this.

'Rape? I didn't …' Finn's eyes flared at his brother.

'You did. I know you did. Why?'

'So you know everything, as usual.' He pointed the scissors at Cillian, away from Mollie, though he still had his other arm around her waist. 'You had Keelan and Saoirse. You had everything and you went and ruined it. Going around sticking it in that Carol slut. And me at home with fucking Sara the cuckoo clock. Tick tock. Time's up.'

He moved swiftly. Lottie was quicker. She rammed her elbow into Cillian's stomach, shoving him back against the steps. Lunging forward, she kicked Finn in the groin and wrestled the weapon from his hand as he doubled over. Mollie fell back and rolled under the bed.

Footsteps hammered on the ladder and Boyd vaulted over the prostrate Cillian, landing on top of Finn. Lottie squirmed as she heard the whirr of a motor. Finn brought the razor up to Boyd's face, shredding his cheek. But he held on to Finn's wrists until the razor dropped to the ground.

Lottie snapped a set of handcuffs on the abductor and blew out a sigh of relief. Then she coaxed Mollie from beneath the bed and hugged her. Boyd pulled Cillian's hands together and cuffed him.

Before reading the two men their rights, Lottie glanced around the hovel and noticed the little paintings on the walls. Saw the name on them.

Then she saw the bones.

CHAPTER NINETY-NINE

Kirby scratched his head and shoved a cigar into his mouth. The lake was churning waves in the wind.

'Don't you dare light that,' Lynch said as she pulled open the door of a mobile home.

'This must be the fiftieth door we've opened today,' he said, looking longingly at the cigar in his hand before consigning it to his pocket.

Lynch said. 'It's the tenth. Nothing here. Have you the key to the next one?'

Kirby checked the bundle of keys they'd found in the unattended caretaker's hut. So much for security. 'This is a waste of time. There's no one in any of them.'

'Give me the key.' Lynch marched over to number eleven.

'What's that over there?' Kirby approached a small caravan surrounded by bushes at the end of the row. The windows were boarded up and the step broken. No sign of any gas cylinder or rubbish bins.

'How the hell do I know?' Lynch snapped the bundle of keys from his hand. 'Maybe the owner died and it's been left to rot.'

She went off with the keys and Kirby made to follow, but paused when he noticed a new lock on the door.

'Lynch. This looks odd.'

'Everything looks odd to you today,' she called back.

He moved closer, tried to see in through the boards nailed to the windows. No cracks. He could see nothing. He rattled the handle of the door. 'Anyone in there?'

He stuck his ear to the timber. Not a sound. Still, his gut told him to investigate further. A vice grip would be handy, he thought.

'Any padlock keys on that ring?' he yelled to Lynch.

'No.' She joined him.

Kirby thought for a minute. 'Stand back.'

The wood splintered as his boot went through the rotten timber. The lock held firm, but he tore with his bare hands to make space to enter. The light cast shadows on a shape on the floor.

'Call an ambulance,' he whispered.

*

Crime-scene tape fluttered around his burned-out home. Paddy McWard shoved his hands deep into his jacket pockets and blinked away his tears. All his life he'd stood up to discrimination and prejudice, but he'd never got a chance to stand up for Lynn. And because of his love for her, he'd never allowed himself to love Bridie. But his son, little Tommy …

He choked the sob back down his throat.

He had fought long and hard to rescue young lads from the dangerous underworld after he lost his brother. Now he had to do something about the ill his people were suffering. He didn't know what yet, but he would not be broken completely.

He turned at the sound of footsteps behind him. A priest stood there, his eyes twinkling in the light of the moon.

'Hello, Paddy. I'm Father Joe Burke. I know something of the torment you're suffering. I'm a good listener if you'd like to talk.'

'You know what, Father, I think that would be a good thing.'

CHAPTER ONE HUNDRED

Boyd had a large white plaster taped down his jaw.

'Goes well with the bruise on the other side,' Lottie said. 'That Finn really didn't like you.'

'It's not funny. It's painful.' Boyd looked up as an ambulance siren wailed outside the A&E before cutting out.

Lottie checked the message on her phone again. 'That should be them.'

Boyd rushed forward as the paramedics unloaded the stretcher, secured the wheels and pushed past them. Boyd grabbed Grace's hand and followed the stretcher inside.

'She's going to be okay,' Lottie said.

But Boyd was gone.

Back in the office, Lottie tried to make sense of what had happened in the old nursing home. Finn and Cillian had been arrested, though she now suspected that Cillian had not been involved in the abduction of their sister. That was all Finn. And he had wreaked havoc on the McWards because of his insane jealousy. She still had to interview Carol and take her statement. But once Finn started talking, he would be charged with rape along with his other crimes.

Mollie was in hospital, as was Grace, and both were expected to recover physically. Their mental health was another issue. Boyd's mother had arrived from Galway, so Lottie expected him to return to the office any minute.

The door opened and in he walked.

'You look like shit,' he said and pulled out a chair and flopped down.

'You can talk,' Lottie said. 'Is Grace okay? Are you okay?'

'She'll be fine. It's hard when your family is involved,' he said.

'You can say that again.'

'It's hard—'

'Boyd!' She stretched her legs out under her desk. Her foot snagged on the strap of her bag and she dragged it towards her. She'd forgotten to bring it home last night, so she still had the envelope containing Katie's money. One thing that had survived the fire.

'That O'Donnell family was seriously dysfunctional,' she said.

'I can't help thinking that Carol could have prevented Elizabeth's death if she had reported the rape.'

'Wasn't her fault. She was terrified. Like a lot of rape victims, she thought it was her own fault, and to complicate things, she believed it was her lover, Cillian, who'd raped her. She kept quiet thinking she was protecting him.'

'Poor girl.'

'And when his nut of a brother realised he'd lost the chain and ring, he started searching and questioning, seeking out anyone Carol was in contact with.' Lottie sighed.

'But it all started with Lynn falling in love with Paddy McWard, whose only crime was being born into a community despised by the O'Donnell men.' Boyd slammed the desk in frustration. 'Prejudice!'

'No, it started before then. Jealousy between two brothers. Jealousy within their family.'

Kirby barged in the door. 'Sorry, boss. We found a body.'

'Where? Who? Everyone is accounted for.'

'On the train tracks. Just by the cemetery. Reports came in a half-hour ago.' Kirby was out of breath.

'Who is it?'

Kirby placed a photo on Lottie's desk. 'That's his photo, from the incident board. He was hit by the evening train.'

'Matt Mullin,' Lottie said. 'Poor man.'

'When Grace is well enough, I'll get her to have a look at his photograph,' Boyd said. 'It was probably Mullin who caused Mollie to move seats and sit beside her.'

'Thanks, Kirby,' Lottie said. 'Will you inform his mother? Take a family liaison officer with you.'

'Will do. Oh, one other thing, boss. SOCOs have been going over Finn O'Donnell's car. Found flecks of skin in the footwell and on the front and back seats.'

'Links Finn directly to Elizabeth Byrne. She suffered from psoriasis.'

'DNA should link him to Carol's rape,' Boyd said. 'Where's his brother now?'

'We released him on bail, so he's probably at home, either patching things up with Keelan or packing his bags. Either way, Cillian did nothing wrong that we can prove, yet.'

'Not unless Keelan makes an official complaint for domestic abuse.'

'Time will tell,' Lottie said.

'But how did he know Finn was at the old nursing home?' Boyd rubbed his jaw, and winced as his fingers snagged on the plaster.

'His story is that he was out at the lake with Carol and she told him about being raped. When she mentioned the chain with the ring, he immediately suspected his brother. He knew there were only two places Finn had an interest in. One was the old railway, so he checked that first, and then he made his way to Finn's other favourite haunt. The old nursing home.'

'Had he not been there before? Surely he would have come across Lynn?'

'He says he never went there, but both of them had worked there when they were younger. He said Finn often talked about the old incinerator and how one day he wanted to restore it.'

'I still believe Cillian was involved.'

'I don't think so,' Lottie said, just as her desk phone lit up with a call. She answered it, her head as weary as her hands. Last night's fire drama seemed to have shrivelled her brain.

It was Jim McGlynn.

'Any news on who tried to murder my family?' Lottie asked.

'Fire started in your utility room. Probably a clothes dryer.'

'That can't be right.' Lottie felt her cheeks burn with embarrassment. 'It can't be my fault.'

'We're still working on it. We may find something else. Just wanted to let you know that.'

'Thanks, Jim.'

'You'd want to check your insurance, though.'

'Oh, won't it cover the fire?'

'How would I know?' McGlynn hung up.

Lottie glanced up. 'What?'

'Your fault?' Boyd said.

Feeling tears building up, Lottie sniffed them away. 'Jesus, Boyd. What have I done to my family? I never have time for maintenance or household stuff. It's always rush and fuss. Oh God. It's all my fault.' She laid her head on the desk and wrapped her hands about it.

'Shush, Lottie,' Boyd said. 'Don't blame yourself. It might still turn out to be the work of that bastard Finn O'Donnell.'

She raised her head. 'Maybe you're right. I don't know which is worse. Thinking it's my fault, or that someone targeted me and my family.'

Kirby stuck his head around the door. 'Lynch is buying the first round in Cafferty's. That right, Lynch?'

'Piss off, Kirby. I can't drink and you know it.'

'Why not?' Boyd said.

'I'm pregnant,' Lynch said, her cheeks flaring.

'Ah, a bit of good news at last,' Boyd said.

'Grace doing okay?' Lynch said.

'She'll be fine. My mother is with her. I better get back to the hospital.'

'Suppose I should give Gilly a call,' Kirby said. 'Don't like celebrating the end of a case on my own.'

When the office emptied and she was alone, Lottie called Chloe.

'Hey, hun. You and Sean okay?'

'Fine. Had a fab day with Gilly. She's cool. Bought loads of clothes in town. Wait till I show you. And we got Sean a hoodie and shirts and a pair of jeans. He's going around in his bare feet, though. We forgot to buy him shoes.'

'I'll get him some tomorrow.'

'He spent all day watching old films on the telly with Granny. You know what? He actually enjoyed it.'

'That's great.' Lottie felt a stab of jealousy. 'Will I bring a takeaway?'

'Is Boyd paying?'

'No, I found my handbag with Katie's money.'

'Only joking. About Boyd, I mean. Bring him round. Granny wants a word with him.'

'Really?'

'No, not really.' Chloe's voice dropped to a whisper. 'We can't live here, Mum. She's going to drive me mad, and by tomorrow Sean will be bored of movies. And we have a week off school. What are we going to do?'

'I'm sorry, Chloe, but we'll have to stay there for a little while. At least until I sort out somewhere to rent.'

'Granny wants to speak to you.'

'No, Chloe, I have to run.'

Too late.

'You're always running.' Rose Fitzpatrick had her mojo back. 'You don't have to bring any takeaway into my house. I've cooked a turkey and a ham.'

'But it's not Christmas.'

'It's Valentine's Day. About time we had a little love around here. And bring along that lad with the big ears.'

'Who? Boyd?'

'Yes. I like him. Are you on your way?'

Lottie hung up and noticed Boyd lounging in the doorway.

'I thought you were gone to the hospital,' she said, moving files around her desk. She found the little paintings in their plastic evidence bag.

'Wanted to make sure you weren't staying here all night.'

'It must have been hell for Lynn being held in that tiny space for ten years. And the bones of her baby beside her. How cruel can people be?' Lottie wondered.

'The baby can be buried with his mother, once Jane runs the DNA tests.'

'I'm trying to make out the signature.' She picked up another painting, one of a train. She glanced up with tears in her eyes.

'What is it, Lottie?' Boyd leaned over the desk and gripped her hand.

She welcomed the contact, needing to feel the touch of a good human being. There was too much evil in the world. But she pulled her hand away all the same.

'Lynn never stopped loving the father of her child.' She turned the painting around for Boyd to read. 'See the word on the train. It's his name. Paddy.'

'Poor bastard. He's off organising funerals. But he probably won't get to attend Lynn's. Donal O'Donnell won't have him near it.'

'If Keelan has anything to do with it, Paddy will be there. I'd say she's sick of their jealousy and prejudice. And frankly, so am I.'

Kirby rushed in, his unlit cigar hanging from his lips.

'What now?' Lottie said.

'McMahon. He's on the warpath. Worse than Corrigan ever was. Coming this way. I'd make a quick exit if I was you.'

'Arsehole,' Boyd said.

'Shit,' Lottie muttered.

EPILOGUE

With Boyd by her side, Lottie stood in the road, looking at the remains of her burned-out house. It was dark, and the heavens were in a tormented mood.

'Why do the gods continue to conspire against me to take everything away?'

'You have your family and you still have your job,' Boyd said. 'You're lucky McMahon's not pursuing your television debacle any further.'

'It's only so he can wallow in the success of closing the murder investigation so quickly. I wonder if Cynthia Rhodes is sticking around.'

'I'm sure she will.'

'Any word on Corrigan?' Lottie said. 'Never thought I'd say this, but I miss him.'

'His surgery was a success, but I don't know when he'll be back, if ever.'

'That means I'll have to suffer McMahon!'

'Or he'll have to suffer you,' Boyd laughed.

'Boyd, I've no home. It's been swallowed up in black smoke and flames. It's all ashes.'

'You have Katie's money from Tom Rickard,' he said with a laugh.

'It's not funny.' She shoved her hands deeper into her mother's wool coat.

'I know, but sometimes you have to laugh or you might cry,' he said.

Her phone vibrated in her pocket as rain began to come down in a diagonal line, cutting her face like shards of glass.

She answered the unknown number.

'Am I speaking to Lottie Parker?'

'Yes.' She walked in small circles. 'Who is this?'

'Captain Leo Belfield. I'm with the NYPD. New York Police Department.'

Lottie dropped to her knees on the hard tarmac, rainwater flowing around her. She clenched the phone to her ear.

'What's happened? Oh God Almighty. Please tell me they're all right?' Boyd bent down and wrapped his arms about her. She shrugged him off.

'Sorry, I don't follow you,' the caller said. 'Slow down.'

'My daughter and grandson are in New York,' she sobbed, all control draining away. 'Tell me nothing has happened to them. Dear God, Jesus …'

'Eh, not that I'm aware of, ma'am.'

'Oh.' She slumped down on the kerb, oblivious to her saturated clothes. 'Why are you calling me then?'

'I found your number among my mother's things.'

'Your mother? What's this about? You scared me half to death.'

'My mother's name is Alexis Belfield. She's suffered a heart attack, though it's nothing to worry about. The doctor says she's going to be fine, with medication. I had to look through her papers and computer files to locate her medical insurance details. I sent you an email, but you didn't reply. After some detective work, I found your number and decided to ring. I don't think I was ever intended to see some of those files …'

'Hey, slow down there. Did you say Alexis Belfield?'

'One and the same. My Mom.'

'Oh!' Lottie stared up at Boyd, wide-eyed, her heart crashing against her chest.

'So I just wanted to introduce myself and say hello. I believe we are related, if I can believe this stuff I've read here.'

'What did you say your name was again?'

'Leo Belfield. You know what, Lottie Parker, I believe I may be your half-brother.'

'What?' She almost dropped the phone.

'Are you coming to the States any time soon? Or hey, I can come visit you. I'm sure Mom would love that.'

I'm sure she wouldn't, Lottie thought.

'Are you for real?' she said.

He hesitated for the first time. 'Sorry, have I upset you? I know a phone call isn't the best way to do introductions, but I was excited and—'

'I need to digest this.' The words tumbled from her mouth. 'You see, my house burned to the ground last night. I'm living with my two teenagers in my mother's house and she isn't the easiest person in the world to get along with, but that's another story. My eldest is in New York with her son, my grandson, and that's why you scared the shit out of me. I've just solved a major case and I'm sitting in the rain, on the side of the road, and I don't know what the future holds for me. I need time to think. Please, Leo, don't come here. Not just yet, anyway.'

She hung up and stared at Boyd.

'I don't believe it,' she said.

'Neither do I. What was that all about?'

Lottie looked up at the sky as the rain turned to sleet.

'I thought … I thought something had happened to Katie and Louis …'

'But they're just fine.'

'Yes. But he said … this Leo guy on the phone … he said he might be my half-brother. Jesus, Boyd. What am I going to do?'

'You're going to get up out of that puddle. Here, grab my hand. You need to go to your mother's and hug your children. And you don't have to meet this Leo if you don't want to.'

'This will finish Rose off.' Lottie pulled away from him. 'I'm not going to tell her. And you're not to either.'

'I won't. But Lottie … you need to think seriously about the implications of that phone call.'

'I will.' She caught the look of hurt skimming across his eyes. 'Just not tonight.'

She linked her arm through his and, leaning into his shoulder, walked away from what had once been her home.

And she truly had no idea where she was going.

A LETTER FROM PATRICIA

Hello dear reader,

I wish to sincerely thank you for reading my fourth novel, *No Safe Place*.

I'm so grateful to you for sharing your precious time with Lottie Parker, her family and team. If you enjoyed it you might like to follow Lottie throughout the series of novels. To those of you who have already read the first three Lottie Parker books, *The Missing Ones*, *The Stolen Girls*, and *The Lost Child*, I thank you for your support and reviews.

All characters in this story are fictional, as is the town of Ragmullin, though life events have deeply influenced my writing.

If you enjoyed *No Safe Place*, I would love if you could post a review online. It would mean so much to me. The amazing reviews my books have received to date inspire me to believe in myself and to keep writing.

You can connect with me on my Facebook Author page and Twitter. I also have a blog (which I try to keep up to date).

Thanks again, and I hope you will join me for book five in the series.

Love,
Patricia

 www.patriciagibney.com

f trisha460

🐦 @trisha460

ACKNOWLEDGEMENTS

This is my fourth book in the Lottie Parker series, following on from *The Missing Ones*, *The Stolen Girls* and *The Lost Child*. As a writer, I am dependent on many people, and I'm grateful to have a great team working with me.

But first let me say, *you* are the most important person in my writing journey. You have bought my books and read them. I hope you enjoy *No Safe Place*. Readers give me the confidence to keep on writing. Thank you.

To me, Bookouture is more than a just a publishing house. It's like a family, where everyone supports each other and offers advice. My writing and editing are a lot more manageable because of it.

Helen Jenner and Lydia Vassar Smith were my editors on *No Safe Place*, and I want to thank you both for your insight into my writing and for guiding me in producing a book I am proud of. To everyone else from Bookouture who worked on *No Safe Place*, thank you. I want to give special mention to Kim Nash and Noelle Holten for their incredible media work and for organising blog tours. Kim, thank you for always being there for me and checking up on me. I really appreciate it.

Thank you also to those who work directly on my books: Lauren Finger (production), Jen Hunt (publishing), Alex Crow and Jules McAdam (marketing) and Jane Selley.

All my books are published in audio format, so I want to thank Michele Moran for her magnificent narration, giving voice to Lottie and my cast of characters, as well as Adam Helal at The Audiobook Producers.

Fellow Bookouture authors, you are the most supportive group of people I know. Special thanks to Angie Marsons for all your support and advice.

Thank you to each and every blogger and reviewer who has read and reviewed *The Missing Ones*, *The Stolen Girls*, *The Lost Child* and *No Safe Place*. I hope I can continue to keep you busy!

Thanks to my agent, Ger Nichol of The Book Bureau, for looking out for me and promoting my interests.

To my sister Marie Brennan, thanks a million for taking the time to read early drafts of my work and for your insightful comments and support.

John Quinn, you're always available to advise me on policing matters. I take huge liberties with most of it, so I take full responsibility for the fiction!

Thank you to my friends. Jo and Antoinette for always being there. Jackie for the writing escapes. Niamh for your informative phone calls. Grainne for your calming influence.

Others in the writing world who inspire and motivate me are: Louise Phillips, Liz Nugent, Vanessa O'Loughlin, Arlene Hunt, Carolann Copeland, Laurence O'Bryan, Sean O'Farrell and many more.

To local and national media, I cannot thank you enough for the coverage you have given me and my books. Olga Aughey, Claire Corrigan and Claire O'Brien, thank you.

Thanks to Dr Clodagh Brennan, Eric Smyth, Kevin Monaghan, Sean Lynch, Rita Gilmartin, Marty Mulligan and Shane Barkey. Also Stella Lynch of Just Books, and a special thanks to libraries and their staff everywhere.

Thanks to Lily Gibney and family for always supporting me.

To my mother and father, William and Kathleen Ward, for many years of listening to my dreams and believing in me.

I am so proud of my three children, Aisling, Orla and Cathal. You three have proved time and again how strong you are. Your dad, Aidan, would be so proud of how you are now coping following his untimely death. And Daisy and Shay have brought oodles of joy and love into my life. Love you both.

Finally, I dedicate *No Safe Place* to my sisters Marie and Cathy, and my brother Gerard. This book touches on the relationship between brothers and sisters. And mine are the best.

*Read on for the beginning of Tell Nobody,
the next book in Patricia Gibney's
Detective Lottie Parker series.*

PROLOGUE

The smell of smoke from the chimneys in the housing estate clogged her throat. She hurried on, and tried to keep a tally of the seconds and minutes as they passed. But she became confused and lost count as another pain pierced her abdomen. She fell to her knees, her hands gripping her belly.

Street lights directed her along the desolate lane that ran behind the terrace. Her jeans were saturated, and she wasn't sure if it was blood or water. She hoped it wasn't blood. As another pain ripped through her, she bit her lip to stifle the scream that threatened to erupt from her throat and escape out into the smoggy air.

Rain pricked her skin like pellets from a gun. She was surprised by the feeling. Because before the shower had started, all she could feel were the sharp twinges in her lower body. It was pelting down and she had no coat. Her thin T-shirt quickly became saturated like her jeans and shoes.

Turning left, she headed for the football pitch, but the lights were on and a crowd stumbled around the side of the clubhouse. Must be a party, she thought. As she headed back the way she had come, another shooting dart of pain creased her in two.

'Not yet. Please!' she cried at the rain-laden sky.

The shower passed over. Within five minutes she had reached the tunnel snaking beneath the canal. No, she couldn't go towards town. Someone would see her, and she didn't want to be seen in this state. People gossiped enough as it was. She climbed the slippery slope towards the water. On reaching the gravelly footpath, she started to run along the edge of the canal, surrounded by reeds and cans and dirt. She thought she heard someone behind her. She hadn't the energy to look back. There was no one there, she told herself. It was only the rats in the waters of the canal.

And then there was another pain. And everything changed completely.

SUNDAY

'Goal!'

Mikey Driscoll thumped the air as the ball landed in the back of the net. He was immediately engulfed by his teammates. Yes! He was a hero. At last. For the remaining five minutes of the under-twelves match, he played with a smile spread across his face.

The referee's whistle sounded, and whoops and cheers chorused through the air as the crowd filled the pitch. Mainly parents and families of the victorious boys. Mikey was hauled up onto someone's shoulders. He no longer felt the smallest on the team. Now he was a giant. Yeah!

He spied his friend Toby smiling up at him from the crowd, and he grinned back. As he was carried towards the gable end of the clubhouse for the presentation of the cup, he scanned the crowd for his mother. His heart dipped slightly. Of course, she wasn't there. She'd never come to any of his matches before; why would she now? But it was a *final*. He'd sort of hoped ... He gulped down his disappointment.

Sliding to the ground from the unfamiliar shoulders, he sought out his teammates. Mikey might have scored the winning goal, but Toby was the captain and he'd get the cup. Mikey rushed to his side. Toby was taller by a good head, and Mikey had to look up at him, shielding his eyes from the setting sun with one hand.

'Great goal,' Toby said.

'Ta,' Mikey said. 'Is it okay if I stay at yours tonight?' He crossed his fingers. He'd already told his mother he was going to be staying over at Toby's. Please say yes, he prayed silently.

Toby hesitated. 'I'll have to ask my ma.'

'Sure. Don't worry.'

'Why d'you wanna stay anyway?'

Before Mikey could answer, he and Toby were jostled to the front of the crowd by the team coach, Rory Butler.

'Come on, lads. Presentation of the cup and medals, then I'm treating you all to a McDonald's!'

A cheer went up, and Mikey was swallowed up by the rest of the team, quickly becoming separated from Toby. He was sweating from the exertion of the game and the evening heat. Should he run home for a shower first? No. He'd told his mum he'd be staying at Toby's, so he better not put in an unexpected appearance. Ah well, he thought, all the lads would be smelly, not just him.

He took his medal from Rory Butler, and then Toby raised the cup. The crowd dispersed, and some of the parents sat in their cars waiting to bring the boys to McDonald's. The team mini-bus was also ready to ferry whoever needed a lift. Mikey followed the team into the dingy changing room.

'That was the best game of the season,' Rory said, clapping each of them on the back as they entered.

Mikey liked their coach. Rory was maybe the same age as his mum. Thirty-something she always said when anyone asked.

'I'm so proud of you lads. No more team talk, it's time for celebration. Grab your things and I'll meet you all at McDonald's. Nuggets and chips are on me!'

The boys cheered again before collecting their bags, then, still in their jerseys and shorts, and with their medals hanging on green ribbons around their necks, they set off with a cheer.

*

Toby felt bad. Yeah, they'd won the final, and yeah, they were all sitting eating their nuggets and chips, and yeah, they had the coolest coach of any team in the county, but …

Mikey was eyeing him across the table with his big, sad brown eyes. Shit, Toby thought. Maybe he could bring him home to stay tonight, like he'd asked. After all, Mikey had often stayed over before. But Toby didn't want him there tonight. His big brother, Max, would be home, and Toby didn't like how things felt in his house when Max was around. None of his family had come to the match, but that didn't bother him. He was better off without them.

He pushed his fair hair out of his eyes, his special cut, shaved all around with a mop on top, as his ma described it. Mikey had tried to keep up with him by getting his mother to put blonde tips on his. Looked shocking. Awful. But Toby never told Mikey that.

Stuffing a chicken nugget into his mouth, Toby chewed hard. He'd known Mikey since junior infants; they'd been in the same class right through primary school. Now they were growing up. Moving on. Would Mikey still be his best friend once they were at secondary school? He hoped so. He felt sad now when he saw Mikey gathering his food wrappers, his medal swinging proudly as he went to put his rubbish in the bin.

Laughter and chat surrounded him, but all Toby could hear was the silence between himself and Mikey. He kept watching him. Mikey was chatting to Paul Duffy, the team physiotherapist. Well, he wasn't actually a physio, but he was a doctor. Next best thing. Everyone was here. Barry, the doc's son, always tagging along and giving orders like he was the boss. He's only fifteen, Toby thought, not the boss of me! Paul's wife Julia, who washed the kit sometimes. Creepy Wes, the bus driver who brought them to away games. Bertie

Harris, who thought he was the coach but was really only the club caretaker. And of course, Rory Butler. The real coach. Toby liked Rory and grinned over at him when he smiled his way.

Stuff it, he thought. Mikey *can* stay with me. Max can piss off. His whole family could piss off. He gathered his empty nugget box and the remains of his fries and was heading to the bin when he felt a hand on his shoulder. He swung round.

'Toby, you played so well today.'

Toby shimmied out from under Bertie's grip and grinned uneasily at the caretaker. 'Yeah, thanks. It was a good match. Great fun.'

'You played a stormer.'

'But Mikey scored the goal.'

'Great goal it was too. Young Driscoll doesn't score too many, but that was an important one. Don't forget the celebration party next Saturday night.'

'I won't.'

Toby picked up his bag and looked around for Mikey. The place was packed and noisy. He was tall enough to see over the seated heads, to search and scan. But there was no sign of his friend.

'Shite,' Toby said. Just when he had decided to let him stay over. Ah well, it was Mikey's loss.

*

Mikey remembered that his mum would be at bingo, and anyway, she wasn't expecting him home. But he had a key to the house. And Toby was being a dick.

He hitched his bag on his shoulder, one hand on the medal around his neck, and talked to himself as he walked. So, first he'd have a shower, then he'd update *FIFA* on his PlayStation, and while that was running, he'd see what was on Netflix. One of the lads had mentioned a series called *Stranger Things*. It sounded really cool. He knew his mum would never allow him to watch it, but she'd be out, wouldn't she? Yeah! He punched the air and began to jog. With the rest of his evening sorted, he felt a lot better.

He crossed over at the traffic lights and headed towards the tunnel to take the shortcut home. He hated the tunnel under the canal. Yuck. He was always thinking the walls would crack and he'd drown in the muddy water.

He kicked an empty beer can, and as it echoed back at him, he heard a vehicle rumble up alongside him. He kept walking. It kept pace with him. Turning around, he peered in through the side window. When he saw who it was, he smiled.

'Hi,' he said.

'Jump in. I'll give you a lift home.'

'Ah, it's okay. It's not far.'

'You must be knackered. I'm headed that way.'

'Okay, so.'

Mikey walked round to the passenger side and opened the door. He sat in and snapped on the seat belt. He heard the click of the automatic locks sliding into place.

'Good Lord, Mikey, you stink.'

'I do, don't I?' Mikey laughed nervously.

'I can fix that.'

'What do you mean? I'm nearly home. Plenty of hot water there,' he said, though he knew he'd have to wait half an hour for the immersion to heat up the tank.

The driver took a left when the traffic light turned green and headed up over the Dublin Bridge.

Mikey looked out of the window, confusion knotting in his chest. 'Hey, *that's* the way to my house. Back there.'

The driver stared straight ahead. Silent.

'You're going the wrong way.' Alarm spread through Mikey's body.

'Oh Mikey, this is the right way. Don't you worry your little head. Trust me.'

Mikey slid down in the seat, his feet resting on his bag, and risked a look sideways at the driver. Trust me? No, Mikey did not, but there wasn't much he could do now, was there?